THE
INSIDE
OF
OUT

Jenn Marie Thorne

DIAL BOOKS

DIAL BOOKS
An imprint of Penguin Random House LLC
375 Hudson Street
New York, NY 10014

Copyright © 2016 by Jenn Marie Thorne

Printed in the United States of America
ISBN 9780803740587

1 3 5 7 9 10 8 6 4 2

Design by Mina Chung • Text set in Kepler

For Rob, my person

1

The day she told me, Hannah showed up with iced lattes and chocolate croissants, as if nothing had changed. The day began at eleven, like all of our Sundays, except instead of travel mags, she'd brought a tote full of college brochures she'd collected all summer. We ate on our stomachs, feet kicked up, making stacks on the foot of my bed—left for "stretch," right for "safety," floor for "how is this even a school."

I was folding Charleston University into an airplane when I noticed Hannah staring at my TARDIS desk lamp.

I tossed the plane at her face.

"Command to von Linden," I said.

"Nothing to report, sir." She went nuclear-sunset pink. "I mean—there's one thing? Maybe? Tell you later?"

I squinted at her until she hid her face against her outstretched arms so all I could see was her cropped black hair.

Today was the day, then. Channeling my tiny inner Zen master, I closed my mouth and resolved to count the seconds till "later."

When it started to sprinkle, we ran to Hannah's car for the seventeen-minute drive to Folly Beach, debating West Coast vs. East Coast schools and whether we were too soft to face a northern winter.

"I mean. We're not even that great at summer," Hannah said, blasting the AC.

I saw her point. We only went to the beach on days like this, when the rain cleared it of tourists, leaving it poetically bleak.

"Pshhh," I protested, kicking my bare feet onto the dashboard. "We're great at everything."

The country station was on, but it took me half the ride to notice. For once, Hannah wasn't cranking it up, warbling off-key. When we pulled into the lot, she still had her lips buttoned, eyes glittering with that pent-up *later.*

On the beach, she got out the camera I'd bought for her birthday and snapped shots of seagulls swirling, shouting encouragement at them like they were fashion models. When she turned the lens on me, I tried to do a handstand, remembered one second too late that I had no idea how, and fell directly onto my face.

Hannah let out a series of hysterical snorts, trying to clean sand off me, then leaped up, horror-movie screaming at a sudden blast of thunder. I laughed so hard my nose started running. The rain let down for real then and we sprinted, hunched together, to the Grub Hub by the parking lot. I kicked the door open with such an apocalyptic bang that we both lost it completely.

The only other person in the snack bar was a middle-aged guy in an oversized polo shirt manning the counter. He shook his balding head. "You girls are crazy."

Hannah got embarrassed. Stopped laughing. She buried her soggy hair in my back while I ordered us nachos to go.

"He meant 'crazy' as a compliment," I said as we ducked into her steamed-up car.

"He meant me." She tugged her wet do so that it spiked into a floppy faux-hawk. "I do look crazy." A few months back, Hannah had chopped her long hair off so that it barely covered her ears—and cried the whole way back from the salon. It looked awesome, actually, especially now, but Hannah smoothed it as soon as she caught sight of herself in the rearview mirror. "Like a hedgehog. Or an alien. A *hedge*-alien."

"Okay. Yes. You are crazy. Certifiably. But you don't *look* crazy. And—*hello?*" I pinched a clump of my own hair, dingy blond until the bottom, where two inches of faded blue dripped onto my shoulders. Last year, it had been all blue, bright and bold. It might have stayed that way too, except my mom had faked an aneurism, hollered something about carcinogens, and handed down one of her most effective punishments ever—I had to *grow it out*.

I'd agreed, thinking two-tone hair would look pretty cool. I was wrong.

"We're both crazy." Hannah let me feed her a nacho as she pulled out of the lot. "We match."

I curled my legs under me, warmed by the sound of that. "So. You were going to tell me something?"

"I was. I am." She drew and held a breath. "When we get to your house."

I turned up the radio as a distraction. Met with an over-produced mess of banjos and auto-tune, I made a vomit noise and switched to a station playing normal music. Hannah swatted at me until I changed it back.

"I will never understand your obsession with country," I said.

"How could you not understand? *You* made me listen to it when I moved here."

"I introduced you to barbecue and Halloween and trashy American TV too, and you're not addicted to those."

"I *am* addicted to Halloween."

"And trashy TV," I admitted. "Okay, my fault, whatever. There *is* better American music out there. There's probably better *Austrian* music out there. Like . . . um . . ." I tapped the dashboard. Was polka Austrian?

"Mozart." Hannah went full Smug Face. "Eighteenth-century Austrian composer. Kind of a big deal, you might have heard of him."

"Nice. Mozart." I licked nacho cheese off my pinkie. "I love how you just won that argument for me."

"I do like country." She shrugged. "It's unpretentious."

"A lovely word for 'without merit.'"

Hannah stuck her tongue out and turned up the radio. But she didn't sing. And her hands stayed clenched at ten and two the whole ride home. She was nervous and I was catching it. Why couldn't she just blurt it out?

I glanced at her canvas bag and spotted the bright blue corner of this month's Moleskine poking out. The sacred notebook—repository of all of Hannah's lists, thoughts, preparations, neuroses, and other evidence of her brilliance. It was always with her, but today it felt more present than

4

ever. If I were the betting sort, I'd have wagered my cat that somewhere in that book was an outline for the conversation to come.

It took her another hour to work up the nerve, Moleskine dangling from two taut fingertips.

"Daisy." Pause. "There's something important I've been wanting to tell you for a little while now, but I wasn't sure what the right moment was. Since school's starting again tomorrow and things are about to get frenetic—"

I snorted. Hannah froze.

"Sorry!" I clamped both hands over my mouth. "I just think it's adorable that you wrote a speech to come out to me and it has the word 'frenetic' in it."

Silence. Then Hannah sputtered a series of non-words ending in *"Daisy!"*

"Oh. Shit." I winced around my fingertips. "I stole your line. That *is* what this is, though, ri—?"

"I like girls!" She waved her arms. "There. Let *me* say it." Hannah drew a breath. *"I like girls.* That's the, um, abbreviated . . ." She held up her Moleskine and let it flop back down, along with her head. "Ugh, life is so much easier on paper."

I grinned. She'd done it. I was probably supposed to hug her. Instead, I cocked my head. "Wait. You like them as . . . lab partners? Presidential candidates?"

Hannah crumpled until she was sitting, pressing her face into her wrists to muffle her laughter. "Oh my God, I think I hate you."

"You love me and I love you and I am dying to hear the rest of your speech."

"This is serious."

"I know." I dropped my smile as she looked up at me. "It's huge. Go on."

I motioned to the notebook. She flipped to one of the last pages.

"This is just one aspect of who I am and it took me a long time to figure it out. Now that I have, I wanted to make sure . . ." Hannah's voice dwindled, her eyes rising from the book. "How did you know? I thought this would come as a *little* bit of a shock."

"You had a plan for that, didn't you? For if I fainted?" I peeked at her Moleskine, grinning. "Cold water on pulse points? Smelling salts?"

Hannah sat up all the way. "Seriously, Daisy, have you known all along? Were you just waiting for me to—to announce it?"

"I've had my suspicions," I admitted. "Little things. Like you stopped participating in Who's the Hottest Actor on *Triplecross*. And you'd get flustered when that one waitress would come to our table at the coffee shop. What was her name? Kenzie? You're not dating her, are you?"

I glanced over to see Hannah's face purpling.

"No!" she groaned. "Oh my *God*, Daisy."

"I'm kidding!" I crouched, pressing my hands to her cheeks to stop the flood. "Hey, listen, it's because we're us that I guessed at all. I mean, come on. How much do we hang out? Like, every day for the last five years."

6

"Not *every* day."

"Thus the '*like*,' Miss Literal."

She scratched her nose with her shoulder. "It took *me* a while to figure it out, is all. I didn't realize it was so obvious."

"It's not obvious. I'm just terrifyingly observant. Like Sherlock. But less of a sociopath. Slightly." She didn't laugh. "Seriously, Hannah. Nobody else would know unless you told them."

That thought seemed to slow her heart rate. It sent my own ratcheting up.

"*Are* you going to tell them? The world, I mean? Or is this just a you and me thing?"

"No," she blurted. "I'm out, or whatever. I mean, I'm not planning to hide anything."

"So . . . what's next?"

Hannah looked confused. I bumped her with my knee.

She blinked. "Junior year starts tomorrow?"

"Not that. Oh wow." I covered my mouth. "Hannah. We need to figure out how to tell your mom."

Hannah looked bewildered. But just as I was about to suggest shooting a heartfelt confessional video for maximum impact, she shook her head.

"Oh. Daisy, no. I told her already. She's the first one I told. I mean, obviously."

"Oh."

Right. Of course she'd want to tell her mom first.

"Don't get mad."

"Why would I be mad?" I forced a smile. "So how did Mama Tan take it?"

"*Well*, I guess?" Hannah picked at her thumbnail. Bit it. I nudged her and she stopped. "Almost too well? She had this weird look the whole time, like I was joking and she was humoring me. Like I would take it back later."

I could just picture Tan von Linden, Hannah's stylish Vietnamese American mother listening to her daughter's revelation, eyebrows arched incredulously. I'd seen that expression so many times, starting from sixth grade, when we'd run into her antiques shop in downtown Charleston claiming to have seen the ghost of a Civil War soldier prowling the Battery. To be fair to Hannah's mom, I might not have believed her either.

"Does she think it's a phase or something?"

"I guess." Hannah rubbed her temple. "All she said was 'Okay.' And then she changed the subject. Asked me if I needed new clothes for the school year." Her forehead scrunched. "Oh God, I *hope* that was a subject change."

"You know what, Han?" I rested my head on her shoulder. "It could have been way worse. She could have started crying. Or *disowned* you."

Hannah craned her neck to stare at me. "Thank you. So much."

"No! All I'm saying is…" I inched away, drawing a frustrated breath. "It's gonna be awesome. It already is. I'm so glad you told me."

At last, those seemed to be the magic words. I could tell by the way Hannah's shoulders relaxed that we were back on the script she'd planned.

"I want you to know," she said, her voice resuming a rote

quality, like a kid in a school play. "This doesn't change anything between us."

"Of course not!" That was loud. It echoed weirdly against my bedroom walls, and Hannah read it as a cue to go.

"You want me to take these?" She motioned to the piles of college pamphlets on my bed.

"Leave 'em. We can divide them up geographically next time you're here."

"Keep them sorted." Hannah eyed them as I shut the door behind us.

"I'm making no promises."

The sound of gunfire erupted from my dad's office down the hall. Hannah jumped.

"I'll never get used to that." She laughed. "What's this one?"

"*Warpath Seven. Eight*?" I sighed. "Best not to ask."

We hopped down the steps in a synchronized trot. Old Zelda was stretched on the bottom step, waiting. At Hannah's ouch, she let out a gentle purr, then turned to me and hissed with the frothing fury of a rabid possum. Zelda liked two humans, Hannah and Dad. She tolerated Mom. And she plotted dark, dark things against me. I kept my ankles out of range as we beat a retreat.

Out in the driveway, Mom was finally replacing her yellowed *Reelect Lawrence* bumper sticker with one that said *Broccoli, Not Bombs*.

"Hey girls," she called.

"So you're officially out?" I whispered. Hannah shrugged. "Can I tell her?"

"Um." Her mouth got really small. "Yes."

9

"Yes?"

"Yes."

"Hey Mom, guess what."

Mom's head rose above the trunk of her vegetable-oil-powered Mercedes, her gray/blond ponytail tumbling over one shoulder.

"Hannah's gay!"

"What? Wow! That's—excellent!" Mom said, her eyes cutting to me, then back to Hannah. "Good for you!"

I grinned like a maniac, hoping Hannah was seeing how easy this all would be—how she *really* could have just told me as soon as she got here this morning. But Hannah seemed intent on the driveway, hair swinging so I couldn't quite see her face.

"Still picking me up tomorrow?" I asked, mainly to change the subject.

"I actually have a tennis thing in the morning. But after school, if that works?"

"Of course!" I chirped. "See you tomorrow."

As she pulled her Honda away from the curb, I waved, lifting my chin while the rest of me started to sink.

Everything was normal. Not normal—amazing. Hannah had come out at last. So, okay, we wouldn't be walking into school together the first day of junior year. She had a tennis thing. Not a big deal.

But when her car rounded the corner and vanished, I had the weird sense that she wasn't driving home. She was driving away.

I looked down and spotted two ugly sets of initials in front

of my feet, a lopsided heart scrawled between: "DBS ♥ NEB."
I turned back to the house, daydreaming of a jackhammer
obliterating that square of cement once and for all.

At one in the morning, I was still awake, fighting with my
pillow. Did Hannah *really* feel like we matched? It wasn't like
we'd ever been identical. But when she'd taken a perverse
interest in country music, I'd sucked it up and bought us
festival tickets. When she got into photography, I'd found her
a camera and posed for photos. We weren't a pair of shoes—
more a wallet and clutch in the same shade of red.

   We went together.

2

Navigating the throng zombie-marching into school the next morning, I wondered, as I did every year, if there was any chance I'd undergone a miraculous transformation that would cause everyone to turn and marvel at how gorgeous or impressive I'd become.

"Smurfette!"

Alas.

Two steps out of the marsh-scented humidity and into the climate-controlled hallway of Palmetto High, QB Saunders spotted me. He always spotted me, even with his eye-line blocked by slightly larger football buddies. Whatever you might say about QB, he was a good-looking guy, especially now, at the end of summer and the start of team training—chiseled, dimpled, bronzed, like he'd been bred in an alien lab to become homecoming king and later destroy humanity.

"SMURFETTE!"

I suppose all the attention might have been flattering if it weren't the verbal equivalent of Chinese water torture.

I kept walking but he called again, hands buried in the pockets of the plaid hunting jacket that served as his daily uniform, no matter how meltingly hot it was outside.

"Smurfette! Still your name, right?"

He was referring to my hair. I suppose it made a little sense back when my whole head was blue, although the real Smurfette had blond hair. So. And this coming from a guy nicknamed "QB" who played *wide receiver* on the football team.

"Call me Handy Smurf." I slid my bag off my shoulder and searched for my locker assignment. "I learned carpentry over the summer."

QB's mouth fell slack. "Wait, for real?"

Before I could reply, some poor freshman kid walked by— and QB shoved him over. Onto the floor! I muttered "*Ass*hole" into my locker—number 235, only a few steps from QB's, yay—but then heard the freshman saying, "Thanks man, sorry 'bout that," as if he'd tripped and QB had helped him up. Pathetic.

Okay, I supposed it was possible he'd *actually* tripped and QB had *actually* helped him up. Whatever. QB was probably just showing off for . . . whoever he was currently staring at, past my shoulder, blue eyes wide like a baby seal in a PETA ad.

I couldn't help but glance over. And then regretted it.

Seven lockers down, Natalie Beck was taping her schedule into her locker door, manicured nails clicking against the metal. Back turned, her auburn ponytail swung from shoulder blade to shoulder blade like a pendulum.

The sight of her was such a shank to the gut that I almost didn't notice QB's giant friend Pete creeping up behind me.

"D-D-Daisy." Chuckle, snort. "QB asked you a qu-qu-question."

Ah yes. The stutter routine. It was a seven-year-old joke. Dusty. Stale. Nobody was even laughing. But it still managed to send flames racing from my ankles to my cheeks.

"Come on, man," QB said uncomfortably, mad that his own joke had been shown up by a creakier one.

Even without looking, I could tell Natalie was watching. Before she could chime in, I slid my locker shut and walk-fled to homeroom.

Shake it off. Twenty-one more months of high school and they are out of your life forever.

As much as I resisted renting QB and Natalie space in my brain, I couldn't help but wonder about the scene I'd stumbled into. QB had looked downright tragic. They must have broken up. After two years.

So at least one thing had changed over the summer. No—two!

Between *bonjour*s and *je m'appelle*s with jittery freshmen in French 1, I wondered how Hannah's first "out" school day was going. I'd called her before I left the house to see if she wanted to meet up after her tennis thing, but she said she'd be fine. I hoped she was right.

On my way out of the classroom, Prof Hélène stopped me.

"Daisy Beaumont-Smith," she read from the class roll, pronouncing my name as "Dizzy Beaumaw-Smeeth" even though she was only French Canadian, not even French French. "I'm curious. You're a junior, yes? And yet you've chosen to take basic French this year?"

"Yep. I did Latin 1 in eighth grade, then Spanish 1 and 2, so I thought it was time to give French a shot." She blinked.

I went on. "Everyone says that to really become fluent in a language, you have to live there. So I'm going to become conversational in every language and then travel the world and become fluent that way."

Hannah was conversational in German, so we had that covered.

"That's a very . . . interesting plan, Dizzy."

I'd heard the word "interesting" enough in my sixteen years to know what it really meant. I sighed, said *"Merci,"* and headed out the door before she could correct my pronunciation.

As I navigated to next period, I scanned my schedule. Yep—one class with Hannah, AP bio. I despised lab reports, and my B-minus average in physics last year had been agony to maintain. But I knew she'd be taking it, so I'd signed up. I only wished we had more classes together, that I didn't have to go through so much of my day alone.

I spotted her on the way to the gym, headed down to our annual first-day-of-school Club Fair.

She nodded soberly as we took to the stairs. "So what's it going to be?"

For a serial hobbyist like myself, club life made school life bearable. If you'd asked me last week, I'd have declared for the Palmetto Foodies. But now I had other ideas.

"Drama?" Hannah suggested. "Parapsychology?"

I waved my hand at the mere mention of last year's club. "They were just a bunch of debunkers."

"Still have the gear?"

"The EMF meter's in the garage somewhere."

"I'll hunt ghosts with you anytime."

I smiled at her lie. The idea of preppy Hannah holed up in an abandoned mental institution for two minutes, let alone an entire night, was ludicrous. Frankly, it didn't sound that great to me anymore, either.

"It's the Foodies, then." Hannah whapped my shoulder. "You know how I knew? Every time you came over for dinner this summer, you asked my mom what restaurant the meal was from and tried to guess what spices the chef—"

"Actually . . ." I interrupted gently, watching her from the corner of my eye. "I was thinking the Alliance?"

"Which Alliance?"

"The Rebel Alliance." Hannah looked blank. I smiled, nudging her. "Is there more than one Alliance in this school?"

"No, I . . ." Hannah shook her head. "Wait, I'm legit confused now."

"I was thinking maybe *both* of us could check it out?"

"*Oh,*" she said, her face going pale. "Right."

At the doorway to the gym, a bustling mecca of booths, banners, and bored kids, I stopped to whisper, "Are you not out, Han? Am I reading this wrong?"

She scanned the room. Tugged peevishly at her hair. "No, I'm out. It's . . . yeah. Let's go say hi to the Rebel Alliance."

With arms looped, we sauntered past 4H, Green Thumbs, and the Football Boosters. When we passed the Homecoming Committee table, Natalie Beck peered up at us, eyes darkening as if we owed her a goat for crossing her bridge. Hannah tensed, but I lifted my chin and tightened my grip, marching us straight to the gayest booth in the room.

Not that it was all that gay. The Alliance's folding table was festooned with a miniscule rainbow banner and a laminated sheet of paper bearing the name of their club that you couldn't read until you were standing right in front of it. At the table were two girls dressed so differently and sitting so far apart that I wondered whether the school had stuck two groups together to save space.

I knew the girl on the left, a senior. Raina Moore. She was one of the few black kids in my World History class last year, where she'd entertained everyone by picking fights with the teacher whenever he voiced the mildest opinion about *anything*, from U.S.-Saudi relations to where he was planning to take his kids for spring break. Today, wearing a lilac button-down and suit pants, hair ironed flat and tied into a pristine bun, she looked like she was interviewing for a job at a law firm.

On the right was a girl I'd seen in the halls but never talked to. She was probably a sophomore, but somehow all the guys in the school, no matter their year, acted as if they knew her—intimately. Today, she was wearing what seemed to be her usual wardrobe—beige peasant shirt, thick honeyed side-braid, slouchy skirt, a pendant necklace bearing a huge symbol from a culture I didn't recognize. If Raina Moore was a lawyer, her tablemate was a pagan milkmaid. Maybe even the goddess of milk. The girl was pretty.

I shot Hannah a look, but she had her glassy-eyed I'm-meeting-new-people face on. I made a mental note to grill her on her type so I could be a more effective wing woman.

"Welcome!" the milkmaid said, just as Raina asked, "Can

we help you?" Raina's eyes were narrowed, like we'd walked over with baseball bats and brass knuckles.

"We'd like to sign up for the Gay-Straight Alliance," I said.

"We're not a GSA." Raina's eyebrows rose. "We're a *gay* alliance."

"Great! We'd like to join that. Do you have a list, or—?"

"We don't believe in lists," Raina said, clasping her hands in front of her. "A physical list could be used as a tool by those who seek to categorize, ghettoize, and oppress."

I stared at Raina. She stared back. Meanwhile, the milkmaid was staring meditatively at the far wall.

"So do you keep a *mental* list? I'm Daisy . . . Beaumont . . . Smith. And this—"

"I'm Hannah." Hannah raised her hand in a tiny wave, and I had to stifle the impulse to cheer. This was a big moment in Hannah's outness, right? It seemed like it should be a big moment.

"*Fine.*" Raina sighed, spoiling it. "We meet Tuesdays and Thursdays, Room A2. If you want to come, technically we can't stop you."

"Thanks so much—we'll be there!" I beamed at Raina to piss her off, while Hannah waved to the milkmaid, clutched my arm, and steered me away.

"That was awkward," she muttered.

"They were kind of off, weren't they?" I agreed, then winced. "Not because they're gay. They didn't even *seem* gay. I mean, not that you *can* seem gay—"

"Daisy. Stop." Hannah shoved me, laughing. "Yeah. They were weird. Not gay-weird, weird-weird."

"Could be good, though," I said, hip-checking her as we passed through the rest of the booths. "Having people to talk to who understand what you're going through? And I'll be there too, as a buffer."

"You don't have to buffer me," Hannah said, lingering in front of the Chess Club booth. "It's sweet—"

"It's not just for you," I lied. "It'll look amazing on my college applications."

She squinted dubiously as she scribbled her name onto the Chess Club's nice, normal, physical sign-up sheet. But just after she set down the pen, she glanced vaguely back at the Alliance table and said, "You're probably right."

As we were walking to bio, I brainstormed ways to ask her which club she was going to choose without making her feel like I was pressuring her. But then Hannah smiled in this intense way that shut me up.

"Moonlight after school?"

"Obviously," I answered. We hadn't been to the Moonlight Coffee Shop all summer. It was time to reclaim our clubhouse.

Hannah looked nervous. "There's something I want to talk to you about."

"Sure." I faked a smile. Had Hannah forgotten that she'd already come out to me yesterday? Or . . .

My throat went dry.

"I'll, um . . ." She bit the corner of her thumb. "I'll meet you there."

"Oh. Kay." As she slid into class ahead of me, I stayed behind, watching her find us a lab table. What the hell was I going to do?

What I came up with by last period went something like:

"Hannah, you know how much I love you. You're the most important person in the world to me and I will always be there for you. But I'm not gay. I can't feel that way about you. And you'll meet someone else one day, someone amazing."

It seemed inadequate. How could I explain how I felt about Hannah? I mean, her looks *were* a part of it in a way, those flashing angular eyes, black hair, slow smiles, the way she twirled her ankle when she was thinking. It drew people to her. Poor Hannah wished she were a wallflower—hated having every stranger at a checkout counter ask her where she was from, as if it were some fairy-tale kingdom between Europe and Asia instead of "just off Harborview"—or, worse, *what* she was, like they saw her as some other species entirely.

You'd never know Hannah was annoyed. She was Palmetto's concierge, impeccably lovely, polite, mature around absolutely everyone—except me.

Around me, Hannah pretended seagulls were top models. She came up with elaborate evacuation plans for MERS outbreaks and tsunamis. She referenced country songs to describe her emotional state—without irony.

I loved every one of Hannah's quirks. Even her nail biting, although we were working on that. More than anything, I loved that she let me get close enough to witness them.

All I wanted was to stay that close. I didn't need anything else. But apparently, she did.

I beat her to the diner on foot and peeled apart the edge of a plastic menu while I waited. True to form, the only people in

the place were the somnolent staff and one other customer—
some kid with glasses who was either in college or in high
school trying to *look* like he was in college.

He glanced up from his laptop and raised his eyebrows,
like he'd caught me gawking or something. Whatever, buddy.
I was only looking because he was blocking my view to the
door Hannah was due to walk through any second. But now
that he'd clocked me, I stared more brazenly.

He had dark, messy hair, sharp eyes behind black hipster
frames, and he was typing on his MacBook with such loud
clicks that I began to form theories. *Angry email to an ex?*
Slasher screenplay? Shocking exposé for a newspaper?

He looked up again, but this time, I had the menu ready to
block my face. Not that I needed to read it. Hannah and I always got the same combination of items to share: mozzarella
sticks, chicken fingers, side salad that we would pick at so we
didn't feel too guilty about the other selections.

I'd just ordered when the door dinged, and of course, that kid
with the laptop glanced up expecting me to look at him, and
of course I did, stupidly, so it took me a second to break eye
contact and peer over his shoulder to see Hannah walking in.

With someone.

Not just anyone.

Natalie Beck's copper blade of a ponytail was swinging back
and forth with OCD precision as she trailed Han through the
door. I mentally *ughed*. Possibly audibly. What were the odds
of that vulture turning up here—our secret hideout—the one
place that the plebs of Palmetto didn't invade as soon as the
last bell rang?

21

I was shooting Hannah a sympathetic wince when I saw it. Her hand. Doing something strange.

It was holding Natalie's.

The booth pinned me in like a carnival ride. I couldn't move. Not until Hannah led Natalie over like a show pony, ushered her into the booth, and said:

"Daisy, this is Natalie."

"I know her." I laughed, because it was such a weird thing for Hannah to say. Of course I knew Natalie. I'd known her since pre-K.

Hated her since fourth grade.

Hannah knew the entire sordid history, but now she flushed her trademark neon, and Natalie—*Natalie*—ran her fingers along Hannah's shoulder to, like, calm her down.

What was happening?

"Right. Of course." Hannah shook her head. "What you *don't* know is . . ."

Natalie smiled encouragingly, insipidly.

No no no holy no . . .

"She's my girlfriend."

3

My earliest memory is one I'd rather forget.

I'm lumbering through a maze of clothespinned sheets, like an outtake from a detergent commercial, and she's calling, "You can't get me!" But then there's her hand, and once I've grabbed it, she smacks her head into my shoulder and we fall down hard and giggle until we can't breathe, watching the sun flash between the leaves of the big oak above. Then she rests her arm on my face and says, "Oscar's not my best friend anymore. You are."

Oscar was her stuffed bunny. And she was Natalie Beck.

Natalie, back then Nat-Nat, who didn't care what anybody thought, who once wore a pasta strainer as a hat for an entire school day because I'd dared her, who had the loudest laugh in South Carolina, who wasn't, you know, evil.

I can't remember when we met or how, just that we did everything together from preschool on. We forced our parents to watch our terrible living room musical performances—our version of *The Wizard of Oz* was longer than the film itself—signed up for the same horseback-riding/berry-picking/hand-loom-weaving summer camps. We were so close that our mothers pretended to like each other, a marvel of social engineering that I still can't wrap my brain around.

It seemed at the time to come out of nowhere, but looking back, it must have all kicked off the summer after third grade, with the Giselle Chronicles. TGC was a book series about ballerinas in space. Ridiculous? Yes. Awesome? Hell to the yeah. Every weekend, Nat and I dressed up as the main characters and acted out each book's plot from beginning to end in a continuous loop.

Our dream for the summer after third grade was to stage elaborate space-ballet productions all over the greater Charleston area. But Natalie's family had other plans. Hours before she left for an eight-week Mediterranean cruise, we forged a pact: On the first day of school, we would dress in character, Nat as poofy-haired Xippie and me as rosy-cheeked Lida. To while away the empty hours alone, I spent the summer perfecting my *grands jetés* and my costume—a new dress, short and metallic green, with slippers that crisscrossed to my knees.

The moment I walked into Mrs. Morris's fourth-grade classroom, I sensed trouble—a vestigial instinct—my eyes, bones, skin prickling like a tiger was stalking me. No tigers here, though. Just Natalie. She was sitting in the back, which we never did, and she was dressed . . . not even normally, *stylishly,* in a striped top and pleated skirt with a matching headband, like she was pretending to be a French fifteen-year-old. And when I said hi, she mumbled it back but wouldn't look at me.

At recess, she was talking to other girls, including a few she'd declared "stuck-up" the year before. When I came up and did a *grand jeté,* Nat got the strangest look on her face.

I'd only ever seen it when we were playing pretend. She was sneering.

"O-*kay*, psycho," she said, and turned her back.

And all the other girls laughed and followed her across the playground.

I still remember that feeling of being stuck to the asphalt, pulled down by more than gravity, the very breath sucked out of me. It was like when Lida went through the black hole in *Swan Planet* and came out a swan, except I wasn't a swan. I was a psycho.

And it must have been true, because the girls I didn't like took it up as a chant—*psycho*—repeating it enough at recess, and whispering it enough behind cupped hands that by the end of that week, a lot of the boys, sensing a fight, had picked it up too. And if my remaining friends weren't name-calling, they weren't exactly leaping to my defense. It took two days for them to start saving seats at the lunch table so that I couldn't sit with them. And it took until the day after that for me to gather enough courage to walk up to Natalie in the after-school pickup line. I was terrified, my hands shaking, my life unraveling, so I stumbled over the "mean," saying, "Why are you being so m-mean to me?" and Natalie just blinked, empty-eyed and said, "I d-don't kn-know, D-Daisy. W-why do you th-think?"

That was as close to an answer as I ever got. My best friend had been replaced by this stranger who didn't laugh at all, whose red hair was never tangled, who'd decided somewhere between Ibiza and Crete that she hated me.

And for years, people teased me for a stammer I didn't

have. Still did—if you counted Pete Brandt as a person. The other taunts evolved. It took them more than a month to realize that Psycho Daisy didn't rhyme but *Crazy Daisy* did, so that one was a big hit, along with the standard synonyms, *freak, loser, weirdo.* Occasionally I'd get a "Hey" in class from someone who felt sorry for me, but never much more.

It wasn't worth talking about. Talking meant thinking and that led to mulling and mourning and honestly, what was the point?

The only day worth thinking about was the first day of sixth grade. As I was settling down to eat lunch in a hidden corner of the schoolyard, I glanced up to a dizzyingly unfamiliar sight: Someone was walking up to join me.

She was new. She had long black hair clipped back with barrettes, warm green eyes. She'd just moved from Europe— *Europe!*—a place where that pretentious cow Natalie had only vacationed.

And she was wearing a Giselle Chronicles backpack. *In sixth grade.* Apparently this was acceptable in Europe?

"Can I eat with you?" she'd asked.

It turned out we had a lot in common. We found this out astonishingly quickly.

"What's your last name?"

"Von Linden. With a small *v.*" She flushed bright, electric, beautiful pink. "It's a common name in Austria, but here I guess it's long?"

"My last name's long too! Beaumont-Smith. With a dash. I always have to explain the dash." I dared a smile. "You moved from Austria?"

"Yeah, me and my mom. My dad's still there, so . . ." She looked down, turning a baby carrot over and over. "I don't know if I'm going to see him much."

"My dad lives at home," I offered. "But I don't see him much either. He stays in his office all day playing video games." I peeked in her lunchbox, spying something that made my eyes water. "What's *that*?"

Hannah picked it up. "Um . . . I don't know the words. In German, it's *kartoffelpuffer*?"

"What's it made of?"

"Potatoes. And fat. Is that the right words?" Hannah's grin flickered. "My English is rusting."

"I *love* fat. Anything deep fried is my favorite."

"*Me too!*" She beamed. "Sometimes I daydream about, sort of, regular food and picture what it would taste like if you fried it. For example, salad and things."

I reeled, amazed. "I bet it would be better."

We talked about fried food all day. And then, when school let out, we exchanged numbers so we could keep talking about it after we got home. On the phone, back at school, back on the phone, we talked in sometimes halting English about ballet and black holes and whether ladybugs bit and our moms and our worst fears and how glad we were to have met. Within forty-eight hours, Hannah von Linden and I were best friends.

It was enough to elevate me from *Status: Pariah* to *Status: Other*. As the years passed, Natalie was ever-present, the gnawing ulcer in my gut that made me feel like nothing I did would ever be right again, but with Hannah around, we'd at least stopped interacting.

27

Until now.

"Daisy . . ." Hannah had risen with me, dropping her Moleskine to reach out and steady me.

"I'm not feeling so well," I heard myself saying, barely managing to sidestep the waitress without knocking the tray from her hand. "Eat the . . . food. I'd better get home. You two crazy kids enjoy."

I was halfway across the diner when it hit me that I'd said "crazy kids"—and one millisecond later that a power cord hit my leg, sending me and something silvery careening to the floor with two sharp cracks.

"What the hell!" Glasses guy jumped from his seat, spilling coffee on his leg. "Gaaah!"

I'm fine, thanks for asking! I yelled from the ground, elbow throbbing. "Why are you plugged in halfway across the freaking room?"

"Because my battery's dead," he yelled back, turning his laptop over and shaking it. "And now my computer is too."

After a moment of paralysis, Hannah was recovering—and approaching fast. Natalie sat in the booth with her eyes closed, like she was practicing a mantra, like I was something you needed happy thoughts to get through.

The guy was offering me a hand. "Listen, I'm sorry—*are* you all right?"

I pulled myself away using the back of his chair, knocking it over in the process, muttering, "Sorry-about-your-computer-I-really-don't-have-time-to-talk."

Then I rushed out the door.

Once the thick street air hit me, a current pulled me

28

along the sidewalk, out of sight of the diner's corner windows. After a few blocks, I realized I'd made a pointless circle, my brain stuck stuttering, "How? I . . . how? But *how*?" My backpack felt impossibly heavy. I put it down on the sidewalk. Sighed. I'd left my ride back at the diner. Along with her girlfriend.

Get home, I thought. *Figure the rest out later.*

I called Mom. She took three rings to pick up, then shouted, "I'm at your school!"

"Why?" I asked carefully. She didn't seem to hear.

"Across the street. Can you see me? I'm with my CFOA group . . . I'm waving!"

Rather than trying to decipher that, I shouted, "See you in a minute," skirted the school's parking lot, and headed across two lanes of sparse traffic to the neighboring field, where Mom and six other ladies were staggering around squinting at the ground, picking up pinches of scrub and soil and stuffing them into tiny canvas bags.

This was possibly a new level of strange.

Mom waved so excitedly that I knew she was misreading the reason I'd stopped by.

"Just wanted to see what you were up to!"

She threw her arm around me and squeezed, shouting to the others, "Activist in training here!"

The ladies whooped, and I did a stealth check across the street to school to make sure nobody had overheard. What would my nickname be if QB or Natalie could see me in a vacant lot with a bunch of middle-aged eco-warriors?

Natalie. She couldn't say anything. Because she was *dating*

29

my best friend. My brain whimpered *How?* one last time and short-circuited.

I spent the ride home dimly registering Mom droning on about her eco group and how there was going to be a minor-league field across from Palmetto, but the deal to bring in the team fell through, and Community Farmers of America and some game app something-something to fund-raise and then she fell silent, which snapped me back just in time for her to say, "It was awfully brave of Hannah to come out."

"Yeah." I blinked. "She's a rock star."

Mom had a dangerous sparkle in her eye. "If you had something to tell me, I'd be very proud of *you*. And supportive. You know that, right?"

"Sure."

"So . . ." She was watching me, not the road. "Is there anything you want to say?"

"Yeah. *Brake.*" I pointed to the light ahead and she slammed the car to a stop just as it turned red. "Apart from that, no. Nice try."

"Okay," Mom said, an irritating note of patience in her voice, as though in time, I'd come to know myself as well as she did.

"When I realize I'm gay, you'll be the first to know. I'll wake you up and tell you the exact moment it occurs to me."

Mom rolled her eyes and turned into our driveway. "Just wanted you to know I'm here for you."

"I appreciate that."

I did. Honestly. Even so, the moment we got into the house, I ran upstairs, locked my bedroom door, and tried my best to pretend nothing outside my walls was real.

4

I practiced a normal expression in the hall mirror before daring to step outside the next morning. Good thing too. As soon as I'd fastened my seat belt, Hannah squinted at me.

"Feeling better?" she asked.

"Yep. Just lady trouble."

Our old-timey way of saying we had our period, but in this case, the lady *and* the trouble was Natalie.

"Listen," Hannah started. "We wanted to explain everything yesterday."

We. They were already a "we."

"We didn't expect for it to happen. *Us,* I mean."

They were an "us."

I turned on the radio. Hannah glanced at me as she changed lanes.

"It was just, spending all that time together on the team last spring . . ."

Right. Natalie was the tennis captain and Hannah's doubles partner. What a cliché. I turned the volume louder, gritting my teeth against the twang.

"And then we did that retreat last month, and one day, it just . . . *Can we turn this down?*"

Hannah's fist slammed into the power button, silencing the speakers. Her nostrils flared. I'd seen her angry like this before, but at malfunctioning electronic equipment, uncrackable algebraic equations.

"Sorry," I muttered.

She was quiet for a few blocks, the air in the car thickening, cementing my mouth shut while my mind scrambled for what to say next.

She shook her head. "I shouldn't have brought her. I should have just told you."

"I sort of had to see it for myself."

"What does that mean?"

I shrugged. If she didn't already *get* what it meant—how ludicrous the entire situation was—I wasn't going to spell it out for her.

Hannah didn't say anything until we pulled into the school lot. Then she cut the engine with a sigh. "I know you and Natalie have . . . a history."

You and Natalie. As if we were both to blame for it.

"Things were awful for you," she went on. "And I hate that it happened. Like, I wish I had a time machine, so I could go back and give little-kid you a hug, tell you it gets better, except little-kid you wouldn't know who this stranger was hugging you, so maybe more like a handshake or a high five . . ."

Weird, I thought. *But okay.*

"But you know that Winchaw Junction song? *The longest road leads to the highest mountain, and you never—*"

"*Yes,*" I yapped, *really* not in the mood for inspirational country lyrics. "I know that song. Unfortunately."

"To me, it means that sometimes things happen the way they do to make you a stronger person. It was a long time ago and now . . ." She turned to grin stiffly at me, eyes manic-bright. "You're you! And . . . you're awesome!"

She held on to her pose, still smiling like a pageant contestant.

My eyes narrowed. Was Hannah seriously trying to argue that Natalie destroying my life was a *good* thing? I was speechless, but Hannah must have thought I was going to interrupt, because she put one jittery hand up to stop me.

"Also? Okay, I have to say this. Natalie's not who you think she is. I mean—people change, right? People are constantly evolving. Actually . . ." Her forehead scrunched. "That's not really how natural selection works, but you know what I'm saying. I just . . ." She blinked quickly a couple of times, so I knew she was about to lie. "I think you might really like her now."

I stared at Hannah, numb with the realization of how candy-colored her view was of my "history" with Natalie. All I could spit out was a muffled "Maybe" while I tugged my backpack from her car.

Hannah seemed to think that the conversation had gone swimmingly. She linked elbows with me as we turned toward school. "You know, you should learn to drive, Daisy. You've got a car. It's getting ridiculous."

She bumped my hip to soften the blow. It didn't work.

I did, in fact, have an ancient Jaguar, a sixteenth birthday gift from my dad. After a trip to a used car lot, I'd selected a sleek green beauty because it looked like a car you'd drive along the French Riviera with a scarf holding your hair. Mom didn't know how to drive stick shift, and Dad kept promising to teach me "next weekend," once he'd finished whatever game he was working on, so I'd looked up some techniques online. I gave it a try—and never left the driveway. In my Hulk-rage at stalling out, I swore off driving altogether.

While I was having my manual meltdown, Hannah was graduating from the driving course at school, taking the test, getting her license. She'd inherited the family Honda when her mom got a new car, and she'd never minded chauffeuring me around.

"You're right," I said. "I should try again."

"I'm going to get you driving gloves." Hannah held up her hand as if to model one. "And I'm going to tell you they're magic and that they'll learn stick shift *for* you."

"That will definitely work," I said.

Hannah kept describing the gloves she'd get me, soft ivory with blue buttons on the wrists. It wasn't until she got a few steps ahead that I allowed my oh-so-delighted smile to sputter out.

One awkward non-argument, one lecture that rewrote my biography, and one loaded comment about "learning to drive myself." Good morning to you too.

We ate lunch together at least. It was rainy again, so we didn't claim our usual spot on the steps between the cafeteria and the faculty parking lot, settling instead into a table in the corner with some random sophomores.

Hannah peeled the paper from the gourmet sandwich her

mother packed her every morning, and I went to get something unhealthy from the lunch line for us to share. When I came back, there were two seats open around Hannah.

My stomach clenched. *And it begins.*

"I've been thinking," Hannah said, and I held my breath. "Am I a real photographer?"

It took me a good three-count to realize this was our regular flavor of chitchat. "Of course you are. A good one."

"No, but . . . my camera." She grabbed a chicken nugget from my plate.

"Your birthday present?"

"I love it," she said quickly. "But it's so easy to use. I was thinking maybe I need, like, a thirty-five millimeter. And a darkroom."

"*Oh,*" I said, leaning my chin on steepled fingers. "I see what you're saying. Yes. But what you really need is a daguerreotype."

"I'm serious!" She tossed her napkin at me. "You're the one who's always saying that there's no point in doing something—"

"If you're not going to do it awesomely. Exactly. Which is why you need a nineteenth-century camera and me posed as a Civil War soldier, otherwise no, you're not a real photographer."

Hannah laughed. "Is it weird that this seems like a good—"

She cut off midsentence, her face freezing into nothingness. I looked where she was looking. Natalie had just walked in. I braced myself. But instead of smiling or waving her over, Hannah crossed her legs to face me.

Natalie surveyed the room in a slow Terminator scan. When she saw my raised eyebrows and Hannah's back, she spun so quickly her ponytail slapped her in the face. Then, trailed by her usual coterie of sycophants, she selected a window-front table in the middle of the cafeteria—the same place she'd sat since freshman year.

The football team had picked a new table clear across the room. The moment Natalie sat down, QB's voice rose, cracking jokes, letting everyone in earshot know that his life was one big, raucous rodeo that no woman could possibly derail.

She'd dumped him for Hannah. I wondered if he knew.

When Hannah's silence tipped from oppressive to maddening, I tossed a crinkle fry at her.

"Aren't you gonna say hi to your girlfriend?"

Hannah didn't react, didn't seem to realize how hard I'd had to focus to say it. She glanced furtively at Natalie, then returned to picking at her watercress sandwich.

"Hang on." I grabbed Hannah's arm. "Are you two a *secret*? Is Natalie not out?"

"Keep your voice down." Hannah's own had slid into a whisper. "Her friends . . . they're not like you. She needs to be careful with how she tells them."

"Because they're assholes and I'm not. Got it."

Hannah smiled faintly. I gave her a couple minutes to relax, finish her artisanal lemongrass iced tea and the rest of my fries. Then I whispered, "I just think it's lame that you've come out and she hasn't. Are you sure she's—"

"*Yes!*" Hannah hissed, when even *I* didn't know how that question was going to finish.

Are you sure she's fully committed to your relationship?

Are you sure she's human?

Are you sure she's not pretending *to be gay in order to steal you from me, thus destroying my life once and for all?*

In any case, I'd seen enough. There were chinks in the armor.

As the bell rang, Hannah stood to bus our trash—a peace offering.

I cleared my throat. "So I'll see you seventh period? Alliance meeting?"

"Right," she said. "See you there."

I had to look up Room A2 on a school map. It took several wrong turns into a faculty lounge and the vice principal's empty office for me to locate the sign reading A2, and taped underneath it, a printout: "Student Club Meeting: 1:30–2:40."

I hesitated. This was a conference room, the kind where teachers held meetings on how to ratchet our test scores up to levels that would prevent them from being shamed in the local papers.

"Come on in," a male voice said behind me. Before I could turn, his hand met my back, nudging me in with him. "We won't bite. Unless you ask nicely."

I knew this kid. Or *of* him, I guess. His name was Jack Jackson—easy to remember, especially since QB used to recite it in a high-pitched voice every time he passed Jack in the hall, like it was the height of wit to call someone by his actual name. I'd been proud to bear witness to the day last winter when Jack Jackson had put an end to it by murmuring back in a sultry voice, "You know I love it when you scream my name."

It was no secret that Jack was gay. He wore it proudly, along with his unofficial uniform of khakis, polo shirt, and weathered boat shoes. I'd always liked him for it. But I'd never talked to him before today.

"I take it back." Jack's face darkened as he leaned in to whisper to me. Leaned up, really. At five-six, I had a good inch on him. "*She* might bite."

He nodded to the end of the long conference table, where Raina Moore had claimed the power seat. Riffling through pages of an old legal pad, she barely gave us a glance as we walked in. But a few seconds later, she froze, brow furrowed, and peered back up. At me.

"Interesting," she said.

"Interesting" was a better reaction than, say, "Go away," or "Kill it with fire!" Still, it took a little courage to pull out one of the roller chairs on the far side of the table and claim it for my own.

"I'm Daisy," I said to Jack.

He raised his eyebrows. "I know. Wondered when you'd show up here."

Before I could ask what that meant, the door opened again, and through it walked the milkmaid, chatting with someone whose face rendered me speechless.

Sean Bentley—the most beautiful boy in the Greater Charleston Area.

When I was a freshman and Sean was a sophomore, he played Billy Bigelow in *Carousel*, while I was cast as, like,

38

New England Townsperson Five. The only reason I didn't quit Drama Club right then was the possibility of "accidentally" touching the lead actor during a late-night rehearsal.

Two years later, Sean was still 1950s matinee idol dreamy, with wavy hair somewhere between bronze and burnished gold, lightly tanned skin, a gleaming smile that crinkled at the corners. An army of girls trailed him like a parade, vying to be his Number One Strictly Platonic Girl Who Was a Friend. Sean was out, in the way that the singing, dancing lead of every school musical who openly dates guys is clearly out, but still they followed, hoping against hope that they could change his mind.

I myself had quit stalking Sean after a firm but gentle intervention from Hannah late freshman year. But I didn't blame the ones who'd kept trying. After all, I'd written two-fifths of an opera for the guy. That was devotion.

"We've been *Skyping*," he was sighing to sympathetic noises from the milkmaid. "But it's just really hard, you know? Having an ocean between— Jack! My man!"

Sean Bentley high-fived in my general direction.

"And . . ." Sean pointed at me. "Daisy, right?"

He remembered my name.

"Daisy Beaumont-Smith," the milkmaid said, a smile lifting the corner of her mouth as she recited the name I'd given them at the booth. "I'm Sophie. So glad you came."

"Did you ever finish that opera?" Sean asked, and even though he was just being polite, I felt the blood drain from my face as I scrambled for an answer that sounded better than "Nope!"

Luckily, Raina picked that moment to gather her legal pads and smack them against the table in a smart stack. "Should we get started?"

I glared at the clock mounted above the whiteboard. Where was Hannah?

The door squeaked and I twirled in my fancy conference room chair to wave hello. But, again, not her. A younger kid with short-cropped brown hair re-shouldered his giant backpack and stared around the room. I wondered whether he'd gotten lost looking for the nurse's office.

"Welcome!" Sophie's voice was just this side of cult leader.

"Um . . ." The kid moved back a step. "Is this the club for if you're gay? The sign doesn't say."

"It's for quilt bag students, yes," Sophie said, and I glanced around, wondering if that had made sense to anyone else.

Raina smiled tightly. "Come in and shut the door, please, we're about to get started."

The kid fumbled for a chair, his eyes everywhere but on us.

"I'm new too," I offered. "Daisy Beaumont-Smith."

"Cool. Kyle Hornsby. I'm a freshman." He winced, as if it were a painful admission. "This room is super nice."

Raina nodded. "They tried to marginalize us last semester by putting us next to the wood shop. We lobbied the administration, citing noise violations and health concerns, and . . ." She gestured to the room with a smirk. "We won."

"Awesome," I said, guessing from Sophie's flat expression that the "we" in this case was one Raina Moore, Attorney at Law.

"So. Daisy," Raina said, her voice notably sharper than a moment ago. "Why don't *you* go first?"

Everyone turned to blink at me while I sat there trying to figure out what exactly constituted "going first."

Hannah wasn't here. And Hannah was prompt. The promptest. That squeaky conference room door to the rest of the world was looking awfully inviting right about now. But then I looked at Raina—and saw a challenge in her eyes.

Screw it.

I cleared my throat and stood, realizing too late that it was kind of a grandiose gesture for an audience of five.

"I'm Daisy. As you know. I . . . am very passionate about LGBTQ issues," I started, praying that I'd gotten the acronym right. "I want to . . . um . . . fight for equal treatment and rights for every gay student."

They were smiling at me. This seemed to be the right track.

"I mean . . ." I leaned against the chair and it swiveled but didn't fall over. "I feel like this school tries to bury issues instead of dealing with them head-on, so we need to be proactive in making sure our voices are heard."

That was a direct quote from my mother, complaining about cafeteria options with her Real Food activist friends at our dinner table a few nights back.

Raina raised her eyebrows. She was listening. This was my in.

"Like *you*, Raina," I said. "You lobbied the administration for a better room and you got it. I want to be a part of things like that."

Sean leaned forward and I had to brace myself not to fall over from the blinding glow of his smile. "What kinds of *things* do you have in mind, Daisy?"

I swear he made that sound dirty.

"Well . . ." I refocused, wishing I'd thought this through in advance. "I think there should be tougher crackdowns on bullying. I want to go to a school where gay students feel comfortable bringing their boyfriends and girlfriends to dances without worrying about the football team making fun of them."

Everyone glanced awkwardly at each other, and I went hot and prickly, insta-sweating. Had I miscalculated? Despite their losing record, the Pirates were beloved across the social spectrum, for reasons I myself could not fathom.

But then Sophie spoke up.

"Actually, Daisy, students aren't *allowed* to bring same-sex dates to dances. It's in the school rules."

For a second, I was too surprised to speak. I'd always known that the conservative element ran strong here, and that our school wasn't exactly immune to it. But this was the twenty-first century. Marriage equality was a done deal nationwide. How could we *still* have that rule?

"We need to *fight* it!" I shouted.

There was a breath of silence, then everyone in the room started talking at once, except Raina, who squinted at her legal pad as if waiting for an answer to appear on it. I watched her, my veins thrumming.

Her eyes lit up.

Bam. I'd won over the room. I was part of the LGBTQ solution. The only way this moment could be better was if Hannah had actually bothered to show up and witness it. I blinked a quick glare at the door.

"We should strategize," Raina said over the chatter of the others. "Plan for prom, not homecoming."

"Why *not* homecoming?" I was too excited to stop. "The sooner the better, I say."

"Hear, hear!" Jack offered me a high five, but I noticed a beat too late and wound up high-fiving his shoulder. It was fine. This was amazing. I couldn't wait to tell Han. We had an agenda. We would take on the school and we would win. We would enact real, lasting change. And then maybe next year, orchestra? Might be fun to learn the violin, although the larger string instruments were arguably—

"Awww." Sophie beamed at me, going crinkly. "You want to take your girlfriend to homecoming, don't you, Daisy?"

My chair swiveled on its own.

"Hannah von Linden?" Jack waggled his eyebrows. "No need to front, dear, it's obvious you're together."

"Oh!" I laughed. "*Noooo*nonono. Hannah's not my girlfriend. Actually, I'm straight."

The silence that fell was so sudden, I wondered if I'd gone momentarily deaf. Then Raina stood from the table, pointed to the door, and chirped:

"Nope! Out! Go."

5

I fought to keep my smile from shaking loose. "Excuse me?"

Raina leaned over the table. "What part of 'Not a GSA' did you not understand?"

"All of it? I guess?"

She clenched her jaw so hard I swore I heard her gears sparking.

"I'm so sorry, Daisy," Sophie said from the end of the room. "But this group is just for students who identify as queer."

Now everybody was smiling again, but in this *oh it's so sad* way. No, more of an *all the seats at our lunch table are taken* way.

"Okay, yeah, I . . . wow." I picked up my backpack.

"'Wow' is right," Raina said, under her breath, and I was heading toward the door, I really was, but then she added, only a tiny bit softer, "More like *whack job*."

My bag fell with a thud onto the table. "Mental illness is nothing to joke about."

The room went freeze-frame except for Raina's hand flying to her mouth. "I—I didn't—"

"I have *not* been diagnosed with mental illness, but if I

had, I would find the term you used even *more* offensive."
Raina's hand dropped, the tilt of her eyebrows decidedly less impressed than a second ago, but who cared? I'd wanted to say that for *years*. I leaned against the table, revving up. "Also. *Also!* Don't you realize how hypocritical this is?"

Her eyes narrowed to slits. "*Excuse* me?"

"Discriminating against me based on my sexual orientation?"

Next to me, Jack Jackson murmured, "Ohhhh, this should be good."

Raina's face went cheerleader sunny at the prospect of a debate. "Are you seriously standing here trying to appropriate—?"

I wasn't one hundred percent sure what "appropriate" meant as a verb, so I cut her off. "I'm standing here trying to help. Trying to add my voice to yours. If I'm not welcome, so be it, but just know that you're silencing me. You're doing to me exactly what you're fighting against."

"Oh my God," Jack said. "You are one privileged little bitch, but I think I love you."

I blinked down at him. "Thank you?"

"She has a point, Ray." Sean shrugged amiably. "And I know things got ugly when we were a GSA, but—"

"We're not letting cis dilettantes into our group to claim ownership over our narrative. End of story." She scribbled something onto her legal pad as if making it official.

What in the hell did *"cis"* mean? *Should I be insulted?*

Instead of asking, I snatched up my bag, ready to embrace defeat and join Chess Club with Hannah. Getting checkmated by cocky freshmen over and over again for forty-seven minutes had to be more fun than this.

I was two inches from exiting stage left when Sophie's hand crept up.

"I might have a suggestion. In this one case."

Everyone's eyes darted to hers and her lashes fluttered downward.

"It seems like Daisy's sincere about wanting to help change the homecoming rule."

And everybody looked at me.

"I am." I leaned against the door. "I'm a very sincere person."

At Sophie's wince, I shut up.

"So," she continued, "why don't we let her run with this a little? And then we can decide whether being more inclusive makes sense."

"Sounds good to me," Sean said, drumming a swing beat on the table in celebration. "The inclusive part *and* the Daisy part."

When he said my name, he winked. *Shameless.* Jack reached up to shake my hand and Kyle gave a rapid-fire nod, probably afraid we'd ask him to say something out loud. When I dared turn to Raina, her smirk yanked me right back down to earth.

"Fantastic! Go for it. Multiple generations of gay students haven't managed to reverse the dance rule, but hell—you're *sincere*, Daisy Beaumont-Smith. I'm sure you'll succeed where everybody else failed."

"I appreciate that, Raina," I said, partly to show how sincere I was but mostly to annoy her. She glared flaming chain saws at me as the bell rang and we all made our way into the administrative wing.

Outside the door, Sophie motioned to an alcove beside a water fountain and ducked inside. Something in the combination of her furtive expression and peasant garb made me want to whisper *"Vive la Resistance!"*

"You are awesome," I said instead, following her. "I'm sorry if I put you in a weird spot."

"Not at all." Her voice was a normal volume but her eyes kept rising over my shoulder, presumably scanning for Raina. "It might be tricky, though. The last thing we want to be is discriminatory, but—there's a history. Ray was part of the group when it was founded. It was a GSA then, but the response from the straight students was . . . not what they'd hoped. A bunch of seniors got together and showed up to meetings to make fun of them. It became a sort of sick party. And one by one, all the gay kids dropped out. Some of them were only half out of the closet until then, so it wasn't good. Two kids ended up transferring out of the school. One tried to kill himself."

"Oh my God." My hand darted to my forehead. "That's *horrible*. Why didn't I hear about this?"

"I was in seventh grade when it happened. So you were probably in middle school too. And what you said about the school burying issues?" Sophie glanced at the ceiling as if making sure it wasn't bugged. "Anyway, things aren't that bad now. It was probably just a rotten batch of seniors, but when Raina and I talked about restarting the group again last year, we decided we'd create a safe haven for gay students. So while we *love* our straight friends, we don't include them in the Alliance."

"You know I'm not like that, right? I would never do anything to jeopardize the group."

"I know," she said, picking a cat hair off my shoulder. "It's just tricky."

"Wait, hang on," I said. "You and Raina founded the Alliance *together*?"

"We were . . . sort of"—Sophie looked down at her espadrilles—"dating at the time?"

I kept my mouth shut, but my eyes must have flashed *"Shut. Up,"* because Sophie smiled, shaking her head like even she couldn't believe it.

"It didn't last long," she said. "We're way too different. And our visions for the group are pretty different too."

The second bell rang and we both jumped.

"I'll do what I can for you, Daisy," Sophie said. "Either way—thank you!"

She waved and walked off, while I lingered, trying to decipher her thanks.

Oh. Right. I was "running with this." *This* being the huge school-policy battle that I myself had just full-on Joan of Arced. Okey dokey then. *Vive la whatever.*

I glanced at the hall clock, sprinted past a flock of lost freshmen consulting school maps, and caught Hannah slipping out of Chess Club a few minutes late, shaking hands with a knobby-necked boy she'd clearly just defeated. When she spotted me, her apologetic grimace deepened.

"You missed an awesome meeting," I said.

"I'm sorry!" She picked at her nails as we started down the hall. I swatted at her fingers before she could bite them. "I don't know why I said I'd see you there. This week has been . . . yeah, do you ever just feel like your brain's going in so many different directions that your mouth goes into autopilot—or, no, like you're sleepwalking—"

"So you weren't planning to come at all?" I pulled a loose thread on my jeans.

"It's just—" She pressed her lips together as if debating what to let out when she opened them again. "They seemed pretty standoffish."

"They're not," I lied, my head jerking back up. "They were super welcoming. And we have all sorts of plans already."

"Yeah?"

I nodded. "Big ones. Confidential. I mean, you'd have to come to a meeting . . ."

Hannah's eyebrows were about as high as I'd ever seen them. Then she smiled. "It's not too late to switch, you know. I'll teach you to play chess."

"You taught me four years ago. And I'm still horrible. All that *strategy*." I shuddered.

"*Or* you could *skip* clubs this year and . . . I don't know . . . paint a ridiculously elaborate mural for the rec center?"

I glared her down. Her mouth twitched.

"Why would you even bring that up?" I shook my head as she snickered. "So mean."

"You've got options, is all I'm saying. The Foodies? As one example? I'm still mad I was wrong about that."

My stomach rumbled at the prospect of becoming a Foodie.

And yet, all through bio, it was the Alliance I kept thinking about. So Hannah wasn't exactly gung-ho about joining the yay-we're-gay club. So what? Once she found out more about their . . . no—*our* plans, she'd get involved. I could just see her, swept up in our strategy sessions, devoting all her spare time to helping fight the school's discriminatory practices, like a getting-stuff-done montage in an action movie.

And if, say, *Natalie Beck* was too cool to join our cast, then she simply wasn't going to make the final cut, now was she?

Guessing that Hannah's learn-to-drive directive hadn't taken effect within the last seven hours, I waited after school as usual outside the hideous arts wing, its 1970s lime-and-orange walls especially garish under today's overcast sky.

It was still drizzling. Maybe we could hit the beach again on the way home and Hannah could help me brainstorm an action plan for Operation Bring-Down-the-School's-Unjust-and-Antiquated-School-Dance-Policy.

Step One: Come up with snappier code name.

I knew better than to go to Principal Zimmer, at least. Mom had called him an "empty suit" enough during her school-lunch tirades that I knew who held the real power— the school board. They were having their first public meeting next Wednesday. As a member of the public, I would be there. I'd entered it into my little phone calendar and everything.

Basically I was off and running. Hannah would be beyond impressed. I grinned into the sputtering sky. A raindrop landed in my mouth. Gross.

I was staring at a dead hedge, watching a sparrow digging

for twigs in its desiccated center, when it occurred to me that Hannah was late. A few minutes later, she still hadn't shown, and then here I was, facing down a slow stream of fellow students squinting quizzically as they filed past.

"Smurfette!" one of them shouted.

Alert.

I ducked away, hoping to get lost in the sparse crowd, but he found me. QB always found me.

"Nice shirt," he said, making fun of my Kudzu Giants album-cover tee. His friends weren't swarming this time, so I wondered who he was performing for. He dug his hands into the pockets of his hunting jacket, his face clouding. "No, I'm serious. I like that band. And their . . . music."

QB Saunders looked, against all probability, *awkward*.

The only possible response was to out-awkward him by blurting, "I like them too."

Before we could continue this scintillating nonversation, a neon-blue pickup pulled up and the football team's actual quarterback, Darius, waved for him to get in. QB walked backward, dodging the rain, saying, "See you around, Daisy."

And then, dear Lord, he winked. Or tried to. His eye twitched shut, so he had to rub it to get it to open again.

Also—hang the hell on—had he just called me Daisy?

Chilled to my core, I hurried to the school parking lot to see if, against protocol, Hannah was waiting for me there.

She was, thank God. She waved over the roof of her car.

"I was about to leave you!"

Odd. It wasn't like us to get our wires crossed.

But it only took me five steps across the lot to identify the gremlin in the works—Natalie Beck, curled up in the front of Hannah's car, examining her nails with the door shut and the window rolled up, a celebrity waiting for her driver.

"Do you mind the back? Nat got here first, so she called shotgun . . ." Hannah's face started to flood. She was never any good at hiding her nerves.

And although I was empirically better in that area, I wasn't a cool enough customer to sit in a car with Hannah and the Beck making googly eyes at each other without launching into an impromptu intervention.

So I said, "I'm meeting my mom. She's on her way. Sorry for the confusion." And turned on my heel so I didn't have to field Hannah's skeptical glare.

I rounded the corner of the school to the rhythm of my thudding heart. What was wrong with me? Oh! Right! My best friend had been stolen by a scheming ice queen and *not even* a fun one who builds snow castles and sings power ballads.

I called my mom five times and on the last try left a voice-mail.

"I need a ride home. Meet me at the Moonlight—" I winced. "Wait, no, Starbucks. Call me when you get this?" I almost hung up and then added, "I'm *fine*, by the way," but in this intense tone that was going to freak her out even more.

Inside Starbucks, I settled onto a wobbly stool near the window with a schmancy soda and a cookie. I'd just taken out my homework when, two seats down, someone pretended to cough. It was flagrantly fake. Almost insulting.

From the corner of my eye, I made out a mess of black hair, tall, rangy, a restless hand tapping the edge of the counter, and the nape of my neck began to tingle. I ignored the second "ahem" for a full five-count before looking over. There he was, Mr. Power Cord, the guy from the coffee shop.

What a delightful coincidence.

He adjusted his laptop so I could spot the duct tape holding the screen's corner together.

"It didn't *completely* break," he said. "In case you were wondering."

"Did you follow me here to tell me that? How considerate."

"Follow you?" He pushed his glasses up. "I was here first."

"If you say so."

He actually had gotten here first. I would have noticed him coming in, since my chair was facing the entrance.

"It has a blank spot in the corner now," he was saying. "But the tape keeps it from spreading."

"Gotta love duct tape." I turned a page of my French textbook, clearly very absorbed. Then a pesky wave of guilt hit me. I hadn't adequately apologized for knocking his laptop to the ground, had I? I'd been too busy fleeing. I closed my book. "Do you want some money to fix it, or . . . ?"

I let my voice trail off.

"*No* no," he said. "Actually, are you offering? My warranty's expired and I could really use the—"

I stared at him over my soda bottle. "Here you're supposed to thank me for the offer but say that you couldn't possibly accept."

"I was kidding," he said, though he completely wasn't. He squinted at his screen and started to attack the keyboard again, calling to mind my theories about him from yesterday.

I managed to keep my mouth shut for thirty seconds before guessing, "Great American novel?"

"Great American article."

Shocking exposé for the win! I mentally high-fived myself.

Then he sank against the counter. "Actually, it's not a great American anything. I'm reporting on boutiques that sell clothes for cats. Did you know that there are over twenty in the Greater Charleston area alone? This town is cat crazy."

I must have given him a funny look. He nodded at me as if he agreed.

"It's for class." He rested his cheek on one hand, fingers tapping against his temple. "I'm a *journalism* major." He groaned the word like it was a death sentence, not something he could transfer out of next semester. Still, he was more interesting than conjugating *être* and *avoir,* so I snuck another glance as he took a sip from the giant ceramic mug in his hand. I was strangely impressed by the mug. He was the only one in this Starbucks not drinking out of a paper cup. He must have asked specifically. Who does that?

"Are you okay?" he asked, and I looked away, realizing it was a little weird to have been watching him so closely. But he didn't seem confrontational, just curious. Journalism major and all that.

"Not great, actually. Sort of having a quiet meltdown."

"Oh." He smirked. "Here you're supposed to say, 'I'm fine, thank you.'"

"I'm fine," I echoed. "Thank you."

"I'm Adam." His smirk loosened. He extended a hand and without thinking, I took it, but instead of shaking it like a normal person, I held on, thinking, *His hand is so big. Firm grip. If I were dangling off a cliff, he could pull me to safety.*

"I'm Adam," I heard myself say. Then I blinked. "Wait. I'm Daisy. I—?"

My mom's car pulled up outside and I snatched my hand back, gathered my books, and shoved the rest of my cookie into my mouth in record time.

"Sorry about your computer," I chew-mumbled, scrambling away. "I really am."

He was still watching me through the window as I got into the car, a confused half smile on his face. It was hard to tell if "I'm Adam" was actually hot, or just hot by virtue of being a college kid, but what was I even thinking? If I saw him again, he'd probably get up the nerve to *actually* ask me for money, and then I'd have to ask my mom, and it would become this big thing. As it was, Mom was nudging me every stoplight.

"Who was that *boy*?"

"Adam. I mean, I don't know. I don't know him."

"You don't know him from Adam?" She had that mom-instincts smirk going on.

Poor Mom. Of course she'd be hopeful. I was probably one of the only people in my school, let alone my grade, to have never had a boyfriend. Or a girlfriend. Or a hookup. Or, you know . . . a date. Well, *one* date, back in eighth grade, culminating in an *attempted* hookup, but since it ended with me punching Seth Ross in his smugly face, I considered it struck from the record. And there had been nobody else, nobody real, no matter how many times Mom asked. She was just waiting for me to become normal. But her hope made me feel worse.

"Mom?" I gulped. "There's something I need to tell you."

Mom swung her head around. Amazing how quickly she could go from theorizing I had a boyfriend back to theorizing I was gay.

"I think I'm . . ." I bit my lip for maximum drama. "Hungry. What are we having for dinner?"

"Salmon," she sighed, the trials of being my mother descending heavily upon her. "We're having quinoa and salmon."

6

By ten o'clock Saturday morning, I'd sent Han six texts:

Whatcha UP to?

GENIUS IDEA: Let's meet up, do awesome weekend stuff ET CETERA

Or are you working? You might be working.

OMG Zelda has rabies. So sad!!! ☹

Kidding. It would explain a lot, tho, amiright

I'm going to mess up these college brochures! I'm putting Northwestern in the no pile!

When even the last failed to get a response, my phone became glued to my hand, thumb primed.

It rang! I pressed.

"Daisy? Oh." The man on the other end coughed. "Have I got voicemail? I didn't hear the tone, but—"

Crapcrapcrap. I considered reciting my outgoing message, complete with beep, but, guilt sinking into my gut, I gritted my teeth and said, "No, hi, Mr. Murphy. It's actual Daisy. Not voicemail."

Mr. Murphy guffawed. "I was all ready to leave you a message!"

He was so nice. It made my soul hurt.

Late last year, my school had taken part in a volunteer day at the James Island Community Rec Center. After weeding the parking lot alongside a seven-year-old who talked about mythology and Sour Patch Kids for two hours straight, the spirit of volunteerism swept through me like a stomach virus. I took Mr. Murphy, the director, aside and offered to do more.

A lot more.

And now, all summer really, I'd been trying desperately to stall for time, if not get out of it altogether. If I could take some private art lessons, maybe, or watch some instructional YouTube videos or check out some books about the history of public art, study some ancient Greek texts or maps or . . .

"Glad I caught you," he said. "If you're free today, we've got some kids who'd love to help you with your project—"

"That's great!" My heart went thud-thudthud-thud. "I'm tied up this whole weekend, though. Unfortunately."

"Oh gosh."

"Yeah, I'm helping my mom with this . . . activist thing. For the, uh, Community Farmers of America."

I squinched my eyes shut, wincing.

"Well, that's great, Daisy, good for you. I just wanted to say, if you can make some time for this mural, that whale sure could use some company."

Oh God, the whale. *The whale.* The gigantic symbol of my ineptitude.

I you-betcha'd my way off the phone and exhaled loudly only to see Mom standing in the doorway, one hand pressed to her heart, the other holding a fresh white expanse of poster board.

"Did I hear right?" she asked. "Are you coming to the farm rally?"

"Depends. Is it, by chance, being held *across the street from my school*?"

"Yes! It's the property we're hoping to—"

I rolled over and grabbed a book. "Then no. But thank you for the invitation!"

Mom pouted, cradling her blank poster like the progressive child she would never have.

"It'll be *fun*," she tried. "I promise."

"Mom?" I peered over my book at her. "I love you. But not enough to protest outside my own school. Seriously. I'll be Angry Mob Girl until my fiftieth reunion. And since you won't let me transfer to private school—"

"Daisy, you know that abandoning the public school system only perpetuates the socioeconomic divide within the American educational—"

"Exactly, not happening. Sorry."

Her face drooped. Residual shame from lying to Mr. Murphy rose in my throat like reflux.

"Good luck, though," I offered, and I meant it. "I'm sure whatever you're protesting is really evil. And deserves to be eradicated."

"We're not protesting." She waved her poster board. It made thunder noises. "We're rallying! Trying to get the city council to zone Lot 429 for a community farm."

"That's awesome." I shot her a thumbs-up. "But I need to . . ."

. . . be here in case Hannah calls back.

". . . spend time with Dad. I've said like two words to him since school started."

In the end, father-daughter bonding warmed Mom's heart more than collaborative chanting, so I was left waiting for my phone to beep, the quiet of the house growing thicker as the minutes ticked by. When the air conditioner clicked off, the only sounds I could make out were swords clinking and monsters roaring behind the door at the end of the hall.

In the interest of fairness, I should note that this was my father's job.

Judging by the sound effects that had been coming from his "office" for the past day or so, this was some kind of sword and sorcery epic. After a few minutes of listening, curiosity overtook me, and deciding that I needed to make at least one lie true today, I knocked on his door.

"Heya," he called. "I'll take a coffee!"

"Not Mom," I announced.

"Oh. Okay. Come on in."

Dad paused the game and rolled back in his deluxe gamer's chair to pull another over, while Zelda scrambled from the room to escape the sight of me. Up on the giant screen, an ogre dripped blood from one eye. An elf girl with abundant boobage was climbing onto his back, preparing to finish him off with her electrical long-sword.

Dad scratched his stubble, then waved a spare controller at me. "Two player? You can be the elf rogue, she's pretty badass." His face clouded. "Or is that sexist? You can be the hammer-lord and I'll be the elf. I have no problem playing the elf."

"Thanks, Dad," I said, smiling at his continued efforts to coexist in a mostly female family. "I'll just watch."

"Let me know what you think," he muttered, launching himself back into a brutal unprovoked attack on a helpless beast. "Something's not working with this game arc and I'm having the durndest time figuring out what it is."

Eight or nine years ago, my dad sold the indie video game company he'd started out of his parents' basement when he was in high school, raking in enough money to support a family of three for, well, ever. But designing *Bertie and the Bots* and all those *Farzone* games had made him such an icon in the field that he'd been besieged by consulting requests ever since. He spent most of his waking hours playing beta versions of new games, then teleconferencing with other high-functioning nerds to find and fix problems.

It was a pretty sweet job. Except for the never seeing sunlight thing. And the fact that his hands twitched involuntarily whenever he wasn't gaming.

I dimly remembered a time when his assignments were only occasional, leaving him enough spare hours to come with me to the park or the movies or even just the backyard play set. He was tanner, I seemed to recall. Athletic, almost? It was possible I'd only dreamed it. Memories were weird like that.

I watched him play for twenty minutes. Once he'd defended the Kingsroad Bridge from an onrush of what looked like straight-up Lord of the Rings rip-offs, I decided I'd filled my quota of father-daughter bonding for the day.

As I was slipping out the door, Dad muttered, "Have fun with Hannah." I didn't have the heart to correct him.

She didn't call until Sunday night.

"I'm so sorry," she said over low voices in the background. "This has been a crazy weekend. I can't talk now, but . . . things went down. I'll tell you later."

I was in shoes and down the stairs by the time she said the word "later." But before I could offer to hitchhike to her house with food and/or medical supplies, Hannah had already hung up.

Monday morning, fifteen minutes before Hannah was supposed to collect me, she sent a text.

"SO SORRY can't drive today. I'll make it up—promise—see you at school!"

Mom was already gone. Her protest group had made some headway, so she was meeting with a city councilman to talk about taking over that field. This meant I was forced to accept a ride to school from my game-addled father, who kept rounding corners so narrowly, I swore we were going to jump the curb.

"Yikes." He chuckled nervously as I stumbled through the car door onto school property. "The last car I drove was a Lamborghini hovercraft. *Galactic Grand Prix: Eternity.* Handled a lot better than this one."

I managed a wave and had nearly regained my balance

when I saw QB Saunders loitering outside the school entrance, messing with the strap of his backpack. I heaved a breath and prepared for impact.

"Smurfette!" QB stepped into my path. "I mean . . . *Daisy*. Hey."

A vein was pumping in his neck, his forehead creased. Holy thundercats—I knew what this was. QB was trying not to make fun of me. It was *work*. He was sweating, little curls of blond hair sticking to his ears. Why didn't he take off that damn jacket?

"Hi." I kept walking.

He fell into step beside me. "Did you, um, have an awesome weekend?"

This conversation had just tipped from strange to delightfully surreal. I had to press my lips together to hold in a squeal of laughter.

"I did!" I got out. "I had an *awesome* weekend, *Chris*, thank you for asking!"

"Cool, so . . ." QB's voice died out. We literally had nothing to talk about.

As we walked through the bustling lobby, I assumed the spell he was under would be broken. But QB stuck to me like a barnacle.

"You excited for homecoming?"

This was too much. I turned to stare at him in utter incredulity . . . then noticed that everyone else was staring at us too.

No, not us. Him. Conversations were falling to a fevered hush, eyes darting to QB and then away, like they couldn't even bear to look at him. *Because of me?* Panic licked like flames at my vision. I knew this feeling only too well.

Before it could progress to shame sweats, I gave QB a nod and a "See ya," and hurried to homeroom.

Weirdly, separating from QB didn't seem to stop whatever eerie mania had taken over the school. The hallways were jammed with kids sharing "Oh. My. God"s and "Shut up, what?!"s before running to the next huddle of people and starting the process all over again.

Even the freshmen in my French class were buzzing like flies around a trash can.

As soon as I sat down, a girl I'd never talked to leaned way over and said, "You will not believe what I just heard."

I hated to admit it, but I was dying to find out.

"En français!" Prof Hélène called out in exasperation.

The girl thought for a second, then said:

"Natalie Beck *est* totally gay."

7

Pre-calc. Fourth period. The Beck sat in her usual spot in back, auburn ponytail hanging perfectly vertical, posture erect, notebooks and pencils arranged in perpendicular rows on her desk. Nothing new. But her mouth was welded shut and her blue eyes focused ahead, like she was trying to drill a hole into the whiteboard with her brain.

Natalie had two underlings in this class, both longtime high-ranking officials in the We Hate Daisy Army. Madison Speiss was a dyed-blond, five-one terror whose father owned a Jaguar dealership or seven, while Dana Costas was a more muted shade of awful, the kind of girl who might have been gorgeous if she weren't constantly fidgeting with her curly hair and her clothes. On more than one occasion, I'd walked into the girls' room to catch her staring sadly at herself in the restroom mirrors and had to fight the urge to whisper, "The problem is with your *souuuuuuul.*"

Today, in her normal back-row seat, Dana was more fidgety than ever. Instead of talking to Natalie—her best friend—she kept exchanging Meaningful Glances with Madison, who had moved two rows up, abandoning the back of the room for the first time in her academic career. Judging by her smug expression, Madison was making some sort of a statement.

No wonder Natalie refused to look at them—or anybody else in the class. Everyone knew. But knowing wasn't enough. They had to crane their necks to stare at her, lean over to whisper between aisles. Even when Mr. Thornton started the lesson, I saw three people sneak out cell phones to message each other under their desks, barely stifling snickers.

The second class broke, Natalie walked briskly to the door, only to face down a hallway crammed with students. At the sight of her, everyone fell conspicuously silent. Natalie pulled her shoulders back and lifted her chin, Anne Boleyn walking to the scaffold. Then I saw her hands clench and unclench at her sides, and we might as well have been seven again, daring each other to knock on the door of the haunted old McLaren house—Nat-Nat in front, willing herself strong.

I touched her arm. "Are you all right?"

She turned to me, impassive as a saint. I waited for her to answer, and so did the rest of the hallway. Instead, her eyes slowly lowered until they were power-drilling into my hand. I flinched, let go, and she walked away. And suddenly, I was the one everybody was goggling.

Served me right. I'd walked directly into this. But as I gathered a shaky breath and huffed away, it wasn't myself I felt disgusted with. It was Hannah.

I'd slipped for five seconds, just long enough to treat Natalie Beck as though she had anything other than Xenomorph acid pumping through her veins. But Hannah? She'd been slipping for the past month. Maybe more. How could she have *fallen* for this person?

My path didn't connect with Hannah's until lunchtime. Once I'd purchased an especially greasy grilled cheese sandwich with an extra plate so we could share, I searched the room for her, wondering how she was coping with all this.

It was an easy room to scan. Hardly anybody was at the tables. At least half the people here had assumed mob formation on one side of the cafeteria, faces crammed against the windowpanes.

The squirrels must be mating again, I thought. *Seems early, but who am I to judge? Maybe they're just enjoying a little off-season friski—*

"Take my seat." I turned to see Jack Jackson gallantly dusting a chair with his napkin. "I was just leaving."

"Oh! Thanks," I said, craning my neck to see past the wall of students, who were, annoyingly, also blocking my view to the steps. "I'm actually looking for . . ."

"Hannah's outside. With Natalie Beck."

Oh, no. Not squirrels. Of course not. This was a much bigger draw.

They were staring at the stoop.

Every cell in my body urged me forward, to join Hannah, to shield her from view—but no. After this morning's altercation, I knew better than to reenter the Beck's ballistic range.

Right. Of course she's eating with Natalie. Natalie's been outed. There's no reason not to. She could eat with Natalie every day from now on.

Which left me with a dizzying array of new dining options. I glanced around, feeling extremely small.

Peppering the room were tables informally reserved by

people I'd barely spoken to, except maybe to ask what the teacher had just said the homework was. A bunch of the Parapsychology Club kids hung out at the table just behind me. We knew each other, yeah, but after the "You're all so *freaking smug*. It must be nice to know *everything about the universe!*" incident that ended my affiliation with the group last year, I doubted they'd clear me a space when they returned from gawking out the window.

To my left was the table where Dan Sawtuck and Mara Thomas usually sat. I'd done an English class project with them last year and we were still sort of friendly, I guessed, but they'd started dating since then and pretty much spent the whole lunch hour making out, so my presence at their table would probably be awkward for all involved.

I spotted some other options that would place me alongside people whose birthday parties I'd gone to, whose jokes I'd laughed at in class, who'd held the door for me on their way out of the restroom. But it felt too weird to walk up and invade their space without Hannah to provide the social niceties. Me by myself was tantamount to, "Hi, I'm Daisy, will you please be my friend?" and I was *so* not up for that today. Or, you know, ever.

Jack had already slipped out of the cafeteria and there was nobody else at the table, so I fell into his seat and picked at my lunch, sliding Hannah's extra plate under my own. It felt disorienting sitting here, like switching from map mode to first-person POV in a video game. I thought I knew the exact social layout of this room, but now that I was fully ensconced, I could make out so much more.

Along the far wall, I saw Raina eating at a table where everyone's heads were ducked, doing homework. A few tables down, Sean was laughing along with his bevy of devoted drama girls. And close to the door, I spotted Sophie carrying on a quiet conversation with a group of classmates in competing earth-toned outfits.

From what I could tell, the Alliance members barely acknowledged one another outside their weekly meetings. But now I saw one thing binding them together—out of everyone in the cafeteria, Raina, Sean, and Sophie were the only three whose faces didn't turn to the windows every few seconds. There was something focused about the way each of them sat in place, refusing to look. A form of respect.

As I polished off my lunch, four gawky guys broke from the window, nudging one another with leering expressions, like they'd just watched a peep show instead of two girls eating sandwiches. At the sight of them, Sophie's serene smile disappeared. I watched them motion toward her, and then, as if drawn in by her discomfort, veer to her table.

For a second, I hoped they were just going over there to set up a pot deal for later, but then one of them said something I couldn't make out and they all started laughing. Sophie's face went pale. A shaggy-haired boy at her table half stood, jaw clenched, then sank again, defeated by their numbers.

One of the four douchenozzles leered over his shoulder, so I got a look at his face—as Slytherin-snide as it was in eighth grade. Seth Ross.

Sophie was fighting to recover a smile and I was steeling myself to march over and slug him again if need be, when somebody slapped a folded piece of notebook paper down on my plastic tray, startling me back into my seat.

I whipped around to see QB striding away, trailing Darius. QB had been getting more than his share of negative attention in the wake of today's bombshell, but right now, Darius's glower seemed to have opened a path in front of them, allowing them to escape without overt mocking. Football had its perks—even if you never won a game.

I unfolded the page they'd left me, expecting to find some taunt, or threat, or accusation about my own sexuality, but it was something far more disturbing.

Please meet me after class. I'll treat for pizza. Need to talk.
~ Chris.

First, I marveled that he'd signed it Chris. Was it because I'd called him that this morning? It wasn't the oddest thing in the world to sign your own name on a note. But QB had been "QB" since sixth grade. His friends would correct teachers on his behalf when they called roll with the standard "Chris Saunders."

But what was I thinking? *Chris* was not what was insane. What was insane was that "Chris" had left me a note imploring me to get pizza with him.

Either this was an elaborate practical joke or QB had been body-snatched.

Hannah had time to give me only the quickest of whispered rundowns before we sat for bio.

"She came out to Madison and Dana over the weekend.

Madison quoted the Bible, said that she was uncomfortable that Natalie was 'choosing this path.'"

Hannah paused for effect, but I could see the irony all on my own. Madison was not the purest lily in God's garden. Not that *I* had any issue with the percentage of the junior and senior class she'd worked her way through, but if you're gonna talk righteous paths . . .

"Dana promised to support her," Hannah went on. "She seemed great about it, apparently. And then she went home and emailed half the school."

"Oh God," I said, and thankfully got shushed by the teacher before I was forced to recite *"Poor Natalie,"* my next expected line.

This situation was horrible. No question. But the Beck wasn't exactly a defenseless victim. She chose her friends a long time ago and set the tone for the way they treated other people—including me. If the situation had been reversed, who's to say she wouldn't have behaved exactly the same way?

I knew better than to expect a Natalie-free ride home from Hannah today, so after the last bell rang, I hid in the girls' restroom and called my mom approximately one million times, getting only voicemail. Dad too. Same result.

The sharp corner of QB's note was digging into my jeans pocket. He was seventeen. He probably had a car. He could give me a ride home. After we ate pizza. And talked. And flew to the moon on giant papier-mâché butterflies.

I was leaning against the bathroom's windowsill, calculating the cost of a taxi, when two girls came in, holding each other up between bursts of debilitating laughter.

A pang scrunched my stomach. Hannah and I always got into giggle fits over the stupidest things—the gym teacher running all over the basketball court trying to catch a possum, the "phallic oak" lecture in English after we'd read *Jane Eyre*.

Then I heard what the two girls were saying.

"Who is he waiting for? He's just standing out there like an idiot."

"He *is* an idiot! How can you not know your girlfriend's a dyke?"

"Maybe he turned her." Giggles galore.

I shoved myself away from the window and past the two banshees, managing to shoulder-check both of them like a cowboy leaving a saloon. Then, ignoring their *"Excuse* me?"s, I slammed the bathroom door behind me, not stopping until I reached the exit beside the arts wing—where QB Saunders was, in fact, standing there like an idiot.

His sad orphan face lightened a fraction when he saw me. Oh God.

I felt sorry for him. For QB Saunders.

"Pizza," I barked. "Let's go."

People were staring, so I walked, hoping he'd have the sense to follow. Mario's Pizzeria was only three blocks away. I had to assume that's where he was planning to take me. It was The Place, full of the very people Hannah and I went to the Moonlight Coffee Shop to avoid.

I had to stop when a minivan blasting death metal rounded the corner, inches from my face. QB caught up beside me.

He up-nodded lasciviously. "You look really—"

"Nope." I put my hand up as I faced him. "What is this? What are you doing?"

His smile flickered. "Um . . ."

"You've done nothing for the past decade but make fun of me. Why are you suddenly friendly?"

QB's brow furrowed with the massive effort of coming up with a reply. The street cleared. I growled a sigh and crossed.

It wasn't until we'd gotten to Mario's, ordered slices and sodas, and sat at a picnic table in the dingy back garden with everyone in the world staring at us that he answered my question.

"I wasn't trying to be a dick. When I teased you, I mean."

I rolled my eyes.

"Seriously!" His face went soft, all innocence. "It was *nice* teasing. Like friends do." At my raised eyebrow, he fell somber. "You're not the easiest person to start a conversation with, you know."

Dozens of overlapping responses sprung to mind, from "That's ridiculous, I am a Class One Loudmouth," to "Tell me something *interesting* and I'll respond," but then I realized I'd just sat there staring at QB for close to a minute without physically saying anything, so he might have had a point.

What I came out with was "Fine."

QB looked encouraged. And then, abruptly, heartbroken. "You heard about Natalie?"

I nodded and took an enormous bite of pizza, determined to eat and get out of here as quickly as possible. The cheese singed the roof of my mouth.

He leaned over the table, his voice low. "Did you know . . . before?"

I shrugged. "Like a couple of days."

"That's it?" QB looked confused. It was a familiar expression. "I thought maybe you could tell by looking at her. Like . . . radar."

It took a sugary gulp of soda for my brain to kick into gear.

I stared at him. "You mean . . . *gaydar*?"

"Yeah!" He perked up. "Like that."

"Oh my God." A laugh got stuck in my throat. "You think I'm gay!"

"What? Well, yeah. Aren't you? You and Hannah von Lincoln or whatever. Everyone knows she's your ex."

"She's my best friend. *Not* ex, current. But that's it. We're platonic soul mates."

"Oh." QB slumped, his expression shuffling between confusion and disappointment. He took a bite of his pizza, but stopped mid-chew like he'd lost the energy to digest it. I pushed his soda toward him. He sipped and swallowed.

When he glanced back up, he didn't look any happier. "So I guess she's with Natalie now."

"I guess. No accounting for taste."

He squinted. "You don't like this either."

"I'm not the world's biggest Natalie Beck fan."

QB recoiled, apparently shocked. "But Natalie's an amazing person! She's seriously the most awesome—"

I motioned for him to lower his voice. A squirrely kid from my homeroom passed with a tray, one ear cocked toward our conversation, and at last QB seemed to realize he was not in

74

the middle of a therapy session. He rocked back in his chair and his face relaxed. Smarmy. Arrogant. The face I was used to.

"I bet you're an amazing girl too, Daisy."

The junior did a double take as he walked past. I didn't blame him. At this point, I questioned whether I was, in fact, dreaming this entire day. "Are you *hitting* on me?"

QB slid his hand closer to mine. "Do you *want* me to be hitting on you?"

"QB." I peered into his eyes. He squirmed. "If you thought I was gay . . . why would you be interested in me?"

He frowned, considering. "I thought maybe . . . I could . . ."

I bit my lip. "Change my mind?"

He shrugged the saddest shrug I'd ever seen.

The mist in my brain lifted, and there it was. His whole misguided plan.

As of this morning, everyone in the school knew his girl-friend of two years was a lesbian. So QB, great philosopher of our time, had decided to take *another* lesbian out to the most visible date spot possible in order to demonstrate to the general public how very wrong they were about him. QB Saunders didn't turn straight girls gay. He turned *lesbians straight!*

Sure enough, QB was scanning the crowded porch. My eyes followed his. None of our classmates were staring, not while we were looking back, but I could feel their attention like a heat lamp. We were the sideshow to Natalie's three-ring circus.

Against all conceivable logic, QB's plan was working.

I shoved my crust away.

"I'm not gay, Chris. *And* you can't change my mind. So thanks for the pizza." I stood. "Good luck with your life."

As I was leaving Mario's, my back itching from the sensation of eyes attaching themselves to it, my phone buzzed. My mom had finally gotten my messages and was on her way. She couldn't resist a second text:

"You need to learn to drive, missy."

I didn't disagree.

A block away from school, QB caught up with me, red plaid jacket tossed over one shoulder. He was out of breath from running, which meant he'd sat and finished his slice before deciding to make a grand gesture.

"Hey, listen," he huffed. "I'm sorry. I just—everybody's making these jokes about me, and I needed . . ." His voice trailed off.

"A buffer?"

He smiled in relief. "Exactly."

I awarded him two points for honesty, even if it wasn't the whole truth. QB could have latched on to any number of willing girls. Homecoming court girls, with beach tans, streamlined waists, expensive haircuts.

I was under no illusions about my own appearance. Average height, average weight, two-tone hair. It wasn't painful to look at me, and with a bit of makeup and the right lighting, I could attract some compliments. But the only way I'd ever stop traffic would be by refusing to budge from the middle of an intersection.

This wasn't about my looks or my social standing. QB chose me because he thought I was gay. I wasn't exactly swooning.

But he was still talking.

"I've always had a thing for you, you know." QB raised his chin so that the Michelangelo-sculpted planes of his face caught the hazy, late-day sunlight, his hair glowing in a circlet like a freaking laurel wreath.

"Really?" I said, cringing at the plaintiveness in my voice. Maybe I was wrong. Maybe I was prettier than I thought, like those girls in movies who just need to take off their glasses to make everyone in town fall in love with them. Except I didn't wear glasses. So.

"Yeah." QB whapped my shoulder. "*Weird*, right? I don't even know why!"

And *poof* the spell was broken.

The fresh-popcorn scent of my mom's bio-fuel car hit me before it even rounded the corner. I ran for the curb, praying that QB could sense from the fact that I was *running away* that this plan of his was not going to work.

But just as I was slamming the passenger door, motioning Mom to hit the gas, I heard QB's voice through the open window, ringing with the confidence that only the dumb and beautiful possess.

"Catch you tomorrow!"

He would too. QB Saunders always caught me.

8

"Where do we stand on the rule change? We all clear to bring our girlfriends to homecoming?"

Raina's eyes were bright with malice as she waited for me to reply. It was Tuesday, club period, and the Alliance had a few questions.

"Not yet," I admitted. She rolled dramatically back from the table, hands in the air. "But the school board is meeting tomorrow night. I'll formally petition them then."

"Whoa," Jack said.

"Really?" Sean pointed at me. "*Daisy!* Yes!"

"Yes," I repeated, trying not to giggle at his repeated use of my name.

Raina's smirk shriveled. "*You're* going to petition the Palmetto School Board. In person. Tomorrow."

"Yep!" I snuggled into my conference room chair. "You guys should come too, if you're free. Solidarity and all that."

"I can be there," Sophie said, glancing at the others.

"I need to ask my mom," Kyle said. "I won't have to talk or anything, right?"

"Nope." I smiled. "I'll do the talking."

"This is a staggeringly bad idea," Raina muttered at her legal pad.

I stared at her. "What? I'm running with it."

"She *is* running with it," Sophie said gently. "You have to admit."

Something about all this "running" talk made me feel suddenly winded.

"You know, it doesn't have to be me," I blurted. "I can assist from the background if any of *you* would rather speak up at the—"

Amid the deafening chorus of "No thank you"s from everybody in the room, I could pick out Sophie laughing nervously, Raina muttering something about waiting for prom in the spring, and Sean sing-saying, "*You* are going to be *fantastic!*"

"So." Sophie gestured so daintily, I expected a bluebird to land on her finger. "Given that Daisy's planning to speak out for the group in public, it would probably be good for us to vote on her *formal* inclusion in the Alliance?"

One by one, the others nodded, except Raina, who appeared to have started her math homework.

"Great," Sophie went on. "Well, we've been talking for a long time about expanding our definition to include the full quilt bag . . ."

There was that phrase again. I nodded, visualizing something one might buy at a craft store. Probably a symbol of . . . different fabrics? Cloths joining together, preparing to be sewn? Yeah, I had no idea.

Sean interrupted, nodding to an equally bewildered Kyle. "You might want to give a definition, Soph."

"For all of us," Jack said, rolling his eyes in my direction. "So many letters. And they're constantly *changing*."

"Of course." Sophie flushed. "Well, *my* understanding is that QUILTBAG stands for Questioning, Unidentified, Intersex, Lesbian, Transgender, Bisexual, Asexual, and Gay. Is it at all possible . . ." Her eyes bored into mine, conveying some sort of secret code. "That you're one of those?"

"Can I be unidentified?"

"But you did identify it," Raina protested, glaring over her textbook. "You told us you were straight."

"Questioning."

Raina set the book aside with a thud. "Since last week?"

"You guys gave me *a lot* to think about."

Jack snorted, Raina huffed, and Sophie kneaded her braid. By pulling out the full rainbow of options, she was obviously trying to find me an in.

"How about asexual?" I tried. "Yes! You guys, I'm *totally* asexual! I never go on dates. I never get crushes on people."

Since freshman year, anyway. Sean had the decency to look at his fingernails.

"The last time somebody tried to kiss me, I punched him in the face!" I clapped in delight. "That's me. Asexual. Sign me up for the quilt bag!"

Sophie looked relieved. Everyone else looked dubious. *Asexual.* It wasn't completely off base, was it? Sure, I'd fantasized about various guys, both real and of the hottest-guy-on-*Triplecross* variety. But at the moment? Nope! Brief musings about QB and Don't Know Him From Adam didn't count. After all, they wouldn't lead anywhere. So today, Tuesday the thirteenth of September, I was one hundred percent—

"You do realize that asexuality is an actual designation, right?" Raina snapped. "*Real* people are *really* asexual. It doesn't mean that you can't get a date."

"Raina!" Sophie, Sean, and Jack shouted in unison.

She picked up her textbook again. "Whatever. Fine. Let's move on."

"Next question?" Sophie offered.

Sean raised his hand to ask it. "Do you, Daisy Beaumont-Smith"—*my full name this time!*—"promise to be respectful of all gay students, whether they're members of this group or not?"

"Of course," I said, and he double-thumbs-upped his approval.

"Raina?" Sophie smiled tightly.

Without looking up, Raina intoned, "Do you promise to keep confidential *everything* we say in this room, unless we agree as a group to reveal it?"

"Y-yeah." Why did I stutter on that? It made me sound untrustworthy. Of course I could keep my mouth shut. I was *excellent* at self-control. Well, good anyway. Fair, which was better than average, right?

Okay, average.

Everyone turned to look at Freshman Kyle and he shrunk lower in his lacrosse hoodie. "I don't have any questions. You seem okay to me."

I smiled my thanks.

That left Jack Jackson. He narrowed his eyes.

"I think this is the number one question we *all* have."

I nodded eagerly, my sweat glands activating. Sure enough,

everybody was sitting straighter, ready for this final qualifier, which they'd obviously discussed in advance.

"Do you think you could get Natalie Beck involved in the group?"

And oh, the epic battle that went on within me. You could write ballads about it. Whole operas. And I *knew* from opera.

"Definitely! We're old friends, you know. And she's dating Hannah, so . . ."

I cleared my throat, noticing how they were all watching me, little kids waiting for the ice cream truck window to slide open.

"Actually, I already talked to her about our homecoming battle, and she's super excited!" I nodded. Kept nodding. I was maybe nodding too much.

Natalie Beck. Super excited. I couldn't picture it. But the tension in the room broke, so I guess everyone else could.

Except Raina. She leaned in.

"I'm sorry, I've got just one more follow-up question. Teeny-tiny," she added over Sean's and Jack's grumbles. *"Why are you doing this?"*

I opened my mouth, but a brilliant answer didn't miraculously materialize on my tongue, so Raina went on:

"Joining this club, lobbying the school board—why? This is not your fight. You're straight."

"Asexual," Jack corrected, and I swiveled my chair to nod a thank-you, even though he'd made air quotes.

"Isn't it enough that she's an ally, Ray?" Sean grimaced through his smile, like arguing tasted bad to him. "Allies are a good thing. A *helpful* thing. I'm speaking from a whole lotta personal experience here."

Raina spread her hands against the table. "I'm just trying to understand."

Sophie and Kyle stayed silent. I guess they were trying to understand too.

I swallowed. "This is important to me because it's important to somebody I care about."

"Hannah von Linden." Raina motioned around the room. "If it's so important to her, then where is she?"

"Ray," Sophie cut in, her voice calm and soothing. I wondered if she'd used this tone to talk Raina down during the three weeks that they were dating.

Raina smiled. "I just—"

"You want to understand." I stood. "Okay, fine. Yes, Hannah's the person I care about. More than anybody in the world, actually. But . . . we're different."

I felt woozy admitting it, like I was still swiveling in my chair.

"We've always been planners. For years, we've come up with these big ideas, but Hannah always talks herself out of them. And I'm the one who gives them a try. So here I am. Giving this a try. For both of us."

Jack nudged me in approval while across the table Sean pressed his hands to his heart. Next to him, Sophie leaned in.

"We're *glad* you're giving it a try."

Her smile was like a Charleston garden gate—sweet, lovely, forged in iron. I'd never noticed that edge to Sophie before— *any* edge, really. I had a sudden image of her presiding over a dinner table, gray hair in a braided bun, inspecting all her grandkids' hands for grime.

Raina peered at Sophie, eyes warming—and then, more quickly, at me.

"Fine, yes, you're in," she said, reshuffling her legal pads. "Please don't make us regret it."

Now that the pesky business of my sexual orientation had been decided—and since Sean had to sprint hilariously quickly across campus for *Music Man* auditions—we broke early. But as soon as Sophie waved good-bye, I realized we hadn't talked about the school board meeting at all. I'd sort of banked on them telling me what to say.

I mean, I wasn't *that* worried. The school's no-same-sex-date rule was probably some holdover from the fifties that nobody had ever thought to question. I could stand up tomorrow and say, "Ladies and gentlemen of the school board, did you even *know this was a rule*?" and they'd probably be as shocked as I was. Still, figuring it wouldn't hurt to think like Hannah for the next few hours, I zoned out during my remaining two classes and drafted an outline:

Point 1 in favor of allowing same sex dates to dances: Fostering an inclusive environment.

Point 2: Acknowledging the socio-emotional needs of all students.

Point 3: Promoting a positive image for the school as a progressive environment.

Point 4: Not being hateful, backward assholes! I mean, COME ON, people! Marriage equality is officially a constitutional right, so get with the freaking times!! (Note: Find better way to say this.)

Point 5: If you fail to accede to our demands, I will unleash upon this land the FULL FURY of my mother's army of protest-Valkyries. Gaze upon them and despair. *Spooky noises. (Note: Empty threat. Involving Mom would be mortifying.)

Still brainstorming when the final bell rang, I nearly wandered out of the arts wing exit and into an encounter with QB—who seemed to have redoubled his efforts to woo someone, if not gay, then at least lesbian-adjacent.

Checking my step, I veered toward the library and started texting Mom to come get me. But before I hit SEND, Hannah's ringtone sounded.

"Where are you?" she asked. "Did you want a ride?"

"Um . . ." I suddenly felt like I was the one who'd derailed our routine, not her shot-gunning princess of a girlfriend. *Annoying.* "Actually, I've got some Alliance business."

"It's just me," she said. "Nat's out sick today."

I'd noticed. It hadn't stopped people from talking. She was going to have to face the music sooner or later. But since later was not today—

"I could use a ride." That was transparent. I backpedaled. "This Alliance stuff—maybe you could help me?"

"By 'help you,' do you mean, 'buy you shreddie fries from Cluck-Cluck'? Because that's where I'm headed next."

"Deal."

By the time I'd doubled back to the parking lot, Hannah's car was one of few left. Maybe that was why she seemed so jittery when I plonked myself down in the passenger seat.

She started the car and pulled out of the lot, turning off the radio. Weird already. Not Hannah-weird, weird-weird. Then she asked, "How was your weekend?"

"It's Tuesday."

"I know, but we didn't really talk yesterday."

She was right. We'd only discussed Natalie.

"It was good," I lied.

"What did you do?"

Oh, Saturday I sat staring at my phone, worried that something horrible had happened to you. Sunday, I bathed in self-pity.

"Hung out with my dad," I said.

"Wow." Hannah pulled into the drive-thru line. "He actually came out?"

"I went in."

"Ah."

"He's working on some fantasy game. I kept him company."

"That's awesome," Hannah said, her voice thin. "I've always liked your dad. What I've seen of him."

I caught a glimpse of her expression before she turned to the speaker to order an assortment of greasy sides. Her eyes were clouded, wistful.

"We can share him, you know," I said as she pulled the car to the next window. "My dad's pretty low-maintenance. And he's good at pep talks if you tell him exactly what to say."

A smile fluttered on her lips. Didn't quite land. "I appreciate the offer, but I've sort of leaned into the whole 'fatherless child' thing. Or how did I put it?" She turned to me, eyes brighter

86

than they should have been. We'd had this conversation before. Every time, I hoped it would be different.

"'Half-foundling,'" I supplied.

"Right!" She put her hand to her forehead. "Abandoned, discarded, cast away."

The Cluck-Cluck window slid open. She broke pose and smiled like a normal person as she paid.

"No word from Austria, then?" I asked quietly, as if that would make the subject less delicate.

"I assume someone has heard something from Austria lately," Hannah said. "Just not, you know . . . me."

She shrugged.

I shouldn't have asked. If Hannah had spoken to her dad, her very next call would have been to me. I was only depressing her by bringing him up. While she turned to grab our food, I racked my brain for a subject change. But she beat me to the punch.

"So what's this Alliance business?" She grinned, her teeth waggling a chicken finger like a cigar. "And how may I be of assistance?"

"Oh! Right!" I took the bag of shreddie fries she offered. "I've got this thing tomorrow night. The school board's having an open meeting, so I'm gonna show up and ask them to change the rule banning same-sex dates at dances. Hopefully by homecoming. We'll see."

Hannah stared at me. "The *school board*. The governing body for the entire school district."

"That's what 'school board' means, yes." The huge truck behind us honked. We were blocking the drive-thru.

"And . . ." She shook her head. "*You're* doing this."

"Yeah. You might wanna . . ." I motioned forward while glancing back. "That guy's getting a little road-ragey."

She turned her head and drove, eyes on the road but wide, like she was steering us through a forest of lollipops and unicorns. It was hitting her in waves, a series of incredulous blinks. I smile-chomped my way through a handful of shreddies, waiting for her to congratulate or thank me, express wonderment at my dedication and bravery. But what she said was:

"Natalie's mom's on the school board."

Natalie. Amazing how the Beck could claim shotgun even when she wasn't riding in the car.

The news wasn't that surprising. I seemed to remember Cindy Beck going hog wild with parental responsibilities when we were little kids. When she was snack mom, she'd bring in petit fours and pinwheel sandwiches. Natalie's birthday parties were the biggest productions you'd ever seen, Mrs. Beck front and center as the gracious, lovely hostess. Once, they'd thrown me a party at the tearoom of a fancy hotel. All the girls from my class had come, and Natalie and I both wore Alice costumes with little White Rabbit purses, and why was I even thinking about this?

I locked my grin, remembering my promise to the Alliance. "Maybe Natalie could get involved? She could talk to her mom for us—pave the way?"

"Maybe." Hannah sounded doubtful. "I think they have a pretty complicated . . . yeah."

She pressed her lips together and I pretended not to notice. We never used to have glitches like this in our conversations.

There was an object between us, a speed bump, desperately in need of bulldozing.

"How are things with the old ball and chain?" I asked.

"She'll be back tomorrow. Just a stomach bug."

Odd response.

"She's really sick?" I raised my eyebrows. "Gotta admit, I thought she was faking."

Hannah slammed the brakes as the light ahead turned yellow.

"Hang. On." I pried the seat belt off my collarbone, gaping at her. "What was *that?* Did you just *lie* to me?"

"I—I—" Hannah sputtered. "It's not exactly—"

"So this is a thing we're doing now?" I forced a fry into my mouth. "Casual lying? Or has this been going on all along? Is your name really Hannah? Are you and your mom in witness protection?"

Hannah's cheeks grew redder with every blink. "It's just, Nat's having a hard enough time and she asked me specifically not to talk about it with you. Which . . . is . . . what I'm doing right now and I should really stop talking."

"*Specifically?*" I hacked a cough. "'Anybody else is fine, but don't talk to Daisy'?"

Hannah let out a slow breath. "You two have this awkward history, and as much as it would be *nice* to help you work through it, I really don't think I should get in the middle."

"Um, Hannah? You are the definition of in the middle."

She stopped the car. We'd arrived at my house. And the shreddie fries were gone.

"Changing the subject," she announced, taking off her seat

belt so she could face me. "You're lobbying the school board for gay rights."

For your *rights,* I mentally corrected. She'd been out a full week now, but she still said "gay rights" the same way she'd say "the European Union."

"I am," I said, sitting up straighter. "On Wednesday."

"This is seriously your next hobby, then. Protesting."

"What?" I squinted at her, wondering how this conversation had gotten so off track so quickly. "I wouldn't call it a *hobby,* no, and it's not protesting exactly. It's . . ."

As I searched for the right euphemism for "grand declaration of love," she sighed and said, "It's the Stede Bonnet opera all over again."

And I reeled like she'd slapped me.

The opera. She knew I didn't like talking about it. Or thinking about it.

Well, here it was. Early freshman year, in the throes of my longing for Sean Bentley, I'd told the music teacher, the drama teacher, and Sean himself that I was going to write a rock opera about Stede Bonnet, Charleston's most notorious pirate, and that Sean was going to star in it. I'd scribbled some lyrics to show them, and outlined a whole first act—the juicy part, in which Stede transforms from Barbadian landowner to Gentleman Pirate.

The school got a little excited. Found a slot for it in the production schedule. Made an announcement in the school paper. And the local paper. With a photo of me, and the caption: "Young Composer Spotlights Charleston's Rich History."

A month before auditions, I was forced to admit to everyone that I didn't actually know the first thing about musical composition. At the time, I hadn't felt all that guilty. If these so-called experts wanted to rally around an untested freshman with a half-baked idea for a musical, it was their funeral. But now, every time I passed the Stede Bonnet plaque in downtown Charleston, I felt his ghost staring back at me, whispering *"J'accuse . . ."*

"Or the banjo Christmas carol thing." Hannah was still talking. "Or the *mural*. Daisy, you promised that guy you'd finish it over the summer and you only painted one whale. Are you just planning to bail on that completely? I mean, what's the deal? Why don't you just change it to something easier to paint? Not everything has to be—"

"This isn't any of those," I snapped, blocking out her last set of questions. "It's show up and give a speech. I'm more than capable of that."

"Of course you are," she said. "You're capable of anything."

I let out a breath, finally hearing the response I'd wanted all along. But then her eyes drifted, fixing on the branches of the old oak tree stretching across my front yard.

"If there's anybody in the world who can pull this off, it's you." She scrunched her forehead, straining for words. "I'm just . . . I guess I'm not sure it *should* be you?" Before I could analyze that, she refastened her seat belt. "Ugh, don't listen to me, I'm . . . I don't even know what's going on with me lately. Just—text me the details."

My hand paused on the car door. "You'll come?"

"Of course." When she smiled, her eyes went blank. "Can't wait."

9

I was making popcorn to bring up to Dad, who'd just restarted *Everwander II: The Glimmering,* when Mom blocked my way to the stove with a piece of notebook paper.

"When were you going to tell me about this?"

Her voice was dangerously quiet. I was forced to take the page from her to figure out what she was even talking about.

Aha. My list of arguments to put before the school board. On the top, I'd written in curling calligraphy:

School Board Open Meeting: Wednesday 7 p.m.

"This?" I said. "Um. Probably right beforehand, so you could drive me."

Her foot was tapping furiously on the kitchen tile. But when I looked up, it wasn't anger flashing in Mom's eyes. It was pride. Mounting, steaming pride, frothing into maniacal glee.

"I can help, you know!" She gripped my arm so hard it hurt. "You've made a good start, sweetie, but four and five need rewording, and you should flesh out the legal aspect—hit them where it hurts."

"Obviously!" I snatched the page back. "I'm not done yet."

This was a lie—I was one hundred percent planning to walk into the school board meeting with this document as my only armor. But as I retreated upstairs, I realized that I hadn't even considered a legal aspect. Was the school's policy against the law? If so, this would be even easier than I'd imagined.

When I shut myself in my room to "prep" alone, Mom took the hint and backed off, which for her meant poking her head in every half hour to ask if I wanted a snack. She also couldn't resist sending email after email from her iPhone with links to "articles you might find useful!" I let them sit unread. I was plenty prepared. Cramming would only elevate my nerves, throw me off my game.

But after dinner, after homework, just as I was brushing my teeth, it hit me.

What this would mean for Hannah. For the Alliance. For every gay student who would follow us at Palmetto. Not just gay students, *any* student who wanted to speak his or her mind and be heard by those in power. Basically: Every. Student. Ever.

Tomorrow, I would either become the heroic junior who forged a new path of empowerment for generations to follow or I would be Crazy Daisy, that psycho who showed up unprepared to a public forum, was laughed out of the room, and forgotten forever.

The toothbrush fell from my mouth. I attacked my inbox.

At four a.m., I was still working my way through Mom's articles, scribbling notes and assembling them into an argument. Sometime between then and sunrise, I fell asleep on my keyboard, my cheek typing 1``1111`1 until my alarm woke me up and I had a speech of 475 pages, only two of which made any sense.

Without the benefit of nine-plus hours of sleep, the morning was rough and the rest of the day a queasy slog. At lunch, Raina tried to flag me, but I feigned blindness and ducked outside to read through my speech with Hannah. I'd expected a few notes, but she just stared ahead at the faculty parking lot while I recited it, then smiled tightly and said, "Sounds good. Fingers crossed."

Maybe she's nervous too, I thought. *This is her fight, after all. I'm just her champion.*

I was way too tired to perk her up. "Fingers crossed" would have to suffice.

Back home, with two hours to go until the big showdown, I tried to take a nap, but my brain would not. Shut. Up.

So instead, I downed like seven Coke Zeros in quick succession until each individual thought blurred, becoming a nice, low hum of white noise, perfect for nodding off. Unfortunately, that only happened after I was sitting next to Mom in the Veggiemobile on our way to the school board meeting in—I pinched my leg to stay awake—nineteen minutes and thirty-six seconds. Thirty-five. Thirty-four . . .

When we entered the municipal hall, a wide space with a dais in the front and folding chairs lined up in five neat rows, I thought, *Maybe this isn't actually that big a deal. They probably won't show.*

But there they were, clumped along the right side of the

room, eyes fixed on the doorway as if they'd been waiting hours for me to appear. Kyle "I'm a Freshman" Hornsby sat flanked by two cheery adults who had to be his parents. One row up, Raina, Jack, and Sean craned their necks to greet them.

I wondered whether their families knew where they were tonight. It was hard to imagine Raina having parents at all. I pictured her living in an apartment by herself, doing SAT prep amid ultra-modern chrome furniture while sipping a nice glass of Cabernet.

Next to Sean sat Sophie, and beside her, *another* Sophie, thirty years older—thick braid, peasant shirt, milkmaid skin and everything, leaning over both of them to talk to Raina.

"Ellen!" Mom waved wildly.

Future Sophie turned and, the caffeine fuzz clearing from my bleary eyes, I recognized her as one of Mom's community farm ladies, pinching soil samples in the middle of that vacant lot. She sure cleaned up nicely. It took twenty seconds for her voice and my mother's to mingle, crescendo-ing over the hum of the gathering crowd with exclamations of pride over their two activist daughters, and weren't we *so adorable?*

Sophie closed her eyes, drawing a calming breath. I smiled in commiseration—but didn't walk over. There they were, the true, legitimate members of the Alliance, counting on me to make a difference. Ignoring the eager glint in their eyes, I gave a quick wave and continued down the aisle.

Don't think about them right now, I told myself. *Don't think about all the past generations of oppressed students, either. Or all the students to come. So many students. Millions. Gazillions. Oh my God—STOP. Just. Think. About. Hannah.*

The front row was my best option. I wouldn't have to shout to be heard by the school board. And I could pretend I was alone. Focused. An island.

I spun to scan the growing crowd. Hannah wasn't there.

She'll come. She promised.

I sat and laced my clammy fingers together, peering up at the long table in the front of the room, and behind it, the empty row of microphoned seats staring back at me. Stars danced in front of my eyes and I realized I seemed to have forgotten the basic mechanics of breathing.

To make matters worse, Hannah's words from yesterday were suddenly echoing in my head. *I'm not sure it should be you.*

Damn right it shouldn't be me, I thought. Okay, Sophie was petrified of speaking out and Raina didn't want to do it in the first place and Kyle was new, but . . . why hadn't I tried to convince *Sean* to do this? He was an actory actor-person, for Christ's sake, used to giving big bombastic speeches. Also? He was gay! What was I *doing?*

Stop. I gripped the edge of my chair. *This* is *my fight. I'm part of the quilt bag. I'm asexual. I'm asexual. I'm—*

"Fancy seeing you here."

I recognized the voice over my shoulder. It didn't compute. It was male. Northern. It didn't belong here.

But here he was, College Adam, he of the shattered MacBook, shouldering his computer bag to join me in the front row. Uninvited. Smiling so unguardedly it made my heart stutter.

"I'm working on my Southern accent," he said, apropos of

96

nothing. This kid was seriously strange, and seriously cute with his Clark Kent glasses, and possibly actually stalking me. My perplexed stare must have lingered a beat too long, because his grin dropped away. "What are you doing here, anyway?"

Right? I thought, but said, "I *go* to this school." Which was a much better reason than any he could come up with.

"Oh . . . kay?" He dropped himself right next to me and pulled out a notepad and pen.

Even turned away, I could feel him smirking. He probably thought I was some civics groupie, obsessed with local government meetings.

"Actually," I piped up. "I'm here to speak—"

A pocket door in the side of the municipal hall slid open and my mouth clamped shut. Six beige, middle-aged people stepped through, waving to the crowd as if they were expecting a standing ovation instead of awkward sudden silence. As they settled into their name-plated seats behind the table, I took one last anxious glance backward, hoping in vain for a glimpse of the one person who could remind me why I'd thought this was a good idea.

Up on the dais, a bald man in a crinkled suit coughed into his microphone and called the meeting to order. My hands started to shake, so I sat on them. Then, remembering my notes, I yanked them from my pocket and uncreased them against my knee.

In the school board seat directly in front of me, Natalie Beck's platinum-blond mother, Cindy, was adjusting the seam of her peach cardigan so that it ran straight down her side.

When she looked up, her eyes met mine—and was I imagining it, or was there a sparkle in them? Had Natalie spoken to her? Encouraged, I attempted a wave, but as I did, Mrs. Beck blinked over my shoulder like she hadn't noticed me after all.

The suited man smiled blearily at the crowd.

"Today's meeting is an open session, so as always, we'll open the floor to questions and concerns prior to conducting scheduled business."

He scanned the room.

My brain went "Stand up," but my legs went "Nope!" falling asleep in instant pins and needles. *Traitors.* In the time it took for me to bang life into them, an elderly gentleman to my left was already up and talking.

"I know there's budget cuts coming up. Y'all aren't planning to cut wood shop, are you? That's my main question."

A mousy school board member at the far edge of the table leaned into her microphone to answer, but the old man cut her off.

"Because if you're gonna get rid of something, why not *music*? Or . . . those classes where they're sketching flowerpots? They're picking up real skills in wood shop and making real things and that's all I came here to say."

He sat down and the school board members glanced at one another in confusion, until the suited man who appeared to be their spokesman leaned into his microphone.

"Thank you for your input, sir, and we'll certainly take your thoughts into consideration as we look at the budget for next year. Anyone else?"

I hesitated. Again.

"I have a question about those dead hedges outside Palmetto High School," said a woman in the back of the room. "And could I suggest rhododendrons as a replacement?"

I'll stand up after she's done talking about plants, I told myself. After my hands stopped shaking. I just needed to gather my nerves and bludgeon them into submission.

Or maybe Hannah's right. Maybe this is just like every other overreaching idea I've ever had. Maybe I should stay quiet and go home without humiliating myself for once in my goddamn life.

There was a silence, and I realized the man in the suit had asked the room, one last time, for any more comments or questions. I felt eyes on me.

Adam's. His brow was furrowed, his eyes dancing between my nervously clutched speech and my face with something like encouragement.

"If there's no further—"

I stood. "I have a matter to bring before the school board!"

10

All the blood in my body rushed downward, making it excruciating to stand, like my feet were on searing coals instead of musty brown carpet.

As the school board shuffled in their seats, Cindy Beck leaned forward and nodded down the table to the suited man. I squinted at the two of them in panic, wondering whether that was some sort of secret signal.

Then Mrs. Beck looked right at me and smiled, calming my nerves. She wasn't surprised to see me.

She half rose to reach her microphone. "For those who don't know, this is Daisy Beaumont-Smith, one of our eleventh-grade students at Palmetto High School. Go ahead, sweetie."

The crowd behind me murmured appreciatively. I drew a grateful breath, pulse stabilizing, remembering suddenly all those times she'd fixed me lunch and patted my head and tucked me into sleepover trundle beds.

"Thank you, Mrs. Beck."

Beside me, I could hear Adam scribbling.

I cleared my throat and blinked down at my notes. *Focus.*

"I'm here today to request that the Palmetto School Board repeal an unjust and unlawful regulation now in existence that restricts students from bringing same-sex dates to school functions, such as the homecoming dance and prom."

A wave of sound rippled through the room. I glanced over my shoulder, my eyes alighting on Old Mr. Woodshop, who looked like he'd been sucker-punched. In fact, other than the Alliance, the only ones who didn't seem surprised were the six members of the Palmetto School Board. They watched me with indulgent smiles and glassy patience—listening but not listening.

And it dawned on me.

They've already decided. Mrs. Beck practically rolled out the red carpet for me with that intro. Natalie must have spoken to her mother and her mother spoke to them. Whatever I say . . . we've already won!

I stifled an exultant yawp, reeling with a strange new sensation—gratitude toward *Natalie Beck*. Then I smiled politely and continued my formality of a speech.

"In 1979, a group of students in Rhode Island were denied the opportunity to bring same-sex dates to school dances. Instead of backing down, they took the battle to the courtroom. The next year, that state's Supreme Court found that the school district was denying gay and lesbian students their right to free speech, as well as violating the Fourteenth Amendment, which states that the government may not 'deny to any person within its jurisdiction the equal protection of the laws.'"

Here I'd written "DRAMATIC PAUSE." I used the opportunity to draw a breath. In the back of the room, someone coughed.

"This was long before I was born. *Thirty-six years* before the United States Supreme Court ruled that all Americans have the right to marry the partner they choose, regardless of gender. And yet I stand here today asking for the same rights that were guaranteed by a courtroom during the *early* days of the gay rights movement. I know that my request may still seem controversial to some of you . . ."

I glanced at Mr. Woodshop. He blinked.

". . . but the truth is, it's *embarrassingly* overdue."

My confidence growing, I stepped closer to the table and smiled at each member of the school board, pretending I was on one of those legal shows where the sexy attorneys all wear designer suits to deliver their final arguments.

"I recognize that we live in a community with strong ties to the values of the past. I could list the many ways in which enacting a more progressive policy for Palmetto students would benefit the school and create a more effective learning environment for students."

I held up my speech to show them my list of pluses, which I was totally going to skip now, because I was on a roll.

"But there is a more important fact that overshadows all of that. By denying all students the right to enjoy themselves as equals at a school function, you are denying a group of Americans the rights guaranteed them by the Constitution of the United States. *Those* are the values we should cling to and uphold—the ones our forefathers fought for. The ones we still fight for today. And so, on behalf of all of the students of Palmetto High School, I ask you to repeal this unjust regulation and allow same-sex dates to dances—effective immediately."

Behind me, I heard a mass shuffling. Just as I froze, wondering if everyone was leaving the room in disgust, there came as much of a roar as a crowd of twenty-four could make. They were standing, cheering. Jack was wolf-whistling. Old Mr. Woodshop was grudgingly clapping. My mother was hyperventicrying! And in the back row . . . was that Hannah?

"That was very nicely put, Miss Beaumont-Smith," said the suited man, his grin bright, but his voice wooden, as if he were reading from a printout of his own. "And it's always an honor to hear from our students directly. Can we get one more round of applause?"

They clapped. I nodded graciously. Then he cleared his throat.

"As you yourself acknowledged, this is a controversial issue with no clear path to take."

No clear path? Obviously, *repealing the rule* was the clear path. Did he not just hear my awesome speech? I opened my mouth to retort, but he spoke into the microphone again, sending a squeal of feedback through the speakers.

"As a matter of fact, we discussed the rule prohibiting same sex dates in a special session yesterday evening . . ." *Nailed it!* "And it's our collective decision that we don't want our schools to be caught in the middle of such a hot-button issue. It would be a distraction to students and a headache for our community."

A headache? This dude's announcement was taking a strange turn.

Whatever, I thought, lacing my fingers behind my back. *Just get to the part where you change the rule.*

"In the end, with the additional tightening of school budgets, the decision that makes the most sense is to abbreviate this year's homecoming festivities. All *other* homecoming activities will proceed as planned—the football game, the parade and court, et cetera—but there will be no dance. I hope that answers your question."

I either sat down or my seat rose to greet me. Either way, I couldn't move.

No. Dance.

So I was half right. The school board *had* known in advance. They'd held a "special session." But the answer wasn't yes. It was the opposite of yes.

And Cindy Beck was still smiling serenely.

I lifted my printout and tried to control the shaking in my hands long enough to read it, desperate for more talking points, any viable ammunition. But there was nothing written there that could possibly uncancel the homecoming dance.

Behind me, I heard the room bubbling with dissent, gasps becoming angry grumbles. The suited man ignored them.

"If there are no more questions, we'll proceed to regular—"

"I have a question!"

Adam stood, his iPhone outstretched like a real reporter. His hands were shaking too. I wondered numbly if he'd remembered to hit RECORD.

"A clarification, really. Are you saying, sir, that you are preemptively canceling the homecoming dance . . . in order to *prevent* gay and lesbian students from attending?"

Red crept up the suited man's neck. "They can attend. They were always welcome to attend." And now his forehead was beading with sweat. "But if they want to bring a date . . ."

Cindy Beck caught the eye of the suited man and his words faded to nothing. Relieved, he slumped into his chair. Mrs. Beck leaned calmly into her microphone.

I wondered if she would acknowledge the elephant in the room—that her own daughter had come out of the closet less than a week ago. But there was something strange glittering in her mascaraed eyes. Something like triumph.

"We're a little community, Mr. . . . ?"

Adam swallowed hard. "Cohen."

Her smile became a wince, as if she pitied him. "I'm guessing you're not from around here. We don't like to *stir the pot. Make waves.*"

She was really laying the Charleston accent on thick.

"We prefer to keep school operations as removed from *politics* as possible."

She wrinkled her nose on the word "*politics,*" like it was a dirty diaper. This wasn't about politics, though. This was about the lives of students like her daughter. How could she not see that?

Adam perked up. "In that case, follow-up question! Is it true that you're planning to run for Congress in the next election?"

Cindy Beck pretended to blush. "I have no comment about that at this time."

A murmur ran through the mini-crowd.

She was running for office. As a conservative, no doubt. And so, to further her political aspirations, she was holding this issue hostage. Her daughter's issue. *My* issue.

The room was in an uproar, at least. This time people really were getting up to leave in orderly disgust. I waited for some-one to hoist their folding chair and chuck it across the room, starting an uprising, but that didn't quite happen. All I saw were heads shaking. People picking up their purses.

And in the back, Hannah von Linden rising from her seat, her disappointed smile gleaming across the room. She'd seen me try.

Try and fail.

Worst of all, she'd seen exactly what her community thought of her. To them, she was an Issue. Capital *I*. A nui-sance. A headache.

"No," I muttered. Adam was putting away his phone, but, glancing at me, he hesitated.

This couldn't be it. All this build-up, to get shut down on a technicality?

Up at the table, the school board had returned to scheduled business, the mousy woman squeaking into her microphone.

I stood up, and said, again, louder, *"No."*

Adam's eyebrows were raised. He gave a little motion with his head.

Do it.

I drew in a breath. "I have an announcement!"

Now everyone else in the room seemed to freeze, locked in expectant silence. In the back, Hannah mouthed "Daisy," her eyes flashing alarm and head shaking no.

I was alarmed too. I didn't have an announcement. My announcement was that I was *so mad*.

But instead of stomping my feet, I clenched my fist—and said the first thing that popped into my head.

"The homecoming dance *will* go on!"

Cindy Beck tittered, then grabbed the microphone, nails scratching against it with a long thud. "We just said it *won't*, Daisy. Now please—"

"It will *not* be the official Palmetto High School homecoming dance."

Somehow I'd found myself standing on my chair, facing the back of the room. Facing Hannah. My voice was erupting out of me without direction from my brain, a medium channeling an avenging spirit.

"It will be *better!* It will be a homecoming that welcomes home all students, regardless of race, creed, or sexual orientation."

This was surprisingly good.

Before my brain could catch up with my mouth and shut it down, I said it. *The idea.* The only possible solution.

"On October twenty-second, we will throw our *own* homecoming, open to LGBTQIA students and alumni, their same-sex dates, and . . . anyone else who wants to attend." That didn't seem like a conclusion, so I nodded seriously and added, *"Thank you for your attention to this matter!"*

It proved harder to climb down from the chair than onto it. As the room became louder than ever, Adam hurried to offer me a hand, and I thought he was just being nice until he lifted his iPhone to my mouth.

"Have you really just announced a competing homecoming weekend for gay students?"

"Yep," I said, my cheeks burning with elation. "And *you can quote me!*"

That was what you were supposed to say to reporters, right? Adam seemed to like it. He trailed me down the aisle as I marched out, flanked by a radiant Sophie and whooping Sean.

"While we're at it, do you think I could get a follow-up interview?"

"Sure!"

"I'm free Friday, if you are. Around five? Moonlight Coffee Shop . . . scene of the *incident*?"

"Yeah. Fine. Sounds good." We'd reached the back of the room, and Hannah was gone. Had she ducked out before or after my announcement?

"See you there." Adam waved over the heads of the people pushing in front of him.

Mom was waiting for me outside, alone. I braced myself for more tears of maternal pride, but right now, she just looked stunned.

It wasn't until we'd pulled into our driveway that she cut the ignition and stared at me.

"Honey," she said. "Do you realize what you've just committed to?"

"Yeah." I shrugged. "Our own homecoming."

A weekend-long event. Not just a dance. A parade. A court. A football game. Rallies. The whole high school nightmare in one rowdy, impossible to coordinate package.

"Oh my God." I dropped my head to the dashboard, all the nerves, adrenaline, and seven Coke Zeros finally dropping away.

"I have to throw *homecoming*."

11

I assume big news has always traveled fast, via horses, homing pigeons, that Greek guy who died after running a marathon . . .

What the people spilling out of the school board meeting had were cell phones, so my news traveled across James Island in an instant. By the next morning, "Daisy Beaumont-Smith" was a household name—like Rosie the Riveter or Lysol. But was she the brave champion of student rights who defied the bigotry of our school board?

Nah.

I was the girl who got the homecoming dance canceled.

The backlash began before I even got out of Hannah's car. In fact, it started with Hannah herself.

"I have a question," she said. "What were you *thinking*? Exactly?"

There were so many possible responses that I didn't know which one to grab from the bag, so I pounded on the dashboard and said, "I didn't want them to win!"

"This was about winning, then." Hannah shook her head, as if it were so *typical* of me.

But I was an extremely uncompetitive person. I used to get bored with Monopoly and give my property away to the Community Chest. My scorekeeping in golf was: *Let's see how many times we can hit it back and forth!* Hannah was the one in Varsity Tennis and Chess Club, for God's sake. Didn't she know me at all?

"No, Hannah," I blurted. "It was about . . ."

I couldn't bring myself to say "you." Even though it was the truth, I knew it would sound like I blamed her, which I didn't.

"About what's right. Doing what's right. For all students. I'd think you would appreciate that."

She let out her breath, her head lolling toward me. "I do appreciate it. I'm proud of you. Trust me, I am a Daisy *aficionado*." Her nose wrinkled. "Did I pronounce that right? You're the one who did Pimsleur Italian."

"Perfetto." I unfastened my seat belt. "Except I'm like eighty-seven percent sure *aficionado* is Spanish? I could be wrong . . ." But Hannah was still talking.

"I mean . . ." Hannah looked away. "I'm *always* proud of you. Every time you . . ." She collapsed against the steering wheel. Scrunched her hair. Then sat straight up and stared at me. "Why do you do this to yourself?"

I shook my head. "What?"

"Paint a target on yourself." Her eyes were glistening. "We go along, everything's fine and normal, and then you . . ." She waved her hands in the air. "Make a huge announcement. Start an international society of beekeepers—"

"I've never done that." I wouldn't rule it out in the *future*, but . . .

"Decide that you're going to take over the world—whatever that world is. And people notice. How could they not? It's like . . ." She stared at her lap, then back up at me. "It's like you *want* to be picked on."

"That's not true. At all." I leaned against the door, as far from her as I could get. "That's what you think of me?"

"No! I . . ." She sighed. "I guess I don't know what I think. You're an enigma."

I snorted, but I kind of liked the sound of it. *Eniiiiiigma.*

"I just need to put this out there," she went on. "If you're doing this for me? You really, really, *really* don't have to."

I slumped against my bag. "What do you mean?"

"I'm good. I am fine. I don't need all this."

I shook my head, preparing to lie again. "It's not just for—"

"Okay," she interrupted, grabbing her keys. "I get it. We don't need to talk about it anymore. I just hope you know what you're doing. And that you're ready for the pushback."

Of course I am, I thought. *Jeez.* What could be worse than the pushback I'd just gotten?

Halfway across the parking lot, I found out.

"Hope you're happy!" A frizzy-haired senior from the cheer-leading team smiled at me with all her teeth, her head cocked way over like a velociraptor.

The petite girl next to her slammed her car door so hard the Hawaiian dancer on the dashboard did a shimmy.

"Way to ruin the year, ho-bag."

"What did you use to dye your hair, *toilet cleaner*?"

"Whoa." I eyed them warily as we passed, muttering, "Do I *know* you?"

Hannah put her arm around me. "This is what I'm saying. Brace yourself."

"Nice going," said some puny freshman, shoulder-checking me as he passed.

"Is that her?" A huddle of sophomore girls glared across the courtyard, then dissolved into snickers. I heard the words "nasty" and "shoes" and stared at my Chucks in alarm. They were a little old, I supposed, but . . .

By the time we made it to the school lobby, I'd shrunk two inches, clutching my backpack loops like a shield, hoping they could deflect the dirty looks flying from every direction.

It was bad enough to make me ask Hannah the unthinkable. "Do you think you could get your girlfriend to order a ceasefire?"

"I doubt she'd be much help."

Before I could figure out whether to be offended, I heard a wordless shout ring out from the crowd—and as I turned to investigate, a Starbucks cup hit me in the forehead.

According to my classmates, this was the funniest thing that had ever happened in all of human existence.

"At least it was empty," I muttered. A trickle dripped from my bangs. "Mostly."

Hannah handed me the napkin from her lunch bag, then veered off for homeroom.

"I'm around if you need me," she called behind her.

"Do you have more napkins? For later?" She didn't respond.

QB was waiting by the lockers. As always.

"Hey, Daisy."

112

I braced myself. If anyone stood to be livid about home-coming, it would be QB. He'd been voted into the court two years running. It was Christmas, the Oscars, and Super Bowl Sunday all in one. And I'd ruined it.

"You look nice today."

I have to admit—I melted. By his pained squint, I could tell he'd heard the news as clearly as everyone else. He didn't care. Which made QB Saunders the only one *not* tormenting me at school. It was a topsy-turvy upside-downy world.

"You doing anything tomorrow?" He'd asked me this every day since Monday and I'd found a plethora of creative ways to avoid answering.

Don't say it, Daisy, my brain cautioned. *You've got a thing, remember?*

His smile was wavering, unsure. He looked so vulnerable. But strong too. Like a bodyguard. I could sure use a body-guard today . . .

"You wanna—"

"*Yes,*" I said. "Absolutely."

You're supposed to be asexual, dammit! What is the matter with you? Just because all of a sudden he's "Chris Saunders: Nice Guy Extraordinaire" doesn't mean a tiger can completely change his—

QB winked. "See you at the game."

I jolted alert. Of course. Friday night, when the Pirates held their weekly exercise in losing gracefully. I'd just agreed to be QB's girl in the stands, dotingly groaning after every in-terception.

"Actually," I called weakly after him. "I might have a thing?"

He was too far away to hear me and too surrounded by football buddies for me to scamper up and continue the conversation without humiliating both of us. So there it was. I had a pseudo-date with QB Friday night.

Why did I feel like I actually *did* have a "thing" on Friday?

Oh right. Adam. College reporter. Moonlight Coffee Shop. I'd have to squeeze them both in. I giggled.

Shut up, said my brain.

"Hey Blueberry," said a senior girl down the hall. "Cancel *this.*"

This time, I managed to duck.

The Alliance was waiting for a plan. And apparently I was meant to supply it.

"Don't get me wrong, Daisy," Sean said. "This is an incredible idea. I can picture it already." He lifted one hand, gazing off at an imaginary horizon. "Club lights. A great mix of EDM and deep cuts, minimal Top Forty to get the plebs on board. *Way better* floats and costumes—"

"Plus," Jack cut in drily, "it could, you know, start a conversation about how we treat gay students at this school."

Sean pointed at him, thunderstruck. "Yes! That too! But it's a big undertaking, right? Are we *sure* we can pull this off?"

Hell to the no. Before I could say it, Raina rolled forward, tapping her legal pad with a ballpoint pen.

"In terms of pure logistics, the answer is 'maybe.' If we're on private land, using private dollars, they'll have a hard time stopping us. So the first question is: How do we get that land?"

"And those dollars," Sophie added, her voice dropping as

if "dollars" were a curse word. "My mom said she'd help us fund-raise, but I don't think she's raised more than five hundred for her community farm project—and that's, like, her baby. We'd need a lot more than that."

Everyone turned to me.

"Bake sale?" I suggested. "Or wrapping paper? We could sell . . ." Everyone's faces had fallen. "For the holidays? No?"

Jack raised his hand. "I have a completely unrelated question."

"Yes!" I said, pointing at him. "Go ahead."

He ignored me, looking down the table at Sophie. "Are we still doing Touchy-Feely Time during meetings? Or is that something we've sidelined?"

"No! Oh my goodness, not at *all*. I have the candle with me . . ." Sophie rummaged frantically in her bag. "We've just been so busy with planning, I didn't want to—"

"Oh my Lord'a mercy, the *candle!*" Sean laughed, making air quotes, as Sophie produced a tiny tea light with a flickering electric bulb. "Y'all, I have *missed* this."

Sophie and Raina were staring questions at each other. Raina shrugged.

"Yeah, fine, whatever, it's not like we're getting anywhere planning-wise."

"Touchy-Feely Time!" Jack crowed, spinning his chair. "I have feels and I am not afraid to touch them."

Just as I was slowly raising my hand to ask, *Whaaa . . . ?* Sophie dimmed the lights. Everyone but Kyle seemed to understand what was going on. He looked to me in helpless appeal, but I faked the same serene expression as Sophie. I'd been voted in less than forty-eight hours ago. I was going to *blend* from here on out.

"Who would feel comfortable going first?" Sophie asked, her voice low and soothing. "Sean?"

When nobody objected, Sean cupped the fake candle.

"First of all," he began. "I said this last week, but it's good to be back here. It was a tough summer with Diego back in Spain . . ."

Group therapy!

At first, the realization came as a relief. At least I could identify the format. But as Sean went on, I started to tingle with embarrassment, wondering whether he'd forgotten I was in the room—the new girl. The outsider.

"His family doesn't know," he said. "It's worse for him in a lot of ways and I wonder whether he regrets it sometimes, the person he was when he was here . . ."

He must have been talking about Diego Jimenez, an exchange student I vaguely remembered from last year. I'd had no idea they were together.

"But then he gets so *jealous* too," Sean was saying, rubbing his jaw. "It's that hot Latin temper, I guess." He grinned wolfishly. "We used to sneak into Luxe Lounge downtown and now every time I talk to D, he asks whether I've gone back. Like he thinks I'm out every weekend picking up college guys. He doesn't believe me, but I'm not! I would *never*. He's the only one I want." He raised his chin, eyes starry, and I wondered if he was about to break into song. "I mean, it's this crazy thing. I met my soul mate in *high school*."

I mentally snorted. Immediately felt like an asshole.

The truth was, Sean looked different than I remembered him from back in my stalker days. He'd always had this unremittingly positive glow about him, the kind that transcended tans and teeth whiteners. But right now, that glow was wavering. He looked everything at once—swept away, sad, giddy, terrified, blissful. He was in love. Who the hell was I to knock it? I knew nothing about it.

Not to mention the fact that my own parents were high school sweethearts. Not that they interacted all that much these days. But still.

Sean rolled his shoulders like he was wringing the sadness out of them, tapped the candle twice on the table, and passed it to Jack.

Despite his eagerness to talk just a few minutes ago, Jack's hands shook as he pulled the faux-flame closer.

"Same old same old for me," he started casually. "I actually did hook up with a college kid I met at Luxe Lounge, back in June." He nodded at Sean. "But he was gone by July. Thank God."

His laughter seemed to deflate him. I found myself holding my breath. This was the first time I'd ever seen Jack Jackson without his swagger in effect.

"My parents are still dragging me to church," he said, and as he shifted in his chair, I could make out a tiny silver chain around his throat, glittering in the candle's glow. "I had to do another prayer session with Reverend Tom. Two hours this time. Probably would have been longer, but finally I just pretended to cry and told him that he'd purged me of my sinful ways so he'd let me out."

He was smiling wryly, making his words all the more jarring. Of all the people in this room, Jack Jackson was the last I'd have expected to come from a conservative family. He was so open. So confident.

"I wish I hadn't pretended now," he said. "Because I have to sit there in church every week and act like I'm listening to the sermons, like they're really *purging* my soul." Jack waved his hands like he was at a tent revival. "And when we leave the service, Reverend Tom always shakes my hand extra-long with this *look* in his eye. Like . . . pride. Like I was his big win against Satan. And it's bullshit. But I can't say anything, can I? And it's almost worse that I'm bi. Because I *could* just wait until marriage, find a nice Christian girl, live the way they want me to. But I'd still be lying. I'd still be different."

There was a moment when it seemed like he'd go on. That he'd stand, strengthened by our presence, press his hand to his heart and resolve to be honest at home and at church. But instead, his head sank as he passed the candle back to Sophie.

She closed her eyes before her turn, and I went from holding my breath to feeling it harden into cement in my chest.

"Everything's good at home," she said. "I'm grateful for that. And for my friends." She smiled like it hurt. "It's just hard to stay calm when people at school say things about me. Call me . . ."

She pressed her lips together, unwilling to voice words that should never have been voiced in the first place. But I could see her mentally reciting them, her eyes unblinking, bracing herself against them. My own stomach clenched at the memory of how it had felt for me—not just the first taunt of the day but the sixth, twelfth, twenty-fifth. Bullying worked in increments: annoying, then stinging, then cutting, then scraping bone, then plain-old scar tissue—numb, but ever-present.

But what I'd faced was "Crazy Daisy." "Psycho." "Smurfette." Nothing. I wasn't sure I even wanted to know what Sophie was hearing day after day—the smallest, pettiest part of me wishing she would just pass the candle. Instead, she turned to me and then to Kyle, the two newbies, straining for brightness as she filled us in.

"I went out a couple of times with a junior last year. It was a mistake. He was a jerk. I didn't let it go too far, thank goodness. But I did tell him that I was bisexual. And since then . . ." She played with the elastic band on her braid. "It's just been really hard. People—*guys*—seem to think they can say whatever they want to me. And I haven't figured out how to handle it."

"Punch them in the face," I blurted. "Or hot coffee to the crotch."

"We don't interrupt during this part," Sean said gently, sinking me deeper into my swivel chair. He winked. "But I totally agree."

"I'm not really . . . comfortable with anger?" Sophie gazed at the ceiling. "My mom says I need to work on it." Her eyes drifted down to me. "She's a psychologist."

"Right," I said, *touchy-feely time* making a ton more sense in context.

The candle traveled across the table to Kyle.

"Um, I'm Kyle. I'm a freshman?" He blushed furiously and itched his nose. "And you already know that? Okay, um."

We all smiled encouragingly.

He tapped his hands on the desk and drew a breath.

"I came out to my mom and dad a few months ago. And my sister, Lily. She was there too. Um, and they weren't surprised? They said they'd always known and they loved me or whatever? And it was . . . pretty cool. So."

"That's *awesome*," Sean said. Everyone nodded except Jack. He was staring down at the table, forehead knotted. I wanted to grab his hand, but wasn't sure I had the right.

"They suggested I join the group, so . . . here I am." Kyle shot the candle to me like an air hockey puck.

My turn. Um.

"I'm actually doing kind of okay, apart from the fact that the whole school hates me. Except you guys!" Everyone smiled back except Raina. "So . . . yeah."

I inched the candle away.

"Can I make a request?" Jack asked. "Feel free to say no to touching-slash-feeling, but this is *at least* the second time you've referenced punching someone in the face. I for one would love to hear more about that."

I did feel like I owed the group my dues, a secret to drop in the pot, even if mine was in a less valuable currency.

"Okay. Well. Back in eighth grade, Hann—"

I stopped. It wasn't cool to talk about her behind her back. But there was no way to tell this story—or, really, any of my stories—without her. So . . .

"My *friend* was dating this guy, Max. They'd been together

for like a month, but they hardly saw each other. He was fine, fairly hot, fairly nice, she was sort of *meh* about him."

Oh right, I realized. *Because she's gay.*

"Anyway, she begged me to try going out with *his* best friend, so I did. For one date. We all went to Max's house and rented a movie and . . ." I groaned, curling up in the chair. "I *really* should have known when Max turned off the lights and suggested his friend sit next to me. Max started kissing Hannah instead of watching the movie and then his friend just . . . jumped me. We had spoken like two words to each other. I mean, hand up my shirt, mouth open, coming *at* me. I basically, like, kissed his teeth while fending off his fingers, and I was like, 'Whoa, buddy, slow it the hell down,' and instead of being remotely gentlemanly, he got all mad and said, 'You should be *grateful.*' And as I'm pondering *that,* he comes back at me! For another attempt! So basically, yeah. I punched him in the face. I mean, what else are you gonna do? Broke his nose. He bled all over Max's sofa, it was awesome. Max and Hannah got into a big fight about it and broke up, but I think she was just looking for an excuse anyway. And then Max moved to Texas two months later. Which I don't think was related."

I gazed at the candle, smiling from the memory—then, abruptly, remembered that there was a room of people listening, their eyes fixed on me with a mix of amusement and horror.

"And . . . that was my first and only kiss, The End."

"Cool story." Jack shot me a wink.

"Thank you," I replied, blood racing through my body in an

embarrassed gush. I'd actually just told that story. Out loud. To near strangers.

"I'm sorry that happened to you," Sophie said quietly, and everybody nodded.

"Oh, I . . ." I wrapped my arms around myself. It was funny. I'd always thought of it more as something that had happened to *him,* bloody nose and all that, rather than something that had happened to me—something that could have been a lot worse. But the moment I looked up into everybody's sympathetic eyes, my own started to prickle. "Yeah, thanks. *Anyway.*"

Since Raina was the only one left, I passed her the candle. She took it with a nod, thought for a second, then said, "Nothing today."

Now I was the one scowling.

Raina clicked out the candle and put a fresh legal pad in its place.

"Okay. We've got . . ." She glanced at her watch with a frown. "One minute to decide on next steps vis-à-vis homecoming. Daisy? Suggestions?"

Earnestness had crept into her tone. Not a good sign.

"I . . . think we should all *brainstorm*?" I clasped my hands on the desk. "And then come back to the table . . . and put our heads together . . . and spitball some ideas . . . and figure something out." I was watching the clock over the door, hoping for a reprieve in *three, two, one—*

The bell rang.

Raina stood to go. "You heard her. Everybody come back next week with ideas."

I was taking a heady breath of hallway air when Raina stopped me with a ninja grip to the elbow.

"That includes you, Daisy. We *cannot* be the club who got homecoming canceled." Her face was inches from mine, rigid with panic. "We have to be better than that. Or all of this was for nothing."

I didn't disagree. I just didn't have any bright ideas.

I didn't have any bright ideas, in fact, until I was in bed staring at the glow stars on my ceiling fan, Sophie's dulcet voice ricocheting through my nerve-addled brain.

"Community farm project . . . that's her baby . . ."

The community farm was my mom's baby too. Which, if you thought about it, made me its sister.

I sat up, clutching my comforter, translating my mom's blahblahblahs into actual, pertinent words.

"I think this next meeting will do it," she'd told me at dinner, while I was debating whether my sneakers were too embarrassing to wear to school again. *"All we need is a signature and the land is ours."*

The land.

The flat, vacant plot of land across the street from my school. Big enough for a football field, several stages, a dance tent . . .

Big enough for the biggest, gayest homecoming Palmetto had ever seen.

12

Friday at five, Adam was waiting for me in a corner booth at the otherwise empty Moonlight Coffee Shop, clacking away on his crippled laptop. The duct tape was gone, but now it had a binder clip stuck to the corner.

As I slid into the booth, Adam raised one finger and kept typing with the others.

"Sorry," he murmured, his keystrokes so forceful that the booth began to shake. He looked incongruously passionate, like a concert pianist playing a concerto only he could hear.

A waitress wearing frosted pink lipstick made her weary way across the restaurant, water pitcher and menu in hand. Her name tag said *Becky*.

"Nothing for me." I rested my chin on my hand, gesturing grandly to Adam as she filled my plastic cup. "I'm just here to be interviewed for an *article*."

The only reaction I got was an eye roll before she returned to her lonely post at the counter.

Adam slammed his finger down on one last key and pulled the computer lid shut. I was about to remark that he'd probably caused the screen damage himself with his *virtuoso* typing style, but then he grinned, and I found myself incapable of doing anything but grinning stupidly back. He had a startling smile, sudden and breathless, like a little kid who's been handed a bunny. His glasses slipped a little, and I had to remind myself that it would be inappropriate to reach across the table and slide them back into place.

"Okay, hi," he said.

"Hi yourself."

"You sure you don't want anything?"

"Nah." I hadn't brought a wallet.

"My treat."

I spun so fast the booth squeaked. "Actually, Becky, some coconut cream pie and a ginger ale, thanks!"

The waitress sighed a yes.

"And I'll take some more . . . um . . . coffee." Adam stared into his empty mug as if unsure of what he'd just consumed.

"Is this another school assignment?" I asked. "Am I the follow-up to your award-winning cat boutique exposé?"

"Something like that."

Adam fussed with his phone, then slid it away. There was a red dot flashing. Was he already recording? I smoothed my skirt in readiness.

"My assignment this week was to report on a routine government meeting," he said, his pen tapping against the table in a syncopated rhythm, making him sound like a beat poet. "You had to come back with a story, no matter how boring the context. When I drew 'School Board Meeting,' I wasn't sure I was going to be able to stay awake long enough to find anything worth writing about. But then . . . *you* showed up, thank you."

I wasn't sure if that last bit was to me or to Becky, who was filling his mug, because his eyes were locked on mine. Hot-glued.

"You saved the day," he said, setting down the pen. "For me, anyway. I was sitting there mentally outlining a story on the death of high school wood shop, tying it into faltering American exceptionalism and the decline of the working class."

"Whoa."

"Yeah. But then you stood on a chair. And there was my story."

"Glad I could help." I would have kept staring at those eyes of his—rich brown framed in black—but my pie had arrived, and man it looked good.

"So. Daisy." Adam knocked back his coffee, then recoiled with a grimace. I handed him my water and he downed it in three sips. He shook his head, recovering. "Wow."

"The coffee's not good here."

"I'm realizing that."

"I was surprised you asked for more."

He sniffed his cup as if actually considering another sip. "Caffeine's more of a need than a want at this point. And . . ." He tilted the mug to display the branded logo: *Moonlight Coffee Shop.* "You'd think?"

I nodded in sympathy. "They should call it the Moonlight Mozzarella Stick Shop. Not that catchy, though."

"Ha!"

It took me a second to realize that that was Adam's laugh—a single "Ha," as if he were imitating the sound of someone laughing. This was a thing with him, then. I had to take another bite to keep from giggling.

"Are they good here?" he asked, head craned like he was dubious.

"Um . . . *incredible*. And I'm picky." I put down my fork and leaned closer. "I can always tell when a mozzarella stick is going to be a disappointment. There's something a little sad and soggy about it. Not quite golden enough. Not enough steam. Or *too* much, so the inside is runny and bubbling over and the outside is, like, null. These are always—*always*—perfect."

The diner was unnaturally silent when I finished my testimonial. I turned to see Becky watching me with wariness bordering on fear.

Adam looked unfazed.

"Okay!" he said, picking up his pen and click-click-clicking the end of it. "So you have strong feelings about mozzarella sticks."

"All fried foods, really." I needed to stop talking, or all of this was going to go in the article.

"What else can you tell me about yourself? Hopes, dreams, favorite band?"

He was probably kidding about that last one, but it was the easiest to answer. "Kudzu Giants."

His face dropped. "You like them?"

"Uh, yeah, who doesn't?"

"They're all right. I guess."

How had I gotten *that* question wrong?

"Hopes and dreams, then," Adam went on, pulling out a notepad. "Career goals? College plans?"

"Hannah and I are going to apply to a bunch of schools in major cities and pick one to go to together . . ."

Adam looked confused. "Hannah?"

"My best friend."

"Ah."

He'd started writing, so I added, "Hannah von Linden. Lowercase *v*. She came out a few weeks ago, actually. If you wanted to interview her too, I could set that up?"

His mouth twitched. "That's okay. You were saying?"

"Right. So we'll room together in LA or London or New York . . . maybe San Francisco, although I've heard it's weirdly cold there. And then, after graduation, I'll probably try out a bunch of different professions to see which one calls to me. Right now, I'm thinking I'll start with architecture."

Adam opened his mouth but no reply came out.

"As an intern," I clarified. "You need an advanced degree to actually design buildings, I assume. So I'll just learn the ropes at some firm and then maybe try out zoology? Or costume design. I'll have to see what I'm really passionate about."

"Makes . . . sense?" He cleared his throat. "Obviously gay rights is an issue you feel passionately about."

Adam's voice had abruptly deepened, like he'd prepared that segue in advance. Was this his Reporter Voice? Like Batman Growl?

"Yes," I answered, setting down my fork, and damn if my voice didn't just get deeper too. "But it's about more than gay rights. It's about the basics of how we treat each other. If you're telling a group of students that they don't have the same rights as all the other students, then you're creating an unlevel playing field, and *that's not what America is all about!*"

That was loud. Adam pretended not to notice.

"Was this something you decided to tackle on your own?"

"No, I'm speaking out on behalf of my school's LGBTQIA Alliance. We're pretty active—"

"How many members?" he interrupted.

"Six," I calculated. Then I added Hannah. "Seven." And Natalie, I supposed. *Blah.* "Eight."

He blinked, pen hovering.

"Eight," I repeated firmly. "And we've got a lot of supportive friends and family behind us." I didn't want it to sound like we were powerless. "Like hundreds. Of supporters."

"But the idea? To fight the rule . . . ?"

I smiled. "Yeah, that was me."

Scribble scribble. This was fun.

"Can you share any details about your plans for the alternative homecoming event?"

"As a matter of fact, I can!" I stole a bite of pie, a mini-celebration of what I was about to reveal. "We've found a local nonprofit that's eager to help. They've got a venue for us to use, free of cost." I leaned in to whisper. "It's hush-hush at this point. As you saw at that meeting, there are a lot of people in the community who would love to shut us down, so I really shouldn't talk specifics."

"Got it." Adam's eyes narrowed playfully. "So what's the name of the nonprofit?"

Mine narrowed back. "Nice try."

He laughed again, that single, sudden, "Ha!"

I giggled involuntarily, then took a bite of pie to stop.

What was going *on* with me? If this was the start of a crush, it needed to stop, posthaste. Whatever Adam's type was, it certainly wasn't an average-except-for-her-odd-hair high school junior of middling intelligence, no discernable talents, and questionable charm. I could see him going for a goth feminist-theory goddess. Or a world-weary singer in a smoky, run-down lounge. Or even a perky blond cheerleader— although he'd hate himself for it a little.

Adam flipped his notepad over and started filling another page. His fingers were ink-stained and restless. I pictured pressing my own hands against them so they would settle down.

Adam stopped scribbling and peered up at me. "I want to ask . . . and please forgive me if I'm prying."

My heart thudded for no particular reason. I nodded for him to ask.

"How long have you been out of the closet?"

Oh, right. That. "I'm straight."

"You're . . ." His eyebrows shot up. Then he sank against the banquette, scratching his cheek. "Okay."

"Is that bad?" I forced a smile.

He took his sweet time answering.

"Huh." He squinted at his notepad as if deciphering a code on it.

"If you want, you can put that I'm asexual." I peered around to see what he was writing, but he angled the page away from me. "It's part of the QUILTBAG spectrum?"

He blinked in confusion. "So you're really straight?"

"Last I checked."

"Do you have a boyfriend?"

"Um?"

"Not for the article. I'm just . . . yeah. Curious."

For somebody curious, he sure was avoiding eye contact.

"Why?" I leaned over the table, putting on a fake-sultry drawl. "You interested?"

He went beet red. Jeez, was it *that* embarrassing a prospect?

"Yeah, no, I, uh." He swiped his hand through his hair. "I was just wondering how he felt about all of this."

"My boyfriend doesn't feel anything."

Adam started to write that down, his shoulders sinking.

I squinted at him. "Because he doesn't exist."

He glanced up. "Right. Oh! No boyfriend, then."

Adam's lips parted like he was about to say something else. He didn't. A few seconds passed, and I realized if I didn't do something, we could be stuck in this freeze frame forever, so I glanced at my wrist as if there were a watch there.

"Is this enough for an article?" I grabbed my bag, pulled out a random receipt and scribbled on the back of it. "I actually have to run. But here's my email. And my number. If you need me, for whatever reason."

I felt instantly stupid for offering it. Should I have waited till he asked?

"Thanks." He rose when I did. "You off to a planning meeting?"

"No," I said. "Well, sort of. A football game. I need to . . . um . . . research homecoming conventions? I've managed to avoid going to any school sporting events my entire life, so, yeah."

"Research." His mouth teetered on the edge of a smile. "Exactly."

For some reason, I didn't want to bring up QB. Probably because he was humiliating. Plus I'd just said I didn't have a boyfriend, which was *true*, but also complicated by the fact that I'd be an official Pirates wench-on-the-sidelines for the next three hours.

"High school football. Wow." Adam acted like I'd said I was going to see a Sumo match at my local dojo. "I've never been to one of those either."

"Really?" Call me hypocritical, but that struck me as weird. "You *did* graduate high school, right?"

"Yeah, but in New York. Brooklyn," he clarified, his chin rising on the word. "It was a magnet school. Not the most *sporty* environment."

The way he said "sporty" made me think of a Ralph Lauren catalog. He shuffled, put his hands in his pockets, and I realized he was waiting for something. An invitation?

"Do you . . . want to come?" As soon as I said it, I felt the diner tilt infinitesimally, like I'd upset the balance of the universe.

"I . . . uh . . ." He watched me and I thought for a few fraught seconds that he might say yes—but then his smile curdled into a smirk. "I'm kind of done with the whole high school thing at this point. But thanks."

My exterior remained placid while, inside, I shriveled into a raisin. *Wow* did I misread that situation.

He slid twenty bucks under his coffee mug, massively overpaying, and motioned for me to walk out ahead of him.

I stomped off under my own steam, not turning back lest he see my mortified face.

But as we stepped out onto the humid street, the palms above us whispering with the breeze, he cornered me for a handshake.

"Thank you, Daisy," he said, his glasses sinking in the heat. "That was a very entertaining interview."

My scowl melted despite my best efforts to keep it in place. Why were we still shaking hands?

"Glad I could oblige," I said.

"'Oblige,'" he echoed, drawing the word out like a song. He backed away with a grin, his fingers slipping from mine. "Such a great accent."

I don't have an accent, I thought, but by the time I caught my breath enough to retort, or to giggle, or to cry out "When will I see you again?" he'd already disappeared down the block.

13

As soon as I stepped onto school property, I felt the wrongness of this evening pulsing around me. It was Friday night. And I'd gone back to school. To watch a *football* game.

A little girl wearing a Pirates T-shirt bounced off me in her rush to join her equally fan-spangled family, and suddenly, I found myself pulled with the tide toward the ticket booth. On top of every other indignity, this was going to cost me four bucks.

The freckly sophomore manning the booth glanced up as I was trying to hand him my wadded cash.

"Daisy Beaumont-Smith?" he asked, staring at the blue ends of my hair.

"Yeah?" I shuffled, wondering if he was about to chuck his Gatorade at me, and if so, which way I should dodge.

"No charge for you."

He up-nodded knowingly. Knowing *what,* exactly? I grimaced a smile, pocketed my cash, and continued past him, mentally reciting my new mantra: *"This is not a date, this is not a date, what am I doing here, this is not . . ."*

I climbed the stands to a comfortable distance from the field, and let people fill in around me. I wished Hannah were here. We could critique the stretching techniques of the opposing team's cheerleading squad, or share a "To Benefit the School Band" popcorn, or give each other a meaningful look and by silent assent get up and out of here.

But she was busy tonight. With someone else. Eating fried foods. Watching a movie. Probably one I wanted to see and would now have to rent by myself. Stretching out on her downstairs sofa, ignoring Mama Tan's comments about their food choices, giggling at some inside joke, building walls around themselves to keep pesky people like, oh, *me* out.

Swallowing bile, I texted her. *"You'll never believe where I am . . . cheering on the Palmetto Pirates! Woohoo?"*

It took her six minutes to reply with, *"Cool!"*

That wasn't much of a response. Not even an accurate one. Sitting here was the most uncool thing I'd done in recent memory. And Hannah of all people should have been the one to call me on that.

The crowd was pretty full by now. To my immediate left and right were two groups of rowdy freshmen who kept leaning over me to shout at each other. I almost offered to move, but that would have put me at the end of the row, where they might knock me off the bleachers with the force of their New To This School enthusiasm.

"Daisy!"

Sophie waved from the top row, where she was sitting with a bunch of her natural-fiber friends. They looked as out of place as I felt. I waved back, wondering if they came to every game or if Sophie was doing what I'd claimed to be doing, helping our cause by researching homecoming traditions.

That's what I had to assume Raina was up to when I spotted her two tiers down with a middle-aged gentleman in a Duke windbreaker. Her father! Raina did have parents! Come to think of it, now that I was in CIA mode, was that Jack with his family on the opposite side of the field? They looked surprisingly nice. And, way over yonder, yep—Sean Bentley, trying to politely extricate himself from a conversation with a cheerleader from the rival team.

I was just realizing that the only one missing from our club was Kyle, when I saw him clamber up the bleachers with his own family, all of them dressed in Pirates gear, his younger brother waving a school pennant.

They really were all football fans. They had authentic school spirit. Was it catching? If so, I was about to find out.

The field's speakers roared to life and everyone cheered, drowning out the mumbled announcement and generic sports music that followed. I stood with the crowd and watched our terrible football team race onto the field from the locker room.

As soon as he hit open air, QB turned to the stands. When he spotted me, his face lit up—a little. He jogged to join the team and kept scanning, his smile dropping a centimeter with every stride.

The game was what I'd expected. Lots of half standing, then sitting with a communal groan as the other team's pockets of fans went wild. We lost. We always lost, so I'd come prepared, knowing this would be more tragedy than comedy. The point wasn't the happy ending. It was the struggle.

QB looked so dejected after the game that I decided to tell him this on my way out. It sounded appropriately inspirational. But while I was tiptoeing down the bleachers in my interview skirt, QB got the first word in.

"Daisy! Let's hang out!"

"Now?"

"Yeah."

His teammates were trudging past, watching us with open curiosity.

QB had just lost the fourth straight game of the season. I couldn't embarrass him further.

"Okay, sure."

QB did a gleeful hop that made me laugh. "I'll meet you out front. Just a quick shower. I promise I'll smell better in a minute!"

Thirty minutes later, the crowds had all gone home and I was sitting on the curb of the school's front drive, watching lamplight pool on the dead border hedges and listening to the crickets start up their nightly party.

When they went silent, I knew he'd walked up. His blond hair was damp from the shower. And he'd kept his promise. Even with the nightly scent of low tide and mown grass thick in the air, I could smell QB from here, a mix of clean and sweat-salty that made me want to lean in.

I refrained.

"You wanna go to that diner on Walker?" he asked. "The one that's always empty?"

And so, for the second time in less than five hours, I found myself settling into the corner booth of the Moonlight with a guy who I was most definitely not dating. Becky was still on duty.

"What can I get . . . y'all . . . ?" Pouring our waters, she glanced up—at me, then at QB, then back at me with horrified admiration.

"Just water's cool," QB said.

"Mozzarella sticks and chicken fingers, please," I ordered, opting to skip the salad this time. I needed to drown this awkwardness in saturated fat and fast.

As soon as Becky left, QB let out a leaden sigh. "Thanks. I needed to get away." He balled both fists and rested his chin on them. It was like he'd seen an illustration of "sadness" and was trying to duplicate it exactly.

I stuck a straw in my water. "Don't you usually hang out with the team after games?"

"Only when we win." *So, never.* "And anyway, I kind of wanted to talk."

"Sure," I said, hoping against hope that he wanted to talk movies. TV. Anything but—

"Natalie didn't come."

"She's probably busy. With her *girlfriend*."

"Chief Beck was there."

"Okay?"

"He comes to every game. With Nat. But she wasn't there." He cradled his chin in the crook of his elbow and peered up at me. "I thought about going up to him. You know, asking what's going on? But then I thought maybe that wasn't such a good idea."

"Good call."

Natalie's father was the chief of the James Island police

force. He'd either express sympathy or arrest QB for stalking. I'd say the odds were fifty-fifty.

QB's head was now resting on the table. "I don't know if I can do it."

"Do what?"

"Go on."

"Ugh."

QB sat up. Apparently I'd groaned that out loud.

"You'll be fine." I smoothed my tone, channeling Sophie. "You're QB Saunders. You'll have a new girlfriend in a week."

And I instantly regretted those words.

"Call me Chris." He stretched his hand across the table. "I like it when you call me Chris."

"Okay," I said, not calling him anything. We fell into a silence that grew exponentially weirder the longer it lasted. I was just about to ask him something inane like what kind of music he listened to when I realized he was crying.

Becky chose that moment to bring me my food.

"This looks great," I squealed. "Thank you!"

She shook her head as she walked away, no doubt wondering why someone who looked like me had not only shown up with two different guys on the same night, but had somehow managed to reduce a young Greek god to tears.

And the tears, they were a-flowin'. His forehead was wrinkled, lips pressed together, cheeks streaming. After a moment of profound reluctance, I reached out and took QB's hand. He immediately started talking, like his fingers were the on switch to his mouth.

"You don't understand." His grip tightened. "We were to-gether for two years. She was the only one I ever thought I'd be with."

"Ever?" I asked drily, trying in vain to lighten the mood. "In your whole life?"

"When I . . . *gave* myself to her, I thought it was because she was the one."

Holy. Lord.

"Wow, uh, you were a virgin? I figured you guys were doing it all the time."

And oh my God, I just said that in real life.

He shook his head, unfazed. "She wanted to wait. And I didn't screw around on her. I'm not that guy. So we waited. Until it was perfect."

I tried to pull my sweaty fingers back, but he had a vise-grip on them. I was officially trapped in the most awkward conversation in the world.

"It was a few months back," he was saying, his voice hushed. "We were on my family's boat. It's for fishing, but it's real nice. Fifty-two-foot. I had it planned for weeks. Champagne. Flower petals."

"Scented candles?" I joked.

"They're not safe on a boat." He sniffed back a sob. "It wasn't great, not fireworks or slow-mo or anything, but you know. First time."

I nodded politely, thinking, *Slow-mo?*

"I figured it would take a couple times to get good at it. And I thought . . ." His voice choked again, but he drew a breath and shrugged. "I thought we had forever."

"Oh." I tried to imbue the word with my deepest sympathies.

"The next week, she told me she was a lesbian. I turned her into a lesbian."

"No." This time I was the one squeezing his hand. "No, no, no." I shook my head. "Chris."

He blinked at his own name, as if pulling himself out of a mental flashback sequence and back into the diner with me.

I pressed on. "You didn't turn her anything. It has nothing to do with you. Maybe it took crossing that line for her to come to terms with the truth about herself, but that doesn't mean she doesn't care about you."

"If she cares about me, why didn't she come to the *game*? The first home game of the year! Why didn't she come?"

His fingers loosened and I pulled my own slowly back.

"I don't know," I admitted. "I'm sorry."

"You came." He blew his nose on his napkin, then peered over it with grateful eyes.

"Yep."

At that, he seemed to relax—and the conversation did too. He stole one of my chicken fingers. Started talking about upcoming games and ideas "Coach" had for breaking their fifty-three-game losing streak.

I smiled, *mmm-hmm*ed, and scarfed my mozzarella sticks as fast as I could without choking, praying that I hadn't just accidentally bought a season ticket to Pirates football. What would happen to the boy if he scanned the stands and neither of us was there?

QB drove me home in a gleaming Mustang saturated with

new car smell. As we pulled up to my house, I wondered whether he was going to try for a kiss—and if so, whether I would try to escape it.

But he just opened the car door for me. "I was wrong, you know, Daisy. You're really easy to talk to."

As soon as I got inside, I texted the one person on the planet who would agree.

"Hannaaaaaah. Are you up? You will not believe the night I just had!!"

I went to bed with my phone on the pillow, in case she wrote back.

She didn't. But someone else did. Someone with a number I didn't recognize.

"Who won?"

No amount of staring managed to make that text make sense, so I figured it was a wrong number. I'd just drifted off when my pillow vibrated again.

"What are you guys, the Pirates? Wanna make sure my facts are right."

Facts. Huh. I propped myself on one elbow and typed.

"We are the Pirates, yes. And the other team won. The Pirates never win."

"Pirates never win. I feel like there's a life lesson there. Not sure which."

I grinned, hopeful that this wasn't some creepy stranger, just the near stranger I'd hung out with hours before. *"Crime doesn't pay? Except it totally does."*

"Can I quote you on that?"

"Best not."

"Ha."

He even *typed* a single "ha"!

The phone fell silent after that. I entered his number into my contacts as "Adam," then added "(Reporter)" so I wouldn't be lulled into thinking we were friends. Or worse—more. He was a college guy. I was me. He'd only texted to fact-check.

I kept my phone on my pillow all night long.

14

The next morning, I heard Hannah's faint ringtone and dropped an open box of cereal in my mad scramble up the stairs to answer.

"What's up?" I tried to control my huffs.

Hannah paused. "Have you been exercising?"

"Not on purpose."

"Phew." She laughed. It was a lovely sound. "Wanna see a movie tonight?"

There was something in her voice that set alarm bells ringing.

"Sounds great."

"Awesome. We'll pick you up at six?"

I stifled a sigh. *We.* "Yep. See you then."

When Hannah's car pulled up outside my house at six o'clock, Natalie was riding shotgun. I'd had a few hours to prepare a fake smile, so it was fully operational—until I scooted into the back and found Dana Costas staring over at me with a pained expression, like she'd been asked to ride in back with the dog. She and Natalie must have made up. Funny how Dana outed her to the whole school and it was water under the bridge, whereas I did absolutely *nothing* wrong and became excommunicated in perpetuity.

Hannah spun from the driver's seat to say hi. She looked especially pretty, her overgrown pixie-cut swept back in a tortoiseshell headband and her eyes framed in light makeup I'd never seen her wear before. When I said, "Hey," Natalie turned her cheek in greeting, just far enough to avoid actually looking at me. She was wearing a dangly star earring. It reminded me of something.

Whatever it was, it made my eyes sting. I redirected them to the seat back and started racking my brain for things to talk to Dana about. History class? What brand of cloying perfume she was wearing?

Tonight was clearly intended to be some bizarro double date. Lesbians + Besties = Fun. But thank goodness, Dana wasn't interested in bizarro dating. The whole ride to Mt. Pleasant, she leaned into the middle of the car to try to talk to Natalie. Despite the fact that her coiled curls kept swinging into my face every time the car switched lanes, she didn't say a word to me until we were in line for the concession stand, where she asked in a disapproving murmur, "Did you really get homecoming canceled?"

I was seconds from replying that no, in fact, it was *Natalie's mother* who'd canceled homecoming, when I saw Hannah watching, eyes pleading.

So I shrugged. "Just the dance part."

Dana made an old-lady clucking noise and turned away.

"It wasn't Daisy's fault," Hannah said, bumping shoulders

145

with me. "I mean, it's not like she showed up and asked them to cancel the homecoming dance. That would have been a *horrible* thing to do. If that had happened."

We all turned to stare at her.

"Anyway, two homecomings! This is my real point." She slung an arm around me and shook. "Two homecomings are *obviously* better than just one homecoming. Especially since the first one isn't going to have a dance, right?"

"Um." I smiled. "Thanks, Han."

"Anytime."

Dana didn't seem impressed by Hannah's little speech. But Natalie had finally decided to look my way. Those icy blue eyes of hers were locked on me with a strange intensity, like she was trying to figure out exactly what genus of insect I was.

Her star earrings twinkled in the concession stand lights—and I had it. Her bedroom walls. She'd had them painted to look like the Perseid meteor showers from the Giselle Chronicles, lovely little falling stars, trailed by dust. They glowed in the dark. We used to count them before we fell asleep.

"I like your earrings," I said.

She flinched as if shocked. Looked away.

"Thank you," she mumbled. Then she looped her arm through Hannah's, pivoting her away. "Jumbo popcorn?"

So *they* were sharing a snack. When it was my turn to order, I stared at the overhead menu as if seeing it for the first time. We usually got a large popcorn, Peanut M&M'S to dump into the bucket, a soda to share—medium, not large, so we didn't risk missing part of the movie with a restroom run. It had taken us years to find the perfect cinema concessions combo.

"What are you doing?" Dana snapped from behind me. "Order."

"Pretzels," I blurted. "Please."

The relieved cashier went to fill my order, as I thought, *Pretzels? You hate pretzels!*

Too late. I shuffled away with my bland, overpriced snack, just managing to get into the theater in time to snag a seat next to Hannah as the previews started. Dana snuck in moments later and sat as far from me as possible. The first trailer looked terrible, so I lifted my hand for a thumbs-down, as per our usual routine. Hannah shot me a faint smile and a furtive thumbs-down of her own. When Natalie glanced over, she tucked her hand under her leg and didn't take it out for the rest of the previews. It felt too ostentatious to review the trailers on my own, so I stopped too.

The movie was just okay, a glossy spy thriller with a twist ending I saw coming from the opening scene. But as we were leaving the theater, Dana declared it ah-mazing.

"Don't you think?" She looked eagerly up at Natalie.

Natalie shrugged one shoulder. "Meh."

Dana deflated.

"It was better than meh!" Hannah said, glancing between them. "I liked it too. A rip-roaring roller coaster with surprises at every turn. *Four stars way up.*"

"You mean thumbs, Han," Natalie said, shooting her a sidelong smirk. "Thumbs way up."

I scowled, wanting to smack the smug expression off her face. Even if she was right about the thumbs thing.

"Why not stars?" Hannah walked backward, glaring kittens at Natalie. "Stars go up too. *Way* higher than thumbs. I stand by my review."

"Hannah von Linden." Natalie's smirk swelled into a real smile. "*How* are you real."

Hannah's breath seemed to catch. She smiled at her shoes and looked away. "You have to stop saying that."

Natalie loped closer to Hannah like she was being tugged by a bungee. Their foreheads touched—gently, glancingly—and then I swear, some sort of telepathic message passed between them. They moved apart again, hands shoved in pockets as if they hadn't been about to kiss, as if that had been the furthest thing from their minds.

I felt like I was attending Visitors Day at the Freemasons—I was seeing the polite, public version of whatever went on behind closed doors and it still felt like I shouldn't be watching.

"I don't get it," Dana said, her voice flat and overloud. "Why wouldn't she be real?"

Hannah flushed, shaking her head. "It's nothing." She turned to me, eyes alert, desperate for a subject change. "Hey, what's your review, Daisy? You can do thumbs up or stars up, your choice."

"Or stars down," Natalie suggested, a few steps ahead. "Or thumbs horizontal."

"I'm actually gonna second the 'Meh,'" I said. "Simple and elegant."

Natalie let out a surprised laugh, turned, and looked at me.

Her eyes on my eyes. No ice in them whatsoever, warm for a single blink—so much like fire-haired Lida, twirling across my backyard to attack me with a hug, that the sight of her hit me like a tidal wave. But then came the withering second blink, and the universe snapped back into alignment.

When we got outside, I let my steps stall behind the others, feeling like a loosed balloon. From back here, I could observe—Dana skipping every few steps to match pace with Natalie, whose stride kept veering toward Hannah, both heads bobbing low, away, low, away as they chatted.

They hardly touched. No stranger could possibly tell they were a couple. They just looked like friends. Best friends. Some strange emotion surged through me. It felt shameful, uncomfortable, a wet bathing suit on a dry body.

Then I noticed Hannah's pinkie inching out to graze Natalie's. Her chin dipping, rising, wrenching away. They weren't even making eye contact. I'd never seen *not touching* look so charged. I had to stop walking to process it. They wanted to hold hands, hold *everything*, but they weren't. Why? Because of what people would think? What was the point of being out if you played platonic even on a date?

They must not be all that into each other, I told myself. *Otherwise there would be way more PDA.*

The thought was so hollow it blew immediately out of my head.

The way home was the same as the way there. I'd nearly nodded off when—

"Beach tomorrow?" Dana's voice was like a sneaker scraping against a gym floor.

Hannah grinned back at her. "You beach'a."

Natalie buried her head in her hands, cracking up. "Oh my God, Hannah."

"That was supposed to be 'you betcha'!" Hannah glanced wild-eyed over her shoulder at Dana. "I wasn't calling you a bitch. Eek, sorry!"

"I think she got that," Natalie said, wiping a tear. "You are loony tunes."

Dana looked blank. "So you're coming to the beach."

"Yes!" Hannah and Natalie said in unison, then fell into giggles.

There were about seventy things bugging me about that little exchange, one of which was far too glaring not to point out.

I poked my head past Dana's maze of curls. "It's supposed to be nice out tomorrow. Sunny, low eighties."

Dana snorted. "Um, thanks weather girl."

"Hang on." Natalie whirled on me from the front seat, jaw agape. "I remember this. You never liked the beach on sunny days. You always wanted to go when it was raining."

And you always hated the beach on sunny days because you had to wear ten gallons of sunscreen to protect your freakishly pale skin. But before I could gather the courage to say it, Natalie whipped back around. I couldn't see her smirking, but I could feel it.

"Hannah feels the same way," I said to her headrest. "You can't even see the beach when it's nice weather. It looks like *Where's Waldo.* It's only worth going on gray days, right Han?"

Natalie raised her eyebrows, turning to her girlfriend for a response.

Hannah shrugged. "That's more of a you thing, Daisy. I'm good with the beach either way."

I sat back. Rationally, I knew it was utterly stupid to feel betrayed about this, but it felt like a shove. Another "me thing" to add to the list of ways I didn't know I was different from Hannah. I leaned against the window while Dana jabbered on about plans for tomorrow's beach party. Which, by the way, I was at no point invited to.

But it wasn't until we turned onto my street that I realized what was bothering me most—the overarching bad vibe that had been coloring the entire outing. Hannah was being weird.

Not weird-weird. Hannah-weird.

Charming, silly, off-kilter, relaxed. She wasn't wearing her polite face around Natalie. Not even around Dana. If anything, she was even *more* herself tonight—Hannah 2.0. And it wasn't because of some magical ability I had to draw her out. It had nothing to do with me at all.

When I opened the car door, Natalie said, as if coached, "Bye Daisy. It was good to hang out."

Hannah preempted any possible reply on my part by saying, "Call you later!"

No, you won't, I thought.

"Sounds good," I muttered.

Mom was asleep already, the first floor dark, but upstairs, I could hear Dad playing *Everwander.* Rather than sitting on my bed in a fog of self-pity, staring poetically at the blank wall until I passed out from boredom, I crept into Dad's cave, pulled up a gaming chair, and grabbed a controller. He shot me an appraising glance, then without a word, restarted the game so I could join as Player Two.

I tried playing a vicious Mohawked dwarf character that Dad had created, but after a few minutes, I asked to swap to the hot elf chick. I knew she was yet another negative, over-sexualized representation of women in video games, but her weapons were better.

"I'm not sure if the story's working as well as the first *Everwander*," Dad said, squinting at the screen. "Can't pinpoint why."

We played at half volume with a few breaks for Dad to jot notes and me to grab us snacks from the kitchen until, at some point, I must have fallen asleep, because I woke up in the gaming chair with a blanket over me and daylight streaming through the window.

Dad was still playing. He tossed me a controller.

"Go again?"

After a few battles, Dad swiveled his chair to pat me on the shoulder. "It's nice to have somebody to play with."

It was maybe the saddest thing I'd ever heard him say. And what was even sadder was that I agreed.

15

GOING LIVE TOMORROW!!

Adam Cohen {adam.s.cohen@charlestonu.edu}

to {me}

DAISY-

Thanks again for the interview/article fodder. Here's the piece. Already out to my professor. She passed it off to *The Banner* (university paper). They're running with it! On website Monday. Print edition Tuesday.

They might want to make this a series of articles so

LET'S STAY IN TOUCH!!!

-A

ps go Pirates

"Whoa." I shook my head to clear it. Between this and French homework, my *cerveau* was *rotario*. Or was "*rotario*" Spanish? I kept getting them mixed up.

Adam sure seemed excited. I was strangely nervous. Maybe because the last time my name appeared in print, it was in reference to the Stede Bonnet opera.

"This is different," I said, warding away visions of a target on my chest. I bit my lip and clicked.

PALMETTO SCHOOL BOARD CANCELS HOMECOMING DANCE OVER SAME-SEX FLAP

James Island, SC—On a muggy September evening, in an unassuming government meeting room, the Palmetto School Board holds its first public session of the year—and a high school junior waits to be heard. She sits modestly, her hands smoothing the speech she's written. Her outfit is muted, a simple gray polo and freshly pressed black trousers, in deference to the crowd she's preparing to address, but the bottom two inches of her blond hair are dyed robin's-egg blue. It is the first hint of the defiant spark she'll show the room moments later.

When it's her turn to speak, she does—forcefully and well. She cites the Constitution and the legal precedent for her request. She appeals to the school board's sense of patriotism and justice. They appear to listen. The gathered crowd is silent as she concludes.

"On behalf of all of the students of Palmetto High School, I ask you to allow same-sex dates to dances, effective immediately."

When she sits again, it's out of shock. In response to her request for a change to a rule that was first put in place during the Eisenhower administration, School Board President Harold Tompkins has just announced that they'll be circumventing the topic by canceling the homecoming dance outright.

"We don't want our schools to be caught in the middle of a hot-button issue," Tompkins says. "It would only be a distraction to students and a headache for our community."

And that might have been the end of it, a disappointing conclusion to a student's exercise in free speech. But the student in question is Daisy Beaumont-Smith, 16, the spokesperson for Palmetto High's LGBTQ Alliance—and she is not accustomed to backing down.

"It's about more than gay rights," Beaumont-Smith later tells me at a local diner near her school's campus, her blue-blond hair tucked neatly behind her ears. "It's about the basics of how we treat one another. If you're telling a certain group of students they don't have the same rights as all the other students, then you're creating an unlevel playing field. And that's not what America is all about."

Her hazel eyes sparkle as she talks about her cause, as well as when she mentions fellow junior Hannah von Linden, to whom she is fiercely devoted and with whom she plans to attend college.

Perhaps, Wednesday night, it was with that very friend in mind that Beaumont-Smith climbed onto her chair, refusing to be quieted, and announced the creation of a competing homecoming event open to students and alumni of any sexual orientation.

The Palmetto School Board concluded the meeting early and has refused to comment on Beaumont-Smith's proposed event. In the meantime, plans are moving ahead, says Beaumont-Smith, from planning her homecoming's football game to nailing down a possible venue.

"There are a lot of people in the community who would love to shut us down." Recalling her reception by the school board, Beaumont-Smith falls somber. And then—unbroken—she smiles. "But we've got a lot of support behind us too."

Was it a million degrees in this room? I pressed my hands against my hot cheeks to squelch my furious blushing. And then I read it again. Giggling.

It was so complimentary. He'd painted me with heroic strokes. He hadn't mentioned my fried food obsession, which was charitable. And he called my eyes hazel! Not mucky light brown, no-color. To him they were hazel. And *sparkly*.

The third time I read it, my giggles dwindled. Was my memory acting up, or were some of my quotes weirdly out of context? Was that how you wrote articles, by cutting up interviews and piecing bits of them together into a collage?

I took a breath. Adam was the journalism major. What did I know? And I had said all of those things and meant them. This was a positive slant on our cause. It was perfect.

It wasn't until I'd forwarded the article to my Allies, plus Hannah as a bcc, that I realized what was missing.

Nowhere in the article had Adam said that I was straight.

He didn't lie, exactly, didn't say that I was a gay student, or that I was personally suffering from bullying or discrimination—but he sure did imply it. And that mention of Hannah . . . was I losing my mind, or did it kinda, sorta sound like we were dating?

"I *am* fiercely devoted to her," I muttered, just as a reply came in from the girl herself.

"Amazing article, Daisy!!!!"

And then, immediately, a second text. *"Any chance you could get my name taken out? Ack! :)"*

I decided to focus on the first text and hope she was kidding about the second.

On the way to school Monday morning, Mom kept glancing

over at me with a hint of a smile. I should never have let her read that article.

"So this reporter . . ." she said, her voice trailing out musically.

"Adam."

Her eyes brightened. "This is the boy I saw you with."

Here we go. "Yep."

"He sure seems to think you and Hannah are an item."

I turned to stare. Her eyes danced to mine and away again. Knowingly.

"We're not. Because I'm *straight*." I scowled out the window. "Seriously, Mom, stop theorizing! You're gonna give me a complex."

"Well." She huffed and tugged on the steering wheel to pull us up in front of the school. "*Either way*, I'm proud of you."

I waved good-bye and marched into school feeling like the girl from the article. *Daisy Beaumont-Smith doesn't back down, so get out of my way!*

The seniors blocking the lobby didn't get out of my way. Apparently they hadn't read the article.

I tried to nudge past. "Excuse me."

"Morning, lesbo," said a voice off to the side. I turned to find Madison peering up the steps at me, arms crossed over a low-cut shirt bearing a huge sparkling cross. She smiled sweetly. "You're going to hell, you know."

"I . . ." My mouth opened and closed like a sock puppet. ". . . have no response to that."

"I do." A wiry arm looped through mine and propelled me

through the doorway. "But I doubt she'd understand it. I use a lot of *big words*."

I blinked myself out of my stupor to find that, of all people, Raina Moore had come to my rescue. Even more shocking, as we made our way through the lobby and up to the main school corridor, she began to smile.

"That article," she said. "It was good, Daisy. It was what we needed."

"You think?" I scanned the buzzing hallway for angry faces, but for once, Raina's wasn't one of them.

"If nothing else, we've got that reporter on our side. Better than nobody." She lingered as we reached my locker. "You heard everybody in our meeting last week. And now you've heard"—she nodded to the school entrance, where Madison was still cheerfully blocking traffic—"the other side. You see how important this is."

I rested my head against my locker. "Yeah."

"It might get worse too, for all of us." She looked down the hallway, teeming with bodies making their way to homeroom. "But this article. It'll help." She raised her fist as she turned, like the Statue of Liberty. "I've got a feeling!"

I tried to mentally bottle her confidence and dab it onto my pulse points like perfume throughout the day. It sort of worked.

But then, seventh period, disaster.

"Let's mix things up, make some new friends," our AP bio teacher said, clapping her hands as if rearranging lab partners were her favorite hobby. "Miss von Linden? Table eight, please."

Hannah's new spot was the back of the room with a boy she knew from Chess Club, while I was handed over to Steven—not Steve, *Steven*—who buttoned his shirts to the neck and snorted when people answered questions wrong.

To make matters worse, AP biology had abruptly stopped making sense to me sometime last week, when we'd started breezing through the curriculum at lightning speed, everyone else nodding along like we were reviewing letters of the alphabet.

"Is an organelle a cell?" I asked Steven. "A cell *inside* a cell? Or—"

He shushed me.

Craning my neck, I waited until Hannah spotted me, then fluttered my textbook in the air and mouthed "Help!"

After class, she walked with me to the English wing. "Why are you even taking bio? You hate science."

"I do not."

"'It strips life of its magic,'" she quoted.

"Well, there is that."

"So is this for college applications too?" She looked genuinely perplexed. Apparently the idea of signing up for classes to spend more time with your best friend was foreign to her.

"I guess, yeah," I lied.

Her eyes twinkled the way they always did when she'd arrived at an answer. "I'll help. Dinner tonight? I'll tell you everything I know about cells—in the most magical way possible."

She waggled her fingers.

"Will there be glitter?"

Her fingers stopped moving. "I cannot promise that."

"I accept anyway."

"Meet me after school?" She turned toward her English classroom.

"In the lot?" I called after her, then added, "*Shotgun!*" just in case.

"Just us," she answered drily. At her glare of warning, I restrained myself from prancing down the hall.

Tan von Linden was not a chef. I'm not even sure she'd ever taken down the shining pots that hung above her pristine kitchen island. She didn't need to. She was flirt-friendly with every chef within a one-mile radius of her antiques shop. In a foodie town like Charleston, it had kept her and her daughter well fed for years. And as an honorary member of the household, I got to enjoy the spoils.

Tonight's dinner was grilled bacon-wrapped scallops over fresh fettuccini, with a side of spicy fried Brussels sprouts. I was in heaven. But Hannah was barely touching hers. She'd placed her cell phone next to her plate and her eyes drifted to it every thirty seconds like clockwork.

"We haven't seen much of you in the last few weeks, Daisy." Hannah's mom dabbed the corner of her mouth with a cloth napkin, careful not to muss her lipstick. "Busy year so far?"

"Not really." I tried to stare down Hannah, but all I got was the top of her head. "Not for me anyway."

Hannah dragged her eyes from the phone. "That's not true." She turned to her mother. "Daisy's joined the LGBTQ Alliance. She's really involved."

Tan rested her chin on her hand, smiling dimly. "The LGBT . . . Q . . . ?"

"Alliance," I repeated. Had Hannah not brought up the group before? "We've got some big things coming up."

"LGT . . . Q . . . is the gay group?" Hannah's mom squirmed elegantly in her chair. "I'm confused. Hannah said you were still straight, Daisy."

Still straight. As if you could switch back and forth. Hannah flushed.

"I'm asexual," I said matter-of-factly. "It's the *A* in QUILT-BAG."

Tan and Hannah stared at me like I'd just announced I was a fridge magnet.

"Anyway, it's an important cause."

Hannah's phone beeped and I watched her expression calcify in that polite way that meant she'd stopped listening. A half second later, she snuck a look at it. And giggled. I scooped some pasta, resisting the urge to shove my fork through Hannah's phone and smash it against their reclaimed wood dining table.

"We've been getting a little attention, actually," I announced, a bit louder than necessary. "There was an article about it. I don't know if Hannah showed you?"

Mama Tan shook her head, confused.

"Did I not?" Hannah glanced up. "I'll send it to you. Yeah, Daisy's group is going to throw a competing homecoming as a protest against the school board."

That last bite of fettuccini soured in my mouth. *Daisy's*

group. A protest. Hannah was acting like it had nothing to do with her. Like it *bored* her.

"That's very impressive, Daisy," Hannah's mom said.

"*Thank* you." I glared a smile at Hannah, but she wasn't looking.

"And there's an article?"

"Yes—and Hannah's *mentioned* in it!"

Han opened her mouth as if to retort, but then the phone beeped—*again.*

Her mom's eyes met mine across the table.

"Be right back." With no further explanation, Hannah erupted from her chair and bolted into the other room, clutching her phone like an Oscar statuette.

As soon as Hannah was out of sight, her mom glided from her seat and fetched a porcelain serving plate piled with tiny red velvet cupcakes. I found myself powerless in the face of their cream cheese twirl-topped beauty. And so my mouth was full of not one but two two-bite cupcakes, for a total of four bites, when Mama Tan leaned across the table and whispered, "This lesbian thing? Do you think it's for real?"

She smiled wryly. Knowingly.

It took me an excruciatingly long time to swallow everything in my mouth. "Um. Real, as in . . . ?"

She shrugged, rustling her crisply bobbed hair—one of few gestures she shared with her daughter. "It just looks to me like something she's trying out. When I was in college, I experimented with girls. Kissing, fondling, that kind of thing."

T to the M to the I.

"But it never *meant* anything. I certainly didn't need to define myself. Maybe it's generational." She sighed.

It hit me, not for the first time, or even the fiftieth, how different Tan and Hannah were. Where Tan had probably kissed a girl in college to test the way the visual effect rippled through a party, Hannah would have never gone to that party in the first place.

"I think it's different for Hannah. I mean, she has a girl-friend."

"Right. *Natalie.*"

Judging by her tone, she didn't seem to like the Beck much either.

"She's a *pretty* girl." Tan said it with a skeptical squint, as if "pretty" were a discarded fashion trend from two seasons ago. "I'd have thought if Hannah were *actually* gay, she'd go for someone . . . more like you."

It took me an embarrassingly long time to stop smiling and realize that it wasn't a compliment.

She leaned in. "Were you two ever . . . ?"

I cocked my head as if confused.

Tan waved her hand around. "*You* know."

"Me and *Daisy*?" Hannah's laugh resounded in the hallway as she galloped back into the room, allowing my heart to fall back into its usual rhythm. "God, Mom. No! Daisy's straight, remember? Besides, she's *so* not my type."

I scowled, Tan's "pretty" comment ringing in my ears. "Why not? Exactly?"

Now Hannah's mouth was full of cupcake, but any answer

she could have given was interrupted by the sound of another text.

I groaned. But this time it was my phone beeping.

The text was from my mom: "*CALL WHEN YOU GET THIS YOU ARE ON THE INTERNET.*"

Hannah rested her chin on my shoulder, squinting at my screen. "Does she mean the article?"

I frowned, shrugging, and pushed CALL.

"I don't have time for this, Mom," I started. "I have to learn about cells."

"You're on the *Internet*," Mom said. "Your name and your face!"

The mania in her voice made me snort. This was too good not to speakerphone. Hannah huddled closer, grinning, biting her lip to keep quiet.

"You mean . . . the article?" I coaxed. "I already know about that, Mom. It's up on the college—"

"It's been shared on Facebook one thousand seven hundred and twenty-two times."

I stopped breathing. Hannah made a choking sound. Then Mom said, "Oh shoot, no, that's likes. Shared eight hundred and *sixty*." She sounded disappointed.

My first of many stunned questions was: "How do you know this?"

"Cousin Erica messaged me."

"From *Alaska*?"

"Yes, Daisy, they have the Internet in Alaska."

"What's in the comments? What are people saying?"

Tan murmured something and Hannah wandered over to her.

Mom was huffing, overwhelmed. "Lots of things."

I shook the phone. "Read it, read it!"

"There are too many, Daisy. Seventy-eight comments on this one post alone. Why don't you get your own profile, anyway? I'm on Facebook and so are all *my* friends."

"You just answered your own question. Come *on,* Mom, just read the top one—"

Hannah's voice rang out across the room. "Gay student Daisy Beaumont-Smith fights for equal rights."

She was holding her mother's phone, both of them staring at it, Tan's eyes gleaming with amusement while Hannah's dimmed more with every blink.

"Gay student," Hannah repeated, looking up at me.

I gaped back. "But I'm *not* gay."

She shrugged, pressed her lips together, held out the phone so I could see for myself.

One account had posted an illustration of a girl who looked a lot like me wearing a superhero costume. "Gay Hero of the Day: 16-year-old Daisy Beaumont-Smith."

I was an illustration. A superhero.

"Gotta go," I said, hanging up.

Hannah's phone beeped from the dining room table, but her eyes didn't veer from mine. "Wow. Daisy. You're an Internet celebrity."

At the word "celebrity," I started laughing, my skin prickling hot as if there were actual hordes of people in the apartment angling for a look at me.

"What's the expression?" Mama Tan asked, then smiled, remembering. "You've gone *viral*."

"I guess so!" I giggled again, frantically scanning the screen, and Hannah laughed too—a taut, nervous laugh. A fake one. I glanced up to see her inching away as if "viral" were something she didn't want to catch.

The phone suddenly felt like a lab sample. I handed it to Tan, then turned to Hannah with as convincing a shrug as I could conjure.

"Anyway. *Cells*. Explain them, please."

16

"Can you pick me up?"

There was absolutely no scenario in which I would ask my mother to drive me downtown to meet Don't Know Him From Adam for coffee. It would fill her brain with all sorts of wrong certainties about my nonexistent love life.

"From school?" Adam sounded surprised.

"That's where I am." It was two o'clock on a Wednesday. Where else would I be?

"Um, yeah, sure." Adam covered the phone and coughed. "You can't meet me? Do you not have a car? You drive, right?"

Intrusive questions alert. I flushed, then remembered he was a reporter and therefore socially inappropriate.

"You're sixteen, right?" He really wasn't letting this go.

"Yeah." I felt a spike of indignation at the question. "How old are *you*?"

"Eighteen. What time do you get out?"

He pulled up forty minutes later in a black Toyota with a yellow stripe painted down the side, like he was planning to go drag racing in his sensible sedan.

"I know," he groaned when I sat down, even though I hadn't said anything. "I'm getting it repainted. I've only had it for two months."

"The car or the need for speed?"

"The car."

"Would you say that you're more *fast* or *furious*?"

He adjusted the rearview mirror. "Fast. I have my temper pretty well in check. Although I could probably jog faster than this car."

I laughed, relaxing. "So are you a freshman?"

He nodded. "Do you not drive?"

He sure had the dogged-pursuit-of-truth part of journalism down.

"No," I admitted, fastening my seat belt with all the dignity a passenger could muster. "I tried. It didn't take."

"Kinda hard to avoid driving in this part of the world. Back in New York, I was the only one of my friends with a license."

He put the car into gear. I watched in envy at his mastery of the stick shift. Bizarrely, Adam seemed more comfortable behind the wheel than I'd ever seen him outside of a car.

"My best friend usually drives me," I said, leaving out the part where she'd ordered me to stop mooching rides.

"The one you told me about? Who just came out?"

"Yeah." I smiled. "She's awesome. She's why I'm doing all this."

"I thought so." We'd hit a stoplight, and Adam was staring at me with a funny expression. "Sounds like she's pretty important to you."

"She's everything," I said, but my voice came out weird and hollow, like I was reciting the Pledge of Allegiance.

Adam was quiet until we pulled up to the restaurant. Honestly, when he'd called about a follow-up interview, I wasn't sure I had much of an update to give him, aside from the fact that I was having random attacks of vertigo every time I remembered that my name was all over the Internet—but then he'd suggested Chez Panisse and visions of éclairs started nomming in my head. It was a nice courtyard restaurant in downtown Charleston, the kind of place that had a long wait during tourist season, even for coffee. But Adam had made a reservation.

He pulled a chair out for me and I had to press my lips shut to keep from grinning like an idiot.

"I've gotten a lot of requests for your contact information," he said as he settled into the seat opposite me. "From reporters. Real ones."

"*You're* a real reporter," I said.

His eyes lit up.

"No," he said, burying his smile. "I mean from national publications. Some news stations. CNN, ABC."

"*What?* Really?" *Legitimate news sources? Not just blogs?*

He squinted at me. "You don't go online much, do you?"

"Mostly just to look stuff up," I said, opting not to tell him that I'd googled my name every five minutes until falling asleep at two a.m. the night before. "I don't do social networking. I don't really network. Or socialize."

"You might want to start." Adam pulled a page up on his phone. "Get a Facebook profile at least. Look at this."

This was new since last night. On Facebook, someone—a total stranger, living in New Hampshire—had started a fund for the "Palmetto Alternative Homecoming." They already had more than $16,000 raised.

"*What.*" I grabbed Adam's phone. "I've raised fifty bucks. From my dad!"

"You should link up with these people. They want to help."

"Thanks to you!" *That was corny.* "Your article, I mean." *Stop talking.*

He cleared his throat. "I'm just pointing it out. You do what you want with the information." He took his phone back, eyes drifting to the next table. "It's important for a reporter to maintain a critical distance from his subject. I can't advocate one way or the other."

"You can't get too involved."

"Exactly."

"Is that why—?" I bit the words back.

Is that why you buried the fact that I was straight? Is that the "critical distance" you're talking about?

I wanted an answer, but I couldn't think of a way to ask that wouldn't spoil the moment—the jasmine-scented breeze, the bright chatter around us, the pretense of having this boy as a friend.

He had his eyebrows raised, waiting for the rest of my question.

"Is that why you took me to coffee at Chez Panisse, Mr. Fancy Pants?" I fluttered my eyelashes at him over the menu. "I'm ordering pastries, by the way."

He grinned, frowned, then shoved his glasses back into place, a gesture I now recognized as flustered, all in the space of a second. "So should I pass them your contact info?"

"The reporters?" I shrugged. "Sure, why not?"

Adam asked a few questions about the event and jotted

down my answers, but when I got bored of talking about my-self, I said, "Let's do you now," half expecting him to cite the aforementioned Journalistic Distance Clause. But:

"I'm from Brooklyn. That's a borough of New York Cit—"

I blinked *duh* at him. "I think I've heard of it."

"I was born there. Grew up there. Had enough of there. Applied to every college with a strong journalism program outside a two-hundred-mile radius. Got into . . ." He counted off on his fingers. "UCLA. Northwestern. Bristol University in England. Waitlisted at Stanford . . ."

"But you picked . . . *Charleston*."

"Yeah." He laughed, like he couldn't believe it either. "CU offered me a scholarship, which I needed. And I wanted to see what the South was like."

He said "South" like other people would say "Camelot."

"Is it living up to your expectations?" I asked wryly.

"It's . . . different than I'd thought," he admitted. "But like I said, the accents are pretty great."

"You keep going on about that." I leaned back, arms crossed. "I don't even have an accent."

"You are mistaken."

It was an accusation, but something about the way Adam said it, his dark eyes glowing and shy, his voice low and warm and flat-voweled, made me feel like grabbing a hoop skirt and parasol and Scarlett O'Hara–ing it up.

He drove me home, and bless everything that can be blessed above, my mother's car wasn't in the driveway when we pulled up.

"Thanks for the éclairs," I said. "They were *magnifique*."

Instead of "You're welcome," Adam said, "I could teach you to drive stick shift."

I stared back, stone-faced, in case he was mocking me.

"Seriously," he said. "I taught a bunch of my cousins back in New York. And if you can learn in the city, you can learn here."

I cocked an eyebrow. "This *is* a city."

"Of course it is." He smiled, running his hands over the curve of the steering wheel. "Think about it."

I did think about it. And his hands. All night and into the next day.

Then the reporters started calling.

The real ones.

"This is a message for Daisy Beaumont-Smith. I'm a reporter with the Chicago Sun-Times . . ."

"Daisy! Hello! My name's Mindy Taylor? And I'm a producer for the Today Show*?"*

"Erm, good afternoon. Or I suppose it's morning where you are. I'm a columnist with the Guardian, *here in the UK, and I saw the story about your plans for an, erm, LGBTQ homecoming . . ."*

"Ooohhh, British," Jack said, swiveling in his chair with a lewd grin.

Sophie prettily rolled her eyes. "He's probably fifty."

"Shhht!" Raina raised a hand, silencing the table so we could hear the rest of the message playing from my phone.

". . . I realize you've spoken one-on-one with a local chap there, but I was hoping you might grant me an exclusive as a follow-up . . ."

Raina wrote down his number and email on the bottom of her full legal pad page. "Any more?"

"Next. Message," voicemail voice said. *"Heya Daisy, this is Mr. Murphy over at the rec center—"*

I hit DELETE.

"That's it. But I've got like twelve email requests," I said, so jittery in my chair that I had to hold on to the table to keep from swiveling away. "Or I did this morning. There might be more by now. I sort of had to hide my phone in my locker for a while. It kept . . . vibrating."

And *bzzzz!* went my phone, as if to show off. I dropped it on the desk with a clatter and sat on my still-shaking hands.

"Okay," Raina said to her legal pad. "So far, we've got an invitation to write a Huffington Post column. *The Today Show.* Three local news stations that want interviews. I counted four bloggers, three print publications . . ."

My phone rang—again—yet another number I didn't recognize. Raina paused as I jumped to silence it, then said, "Plus whoever that was."

"Ladies and gentlemen?" Sean rose from his chair, arms extended. "This is officially *crazy.*"

He fell sitting again, tipsy with excitement.

"Agreed." Raina pressed her fingers to the bridge of her nose, like she'd passed from tipsy to hungover several hours ago.

"So!" My attempt to keep the sound of panic from my voice was unsuccessful. "Where do we start?"

"Good question," Raina said, flipping to a new page where

I prayed she'd already written the answer. "Given the immensity of what Daisy's gotten us into, we'll need to meet every day after school to coordinate. I've booked out the room until after homecoming."

Kyle raised his hand. "I've got lacrosse practice?"

"That's okay," Raina said, her voice brightening into something approaching pleasant. "Just help out when you can."

"*Music Man* rehearsals start next week," Sean said. "But I can sneak out. This is more important." He grinned. "And let's be real, I've had the role memorized since I was eleven."

"Anybody else?" Raina looked around the table. We shook our heads. "Good. Then we'll expect you here, rain or shine. Especially you, Daisy."

What, did she think I was going to run out on them? I hadn't yet, had I?

"This is a good time to divide up responsibilities," Raina went on. "I'm happy to handle our legal and political strategy."

We all exhaled at that one.

"My dad's a lawyer," Raina said, and her entire existence suddenly made sense. "He's busy, but he'll help. Sophie—given your mom's connection to the land acquisition project, maybe you can be our site supervisor?"

Sophie nodded, jotting the title down in her little pink notepad. I felt a prick of jealousy at not having gotten that job myself, since I was the one who came up with the idea and was going to have to volunteer gardening hours for the rest of my life in repayment.

"You'll also be in charge of managing the vendors and our budget."

That sounded like a ton of work. I shot Sophie a thumbs-up in congratulations.

Jack volunteered to lead our social media efforts before Raina even assigned it to him.

"No offense," he said, looking around the table. "But y'all are hopeless."

"Make sure you coordinate with the people raising money on our behalf," Raina suggested, just as I was about to shout the same idea. "And work with Sean on fund-raising. He's been great at raising money for the theater program."

"I'm *always* happy to work with Sean," Jack cooed.

Sean balled up a piece of paper and threw it at his head, and with that, everybody started laughing and talking, like the meeting was breaking.

I raised my hand. "What about me?"

Raina looked confused. "You'll continue to be our spokesperson."

"But . . ." I looked around at the others as they fell silent. "I'm straight. *Asexual,* I mean."

"Nobody knows that but us," Raina said slowly. "And I think maybe it should stay that way."

Everyone's eyes were on me, unsurprised, expectant. They'd talked about this in advance.

I swallowed dry. "What are you saying?"

"In the parlance of our people," Jack said brightly, like a museum tour guide, "I believe it's called '*staying in the closet.*'"

"Our homecoming is a month away," Raina said, pointedly ignoring him. "After that, you can be as straight as you want. But we can't let anything derail this. If this event doesn't happen or it's embarrassing in any way, we're a laughingstock. A *headache*. They'll use it as an excuse to bury us again. You get that, right?"

I nodded. "Of course."

"Good." Raina stared at me, unblinking. "Because it sure didn't seem like you got it when you stood up on a chair at the school board meeting."

Sophie cleared her throat. "This is Daisy's decision. If she doesn't feel comfortable . . ."

"It's kind of the group's decision," Sean argued, turning to me with an apologetic smile. "I mean, it impacts us all."

"Why don't we vote?" Kyle rolled back as we all swiveled to look at him. "That's, um, how we settle things in my family. Or . . . yeah."

"Not a bad idea." Raina knocked on the desk. "I vote for Daisy to stay in the closet. Sean?"

"Closet," he said, pointing at me with both hands. "It's just acting, remember? You were so good in *Carousel*!"

Liar.

"Sophie?" Raina nodded down the table.

She sighed. "I vote for the truth. I think forcing her to hide who she is kind of misses the point of what we're doing here."

Raina didn't react. "Jack?"

"Closet."

I blinked at Jack, surprised.

"I lie every time I step into my house." He shrugged. "It's easier than you'd think."

His smile didn't reach his eyes, making me suspect other-wise.

"Kyle?" Raina went on.

"Truth," Kyle voted. *"Honestas ante honores."* He glanced up, eyes wide, like he hadn't meant to say that out loud. "Sorry. Last period was Latin. It means, um—"

"'Honesty before glory,'" Raina translated. Then her head snapped up. "That's two for truth, three for the closet. We need a majority, Daisy. How do you vote?"

I stared at the Alliance, saw the hope in their eyes, registered the weight of the fact that they'd even given me a vote at this table.

"Closet," I said.

Raina stood as the bell rang.

"That's settled then. For the next thirty days, Daisy is a lesbian."

17

Friday morning, September the twenty-third, at 7:52 a.m., Hannah picked me up for school. Natalie was not in attendance.

"This article," she said as we pulled out of my neighborhood. "It's everywhere."

"Pretty nutso, huh?" I rolled down the car window, enjoying the first hint of crispness in the air. "A bunch of reporters have been calling me. We haven't decided how to handle the press yet, though."

"We?" She raised her eyebrows, smirking. "Have you adopted the royal 'we' now that you're FOTI?"

I stared at her. "FOTI?"

"Famous on the Internet." She blinked. "I just made it up."

"Ooh, I *like* it. But no, 'we' is the Alliance. Oh! That reminds me!" I pressed my lips together as she glanced over. "I'm kind of playing gay for the next month?"

"You—wha—ga—" Hannah sputtered. "*Daisy.*"

She closed her eyes. It was a good thing we were at a stoplight.

"Just until the event is done."

"Did it start with that interview?" Hannah's lips were set

tight, her eyes now locked ahead, and I had the sense that she'd been waiting a very long time to ask me this. "Did you lie on purpose, or—?"

"Nonono." I grabbed her shoulder until she glanced at me again. "I was totally up-front, Hannah, I swear. Adam knew I was straight, but he didn't mention it in the article for whatever reason. *But* now that it's out there—"

"'Adam'?" She made air quotes with one hand, steering with the other.

"That's his name. The reporter. The first one, the college guy?"

"Yeah, I know, I just didn't realize you were on an Adam-name basis with him."

I shrugged. "Why wouldn't I be?"

She sighed, turning the corner. "I don't know why you would or wouldn't be. I don't know *anything* about your life right now."

Whose fault is that? I thought, but said, "I'm not asking *you* to lie. I know you're not wired that way."

"No." She clenched her jaw. "I'm not."

"But if anybody asks between then and now, just tell them my sexuality is a private matter and you refuse to discuss my personal life."

"'Them' being?"

"Other kids? The press?"

Hannah let out a squawk. "Don't you think this has gotten a little out of hand?"

"Pshhh," I scoffed. "Picture a hand. Like a giant hand."

She cracked a smile. "Okay?"

"This event is in it."

Hannah shook her head, laughing. "If you say so."

But then we turned into the school parking lot.

"This is *in hand*?" she said, while I could only muster a low, long, "Hooooollllyyy . . ."

In the narrow strip of public land between the road and the arts wing, a conga line of protesters stood waving posters. A printed sign along the edge of the crowd read "FREE SPEECH ZONE," and across the street, a pair of police cars and three news vans were parked, observing the crowd from a careful distance. And it *was* a crowd—way bigger than any protest group my mom had ever assembled. Unless . . .

I leaped from the car, grinning, but turned back to see Hannah hesitating in the driver's seat. "What's the matter?"

She had her fist pressed to her mouth.

"Oh, don't worry!" I waved my hand. "These are my mom's people. They're harmless."

Hannah shook her head. "I don't think so, Daisy."

My eyes traveled to where she was pointing. The biggest sign of the bunch, held high by a beaming old man in a brown, too-large suit, read "GOD HATES FAGS."

"*No.*"

They looked like hippies. But all the signs said horrible things. Nonsensical things, like "Stay strong Palmetto against the QUEER FORCES OF SATAN." It turned out that's what they were all cheerfully chanting, a tiny girl with pigtail braids the loudest of the bunch. It would have been comical if weren't so horrifying.

Several of them wore T-shirts bearing the words "Christian

Values Coalition." I wasn't the most religious person in the world, but I had a hunch they were the kinds of "Christians" who only read the same two sections of the Bible over and over, ignoring all those pesky parts about love and tolerance.

Hannah tugged me backward. "I'm not walking through that."

"It's the way in," I said, squeezing her hand. "We can walk wherever we want. If we hike all the way around the soccer field, the terrorists will have won."

She seemed to accept that, but clung on as we stepped forward. When we drew alongside them, Hannah held her breath, her eyes blinking hard as if to blind herself. I stared boldly back.

I shouldn't have. The little girl's eyes darted to our intertwined hands and a second later, the crowd ignited, red-faced and vicious, no longer in any way confusable with my mother's brand of protesters.

"Abomination!" one woman yelled, spitting in our direction, missing by a few inches. Across the street, I saw the doors to the police car open and two officers get out.

"Daisy," Hannah said as the crowd's roar grew too chaotic to make out individual words. I turned to see tears streaming down her cheeks.

Someone, another student, stepped in front of us and snapped a picture with her phone.

"Almost there," I said. "Two more steps."

And then, thank God, we'd reached the steps of the school and then the doors, and the noise of those hateful bastards was silenced by the ordinary hum of morning in the lobby.

Hannah wriggled her hand free of mine and hugged it like it hurt. I hadn't realized I'd been holding it so tight.

"Are you okay?" I asked.

"Fine," she said. "Everything's fine."

She was shuddering like she had a fever. But before I could reach out a hand to calm her, she'd already hurried down the hall to homeroom.

At 8:15 a.m., a senior on the cheerleading squad with the Twitter handle @tmtpiratewench tweeted the photo she took, tagging it #GoDaisy. I'd later learn that this was the same girl who last week called me a ho-bag.

At 12:25 p.m., I made my way to the cafeteria. A quick glance at the stoop showed me where I wouldn't be sitting today. Natalie was pacing the steps, listening to whatever Hannah was saying with a thunderous glare. Watching her viciously rip her red hair out of and back into its ponytail, I decided now was probably not the best time to butt in.

And besides, wonder of wonders, right there at a table smack dab in the middle of the room, if it wasn't the Palmetto High School LGBTQIA Alliance sitting together for once, their heads ducked over Jack's shining tablet like it held the meaning of life. Kyle waved me over.

"The photo of you," he explained. "People are sharing it kind of a lot."

The cheerleader who'd snapped the shot had done a surprisingly expert job of framing it. On the left, the mob of supposedly Christian protesters, screaming hate. And on the right, two girls walking past, heads ducked, hands linked.

According to the tablet screen, someone in Florida had just retweeted it with the caption: "Gay advocate Daisy Beaumont-Smith with her girlfriend."

No wonder Natalie was mad. *Heh.*

"It's all over the Internet," Raina piped up. "And #GoDaisy is trending."

"Trending who?" I grabbed the tablet and shook it. "This is a Twitter thing? Show me, show me!"

Jack gently pried the iPad back and opened a bunch of sites. People on Reddit were planning counter-protests for as early as this afternoon. The Facebook group Jack created for LGBTQ Palmetto alumni had, nonsensically, grown to over 100,000 members.

"We're on the *Guardian* website," he said, opening another tab. "This must be the guy from your voicemail!" He turned to Sophie. "You were right. Not hot."

"Anything in Spain?" Sean asked, leaning over me to see the screen. "I wonder if Diego's seen this."

"Probably." Jack let out a diabolic laugh. "We've gone global, kids. We're huge!"

I glanced up, then quickly back down. It wasn't just online we were huge. Around our table, a group of fifty or more students had just gathered to steal peeks at Jack's tablet—and at me.

"Bathroom break." I scrambled out of my chair, bracing myself for another angry mob. But as the crowd parted, a few people patted me on the back, murmuring their support.

A week ago, I was the girl who got homecoming canceled.

And now, greeting me in the hallway, the guy I suspected of throwing a Starbucks cup at me was offering me a high five. Why? Because I was FOTI?

"Go Daisy!" said a group of choir members in unison, popping their heads out of the auditorium. *Seriously?* I fled to the restroom and didn't come out until the bell had rung. I wasn't up for eating with an audience. And besides, I'd lost my appetite.

At 1:35 p.m., my stomach growled so loudly during lab that everyone turned to look at me. Everyone but Hannah.

At 2:32 p.m., I was sitting in French, glancing over the quiz I'd just gotten back, upon which Prof Hélène had scribbled *German, Spanish, Latin* next to my wrong answers, when a noise like the ocean roared from outside. We all glanced at the windows, seeing nothing but the eighth-period gym class jogging around the football field.

"What the hell," the boy next to me muttered.

"En français!" Prof Hélène admonished, but the bell rang before we could figure out the translation.

The sound from outside grew louder and louder, mingling with excited shouts of students moving between classes, until I reached my history room on the other side of the building, where everyone, teacher included, stood with their faces cluttering the north-facing windows, riveted by the scene outside.

Almost everyone. Madison sat in her usual seat in the back with prim serenity, as if she alone were above our petty politics. Her eyes narrowed when she saw me, but she was only five-one. I could take her.

From what I could glimpse over my classmates' heads, the crowd of angry protesters seemed to have quadrupled in the past few hours. No wonder Madison looked so smug. My heart was sinking when I heard Mr. Beckett, the history teacher, let out a whoop.

"Counter-protesters! Students?" He spun around to take my hand in both of his. "We're watching history unfold. Right here. Today!"

I swallowed a snort, but as the others shifted to give me a better view, I started to suspect that his enthusiasm wasn't all that overblown. The Free Speech Zone now spilled across the street and down the block. Closest to us, one group was holding up their "God hates you and loves us" signs, and yes, there were more now, but a larger group stood facing them, shouting in much more effective rhythm—and waving the biggest rainbow banner I'd ever seen.

As a siren sounded and two more police cars pulled into the parking lot, the speakers in the classroom beeped for an announcement.

"*Students.*" It was Principal Zimmer. He sounded exhausted. "*Ninth period will proceed as scheduled, hubbub outside notwithstanding. I know it might be tempting, but we're going to ask you not to talk to reporters as you leave school grounds. Thanks for your cooperation.*"

I felt everyone's eyes on me as we returned to our seats.

"Okay." Mr. Beckett sat on his desk, slumping with disappointment. "Let's talk about the Industrial Revolution."

At 4:05 p.m., the final bell had already rung, but I couldn't bring myself to leave the building. The mob outside was bigger than ever, and through an open doorway, I could see at least half a dozen news teams milling around the border of the Free Speech Zone, interviewing protesters. When the first waves of students walked out, reporters swarmed them, scanning the doorway, searching. For me.

A whistle sounded from behind me, and I turned to see QB at the end of the hall, making some sort of secret football signal that I assumed translated to "Onward!"

When I reached him, he huddle-whispered, "Do you have a ride home?"

"My mom." Probably floating somewhere in that sea of protesters.

"Good." He guided me through cracked glass doors into the athletic wing. "Tell her to meet us on the corner of Miller and West."

As I hurriedly texted her, QB ducked into the boys' locker room, reemerging with a football helmet under one arm. When we reached the door that led to the football field, he stuck it on my head. It bobbled back and forth.

"Better than nothing, right?"

"Right." I knocked on the top of it. "Thank you."

"One more thing." QB shrugged out of his hunting jacket and wrapped it around me. To my surprise, it smelled sweet, like wood smoke. Like a fireside, in a cabin in the woods, cozy and . . . huh.

A guy as good-looking as QB should probably have brought

to mind visions of the two of us nestling for warmth. But the most I could picture was he and I playing Chinese checkers or having a thumb-battle for the last s'more. Which actually wasn't that unpleasant a daydream. I'd always wondered what it would be like to have a sibling.

He grabbed my hand and led me across the field toward Miller Street in a too-quick jog. It was a good thing I was disguised, because if any reporters saw us right now, hand in hand, they might get the wrong idea. Again.

"Hey, Chris?" He glanced over his shoulder at me. "If anybody asks, reporters or whoever—*I'm gay*, okay?"

His face registered confusion for a full three count. Then he slapped his leg. "I *knew* it!"

I bit back a clarification. Why was this such a confusing concept for people?

"So . . ." He held out a hand to help me across the dead hedges and onto a block of modest one-story houses, where the Veggiemobile was dutifully idling. Then he removed the helmet from my head, spun it on one finger, and tucked it back under his arm. "We've got an away game, so I've gotta take off, but—you doing anything next Friday?"

Back to gay and he was *still* hitting on me. The boy didn't get it. But hey, he had just heroically orchestrated my escape from a school under siege.

I handed him back his hunting jacket with a smile. "See you at the game."

The second I got home, my cell phone rang—and my heart started racing.

Hannah. Oh my God, how could I have forgotten her?

"Are you okay?" I asked, racing to my bedroom.

"Yeah." She huffed. "I mean, I'm home. But it wasn't good, Daisy. The reporters completely ignored the police barricade. I could barely get into my car."

"Oh, no!" I clicked my computer to life. "But the counter-protests—amazing, right? They're all here for you!"

"They're here for you, Daisy. They have your face on posters."

"*What?*" That called for immediate googling.

"The only question the reporters had for me was how long we'd been *dating*. I tried saying what you told me, that it was a personal matter, but it didn't work at all! There are reporters outside my house right now. I'm looking at them."

"You should call the cops? Maybe?"

"We have." She sighed. "Are you okay? Did you manage to get past them?"

"Yeah, I snuck away. And they don't know where I live." I felt guilt-itchy, admitting it. "All quiet on the Daisy front."

"Oh. That's good. That's . . . a relief."

She didn't sound relieved. And she fell silent for so long that I started to get worried.

"Hannah?"

"This is not how I thought this would go." Her voice was a pinprick all of a sudden.

"How what would go?"

The line echoed with her silence. Then she said:

"My *dad* called me, Daisy."

She was crying.

"Two years and he called me because he read my name on the

189

Internet. That is not right. That is not what's supposed to—"

"Your dad?" I clung to the phone. "Oh my God, when? Did you talk to him? How was it?"

"It doesn't matter."

"Of course it matters, Han. It's your father, it's important!"

"You don't get to decide what's important."

Hannah didn't raise her voice, not a decibel, but something in the sharp measure of her tone stopped me cold. Like so many of her words lately, these sounded rehearsed—like she'd been thinking them and thinking them and finally had a chance to say them out loud.

I held on to my desk with my free hand, fighting the sensation of falling.

"I don't want to talk about my dad right now, Daisy, I just . . ." I heard her sniff hard, and then a thump, feet on wood. She must have been sitting tucked up in her window seat. "I don't want this. I never wanted this, to . . . to be talked about. In Austria? What the hell! And for that to be the reason he calls me? To have *this* be all that anybody can say about me?"

It took me too long to grapple for a response. Long enough for her to say:

"I need a break."

Tears sprung up, stinging and wrong. I forced my eyes wide so they wouldn't fall. "From all the attention? I get that."

"Do you?" She let out a weak laugh.

"Of course!" I spoke quickly, brightly. "And I'll stop, I'll step away from all of this if you want, join Chess. Just tell me what—"

"You can't, Daisy. It's too *late*. This isn't the opera, this is something that actually matters to people. You should have thought about that before . . ." She drew a breath. "I'm gonna go."

"Hannah?"

"Talk to you later," she said, and hung up without any clarification of how much later that later would be.

After staring blankly at my computer for a full minute, I realized that what I was looking at was a blue-and-white graphic of my own face, the word "PRIDE" printed beneath it in red. This was the poster. I clicked the screen off, extinguishing the image. Then I swiped my cheeks dry so forcefully it hurt.

Of course she was upset. Whatever had gone on during that phone call with her father must have been agonizing. And the protesters—she'd woken up this morning and gotten ready for school, only to be ambushed by people who had shown up to tell her they hated her. It was no wonder that, looking at the crowds that had sprung up overnight like mushrooms, Hannah just saw menace.

But she was right, it was too late for me to back down. Too cowardly. Soon our own troops, those hundreds of thousands of supporters online, would mobilize and overpower the detractors, and Hannah would realize how much the world cared. And she'd see how much *I* cared too—more than all of those supporters put together, more than a school full of friends, more than a distant father, more than enough. She'd see.

I just had to work harder.

18

"How many now?"

"Our side or theirs? Ooh!" Jack shook the conference room blinds in his excitement. "Another bus!"

Kyle peeked past me. "'College of' something? On that guy's sweatshirt?"

"Our side," I crowed, doing a quick guesstimate of the teeming masses across the street. "That makes two fifty for us, a hundred for them. *Lame.*"

"Hmmm." Sophie pointed at the young bus riders, now hoisting cheerfully hateful posters as they joined the crowd nearest the school. "College of the Redeemer. Church group."

Jack's face went pale. He turned from the window with a pinched smile. "I'm just glad Reverend Tom hasn't shown up. He'd probably expect me to picket with him."

"Whoa." Kyle's eyes darted upward. "Sorry. Was that a helicopter?"

"Yes!" I laughed. "Because the only way to get all of our

supporters in a picture is to photograph them *from the air.* What *what*?"

I offered Jack a high five. He left me hanging.

"Oh, look!" Sophie tapped on the window. "Another church bus . . . going the other way."

Jack and I bumped heads leaning in. Sure enough, the small white bus branded "James Island Unity Church" had just veered a hard left past the protesters to park near the lot. When the doors opened, the brightly dressed congregants spilled straight into the counter-crowd. I held my breath as their conservatively suited leader hoisted his sign.

"God Loves ALL of His Children," it read. Above it was a bright rainbow banner.

Jack's mouth had fallen open.

"You should go talk to them," I said, nudging his foot with mine. "See what their deal is."

Jack scowled to hide the dawning hope in his eyes. "Maybe. I don't know. If they're still there when we're done."

"Can we get started?" Raina clapped her notepads into a neat stack on the table. We ignored her.

Sean burst through the door wearing a red jacket with spangly epaulettes. "They're rehearsing 'Wells Fargo Wagon,' what did I miss?"

"Absolutely nothing," Raina huffed.

"Awesome!" Sean clapped, hurrying past her to the windows.

Kyle pointed. "Daisy, is that your mom?"

I leaned over his shoulder, spotting a woman at the front of the crowd wearing an oversized rainbow T-shirt and a wide straw hat with the word "PROUD" perched on it like the Hollywood sign.

I shut the blinds with a thwap. "You know, we should really get this meeting going."

"Social media," Raina started, before we'd even sat down. "Jack?"

"Awesomesaucesomeness," he said, perking up. "Close to half a million shares on Facebook, and that is *not an exaggeration*. Some traction on other sites, but we'll need to keep the buzz going."

Raina nodded. "Makes sense. Where do we stand on that?"

Everyone seemed to be looking at me. "Sorry?"

"Interviews." Raina tapped the table with her pen. "Which ones have you set up?"

"I . . . thought we were going to decide on a plan for that . . . collectively?"

Which was why I'd allowed my voicemail box to fill up and had officially become too overwhelmed to check my email as of ten a.m. Saturday. An intrepid college reporter was one thing. But the *Guardian*? The *LA Times*? Even the local news team—*"We've got Charleston on our radar!"*—seemed hopelessly intimidating at this point.

"So. None. Is what you're telling us." Raina put her head in her hands.

Before I could make up something encouraging, Sophie inched out of her chair, one hand raised. "You guys? We need to talk about the land."

The look on her face was the opposite of reassuring. We

were holding our breath, waiting to for her to go on, when a soft knock sounded on the door and Principal Zimmer's bald head poked in.

Raina scooped up her legal pads and leaned against them casually, shielding them from view.

"How's it going, guys?" he asked, to which everybody mumbled "Okay," which probably happened every time he tried to talk to students.

He glanced behind himself, shut the door, and took a seat at the table next to a very uncomfortable Kyle.

"I want you to know that I *appreciate* what you're doing here," Principal Zimmer said, his voice so low we had to crane our heads to hear him. "I've got some information that, in all good conscience, I felt I needed to pass along. The school board's trying to find ways to shut you down."

"Shocking," I muttered, and Raina shot me a *shut up* look.

"They're going to issue an injunction preventing you from using the school's name in your communications."

Raina leaned forward. "Can they do that?"

"I'm not a legal expert. But you might want to find somebody who is."

We all looked to Raina. She cleared her throat. "My dad's a maritime lawyer. Not exactly up on copyright issues. But yeah, I'll ask."

"There's more." Principal Zimmer's voice got even quieter. "They're working on the landowner. Trying to keep him from selling to the Community Farmers Association."

"I'm confused," I said, glancing at Sophie. "I thought that was as good as done."

She flushed. "That's what I was about to tell you guys. The owner's now saying he doesn't want to get caught up in anything political. He'll only sell to the farm if they promise not to let us use the land for homecoming."

The room seemed to sink as the news hit each of us in turn. Then Sean slapped the table.

"Idea." His eyes were gleaming. We all leaned in. "Let's get an *even better* venue."

He beamed around at us, apparently expecting us to clap.

"Brilliant," Jack said.

Raina smiled tightly at the principal. "Thanks for letting us know. We'll figure it out."

Principal Zimmer rose, seeming to understand, and put his finger to his lips. "I was never here. But if I learn anything else, I'll . . . *not* drop in again!"

He snorted at his own joke, stifled it, and left the room.

A silence fell over the table. Then Jack said what we were all thinking.

"Gay."

"Gotta be, right?" Sean glanced back at the closed door. "He came to every single performance of *Footloose* last year. Even the dress rehearsal. Just sayin'."

"Wait, are you guys talking about the principal?" Kyle glanced around the table. "I have absolutely no gaydar."

"You will," Jack said sagely, Yoda to Kyle's Luke, and we all laughed.

All but one of us. Raina stood from the table, clearing her throat.

"We've got *twenty-six days* left. Less than a month."

The smiles fell dead from our faces.

Sophie shook her head. "I honestly don't know how we're going to handle this land situation. My mom and Daisy's are trying their best, but—maybe we should just let them drop out. I don't want them to lose their farm because of us."

I goggled at her altruism. Sophie was a much better daughter than me.

"I wasn't a hundred percent on that field, anyway. I'm not exactly the Bonnaroo type." Sean snorted. "So—what's our backup location?"

Wait. Why was everybody looking at me again?

"Party at my house. I'll provide the Fresca!" Nobody laughed, so I forced my face serious. "Yeah, no, we need to make this land deal happen. Maybe we should go talk to the owner ourselves—help him see our point of view?"

"I don't know." Kyle shook his head. "What if he's homophobic, or whatever? What if he's on the same side as—" He gestured vaguely past the blinds, and we all knew that he wasn't talking about the busloads of supporters who'd shown up.

"If we can't appeal to his sense of basic human decency," I said, "then we'll have to appeal to his wallet."

Everybody seemed to think that was a viable answer, so I scribbled it on my wrist, along with an arrow and a note: "Figure out what this means."

Sunlight attacked me as I emerged from the dim athletic wing onto the football field. A couple of field hockey players spilled out behind me and I jumped like they were assassins.

So this was what "on edge" felt like. I wondered what exactly I was on the edge of.

It wasn't just homecoming—the increased improbability of it, the fact that it still seemed to be my catastrophe to organize. I'd left Hannah alone all weekend, knowing she needed some space. Mom had driven me to school, the new normal. And when I'd walked into bio, I'd kept to myself, allowing Hannah to make the first move.

She didn't. She sat in her new seat in the back and barely looked my way.

I wondered how she'd gotten into the building this morning—and how she would get out now. Did she know a way to avoid the reporters and protesters, like I did? Just as I was scrabbling for my phone to text her about the athletic wing, she came outside through the door behind me and I dropped it on the ground.

While I was rising, she was passing. *I'm going to stop her,* I thought. *I'm going to say something.*

But then she glanced back so casually it hurt, and said, "Hey, Daisy," and kept walking and that was that.

There's this sound an ice cream truck makes when it's driving away. The song warps, becomes flat, the instant it passes. That's what Hannah sounded like. It was the same old "Hey, Daisy," but I knew from the music that there was no chasing it down today. So I stood still and stared at her back as it vanished into the parking lot.

My phone rang, snapping me back.

Adam (Reporter).

I felt a stupid frisson of excitement, even though I knew he was just calling for an update, wanting to know how *swimmingly* all of our plans were going. How *on top* of everything I was. What an *inspiration* we all were, planning this massive event with vendors in place, a hospitality company donating tents and stages, and oh! Right! *No location whatsoever!*

Raina wanted me to give interviews? Here went nothing.

I answered, marching off the field, but before I could even say hello, Adam started scolding me.

"Your voicemail is full. You need to clear it out, Daisy, people are trying to reach you."

"People?" I rounded the corner outside Starbucks and stopped, hands in my hair, trying some deep breathing so I wouldn't sound panicked on the phone.

"Yeah." He paused. "Are you all right?"

"Fine! Why?"

"Because you appear to be hyperventilating."

I turned and sure enough, Adam was waving from the Starbucks window, a concerned line etched between his eyebrows. He held up his pastry bag and mimed breathing into it.

Good idea. I veered through the glass doors, sat with a thud at Adam's table, and gazed out at the cloudy sky, the din in my brain growing louder by the second. He peered over his ceramic mug at me.

"Let me get you something," he said, standing up. "And let's talk? Off the record."

I think I said "Okay," but it's possible I just thought it.

A few tables over, two girls in their twenties were whispering to each other with subtle gestures in my direction.

Their expressions were friendly. They probably thought I was somebody who could accomplish something. Idiots.

"There's a guy from a PR firm in DC who called me a few times," Adam said, handing me a fancy cookie and a blackberry soda, somehow remembering the same two items I'd gotten last time he saw me here. "I gave him your number, but he said he couldn't leave a message, so he wanted me to let you know that he's flying down here tomorrow. He wants to work with you guys to help publicize the event. Pro bono."

I stared at him, my mind cycling between Latin, Spanish, and French. "I'm really hoping that means 'free.'"

Adam nodded, that sudden, bright smile electrifying his face. "He's going to call you tomorrow morning to set up a meeting. This is a huge win, Daisy. I suggest you answer the phone."

"So he's some sort of big shot?" I wasn't sure if that made me feel more or less nervous.

"Let's put it this way—every time he called me, a woman started the call by saying, 'Please hold for Mr. Montgomery.'"

"Classy."

"Extremely." Adam grinned and my heart stuttered. "And now that I've passed along this vital information that could make all your dreams come true, I can go back to maintaining a journalistic distance from my subject."

"Sounds great. So when are you teaching me to drive?"

"This weekend," he answered, and I coughed on my soda in surprise. I'd thought he was just offering to be nice, one of those things you suggest and hope nobody takes you up on, like, you know, paying for his computer. But Adam seemed genuine.

Then again, he was probably angling for an exclusive, now that my story was being reported all over the known world.

I eyed him warily. "How are your *articles* coming?"

He took a greedy gulp from his mug. "Good. Excellent, actually! My reports have been picked up by the Associated Press. I'm getting paid now!"

Bingo. I arched an eyebrow.

"I know, right?" He sat back with a grin. "Pretty crazy."

"So did you tell this PR guy that I was . . ."

I glanced around. Suddenly everybody looked like a journalist. Even the baristas.

"That you're asexual?" Adam peered over his glasses at me. "Like Morrissey?"

I didn't get the reference but chuckled along anyway.

"No." He cleared his throat. "I don't think it would be such a great idea to let the cat out of that particular bag."

"Or closet," I said. "My group agrees. We had a vote."

"Wow. That's . . . official."

"But you . . ." I squinted at Adam so hard he scooted back in his chair. "You're a reporter."

"Sort of," he corrected, then sat up straighter, as if giving himself a mental pep talk. "Yeah. I'm a reporter."

"So why didn't you *report* the truth?"

"Yeah. Um." His fingers tapped nervously along the table. "It was a stronger story without that one detail. Your motivation for doing all this made more sense. Because honestly, Daisy? Even now? I don't really get it."

I looked down at my phone, dodging the question—thinking about all the voicemail messages I needed to delete, and not a one of them from Hannah.

"Is it your friend? Your 'everything'?"

I glanced back up at him, igniting with defensiveness, but he didn't seem to be teasing. He wasn't digging, either. No iPhone recorder in sight. All that was here was Adam, his hands quiet for once against the table, his hair tracing a Superman curl against his forehead, while behind his Clark Kent glasses, those dark eyes of his stared right into mine like they'd known me forever. Like they *cared* about the answer.

Maybe it was the hopelessness I'd felt when I walked in here, maybe the way my brain was rattled from trying to avoid protesters. Maybe the sugar rush from the cookie-soda combo. Or vertigo from Hannah's little "break."

Whatever it was, my defenses were wobbling—and man, it felt good to knock them down completely. So I told him everything. About Hannah. And Natalie. Our histories. How uninvolved they both were in our cause. How, in fact, Natalie might have sabotaged us with the school board. How wrong she was for Hannah. How I was going to bolster Hannah's self-esteem, pull her from this tar pit of a toxic romance, and reclaim my rightful place as Hannah's person.

When I was done, the light outside had grown dim and Adam was staring at me as though I were a strange zoo animal that he didn't know existed. A mouse deer, maybe.

"So you're really doing all of this for . . ." His eyes darted around my face, searching for the answer among my freckles. "*Attention?*"

My breath caught. That word was so stark, so petty, so childish. It thudded in my head like the foot-stomp of an angry toddler.

"That . . ." I stood, sputtering. "That is *really* unfair."

"Sorry." He stood too, glancing around at the nearly empty room. "Badly worded."

I sniffed. "I should go."

"Okay."

For exactly three seconds, I felt like dignity personified. Then I sighed.

"Can you give me a lift?"

On the way home, Adam decided to return the favor of my over-sharing. He talked about his big brother, Eli, how they'd been best friends until high school, when Eli learned to play the guitar and pick up girls.

"He wasn't a dick or anything," Adam said, his voice soft, regretful. "He just had no time for me anymore. I wasn't interesting. I'm still not interesting, apparently. He's always touring, which makes things easier, but when we're back home together, our conversations are just . . . painful. We'll spend all of Thanksgiving this year trying to find ways to avoid each other."

"Oh gosh, that's tough," I said, my pulse quickening—with what? Panic? The idea of Adam spending fall break in New York did not sit well with me. It was the real city, wasn't it? He'd wake up on Thanksgiving morning as if from a dream, realizing that South Carolina was some stupid lark and that it would make all the sense in the world for him to stay at home and enroll in an Ivy League program like Columbia. And I would never see him again.

I stuck my hands in my jacket pockets, fighting the growing urge to grab his shirt and beg him to teach me to drive—right here, right now. He was so *good* at it, with his smooth braking, suave glances over his shoulder before lane changes, and oh my God—that *gear* shift.

Was I some sort of driving fetishist? Where was that in the quilt bag?

By the time we pulled up at my house, I was feeling flushed, distracted, and more than a little bit sheepish. "Hey. So. All that about Hannah? It's—"

He touched my wrist and my voice stopped working.

"It's off the record. Like I said." He thwapped my shoulder, a faux-stern look on his face. "Now start answering your phone."

As I watched him drive away, I wondered if he'd call again, just to test me.

It took him four minutes.

"I'm answering," I said.

"All right." He laughed. "Talk to you later."

It was harder than ever to focus, but I did, clicking my overloaded inbox back into existence. I wrote to the Huffington Post first.

"Thank you for your email! We'd love the opportunity to write a column."

19

"Please hold for Mr. Montgomery."

I scrambled into a vacant hallway, hoping the bustle of students transferring between classes wouldn't bleed through the call, making me sound juvenile.

Except he knew I was a student. That was sort of the point.

"Daisy!"

"Mr. Montgomery!" Too loud.

The man on the other end of the line chuckled. "Please, call me Cal—or I'll have to start calling you Ms. Beaumont-Smith, and that's way too many syllables."

I liked him already.

From what I'd found online, Cal Montgomery was some sort of political strategist in DC. He worked for a big, shady consulting firm—the kind of people, I assumed, who helped cover up shocking scandals and get horrible laws passed for their clients. Cal didn't do much to change that impression.

"Our clients are generally corporations, politicians. I'd give you examples, but then I'd have to kill you."

I laughed. He didn't.

"It's grunt work. But every once in a while, I get the chance to work on something I feel passionate about. When I read

Adam Cohen's piece on your homecoming event, I knew I had to be involved. Bottom line—I'm in town. I'm staying at . . . where am I?" There was a pause. "Charleston Place. I've got a two o'clock call, then I'm all yours."

"We've got an Alliance meeting after school, at three. Everyone will be there."

"So will I. See you then."

Raina passed me, then doubled back, her head cocked quizzically. I grabbed her by the shoulders.

"A VIP-DC-PR guy just flew down to save us! Tell everybody to come to the meeting looking impressive!"

"Impressive?" Raina shook her head.

I motioned wildly to her sweater set and pencil skirt. "Like you!"

For a split second, I could have sworn I saw Raina light up, before she nodded briskly and hurried to spread the news.

As soon as the final bell rang, I raced to the administrative wing, in case the others hadn't gotten the memo. But when I got there, I found a surprisingly young man already settling in, hanging his cream seersucker jacket on one of the conference room chairs.

When he spotted me, Cal crossed the room with his hand outstretched.

"Your hair is *excellent*." As we shook, he leaned away to examine me. "I love the blue. Very creative."

"Thanks," I replied, processing his compliment with suspicion. This was possibly the most clean-cut guy I'd ever seen. But something about Cal's squint told me that his "excellent" meant "I can work with that," not "That is an attractive hairstyle that my sister might want to try out at her wedding." Either way, it was nice to be appreciated.

When the rest of the group trickled in, they were met with equal appreciation. Raina must have gotten to the others in time for them to primp. Sophie's plait was smoother than usual, Sean had changed out of his *Music Man* costume— even little Kyle had his shirt tucked in, no hoodie in sight. Jack was Jack, yacht club casual as always—i.e. perfect.

Once the niceties were done, Cal introduced himself. He repeated what he'd told me earlier, that he'd started his career by working on a bunch of political campaigns, but that now, as a consultant, he was able to seek out the occasional passion project to "vacation with," as he put it. He seemed thrilled to be here.

We tried not to jump up and down in our seats. This guy was the real deal.

Then he clapped.

"Your turn! What's the status of the event?"

A nervous silence fell over the room. As I wilted, Sophie stood, that cast-iron smile seeming to pull her upward and hold her in place.

"We're having a few issues."

While she described the problems that had popped up with our venue, Cal's expression didn't waver, making me suspect that he'd already gotten the lay of the land. So to speak.

After she sat, Jack piped up to report the good news side of the equation—the Twitter account he'd set up, the Facebook horde, the Homecoming Fund growing by the millisecond.

Then it was Raina's turn—and back to somber. The school board had sent a cease and desist to Raina's dad's office, assuming correctly that he was handling our counsel, ordering us to stop using the words "'Palmetto' and/or 'Pirates'" in any of our communications, along with any of the school's logos.

When she was done, Cal rose from his chair and leaned on the table with his fingers like he was about to pounce on it, Spidey-style.

"I have a plan," he said, and we all burst into applause, then stifled it, so the room made a noise like:

"Yuh!"

Cal grinned. "Let's start with . . . Sophie, was it?"

She nodded nervously.

"Don't worry about the field. I'll work on the field. We'll find out who he knows, who can influence him, and we'll mobilize them. You keep focusing on logistics—and it sounds like you're doing a great job so far. Some vendors will donate to the fund in exchange for a presence here, so don't commit to anybody until we set our rates."

We all glanced at one another, barely suppressing our giddiness. He knew what he was doing. And he was already helping us. This was going to happen!

"Jack. Great start. Seriously. The online buzz is what got my firm's attention. Now we're going to take what you're doing and amplify it through traditional media. You just keep going."

As he turned to Raina, she closed her eyes and slumped.

"You're in a tough spot," he said. "And I commend you for taking on the hardest aspect of this." Raina raised her brows in acknowledgment, her head downcast. "But what you see as a problem, I see as an opportunity."

Her eyes flew open. She looked as confused as I felt. How could the school's threat of a lawsuit be anything but bad? We were being disenfranchised, cut off from our identity as Palmetto students, defeating the entire purpose of what we were trying to do.

"This event is no longer Palmetto's Homecoming." Cal looked around to make sure he had our full attention. "It is *America's* Homecoming."

We were all quiet for a long time, then dear, handsome, brave Sean, raised his hand and asked, "What does that *mean*?"

Cal gestured out the window, a sweeping motion that encompassed the protesters, the supporters, the field across the way. "This is big. Bigger than this town." He adjusted his collar, feigning awkwardness. "No offense intended. I'm enjoying my visit, but—"

I snorted. "We get it."

"It's a big field over there, if we can land it, and I have faith that we can. So why not open it up to any gay alum of *any* school? And not just gay. Anyone who felt shut out of their own high school experience because they were different. Anyone who had to hide who they were, for fear of being bullied or worse. This is their chance for a do-over. A do-*better*. This is everybody's homecoming."

"Damn," I said, breaking our stunned silence.

Cal rolled up his sleeves as he pointed at me. "You've got to remember, Daisy. Not everybody is as brave as you, out and proud in eleventh grade. A lot of people are too scared to come out, and this could give them the courage to be who they truly are. You could be a real inspiration to them."

Raina smiled coldly. "She's certainly a daily inspiration to us."

Jack snorted and I kicked him under the table. Cal didn't notice. As he went on to describe a media plan, all of our eyes connected to one another's, drawing a grid, one stare at a time, conveying a clear message.

Daisy. Must. Stay. In. The closet. Cal Montgomery, strategist extraordinaire, hadn't sussed out the big, fat elephant in the room.

"What about your girlfriend?" he asked, peering at his notes and up again. "Hannah, is it? Is she as comfortable as you are with the limelight?"

"Not really," I said quickly as the energy in the room hardened into ice—Translation: Closet (See: Stay in the). "I think . . . she'd rather stay out of all this."

Not a lie. Not a confession. Not bad. I exhaled.

Cal nodded gravely. "I respect that too." He sighed. "Shame, though. She's seriously photogenic."

As he passed, he whapped my arm, like, *Good for you for scoring such a hot chick,* and then launched right into the next part of his outline, so he couldn't see me cringing.

Hannah. Natalie's girlfriend. *My* person. The reason I was here—and honestly, in the blur of everything that was happening, I'd hardly thought about her all day.

When we wrapped up the meeting, the light was fading outside, and many of the protesters had gone home, leaving a skeleton crew of picketers, supporters, and news crews from neighboring towns, along with the football team, which appeared to have just gotten out of practice.

My mom was waiting across the street with the remaining counter-protesters. If I could just get to her without a QB encounter, my day would be—

"Daisy!"

I sighed, turned to say a quick good-bye and be on my way, but before I knew it, QB had his arm slung around my shoulder and was murmuring into my ear.

"Still coming to the game Friday?"

"Yep!"

Cal had actually insisted we all attend the game this week as a photo op for the publications that would want to get some rah-rah Americana shots to go with their story about how the Palmetto LGBTQ Alliance did and did not fit into the traditional high school experience.

"Awesome." QB wasn't letting go. I was steering myself away and he was scraping behind me like a loose bumper. "Maybe afterward . . . we could talk some more? It really made me feel better last time."

"I charge eighty dollars an hour."

QB laughed as if I were joking.

One of the news crews in the parking lot seemed to have clocked us, the cameraman picking up his gear, probably thinking, *Is that the girl? She's got blue hair. But she's got a boy hanging all over . . . does not . . . compute . . .*

Evading QB's grip, I whirled around and punched him on the arm like one of the guys.

It hurt my hand. I hid it.

"Tell you what," I said. "When you guys win, I'll go out and celebrate with you."

"Deal!" In a flash, QB's face lit up, and I was free.

The cameraman from the parking lot lifted his gear as I reached Mom in the field, having obviously decided this was a better photo op—me with my supportive mother on the site of our upcoming extravaganza, rather than me in some ambiguous conversation with a guy who was trying to hit on me. If I could just keep the cameras pointed this way for the next three weeks, I'd be fine.

"Who was that boy?" Mom raised her eyebrows, nodding after QB.

He chose that moment to wave.

"*Nobody,*" I sighed. "I'm gay, remember?"

Poor Mom looked more confused than ever.

20

Hell-beast that she was, Zelda the Cat could be pretty damn cute when she thought nobody was looking. Sometimes I'd catch her snoozing in a sunny spot by the window with a peaceful smile on her whiskered face. The instant a cloud passed by and the sun-triangle disappeared, her body would coil tight. But when the light came back, there was that smile again, a stretch, a grateful purr.

That's what it felt like when Hannah walked up to my lab table after bio.

She did nothing but smile patiently until Steven skulked past her with his giant backpack, but it was enough to bask in as I rose from my chair. Then she said, as if teasing, "You do realize that when I said I needed a break, I didn't mean from you."

"Of course!" I lied, shrugging into my bag.

Her eyes clouded. "Or I guess I did, sort of. At the time. But . . . I didn't like it. I miss you. Is that stupid? It was like a day. You think I'm crazy."

"Me? Not at all! I thought—" In my scrambling, I stumbled backward into Han's lab partner and turned to apologize. By the time my eyes returned to Hannah's, she'd rearranged her face into a casual smile. I missed her weird face.

"Wanna do dinner tonight?" she asked. "Catch up a little?

We could do the Moonlight or get my mom to grab takeout—"

"*Yes*," I said, before remembering. "No. Ugh. I have to watch football."

"You *have* to?" Hannah raised her eyebrows, her mouth quirking as she held the classroom door open for me.

"It's part of our PR push."

She fell into step beside me. "The Alliance 'we.'"

"Yeah, we've got this hotshot from DC working for us and . . ." My voice trailed off as I watched her glance away, fading even further into politeness. "Anyway. I can't do dinner. But let's definitely catch up."

"Cool," she said. "Call me when you're home."

She nudged me with her elbow and continued down the hall to her next class, her stride relaxing the farther she got from me.

The line for tickets looked like the world's worst-dressed movie premiere. Two-thirds of the crowd was in Pirates red and black, countering the opposing team's green-garbed fans, who'd shown up in surprising droves. You'd think this was your average, good old American, Friday night football game. But all around, flashes were popping, a barrage from the army of photographers piled up just outside the school property line. The sight of them was so surreal that I shuffled numbly into the firing line like everybody else, a sheep to my flock.

"*Daisy!*"

"*Is that her?*"

"*Over here!*"

"*One picture, Daisy, can we get a smile?*"

I turned. And smiled. And winced from the flashes, squirming in my brand-new Pirates T-shirt, size XXL. Along with advising we turn up without our parents to show what mature young adults we were, Cal had suggested we all wear Pirates gear, broadcasting school pride in the face of adversity. But when I'd scrambled to the school store after the last bell, the only size left was "tent with arm holes."

"Daisy!"

I turned with a dazzling smile, but it was only Raina.

"Have a pin," she said.

"Thanks," I muttered, grabbing a rainbow-striped pin from her outstretched palm. As she started away, I clung to her, my camera-smile shellacked onto my face. "Don't leave me."

She glared down at my tent-shirt. "I still have to give Kyle and Sophie their rainbows."

"Daisy, look here!"

"Daisy, can we get a quick interview before the game!"

Sensing my panic, Raina thawed enough to say "See you in there" before dashing off to find the others.

The line moved fast. The second I passed the ticket booth, I exhaled, releasing the shaking grin from my face, and made my way up the stands to where the Alliance was waiting.

"This is sort of bizarre, isn't it?" Sophie whispered, linking arms with me as I slid down next to her. "All these reporters? And have you ever seen this many people at a Palmetto game?"

I tried to answer, but a roar rose from the oversized crowd, drowning me out. The Pirates and their archrivals, the Northville Spartans, were running onto the field. QB scanned the crowd like usual, but this time, when I stood to wave, he jumped in celebration. A bunch of people turned around in the stands to take camera phone pictures of me, sending me cringing back into the fold.

"Yes," I finally replied. "This could not be more bizarre."

Hey, guess what, I was wrong.

I'm not sure the Northville Spartans even knew they were our rivals. The Pirates were like a gnat they needed to swat away from their faces twice a year. It was no wonder the opposing team swaggered onto the field—*our* field—waving to the local sports photographers as if they were on home turf.

The Spartans continued to look cocky for the first four minutes of the game. And then QB scored a touchdown.

The Pirates fans in the stands didn't know what to do. We'd stood as one as he approached the end zone, but we were so used to sitting while the ball got picked off that that's what we started to do. It took us a few seconds to even realize what had happened. Poor QB stood stunned beside the goal post, cradling the ball, listening to the sound of a few hundred people holding their breath. And then, in a rush, we let loose.

Awwww, that was nice, I thought, clapping. *Good for them for getting points on the board for once. They can go home happy.*

Two minutes later, the Pirates intercepted a Spartans pass, scoring again.

I don't know if it was the extra people in the crowd who'd bused themselves in to support a cause only peripherally related to football, or the thrumming excitement of having reporters surrounding the field, but QB and his compatriots were doing the opposite of choking. They were swallowing the other team whole.

At halftime, the fans in green had faces to match their jerseys and I was starting to understand why people liked coming to football games. In theory, anyway.

A reporter from the *Post and Courier* climbed the emptying stands to ask for a photo of the Alliance, and when we said yes, a few other photographers joined him. We threw our arms around each other, laughing first at the awkwardness of our pose, then laughing because we were laughing, then laughing even louder thinking about how stupid this photo must look. It was contagious. The photographers started laughing too.

"Thanks guys," the local guy said. "And good luck—we're rooting for you."

Kyle jumped up. "I need a hot dog. Anybody want anything?"

Jack poked his head around Raina. "I'll have a Coke."

"Do they have chicken fingers?" I asked hopefully. "Or cheese fries?"

Kyle furrowed his brow. "Um."

"That's too much for him to carry!" Sophie laughed, whapping me.

He started away. "No, it's cool! I'll see."

Whatever halftime pep talk the Spartans' coach had given them in the locker room did not appear to have worked. We scored again. And again. They got a field goal, woo-hoo. Before we knew it, the game was over—and inexplicably, we had just defeated the five-time state champions for our first win in years. I was cheering, practically teary eyed along with everybody else, when a realization hit me.

I'd promised QB I'd celebrate a win with him. And his entire team.

I have to get out of here.

"Where's Kyle?" Sean asked behind me as I said some hasty good-byes and scrambled down the stands.

"Did he not come back?" I heard Sophie reply.

"Yeah," Jack muttered. "I never got my Coke."

Huh, I thought, hurrying past the stands, through the crowd of dizzy Pirates fans, and into the athletic wing. *Maybe Kyle met up with his parents and forgot about our orders.*

But when I walked into the quiet hallway, something started gnawing at my gut and only grew stronger the farther I got from the noise of the celebrating crowds. *It's the reporters,* I told myself. *They've got me nervous.* To avoid them, I exited the school through a random side door and started making my way to the Moonlight Coffee Shop, where I knew Mom was waiting to pick me up, hopefully with takeout.

As I approached the border of dead hedges, a sound stopped me cold—a low, burbling sigh, and then, so quietly I almost missed it, my name.

"D-Daisy?"

Kyle. He was crouched behind one of the hedges, poking his head around a dead branch to call me over. I almost laughed when I spotted him, he looked so ridiculous—like an inept spy who'd chosen the world's worst hiding spot to gather intel. But then he stood. Or tried to. His knees shook and gave, and the parking lot lights hit his face. I let out a shout as I ran over to him.

He lifted a shaking finger to his split lips, quieting me. I brushed his bangs back from his forehead, revealing an eye swollen shut, a gash below it on his cheek.

"Who did this to you?"

"It doesn't matter."

"Yes, it does. I'm going to go find them and kick their asses."

Kyle almost managed a chuckle at that idea.

I propped him with my arm so he could sit more comfortably. "We need to call 911."

"No," he said, trying to stand.

I bit the inside of my cheek to keep from crying at the sight of him. Tears weren't helpful right now. "You need medical help."

He slumped again, holding his side. "Yeah, okay, just don't tell my parents, Daisy. I don't want them to worry about me."

"*Kyle.*" I motioned to him, shaking my head. "They're gonna notice."

Before he could change his mind, I grabbed my phone from my pocket and dialed 911. "Hi, I'm on the northwest corner of Palmetto High School—my friend needs an ambulance? Yes, he got . . . beat up, I guess?"

"Don't tell them what they said," Kyle was muttering. "Why they did it."

"*Stay on the line until the police arrive,*" said the dispatch lady.

"What they said?" I whispered, covering the phone.

Kyle held his head. "That they called me a fag."

I took a breath. It nearly choked me.

We heard the beep-beep of a police radio before we spotted two officers making their way across the street. They must have been here already, handling the protesters. A middle-aged man in a Pirates jacket was with them. It wasn't until they got within a few yards of us that I spotted the graying red hair under his faded Atlanta Braves ball cap and realized it was Natalie's dad.

This is happening too fast, I thought, suddenly longing to keep everyone the hell away from Kyle. If only I'd had that instinct an hour ago.

"You kids run into some trouble?" Chief Beck crouched beside Kyle, then glanced up at his officers. "Watch out for that ambulance."

"Some guys from the other school," Kyle said, forcing his voice steady. "They pulled me from the hot dog line and took me outside. I tried to get away, but there were too many of them. I didn't know what to do." He started to shake. I clasped his hand, the one part of him that wasn't injured. "So I just did what you're supposed to do with bears when you go camping? I balled myself up and pretended to be dead and they went away?" He looked up at me, as if asking forgiveness and my eyes burned, tears coming fast now. "I've never been in a fight before."

"Me neither," I said, the hedges around us blurring, running.

How did they know he was gay? It could just as easily have been me that they attacked. It should have been me. I was the one who put our faces on the Internet, who'd stood on a chair and made us targets. I should have been the one they'd kicked until I stopped moving.

My hand trembled in Kyle's.

"Do you know what made them go after you?" Chief Beck asked gently.

"Not really," Kyle said. "I think they were mad that their team was losing, and they figured they could take me because I'm not that tall, or whatever."

Oh, Kyle. He was a terrible liar. He'd blinked his one good eye rapidly through that whole speech. Classic tell.

Chief Beck was equally dubious. "You sure that's all there is to that story?"

"Yeah, I mean . . ." Kyle sighed shakily. "Yeah."

Chief Beck glanced at me for confirmation.

I swiped my cheek dry with my shoulder. "I wasn't here. I found him a couple minutes ago."

He turned back to Kyle, lowering his voice. "Just so you know, hate crimes carry a stiffer sentence."

"It wasn't—"

Chief Beck waved one of the officers over, interrupting Kyle's lie. "He's gonna ask you some questions about what these guys looked like, and then we'll make sure you get these injuries taken care of, okay, son?"

"Okay." Kyle relaxed. "Thank you."

I stood with Chief Beck, surprised by how warm, how understanding he seemed to be. Whatever genes he'd passed on to Natalie had obviously been recessive.

He laid a hand on my shoulder. "Look after him until his folks show up. He's putting up a good front, but he'll need a friend tonight."

I nodded.

"Good girl," he said. "Nice to see you again, Daisy."

The EMTs decided to take Kyle to the hospital to make sure his ribs weren't fractured. I rode along, perched beside his gurney. He looked so young lying there, like he'd been tucked into bed for the night. His brow was furrowed with pain or worry or both.

"This is weirdly fun, right?" I said to lighten the mood, rocking onto my heels as we rounded a corner. "I've never been in an ambulance before."

"Me neither," Kyle said, with a flicker of a smile that fell with the next turn. "Did the cops call my parents?"

"I think so."

"I want them to be happy. They were so happy when I came out. This is going to ruin it."

"No, it won't," I said, but I must have had a tell of my own, because he rolled his eyes. His good eye, anyway.

"Thanks for coming with me," he said.

In the next blink, his brow contorted and his skin went mottled. I half rose, thinking something new was hurting him—his ribs? Internal bleeding? But then he let it out. A sob.

"I can't believe this ha-happened. Everything was supposed to work out o-okay. I didn't think—"

He was crying too hard to talk, really shaking now. I glanced at the young EMT, anxious about his breathing, but she just smiled sadly and murmured, "Almost there, kiddo."

"I'm sorry, Kyle," I said, my own voice staccato with tears. "I didn't think . . . I'm just so sorry."

We didn't talk again until we got to the hospital, where his parents turned from statues to sprinters at the first sight of his gurney.

My mom picked me up a few minutes later, her face a terrified mirror of the Hornsbys'. "Are you all right, sweetie?"

"I'm fine," I said bitterly, fastening my seat belt. "Not a scratch on me."

"You're shaking."

I didn't answer. I'd caught Kyle's shock, I knew, and added some of my own. The kind that made my stomach roil, made my chest constrict and burn.

Made me want to hide from my reflection in the dark car window.

Just yesterday, Cal had called me brave. The memory felt like a taunt right now. An accusation.

That night, thank goodness, the late local news didn't report on Kyle's attack. They did report on me.

"Teen gay advocate Daisy Beaumont-Smith bravely cheered on her home team at tonight's match-up against—"

I turned it off and stared at the dead screen. Suddenly, it was another face I saw, her bottom lip split, her beautiful green eyes smashed shut, or worse or worse or worse—

My phone rang, jolting me awake.

It was Hannah. I'd forgotten to call her. What could I possibly say now?

I silenced my phone, buried it under a pillow, and went upstairs to where my dad was fighting bad guys with red circles drawn on their chests so you knew exactly who they were.

21

"Ease off the clutch. Gently!"

The gears ground and the engine sputtered out. Again.

I let out a primal roar.

"It's fine," Adam said. "You're getting it." His voice was soothing. But when I glanced over, he had one hand on the dashboard and the other on the ceiling.

I yanked the brake, tossed the keys at his chest, and got the hell out of the driver's seat. Thankfully, the Sears lot was empty, so there was no one to witness my disgrace. Just Adam.

"What are you doing?" He craned his head over the Jaguar's roof. "Let's try again."

"I'm done. Drive me home."

He raised his eyebrows and I realized how princessy that sounded, especially given that I'd insisted we hold our lesson in my ridiculous vintage Jaguar.

"Sorry." I removed my hands from my hips and tried to calm my breathing. "What I meant to say was, please, please, please don't make me try again? *Dear* Lord, please?"

Adam shrugged wildly, lifting his hands, then rounded the car to the driver's seat, watching me the whole time with a slow, disappointed head shake. I buckled my passenger seat belt, feeling like a slimy speck on the bottom of the universe's shoe, but also deeply relieved about actually making it home alive.

Except Adam didn't start the car. "You're not yourself to-day."

"You don't know me that well yet, so let me fill you in." I pivoted in my seat to glare at him. "I'm Daisy. I suck at everything. Nice to meet you." I smiled sugar-sweet and turned away, but Adam leaned over to catch my eye again.

"Something's up. Tell me."

"Kyle got attacked," I said, my voice blunt, ugly. "It's my fault."

And my eyes were spilling over. Awesome.

"He . . . what?" Adam leaned in, and my guard went up. "Is Kyle from your group?"

"You can't report on this. He doesn't want anyone to know, so when I say off the record—"

"Of course," he said, squeezing my hand, letting go. "Just tell me."

"This online troll collective dug up the Facebook pages for all of the Alliance members to try to shame us. Some guys at the football game recognized Kyle and went after him. Total strangers." I swiped my face, angry at it for being wet. "He's a freshman. He's the nicest kid in the universe. He thought we'd be a support group. I'm the one who made this into a headline and now he's got two broken ribs, bruises just—" I waved my hands from my head to my knees. "I checked on him this morning, and he said he's okay and I didn't need to keep guarding his house—"

"Guarding his—?"

"But I can't stop thinking, what if those guys who found him were even *worse* people? This is real now, Adam. I should never have made it this real."

I closed my eyes, the closest I could get to taking it all back.

"But Daisy . . ." Adam put his arm on my headrest. I could feel his wrist's warmth, centimeters behind me. "This is how change works. It's not smooth, it's not easy, but that just shows you how important it is. This event—"

"It's not going to happen. Or it's going to be terrible. Like hugely humiliating."

He leaned away, apparently amused. "Why would you say that?"

"Because it's me! Because I screw things up. Hannah's right, it's the Stede Bonnet opera."

"Stede . . . ?" He blinked. "Okay, I'm confused."

"I promise things and I can never deliver them. I can't even drive. I can't do anything. And this interview is going to be a disaster."

"Interview?"

I let out a leaden sigh. "I'm going to be interviewed on *The Evening News with Shawna Wells*. On Monday. So like, you know, just a couple days to prep. No big deal."

Adam shook the headrest. "This is amazing! A national platform!"

"I'm already freaking out enough, thank you!" I covered my face with my hair, a wall of yellow and blue protecting me from reality. "The producers are coming to my house at the butt-crack of dawn tomorrow to figure out where to put the cameras. I'm gonna be the little box on the screen she talks to." I drew it in the air, as if he couldn't picture it for himself.

"So is this an exclusive?" Adam nudged his glasses up.

"On-air exclusive, I think," I answered, trying to remember details from the flood of information Cal had thrown at me over the phone this morning. "We're not doing any print exclusives. I'll talk to anybody. Talk talk talk."

"Oh good!" Adam laughed a nervous "ha" when I turned to stare at him. "I'd love to keep interviewing you, is all."

"Yeah, well, make sure you put in your next article that the only thing I'm capable of doing is shooting my mouth off."

"Daisy?" His mouth crinkled at the corners. "Isn't that all they're *asking* you to do?"

"Shoot my mouth off?"

He raised his eyebrows.

"Um." I tucked my hair behind my ears, thinking. "I mean, this is an interview. So yeah, talking will be involved."

"You've got this, then. Stop freaking out."

I must not have looked like I was taking his advice, because he sighed.

"Just think about Hannah. How much she means to you."

I managed to nod.

"Good." He started the car. "Let's take a break from driving. We'll try again another time."

He'd given up. Harrumph. Yeah, okay, I was the one who'd insisted we stop the lesson, but Adam was supposed to urge me to try again and he didn't.

"Thanks for the lesson," I grumbled as we reached my house.

To which he answered, "You're welcome," with no apparent

irony. Then he parked the Jaguar, got in his racer-striped sedan, and smoothly, elegantly drove away.

It wasn't until that night, after replaying and dissecting our conversation no less than twenty times, that I was able to process the silver lining in my afternoon with Adam. He'd given me a new mantra.

"It's just talking," I chanted to myself, panic swelling and ebbing in my chest. "I know how to talk."

Having gotten through Monday morning without heart palpitations, I headed to lunch with renewed confidence. I'd planned to have a prep session at the now semi-official Alliance lunch table, but as I was nearing the cafeteria, a text came in from Hannah.

"Lunch today? Meet you on the stoop?"

My phone did a happy dance in my hand as I texted back a quick "Yes!" But a second after I hit SEND, I wished I could take it back and write something a little less exclamation-pointy. We'd eaten there for the past two years without the need for invitations or planning, and now I was elated to even be asked.

By the time I'd bought my lunch and emerged outside to stretch my legs against the cement steps, my mood was in serious need of boosting. I gazed out to the faculty parking lot and watched as the noonday sun danced and glittered against a field of windshields. It was such a calming sight that it took me a few seconds to realize that Hannah was standing behind me. I startled, then laughed and scooted over to make room for her, wondering how long she'd been there.

"It's Taco Monday," I said, showing her my tray. "I got you one."

"It's okay," she said, sitting down.

I held it out, confused. "You sure?"

"Yeah, I'm good."

This was a first. Was she suddenly watching what she ate? Did I need to be worried about her? Skinny though she was, something told me this wasn't a food thing. More a her and me thing—worrying in a completely different way.

"Sorry about Friday night," I said. "I tried to get you on Saturday, but—"

"Oh, sorry," she said. "I was . . . yeah, it was a crazy weekend."

"That's cool," I said. And then we sat in silence, like now that we'd run out of tiny apologies, there was nothing left to talk about. I drew a determined breath. "So I have an idea."

She raised her eyebrows, her eyes locked on the parking lot. "Okay?"

"Sleepover night!" I tucked my legs under me. "It's been forever, right? Things are a little nuts right now with homecoming, but once it's done, my place—UNO, popcorn, *Triplecross* marathon."

Hannah was too studiously unwrapping her gourmet sandwich to reply. Was she really this pissed off? I'd failed to return one phone call. In five years.

"Friday after homecoming?" I tried.

"I can't." She looked away, unscrewing her water bottle with intense focus, while the two inches between us solidified into Plexiglas.

"You can't because you're busy, or . . . ?"

"It's not appropriate, Daisy." Hannah finally turned to me, her face flushed with exasperation. "I mean, dinner's dinner, but sleeping over? I have a girlfriend."

I coughed an incredulous laugh. "Is she *jealous*? She knows I'm straight, right?"

"Yeah, but . . ." Hannah's brow relaxed. "Okay, so think about it this way. How would you feel if QB had a sleepover with a platonic friend who was a girl? It would be weird, right?"

It took me what felt like a year to realize what she was talking about, why she would think QB's weekend plans, however odd, would affect me one way or the other. Then it hit me so hard it knocked the wind out of me.

"You think I'm dating QB."

"Aren't you?"

I stared at her. "I would tell you something like that."

"Oh. Well." She picked at her crust. "There's a rumor."

"So why didn't you ask me about it?"

"I'm asking you now." Hannah's eyes flicked to mine and then away. She knew exactly how ridiculous this conversation was. "Anyway. We're too old for sleepovers."

I balled my napkin into a marble in my clenched fist. She took a tiny bite of her sandwich.

"What about when we're roommates?" I asked. "Is Natalie going to find that *inappropriate*?"

"No." Hannah sighed, mussing her hair. "I mean . . . there's no point in thinking about that now. Who knows what's going to happen, right?"

My breath stopped, my heart stopped, traffic stopped.

Meanwhile, Hannah shrugged, lifted her sandwich to her mouth, put it back without taking a bite. This was a simulation of a meal. A simulation of a friendship.

She didn't mean that the future was unclear for her and Natalie. She meant us. Our plans for college and everything that followed, sitting in sorted stacks in the corner of my bedroom, untouched as promised, gathering dust.

While I sat staring at the rusted bumper of my history teacher's car, too wounded to find any more words to offer Hannah, she pepped back up like a toy with its battery replaced.

"Listen, I wanted to talk."

I guess talking's on the appropriate list, I thought, turning my attention to my lunch.

"I heard about Kyle."

And the taco in my mouth turned to dust. I swallowed.

"Awful, isn't it? He's pretty banged up, but he'll be back in school tomorrow."

I figured that was safe—a way to tell the truth while still keeping my promise to him. Then I caught the wince creeping into Hannah's smile. I noticed the Moleskine in her hand, her thumbnail anxiously flipping the corners of the pages. And I knew what was next.

"Are you sure all of this is a good idea?" A cloud shot across the sun and the parking lot went dull. "I mean, I know I told you it was too late for you to back out, but I think maybe I was just feeling trapped that day and frustrated and . . ."

I focused on the dead horizon, trying to steady myself enough to talk, while she kept going in her Hannah-rambling way, so familiar and so alien at the same time that it made me want to scream.

". . . It's just such a big thing and it's junior year, right? We should be worrying about our grades and our futures, not, I don't know, politics. Especially *this* kind." She swallowed. "Don't you think they can take it from here? Without you?"

She blinked. Set the Moleskine aside, so I guess she'd come to the end of her poorly reasoned speech.

"I actually have a question for *you*." My voice was so low that I barely recognized it. Hannah raised her eyebrows. "Why is it that the only time you want to talk to me these days is to discourage me from doing something? Or tell me how unreliable I am?"

"Whoa." Her cheeks went rosy, two pink circles. "That is *not* what I'm—"

"Then what?"

Hannah huffed.

I put my tray neatly aside. "My mistake, Han. Finish what you were going to say."

"You don't understand what it's like. For them."

"For you, you mean."

She raised her chin, an acknowledgment.

"Well, I'm trying!" I threw my hands in the air. "In case you haven't noticed, I'm putting *everything* into trying to understand. And to help. But I guess it doesn't matter. *I* don't matter, now that you've got Natalie."

Hannah scrambled away until she was standing. "Leave her out of it."

"She's doing a fantastic job of leaving *herself* out of it." I stood to face her, crackling. "I haven't seen Natalie at any of our planning sessions. Or you, for that matter. We have strangers across the country writing in, donating money, *traveling* here to show their support, but what do I get from you? Nothing. Just constant . . ." I racked my brain for a nice way to say this, but came up empty. "*Whining.* Why?"

"It's just . . ." She sighed. "I know you."

"Screw you, Hannah." I picked up my tray and Hannah's taco rolled off, so I had to race to retrieve the biggest bits of it before storming away, my eyes blurry with tears. It gave me just enough time to utterly lose my composure, spin around, and blurt out, "Have fun with your resting bitchface girl-friend. Maybe I'll see you at the huge event that I'm throwing because I *fucking care about you!*"

And some sophomore girls chose that exact moment to open the doors to the stoop and stand gawking at me while the entire cafeteria went dead. Silent.

Raina motioned to me from the Alliance's table, face clouding at my outburst. I swiped my eyes and turned away. No prep today. I was done. My nerves were too rattled, from the upcoming interview, the mounting crowds surrounding us, the lie I was holding on to, the fact that I'd just full-on fought with the one person I never fought with. The person who knew me better than anybody—and didn't believe in me. To know me, apparently, was to doubt me.

I had an interview in six hours, so I had no time for doubt. Just talking.

Like Adam said, I could do that much.

22

Dad picked me up from school, which didn't help my nerves. By the time we pulled onto our street, my knuckles were white, glued to the backpack in my lap.

"You okay?" Dad watched me instead of the driveway, clipping the curb with two tires.

"Yeah!" I faked a smile. Then I did a double take. Dad was pastier than me. "Are *you* okay?"

He let out a shuddering sigh. "I've been ordered to take the night off."

"No gaming?"

He shook his head.

"Mom?"

A feeble nod.

"Oof." I rested my hand on his shoulder. "When this is done, I'll play two player with you. And I'll try out mage."

That cheered him up enough to get us both into the house.

The *Evening News* crew was already inside, Mom buzzing around, for some reason asking everyone if they wanted lemonade. As Dad dragged a kitchen chair into a distant corner and hid behind a magazine, I waved a quick hi to all the strangers and ran upstairs to change, barely dodging Zelda, who'd been trying to blend into the carpeting.

She hissed. I hissed back. No one seemed to notice.

Once I'd slipped into my Cal-approved outfit, a bright blue long-sleeved T-shirt and khakis, I gave my hair a brush and swiped on some concealer and blush, hoping it would be enough. But when I got downstairs, the on-site producer paired me with a makeup artist.

"Let's just wash this off," she said, and was so sweet and quick about my makeover that I only had about five seconds to feel offended before she handed me a mirror and left me gazing at myself in wonder. So this was what makeup was supposed to do.

I considered calling Adam to meet me after the interview so he could see me all spruced up, but felt immediately idiotic. What would he care? Besides, he'd see me on TV in a few minutes . . . along with millions of total strangers. A gorgeous African-American news icon, Shawna Wells was the most popular anchor in the country and, according to the producer who'd been sent to coordinate my part of the interview, they'd been "plugging" my appearance all day long.

I wondered if Hannah would watch. The thought of her made my throat clench.

This isn't about her, I told myself. *It's about America and other gay students who are not Hannah and the tide of . . . history? Or something?*

"You pumped?" Cal asked as he came into the kitchen.

"Does 'pumped' mean 'about to pass out'?"

He laughed. "Let's get you into place."

From far away, the corner of the living room looked like an art installation. The *Evening News* crew had taken various objects from our house and rearranged them inside the framing of the shot as if they'd always been there. In place of our coffee table—currently on the front lawn—were a camera and tripod, alongside a bunch of lights so hot that the makeup girl had to jump in and de-shine me after about thirty seconds.

Mom was relegated to standing in the hall, wringing her hands, and asking everyone who passed her, "Nobody for lemonade? It's organic! Locally sourced!"

"Could I get a Coke Zero?" I asked. She pretended not to hear me.

"Five-minute warning," one of the PAs said.

I closed my eyes, feeling my breath grow shallow.

No big deal, I told myself. *She's going to ask some questions and I'll answer very positively and then it'll be over and America will be in love with me and they'll love gay people a little more and maybe the crime rate will drop and aliens will decide not to attack and we'll have a huge spontaneous musical number . . .*

When I opened my eyes, Cal was staring down at me.

"You weren't kidding about the passing out, then." He crouched to pat my shoulder. "You're ready, Daisy. It's a point-counterpoint. Stay positive, stay on message, like we talked about, and refuse to engage with her."

"With Shawna?"

How could I do an interview without engaging with her? Was I confused about what "interview" meant? My face began to prickle.

"No . . ." Cal's brow furrowed, but before he could answer, the makeup girl dove in to pat me down with powder yet again, and then one of the assistants started counting, so Cal backed away, mouthing "Good luck!" and the monitor opposite me lit up, and I blinked and there was Shawna Wells staring from the screen as if we were having our own, personal, one-on-one conversation.

Every viewer in the country felt that she was talking to them. It was what made her successful. But in this case, she actually *was* about to start talking to *me*.

Oh. Gah. No. Holy . . .

I could hear the last sound bites of a news story through my earpiece—about us?—and then some sort of countdown on Shawna's end. Before I could catch my breath, she began to talk.

"Thank you, Roberta."

My name is Daisy. Should I correct her?

That's probably the reporter's name. Oh dear God, someone help me.

Behind the cluster of news producers, I could see both Cal and my mother mouthing "Smile!" then demonstrating.

I obliged.

"We're here with Daisy Beaumont-Smith to learn more about her efforts on behalf of the Palmetto LGBTQ Alliance . . ."

My face appeared on the screen. And hey, I was in my living room! And I was smiling too much. I frowned and saw myself frown, then smiled again. This was torture.

". . . and we also have with us Palmetto School Board

member Cindy Beck, who in the past week has been vocal in voicing her concerns about the event."

Another box popped up. And in it was Natalie Beck's mother, blond hair curled prettily, wearing pearls under a Chanel-collared blouse.

My grin locked in place as my brain swam, scrambling to connect the three faces on the monitor. I heard Mrs. Beck drawl, "Thank you for having us, Shawna!"

Not to be left out, I cut in, "Yeah, thanks so much!" like a total idiot.

The point-counterpoint hadn't even begun and I was already losing.

"Daisy, let's start with you," Shawna said, turning toward my hovering image as if I were a hologram in her studio. Maybe I was. That would be crazy.

"Tell us how this event got started—your alternative Palmetto homecoming."

I saw Cindy's smile ossify, like she was already preparing her legal attack against us using the school district's trademarked name. But I lifted my chin, ready to answer. Thank you, Cal!

"Actually, Shawna, we're now calling it America's Homecoming. Because, as you know, it's struck a chord with people all over the country in the past few days, and we want to open it up to anybody who's felt left out of their high school experience. This is a chance to cheer on every teenager who's had the courage to admit to their communities who they truly are." I took a breath. "It all started because of a simple request. I asked the school board to allow same-sex dates to school dances, and knowing the legal ramifications of refusing, they took the cowardly step of canceling the homecoming dance entirely—"

"Shawna, if I can just interrupt."

Instead of gasping at her rudeness, Shawna Wells politely pivoted toward Mrs. Beck's floating head.

"We *wanted* to have a homecoming dance. It's a tradition that's gone on for fifty years, I'm proud to say." Cindy smiled graciously, taking credit for the last half-century. "But when someone comes in and threatens a lawsuit, our hands become tied. For us, it's a question of *preserving tradition* for the vast majority of students who want to have a good time at their homecoming. It's that simple."

Stay positive, Cal had said. Don't engage with her—*that's* what he'd meant.

"You know . . ." Mrs. Beck used my moment of indecision to let out a helpless laugh. "I appreciate you having us on here, Shawna, but most Palmetto students that I've talked to are disgusted with all of this media attention! Their goals are simple—get good grades, play on their athletic teams, support their school, and enjoy that *traditional* high school experience. But their needs are being ignored because of a very vocal minority."

I probably should have let it go. Said something along the lines of: "As a student of Palmetto, I know firsthand that the issue of equal treatment for all students is important to everyone of my generation blah blah . . ."

Instead, I said what I was thinking.

"I'm sorry, can I jump in?" Shawna pivoted back to me. I

raised my eyebrows. "I find it hypocritical for Mrs. Beck to sit here and talk about the rights of straight students when her own daughter came out of the closet no less than three weeks ago."

Shawna's expression wavered between thrown and delighted. She nodded to Mrs. Beck. "Care to respond?"

Mrs. Beck's face had gone very pale. Even for her. "I don't know where this accusation is coming from. It's a *lie*. A blatant attempt to—"

"She's dating my best friend." I shrugged. "That's where the accusation is coming from."

Uh . . . whoops! I guess Hannah wasn't my fake-girlfriend anymore? I mean, I hadn't actually said her name, but if America could put two and two together, it was fine with me. One fewer lie to haul around.

"It's a private matter!" Mrs. Beck wriggled out of frame and back again. "And I don't see how airing it on national television is in any way appropriate, just as I don't think it's appropriate for one *subgroup* to bully an entire *community* into doing what they want just because they yell the loudest!" She sniffed a breath, dragging her chin upward. "Miss Beaumont-Smith has spoiled homecoming for the vast majority of students and we on the school board don't see that as fair."

"We haven't spoiled anything," I replied cheerily. "*Everyone* is welcome at this event. We're hoping to bring students and alumni together in an open, honest way, for maybe the first time ever."

I'd remembered my talking points. Thank God. My heart was flailing like a cornered bat at the sudden realization that

240

I'd just gossiped about Hannah and Natalie on national television, but—*focus, Daisy.* Mrs. Beck was counterpointing.

"I have a hard time believing Palmetto students will have any interest in attending this 'alternative' event," she said, thus demonstrating to America how little she knew about people my age.

But Shawna turned to my picture and said, "Daisy?" and I felt like I needed a better rebuttal than that, so I blurted:

"Our event is going to be amazing. We'll have a red carpet. A lot of celebrities have expressed interest in attending."

Shawna and Mrs. Beck were both squinting in confusion.

"And ... also ..." I gave a mysterious side smile to cover my scrambling. "We have one of the biggest bands in the world playing. Can't disclose who yet, but it's going to be epic. And like I said, all are welcome! That's the entire point."

"Thank you Daisy, Cindy . . ." Our faces disappeared and Shawna said, "Next up, mass protests in the oil-rich region of—"

And the monitor went black.

"Great job," said the producer, who probably said that to everyone, and they were pulling the earpiece from my face and the microphone from my collar and Mom was doing a goofy cheering dance and Dad was looking up from his gaming magazine in time to wave, and my heart started trotting like a dressage horse because it was finally allowed to react to the fact that I'd just been *interviewed on national television.* Then Cal drew me aside and said, "What's this band that's performing? And who are the celebrities?" He grinned. "Kind of a big win to keep from me!"

I laughed. It sounded maniacal. "Surprise!"

And then they were clearing up and we needed to get out of the way, and somehow, miraculously, an hour later, I managed to shuffle both Cal and the news crew out of my house for the evening without ever answering the question.

I ran upstairs and turned my phone back on. It rang right away—Raina.

"What the fuck, Daisy."

I turned the phone over to stare at it. Was this how she expressed enthusiasm? Hopefully?

"What the fuck indeed!"

"One of the biggest bands in the world?"

"Yeah, it just sort of . . . came out."

"We're already playing catch-up with what you over-promised, and now you lay this on us? Celebrities? *What* celebrities?"

My mouth went dry. "Jack said that we'd been getting a lot of retweets? From—"

"That's retweets. That's not . . . ugh, Daisy." She let out a long, low groan. "We'll talk about it tomorrow."

When she hung up, I saw a text from Jack: *"You are one crazy bitch. High fieeeeeve!"*

And one from Sean: *"Celebrities??? Which celebrities? OMG OMG."*

And Sophie: *"Good job, Daisy! We're proud of you!"* with an emoji of a bear holding a heart.

I kept Sophie's text lit up on my phone for as long as I could.

Then Hannah called, and without thinking, I answered. A

242

second after saying "Hey," the memory of our argument vise-gripped my stomach.

Hannah was silent on the other end. Had she butt-dialed me?

"Hello?"

"I don't even know what to say to you."

My fingers curled around the phone to keep from flinging it across the room. "Then why did you call?"

"Natalie's really upset."

"Boo! Freaking! Hoo!" I shot up from my desk. "Maybe she shouldn't have unleashed her hell hound of a mother on us, then."

The theory that had been hovering in my mind for weeks took form and shot out of me like a blow-dart.

"You think I don't know that she tipped her mom off about the school board meeting? They came in prepared. Remember? How do you suppose that happened?"

Hannah went quiet. "You have no idea how hard it is for her."

"I don't care about her, I care about you."

As soon as I said it, all the anger flew out of me. I cradled my head in my hands.

"What *is* this, Hannah? This isn't us. We don't fight. What is *happening*?"

"You tell me, Daisy. You're the one who's gone insane."

"Insane? Because I'm fighting for your rights?" I shook my head. "What's insane is that you don't seem to care at all. It's like you're in denial."

"Maybe I am!" She laughed. It was an ugly sound. An unfamiliar one. "Maybe what I wanted was the *same* life, a normal life where people weren't taking my picture or constantly talking about my sexual orientation. Maybe I wanted my dates with my girlfriend—my *real* one—to be private and not a matter of national discussion." She let out a low moan, almost a sob. "Did you ever think to stop and ask me what I wanted, Daisy? Ever once?"

I could hardly get my mouth to work. "Everything I've done has been for you."

"That's not the same thing." She was quiet for so long that I checked the phone to see if the line was still connected.

"Is this about your dad?" I asked quietly. "You still haven't told me—"

"It's about a lot of things. It's . . ." Her inhalation was shaky enough to hear over the phone. "I feel like . . . the moment I came out, I stopped being *me* to you? I started being an issue. Or, like, a *hobby*."

I flushed, blinking furiously. "That isn't true, Hannah. I promise you, it—"

"Okay." The word was a door slamming. "I know you mean well, Daisy. You always mean well. But you shouldn't have outed Natalie. That was . . . cruel. It wasn't like you to do something like that."

Cruel. That was the word that stuck to my brain like Saran Wrap, until a few hours later, mulling it over, trying to mentally replay what I'd said in the interview, I *still* couldn't understand what Hannah meant. I'd stated a fact—pointed out a flaw in Cindy Beck's argument, a glaring blind spot in the debate. What was cruel about that?

Unless . . .

I pictured Jack, buttoning up his polo shirt, shedding his swagger every time he walked into his house. Mrs. Beck, sunny with confidence at the school board meeting. And her crestfallen, floating face tonight.

Oh. Crap.

Natalie's parents didn't know.

23

When I was little, my heart still intact, the only thing that bothered me about Natalie Beck was that she learned everything more quickly than me. The summer before second grade, we took swim classes at her grandparents' country club, and I watched in grudging awe as she took to the waves like a mermaid, while I stayed behind in the Guppy class for weeks.

One day, I refused to go in her backyard pool, dangling my toes on the side as she did flips in the water. Then her head popped up under my foot.

"I'm your seahorse," she said—and hauled me in with her. Nat was strong enough to stay above the surface as I rode on her back yelling "Giddyup!" every time she turned. She didn't falter once—not until her mom walked out and stood watching us with the oddest look on her face, like her lips had been broken and glued back on.

"I've made some snacks," Mrs. Beck said sweetly. "Help me bring them out for Daisy."

Natalie swam us into the shallow end and slid me off her back. "Mom—"

"*Right now.*" She walked into the house and Natalie scrambled out of the pool, rubbed herself raw with a towel, and hurried after her.

It felt weird to be unsupervised, so I dried off too and crept inside.

In the kitchen, Mrs. Beck was yelling without raising her voice. "Do you *hear* me? *Enough.*"

She stormed out the other way just as I walked in. Natalie's back was turned, shoulders collapsed. There weren't any snacks on the counter.

"Are you in trouble?" I asked.

Nat turned. She was crying. I'd never seen her do this before. It was like finding out her red hair was a wig. This was not who she was.

Just as I processed it, her tears seemed to retreat back into her eyes, her face relaxing, shoulders straightening, making me question whether I'd seen anything in the first place. But there had been something that remained. A tension. An edge. I'd never forgotten it.

I saw that same edge now, the day after the Shawna Wells interview, as I glanced out the open cafeteria door to the lunch stoop, and Natalie happened to glance back. She'd been crying. And now she was pulling it back in. At the sight of me, she picked up her lunch bag and motioned around the building for Hannah to follow. I was too vile to even be permitted a look at them.

As I made my way through the cafeteria to the Alliance, faces turned toward me like a cresting wave, some admiring, curious, others smirking or disdainful. But when I reached the table at the edge of the room, there was only one face I wanted to see.

Kyle looked up at me with a grin. For someone with a purple shiner, he seemed upbeat.

"How are you feeling?" I whispered, my shaking voice barely coming out.

"Deaf," he whispered back. It took me a second to realize he was kidding. "I'm fine! Seriously. I saved you a seat."

The rest of the group was giggling, too giddy to notice me joining them.

"This is *astounding*." Sean idly drummed a swing beat on the table. "The whole cast?"

"The show's publicist called me this morning to confirm." Jack's face floated into a grin. "Did that sound official? Do I sound like I know what I'm talking about?"

Sean clapped. "Yes!"

Raina gave me the barest of smiles. "I take it back, Daisy. You sure can deliver on your bat-shit promises."

"I can?" I leaned over to get a better view of Jack's tablet in the center of the table, seeing only a giant photo of Chase Hernandez, number two on my ever-evolving list of the Hottest Guys on *Triplecross*.

"He came out last night," Sean breathlessly filled me in. "Really, really, really publicly. The press release said he was inspired by the efforts of Daisy Beaumont-Smith." He made a tiny flourish of a bow to me. "And would be making a trip to

South Carolina to come to homecoming. *Our* homecoming. And now the whole cast has said they're coming. The entire. Cast. Of *Triplecross!*"

Sean and Jack linked hands and screamed. Clearly they were fans.

"That's a show," Sophie explained. "On the television, I think."

And clearly Sophie wasn't.

Raina's fork hovered in front of her mouth. "Sometimes I swear you just wandered in from a Disney movie."

Sophie beamed, resting her head on Raina's shoulder. "Aw, thank you!"

"So." I grinned back at Sophie—who did look an awful lot like Cinderella, now that I thought about it. "We've got our celebs. Now we just need a band."

"Yes." Sean snorted adorably. "But not just any band . . ."

Everyone said it together.

"One of the *biggest bands in the world!*"

I cringed, preparing for insults, but they all started laughing. "It could happen!"

In the flush of the *Triplecross* win, everybody seemed to agree with me. So why was there still such an ugly knot in my stomach—like I'd done something terrible and was just waiting for everybody to find out?

Because I was lying to the country, maybe? Seemed like a workable theory.

Stop being neurotic, I ordered myself. *At least until after homecoming. Everything is great.*

Hannah blanked me during bio. And in the hall, after class. I wondered if she heard about *Triplecross*.

I didn't ask.

Everything is great.

Adam looked even nervier than usual as he waited for me outside the Moonlight Coffee Shop, feet tapping, hands stuck deep in his black corduroy pockets. I cocked my head as I neared him, wondering why he wasn't in the corner booth like last time.

Then I heard it. Something inexplicable.

Voices. *Inside the diner.*

The Moonlight Coffee Shop was packed. Every table full, every seat at the counter occupied. It didn't make sense until I pressed my nose against the glass and spotted laptops, tablets, iPhones in front of every customer.

The reporters. They'd *invaded* my hideout.

"Twenty-minute wait," Adam announced.

"This is an outrage!" I shouted.

He laughed. I stared him down. His grin sank into a gulp.

"Should we pick another spot, then?" he offered. "I've been wanting to go to the beach. What do you say? Change of pace?"

I peeled myself from the sidewalk and fell numbly into Adam's passenger seat, saying a silent good-bye to the desolate diner that was. We rounded the corner and sped off before any of the other reporters could spot and accost me.

It took me several sullen blocks to process the fact that it had started to drizzle. I turned to see Adam's reaction, whether he'd order a rain check, but he seemed undeterred. When we got to the empty Folly Beach parking lot, he jumped out of the car, standing on his toes to get a look at the waves.

"It's nice like this," he said, the wind whipping his dark hair into a mop. "Empty. I'd be insulted by sunbathers, if I were the ocean. This ageless, majestic thing in front of you and people bring along neon umbrellas and towels and . . . what do you call 'em? Boogie boards." He shuddered. "I used to go to Coney Island when it was raining, but nobody ever wanted to come with me."

I stopped walking. "Say that again."

He swiped his hair back, one glistening curl dropping down again. "I guess it's kind of a weird preference."

"No." I turned toward the surf in an attempt to stop staring. "It's . . . I get it."

"Thanks for taking time out." Adam put on Reporter Voice. "I know how busy you are these days. With *Evening News* appearances and all that."

I grimaced. "Did you watch?"

"You kicked ass." He squinted over his rain-spattered glasses at me. "So her daughter . . . that's Natalie? The one you—?"

"Yeah." I picked up a shell and chucked it at the ocean. It arced high, landing a few feet away. Leave it to me to miss the Atlantic Ocean. "I didn't mean to mention her on TV. I guess it was kind of a mistake."

Adam shrugged. "It won you the debate."

"Hannah's pretty mad."

Adam picked up another shell and handed it to me, but it was pink and swirly, too nice to throw.

"So Operation Hannah isn't going so well?"

"No," I admitted. "I would definitely categorize it as 'unwell.' We had a fight yesterday, before I even went on TV. She thinks I'm gonna screw everything up. Or bail, like with the opera, among other things. Actually, I think she *wants* me to bail, which is even more confusing . . ."

"Okay." Adam stepped out ahead of me and dug his sneakers into the sand, hands outstretched to stop me. "That's the third time you've brought up this opera. I *have* to ask."

"You ask too much."

"Off the record?" He crossed his heart.

The only way out of this was to answer. Quickly. Pulling off a Band-Aid.

"Freshman year, I started writing an opera about Stede Bonnet. The school got really excited, but I couldn't finish it, because . . . reasons. So we had to cancel and everybody was really mad at me for about five minutes until they forgot all about it. The end."

Adam looked perplexed, as well you might when hearing someone say they'd started writing an opera. "Stede Bonnet?"

"The Gentleman Pirate?" I offered. "Terror of the seas? Hanged on the Battery?"

He shrugged and my mouth fell open.

"How could you not know who Stede Bonnet is?"

He let out a bewildered laugh. "I'm new here."

"He's not a *Charleston* thing. He's a pirate legend!"

Adam did not look convinced. "And you started an opera about him?"

"Kind of half opera, half rock opera," I clarified. "I got like five songs in and realized I didn't know how to make musical notations or play any instruments. So."

"So how did you write the five songs?"

"In the shower, mostly." I bent to pick up another shell that matched the one Adam had given me and tossed it over to him.

"You sang them."

I nodded, my flush creeping higher.

A dangerous glint was in his eye. "You have to sing them for me."

I stopped walking. "Um. No."

He kneeled, offering a chipped oyster shell in payment. "*Please.* Just one."

Apart from the music teacher, the only person who'd ever heard these songs was Hannah. It did seem like kind of a waste.

"One song," I said. "I cannot believe I'm doing this."

Adam flopped onto the sand, waiting for me to start. "Just go."

"Okay, this is called the 'Ballad of Bloody Stede.' It opens the opera and . . . yeah. Picture a bunch of drunk sailors on a dock at night, standing around the entrance to a sketchy pub."

Adam grinned. This was too embarrassing. I gripped the shell and closed my eyes.

"Out on the sea, you see the flag, the flag of Bloody Stede, and you know your fate is sealed as tight as a basket of woven reeds . . . a basket of woven reeds."

I opened my eyes. "There's, like, a musical interlude here."

"Keep singing!" Adam heckled. My eyes clamped shut.

"A wealthy man from Barbados, a married man was he, but Mary proved a rightly shrew, so Stede turned to the sea . . . so Stede turned to the sea.

"A four-gun ship, a purchased crew, and Stede stood on the bow, said 'I will rule the seas one day. You have my solemn vow . . . you have my solemn vow.'

"Aboard Revenge *he sails the coast, a terror on the waves, from Chesapeake to old New York, 'tis plunder that he craves . . ."*

I swished my hand to keep from having to sing the chorus again, then Adam did it for me. Emboldened, I kept going.

"With dandy clothes and hired ship, a gentleman is Stede, but don't mistake him for a fool, you'll walk the plank indeed . . .

"On Nassau Isle a pirate lives, more famous yet than he. 'Tis Blackbeard, Edward Teach, by God, who'll teach him verily . . .

"Now Bonnet sails with foolish pride, and feels so wild and free, but in Charleston Bay a gallows sits, on the Battery . . . Waiting there for . . . Stede . . ."

When I was done, I opened one eye, then the other. Adam was staring at me with a look I'd never seen before, face slack, muscles primed—like he was about to rush over and kiss me.

So. Mean.

"Hey!" I lobbed the shell at him. It hit him in the nose, wiping the faux-longing right off his face. "Don't make fun of me.

I know it's terrible, that's why I didn't go through with it."

"It's not terrible!" Adam jumped to his feet, dusting off sand. "Daisy. It's the opposite of terrible."

"Are you an expert?"

"Nah, that'd be Eli. Musician of the family. Big shot guitarist."

"Fancy."

"He is. Very fancy. Didn't used to be. But." His face clouded, but before I could blurt something sympathetic about how I sometimes fantasized that I had an older sibling I could squabble with, instead of just my cat, he brightened again. "You've got to record that song for me. I want to listen to it again. At least seven more times."

"Ain't no way."

"Oh, come on, Daisy." He clenched his hands together, pleading. "I'm your biggest fan!"

Hannah used to be my biggest fan. Now, improbably, it was Adam Cohen, ace college reporter, Mr. Journalistic Distance himself.

I crossed my arms. "I'll record it for you if you can prove your investigative mettle by bringing me concrete proof of Bigfoot's existence."

Adam extended his hand. "Deal."

I shook, and he held on and I held on and we stood watching each other like something was supposed to happen but neither of us knew what. Suddenly, and horribly, and wonderfully, I knew what I wanted it to be. And I knew he was thinking, *Why is she still holding my hand? This is awkward.* So I let go.

Then he clicked his car open and drove me home.

It wasn't until I was back in my house that I realized Adam hadn't asked me for homecoming updates. I texted him to let him know, and he wrote back: *"You're right! Does tomorrow work?"*

I made sure at least five minutes had passed before I replied, *"Sounds good,"* then read his collected texts again, perusing them like old photographs.

When my homework was done, I brushed my hair, sat in front of my computer at just the right angle—and sheepishly recorded *"The Ballad of Bloody Stede,"* emailing it to him with the explicit warning of pirate-level violence should the video ever find its way onto the Internet.

He wrote back instantly: *"You have my solemn vow."*

That Adam Cohen was too much.

24

I was bound to bump into Natalie Beck between classes, no matter how diligently I schemed to avoid her. I knew this. I just hadn't expected to *physically* bump into her on my way into the cafeteria, so hard that we both ricocheted off the sides of the open doorway.

"Jesus, Daisy." She let out a near-silent cry, somewhere between a laugh and a sob.

"Sorry!" I bent to pick up her little designer lunch bag, but she snatched it back before I could. "My mind was wandering. I wasn't trying to start a rumble or . . ."

I stared at her hands. They were balling, unballing, tapping her sides, trembling.

"Are you okay?" I asked.

She looked incredulous for one-tenth of a second.

"I'm *spectacular.*" She motioned grandly to the open doorway. "You going?"

Natalie was barely keeping it together. Because of me. What I'd done.

"I'm actually . . . not hungry," I said, then spun around—and let out a cry as my forehead connected with somebody's rock-hewn chin.

QB laughed. "Hello to you too."

"Gah," I said, staggering back. "Sorry. I'm like a pinball to-day."

He caught my elbow. "You going in? Wanna sit together? Darius is sick, so there's room at my . . . table . . ."

His voice trailed off as his eyes wandered past me to where Natalie was still standing, her escape thwarted by QB's arrival.

"Oh," he said. "Natalie."

"Hey, Chris," she said.

She called him Chris too.

"I'm gonna eat upstairs, actually," I said, inching myself out of the Bermuda Triangle of awkwardness. "In the math wing. I have a test."

As if that made any sense at all.

"Yeah, cool," he said. "I'll come with you."

QB pressed his hand against the small of my back as we retreated, and I glanced behind me to see Natalie's brow furrow, more with confusion than the jealousy he was obviously trying to incite.

And, of course, the instant we walked out of sight of the cafeteria, my stomach started to growl.

After we'd settled in an empty hallway, QB unzipped his lunch container, revealing a pristinely packed meal. There was a folded napkin on top, on which his mom had scribbled: "I love you, Mr. Awesome!"

He quickly turned it over. "Where's your lunch?"

"I'm on a diet," I lied. To my disappointment, he believed me.

"Are apples okay? I'm not gonna eat this . . ."

"Oh my God yes thank you," I said, snatching the Golden Delicious from his outstretched hand and polishing it against my jeans. "So. How are *things*?"

QB took a bite of his chicken drumstick. "Good, actually. Better."

He didn't sound better. Maybe because he'd just seen the ex. I hoped my smile would be contagious.

"Enjoying your winning streak?"

"It's not a streak until you've won more than one," he said, nudging me. "But yeah. Practice has been awesome. We're like a new team. Darius even has a college scout coming out to the next game."

"How about you?" I asked.

QB flushed. "Nah, I'm not that good. But my grades are okay and I don't need a scholarship, so I'm not worried." His face fell. "Don't know where I'm gonna go, though. I was going to apply wherever Natalie did."

He eyed me cautiously, waiting for me to mock him.

"Yeah." I rested my head against the cement block wall. "I was going to apply wherever Hannah did."

We sat in silence, staring at the empty hallway. I straightened.

"But actually, I've been getting a lot of college brochures all of a sudden, now that I'm an Internet celebrity. I'm thinking maybe NYU, if I can get my grades up. New York seems pretty cool."

"I could see you in New York," QB said, and I locked it in my memory as the nicest of many nice things QB had ever said to me.

Between carefully rationed bites of my apple, I watched him polish off what looked, agonizingly, like homemade sweet potato chips, then said, "Can I ask you something?"

He nodded, but I flinched, too shy to voice the real question that had been tormenting me since the first week of school. Instead, I asked, "Why does everybody call you QB?"

QB cleared his throat, his eyes going wistful. "The first year of football, fifth grade, I played quarterback. I thought I was pretty good till I got to high school and saw Darius throw the ball."

"You're a great . . . um . . . line? Wait—no—wide receiver."

"Thanks," he said wryly, returning the favor of not mocking me. "It was fun to be QB, though. Still is fun to be QB, I guess."

"Okay." I drew a breath, feeling braver. "Question two."

QB crumpled his trash into his lunch container, shrugging a go-ahead.

I copped out again.

"What's with the hunting jacket?" I asked, pinching his red sleeve. "This isn't exactly the right climate for flannel."

"It was my dad's." He glanced down at it. "He died when I was five, so it's—"

"Oh my *God*, Chris." I covered my mouth. "I did *not* mean to pry."

"It's stupid, I guess."

"Not at all!" This poor guy. What the hell was wrong with me?

He managed a lopsided grin. "Any other questions?"

"Okay," I said, figuring it couldn't get worse. "Why do you hang out with me?"

He blinked, confused.

I nodded to the hallway, where Pete Brandt had just passed us, tripping over his own giant feet as he rubbernecked, jaw agape.

"You're Palmetto royalty," I said, lowering my voice. "Aren't you worried I'll spoil that for you?"

I steeled myself for his inevitable reaction. Pity. Disdain. A long speech about how important it was to be kind to the little people in life.

"I'm gonna be honest," he said. "I'm not really following this conversation?"

I squinted. Behind the blank veneer of QB's eyes, I could only make out . . . more blankness.

"I'm *not popular*," I explained, the understatement of the day. I'd had one friend for the past five years. And lately she was more one-third friend.

"You're not *un*popular. You just do your own thing," he said. I gaped at him but he shrugged, daring me to contradict him. "There isn't really, like, a popular, unpopular thing at this school. We all just hang out with who we hang out with. Right now I'm hanging out with you."

"Are you kidding me? I'm *Crazy Daisy*."

He rubbed his temples. "From grade school? That was forever ago. Nobody calls you that anymore. I mean . . . you've always seemed pretty cool to me."

The hallway seemed to splinter into component parts—carpet, doorknob, fire alarm—and then reassemble itself into something that suddenly made a hell of a lot more sense. Grade school *was* forever ago.

"Wow," I said. "Thanks for . . . yeah. Huh."

The bell rang and we stood with a mutual sigh. I was just about to say something horribly sincere, like that this was one of the best lunch breaks I could remember and did he want to be my pretend-brother, when Dana Costas walked by and the words died in my throat.

Spying us, she doubled back.

"Hey QB," she cooed. "You got my birthday invitation, right?"

"Yeah," he said. "Sounds cool."

"Don't forget," she said, backing away. "October twenty-second. Ravenel Country Club. Gonna be *swanky*!"

Then she tugged at one side of her dress like it was itching her, blushed for no reason, and scampered away.

"My invite must have been lost in the mail." I chuckled. Then it hit me. "Hang on."

"It was an email," QB was saying. "You should check your junk folder."

"*October twenty-second?*" I gawked around the corner, watching Dana squirm down the hall. "She's *seriously* having a birthday party the same night as the homecoming dance?"

QB shrugged. "The dance is canceled."

My heart stopped. "No. QB. *Our* homecoming."

"The gay one?" He ran his hand through his hair. "I didn't think we were invited."

"Of *course* you are," I said, and he brightened.

"Because I'm friends with you?"

"No!" I shook my head, frantic. "Because you're a Palmetto student. This is for all students, regardless of—"

"Yeah, I've gotta get to class," QB said, wincing. "But tell me more about Gay Homecoming later!"

He fled with impressive grace. It could have been his football training—or maybe two years of dating the Beck had taught him a thing or two about how to escape a withering glare.

As I was settling into a desk in French, Raina poked her head through the doorway, motioning at me.

Prof Hélène looked miffed. *"La classe va commencer en deux minutes!"*

I stood with my mouth slack, trying to form a reply *en français,* when Raina rattled off a stream of fluent Gallic gibberish that made Prof Hélène laugh. I chuckled too, pretending to understand, and she waved me out with a wink.

I shut the door behind me. "What was that about?"

"I said you have an interview with *Le Monde* and I needed to make sure you wouldn't embarrass the school with your terrible French."

"Gee, thanks."

"De rien. Listen, you missed yesterday's meeting. Are you going to be there today? Cal wants to go over plans for a rally this Saturday. It's going to be grassroots—a bunch of supporters and speakers outside the City Council building. We need to figure out a speech for you to read. Cal will write it, but he wants you to have input."

I leaned against the classroom door. "Great. Yeah. Speech."

Raina squinted. "You okay?"

"Yep, fine. It's just . . ." I blinked hard. "I can't today. I have an interview with Adam."

"I thought that was yesterday."

"He forgot to ask me some stuff, so we're having a round two. I'll be there tomorrow, ready to speechify, I promise!"

Raina stepped back. "A round two. With 'Adam.'"

I gulped. "Yeah?"

"Is there something I should be nervous about here, Daisy?"

"Um . . ."

"We are seventeen days out. If there are any . . . loose ends . . . I need to know about them."

"Oh wow." I laughed, fanning myself. Why was this hallway so hot? "Okay, no. What you're thinking? Not happening. He's just a . . . not even a friend. He's a reporter. He's my reporter."

Raina covered her face with her hand and peeked through her fingers at me.

"I mean, not mine," I sputtered. "He's . . . there's nothing going on. On his end. Or mine. Our ends are staying completely . . ."

Raina's wince deepened.

"I'm the spokesperson!" I said, throwing my hands in the air. "I'm spokespersoning!"

"Fine." She slumped like she'd run out of gas. "See you tomorrow."

But before she could go, I grabbed her arm. "Did you hear about Dana Costas's birthday party?"

Instead of answering, she narrowed her eyes and scanned me for signs of mental illness.

"Never mind," I said, waving at her back as she walked away. "Not important!"

"Where to today?" Adam drummed on the steering wheel.

"You wanna show me where Stede Bonnet was hanged? I'm curious now."

Out on the front drive of the school, I could see Dana standing a few feet away from the Christian Values Coalition mob, her arms crossed over her chest like she was worried they were ogling her. A few seconds later, a miniscule blonde jogged out to join her.

Madison.

She whispered something in Dana's ear, they both giggled, then Madison veered left and disappeared—*into the crowd of protesters.*

"Daisy?" Adam leaned over the passenger seat to get my attention.

"She's one of them."

He froze. "I'm sorry?"

"Madison said I was going to hell and now she's *whispering* things to Dana Costas!"

"I . . . don't know these people."

I leaned against the dashboard. "There's a competing party, event . . . thing. The same night."

Adam looked confused. "There's a party that's competing with your competing party?"

"If my party even *happens,* with the land still up in the air . . ." I gasped. "A party *above* the land! Then they wouldn't have to buy . . ." I sank. "Yeah, whatever, I'm tired."

"Whoa." Adam spun to face me, his brow furrowed. "The land deal hasn't happened?"

"Nope." I sighed. "The owner's stalling. The school board's working on him. That's all I know."

"I'll find out more. That sucks, Daisy, I'm sorry." He didn't look sorry. More elated, actually. He started the car, ignoring my glare. "All right then, consider that our interview. Now I can ask you more important things. Question number one: What's the best pizza around here?"

"Mario's," I admitted. "Unfortunately, it's crawling with high-schoolers."

"Terrifying."

"Yeah."

"That's a shame. I haven't discovered any pizza even approaching edible since I flew down here."

I leaned back to smirk. "What, are you some kind of pizza snob?"

"Have I mentioned that I'm from New York?"

"Seventy-three times. Is how many times you've mentioned it."

Adam laughed. Then he glanced down at his knees and back up, his eyes searching mine. He moved a centimeter closer, and I froze, breathless, desperate for some latent telekinetic ability, so I could will his hand off the central console and onto me. *Any* part of me would do. But instead of inching closer, bridging the gap for him, I blurted, "That thing about the land deal? It should probably stay off the record."

"Oh," he said, tensing up. "Yeah, okay. You got it."

"Sorry." I glanced out the window. "It's just my group . . . we've got this confidentiality thing—"

"It's cool," he said. Then he tapped the wheel. "You know, I'll drive you home, but I should probably get back to campus.

I've got to post something homecoming-related by tomorrow and I have a draft of a term paper due."

I forced a smile, while the last of my nerves unjangled. "On what?"

"Stolypin's agrarian reforms in turn-of-the-century Russia."

"Ah." I stroked my chin. "I would give you my thoughts on that, but I wouldn't want you to be accused of plagiarism."

Adam nodded seriously. "I appreciate your foresight."

"Anytime."

As we pulled up to my house, I saw the Veggiemobile in the driveway, but Mom didn't seem to be peeking out the front window, so there was a small chance I could sneak in without having to tell her Adam and I weren't dating for the fiftieth time this week.

"Listen, Daisy," Adam said, putting the car in park. "Forget about that other party. Or the Madisons at your school. Did I get her name right?"

"Yes," I laughed.

"The Cindy Becks, even. They're not going to stop you."

His brown eyes weren't angry at me for quashing his story. They were warm. Easy to misread. I was blushing, and embarrassed that I was blushing, thus creating an inescapable blush cycle, so I flashed him the Black Panther salute and dashed out before he could say anything else nice to me.

He's right, I thought as I walked up the driveway. *Forget about Cindy Beck.*

Except, um, there she was, in my living room, her entire face taking up our television screen. It was the local news, but my mom was yelling at her like they were having a video chat.

"How can you *stand there* and—"

"This event is about bullying," Mrs. Beck drawled. "Bullying our community. Bullying this *poor* landowner, whom I've had multiple conversations with, and who is being pressured to act against his conscience!"

"Do you even believe the words coming out of your mouth?" Mom whirled around, her face purpling. "Are you hearing this?"

I staggered to the TV. "*She's* meeting with the landowner?"

"At Chez Panisse, no less. Wining and dining him along with half the Republicans in Charleston County."

"I can't believe she hasn't gone away," I muttered, stopping myself from finishing the sentence: *After what I revealed on national television.*

"Throwing Natalie under the bus for her own personal ambitions. It's disgusting." Mom pointed the remote at the screen and eviscerated Mrs. Beck's face with a cathartic click. "I *never* liked that woman."

That was about as mean as my mom got. And if she was pulling out the big guns . . .

"How much trouble are we in?" I asked, my hand frozen on the staircase banister.

"That depends," she said drily. "Do you have a backup location?"

Instead of replying, I decided to focus my energy on not throwing up. Then I shut myself in my room and texted Adam.

"What I told you about the land deal? Go ahead and run it."

"You sure?" he texted back.

"Yep. And FYI—you might want to look into Cindy Beck's political connections. I wonder if anything shady might be going on here."

I was completely making that up. But Adam texted back:

"You are my favorite person right now."

I blushed so hard it hurt, then wrote, *"I bet you say that to all your sources,"* and felt really cool for about an hour.

25

I was running exactly five minutes late to the Alliance meeting. In my mad rush to get there early enough to avoid Raina-glareage, I nearly barreled right into Cal. This was becoming a thing with me.

"Glad I caught you," he said, glancing at his watch. "I've got to head back to DC. Something's come up with one of our clients. We need all hands on deck."

"Ooh! Tell me! Politician? Sex scandal?"

Cal chuckled uneasily. "Nothing you'd guess. And if I do my job, nothing you'll ever find out about."

I was mulling that when panic struck.

"You're leaving?" I grabbed his sleeve. "What about this rally? I'm supposed to give a speech? What do I say?"

"I'll send you something tomorrow," he promised, prying himself and his expensive shirt politely away. "Tweak it as you see fit. Other than that—you guys can handle the rally. And homecoming, for that matter. I'll run damage control as needed from my office, but I have total faith that I'm leaving this event in more than capable hands."

"You have . . . faith?" I sputtered feebly. "We don't have a *venue* and—"

"Sure you do," he interrupted, backing away. "You'll find out in the meeting. Gotta run, talk soon!"

Fixated on the spot he'd vacated, I jumped when Raina murmured over my shoulder, "Did I just hear what I thought I heard?"

"I hope so," I said. "Guess we're about to find out."

When we opened the door to the conference room, we found a sharp-suited woman with an awesomely huge poof of hair waiting in Raina's usual seat, typing on a red laptop.

"Daisy." She leaned to shake my hand as the others trickled in behind us. "Pleased to meet you—all of you. I'm Ivy. I work for the ACLU." At Kyle's bewildered blink through the doorway, she added, "The American Civil Liberties Union. We're a group of attorneys and advocates who work to protect constitutional rights. Like *your* right to free assembly and equal protection under the law."

"Oh. My. God." Raina grabbed a swivel chair for support. "I knew I recognized you. You're *Ivy Diaz.*"

Ivy cocked her head. "Yes. I'm—"

"AVP for Grassroots Advocacy! I am a *huge* fan of your work."

Raina clapping, giggling, like a three-year-old meeting Santa.

"I'm honored." Ivy smiled to hide her bemusement. "Well, if you're a fan already, you're going to love the news I'm here to deliver. I got in late last night and had an early-morning sit-down with Bill Levitt."

The name was ringing faint bells when Sophie piped up, "The landowner."

271

"I showed him this," Ivy went on, sliding a printout to Raina, who slowly grinned as she scanned it. I craned my neck, but could only make out the word "DRAFT" stamped across the top. "It's an editorial, scheduled to be published in tomorrow's *New York Times,* criticizing Levitt Holdings for pandering to conservatives and urging a boycott of one of his side businesses . . ." She squinted over at the editorial. "Cluck-Cluck Chicken Shack?"

Not Cluck-Cluck. *Anything* but Cluck-Cluck.

"He owns Cluck-Cluck?" Sean asked, pulling on his cheeks. "This cannot be happening."

Kyle's eyes went hollow. "But . . . but . . . *shreddie fries.*"

"Wow." Ivy raised her eyebrows. "Sounds like I'll have to try this place out."

We glanced at each other, her words not computing.

"No need to boycott," she explained. "Mr. Levitt is planning to expand Cluck-Cluck Chicken Shack to twelve new states in the west, so he agreed that it was not the best time for his company to become mired in scandal. He signed the land deed on the spot. And we buried the op-ed."

"We have a venue," I muttered.

"You have a venue," Ivy repeated. "Thanks to your trusty local college reporter."

I gasped. "Wait, Adam Cohen? *That* trusty local . . . ?"

My voice died out with the realization. Adam had written the op-ed? Did he know it was going to be buried? Leverage was one thing—but he'd just come thisclose to having his byline in the *New York Times.*

Ivy stood, gathering her laptop and bag. "I've got some calls to return, but I'll be there Saturday to help. I owe Cal several favors, but even if I didn't, I wouldn't miss it. This is a big moment. You guys should be proud." She passed Raina a business card. "If you need me."

Once the door shut, Raina cradled the card like a newborn chick. And the rest of us let out a scream.

After a lengthy round of high fives, the Alliance settled happily down to talking details—the rally, homecoming court, football game, dance. All of which were *actually going to happen.*

"Are we doing a bonfire?" I asked, woozy with hope.

"Not happening." Jack laughed. "Let it go, Daisy."

Cal had been advising us to drop the traditional bonfire from the beginning. Given how desperately everybody was scrambling for reasons to shut us down, we didn't want to hand them something as obvious as a fire risk.

"Maybe we could build a symbolic fire," Sophie suggested. "Make it out of cloth and lights."

I nearly snorted at how fantastical Sophie made it sound, her hands tracing flames in the air. But then Sean leaned forward.

"Diego did something like that for *Brigadoon*! It was gorgeous. He's an *amazing* artist. I'll email him and see if he has any . . . ideas . . ."

His voice sank into a minor key. Poor Sean. Meanwhile, weirdly, Sophie's face was twitching, wrestling down a smile. Odd. I mean, this was *Sophie*, but even for her . . .

"We've got our football teams," Jack said, distracting me. "I posted on Facebook and got hundreds of responses. We're going with: Eastern vs. Western Conference."

"Sounds professional," I said.

"It should," Sean said, emerging from his poetic stupor to slap the table. "We've got three pro players coming out!"

"Not coming out of the closet," Jack clarified. "Coming out to support us." He blinked. "Which might mean the same thing, actually."

"Any Pirates players?" I bit my thumb.

"Not yet," Jack admitted. "I'm working on it. Maybe once they hear about the pro players? We'll see."

"Sounds like we're in okay shape," Raina said, back to her usual level of exuberance.

"Okay?" Sean stood. "We've got our venue! This is gonna be . . . *the best night . . . not the first night . . . but the only night we need . . .*"

Sean had broken into song again. It was half-familiar . . . a musical? *Wait, no.* Winchaw Junction. Hannah used to recite-sing it before we went out for a wild night of mozzarella-stick eating and board-game playing. The realization made me smile and fight back tears in the same blink.

Stop. Everything is great.

"Um." Kyle cleared his throat, eyes darting between Sean's performance and Raina. "I actually have an update too?"

The table went silent.

Sean sat down. "Did they find them? The people who—"

He gestured to Kyle's face. His bruises had faded quickly, thank goodness, but we all understood.

Kyle ducked his head. "No. Not that. They haven't, but . . ." He perked up, changing the channel in his brain. "Anyway, this is better. I, um, got a speaker for the rally?"

"Yay!" Sophie said, clapping. "Good for *you*, Kyle, that's wonderful!"

"My sister did, actually," Kyle went on. "She goes to Harvard with . . ."

I tuned out, staring down the table, my mind stilled by the wonder of the sight before me.

Raina was leaning back in her chair, watching the ceiling, her eyes bright and wide and hopeful. She looked like a completely different person. Someone you could befriend. Someone you could wound.

She caught me looking and scowled.

"Hot *damn*," Sean was saying, rising from his chair to shake Kyle's hand.

Jack leaned over me to give him a high five. "I see national news crews in our future."

I grinned along, pretending to have followed the conversation. "Sounds like Cal's right, then."

I turned to Raina and the ghost of a smile reappeared in her eyes.

"Yep," she said. "We're ready."

My speech was good.

Too good. I had to look up what several of the words meant. But tweaking it didn't feel right. Cal was the expert speechwriter. Who was I to screw with his masterwork?

Then again, how on earth was I supposed to pull off a

line like: *"In the years to come, the seeds we plant today will burgeon forth, germinating orchards for future generations of teenagers, so they too can taste the fruits of freedom"*?

With seven hours to go until this evening's rally, unable to keep a straight face while reading Cal's speech into the mirror, I realized I needed a practice audience.

My first thought was Hannah. Of course it was. She'd been my one and only audience member for the past six years. But—maybe this could reboot us. I'd apologize for outing Natalie. And then I'd ask for help. *Anything* was worth a try at this point.

Mom was heading out to celebrate the land deal with her farm group at an organic cafe in downtown Charleston. I stopped her as she was looking for her sunglasses.

"You mind dropping me at von Linden Imports?"

"Visiting Hannah? Haven't seen much of her lately."

"I see her at school every day."

I must have sounded defensive, because Mom had a pitying look in her eye when she joined me in the Veggiemobile.

"You know . . . friendships are living things," she said, her voice singsong, like she was reciting a greeting card. "They evolve over time. That's how they get stronger. But I know how hard it can be when one person evolves a little faster than the other."

Was she seriously calling me unevolved? I leaned down, pretending to tie my shoe.

"I remember when my best friend had her first boyfriend. We were fifteen. Cassie was two months older, but all of a sudden, seeing her with him . . ." She started the car, shaking

276

her head. "I felt like she was about a *hundred* years older than me. I couldn't understand her anymore—the things she was interested in, how distant she was, even when we were doing the same things together that we'd always done. But then your dad came along that next year and I thought, *Aha. This is what happened.* She'd just . . . leveled up before me."

The engine revved too fast as we turned onto the highway, my heart lurching with it. *Leveled up.* Did that mean I was losing the game?

"In the end, we got through it better than ever." Mom clumsily patted my head, then glanced at me. "Aunt Cassie. Your godmother."

"Yeah, I got that." I pulled out Cal's speech and stared at it. "I'm sorry, I really need to memorize this."

"Okay." I could sense Mom pressing her lips together. "I'll be quiet."

Her voice was so pinched—so careful—it made my heart twinge. If we'd been home, I might have thrown my arms around her waist and closed my eyes and pretended I was five again. But we were in a moving car, so I swallowed the feeling and kept my head down.

Hannah would be helping out in the shop today. Tan liked to "visit" on the weekends, gossiping with the neighboring business owners along Broad. Sure enough, as we pulled up alongside the shop, I spotted her across the street at a new bistro. The chef looked way too young for Tan, almost too young to cook, but he was grinning like an idiot as he chatted with her on the sidewalk. Tan had her hair swept back with a red scarf, her tunic dress flouncing off one shoulder. I'd never known Hannah's mom to date—Hannah thought she was still too wounded by the divorce—but lordy, the woman could flirt.

"Pick you up after lunch," Mom called as I stepped out of the car. "Then we'd better get you ready for the rally!"

I shot her a sarcastic thumbs-up as she drove away, then stared dizzily at my reflection in the shop-front window, scrambling to think of the best possible way to say "I'm sorry" without it sounding forced.

As usual, the door was propped to draw in window-shoppers. Why did it feel like an impenetrable barrier today, like I was a vampire who needed a formal invitation to step inside?

Bingo, I thought as a flash of red hair bobbed between the aisles, vivid as a flashlight through the glass.

Natalie Beck was here. Visiting Hannah. Skipping through the store. She sure made herself at home.

I growled and walked away, wondering where I should loiter until my mom's meeting was done. I'd hit the corner when my phone rang.

Hannah.

I cleared my throat before I answered, glancing behind me. "Hey, what's up?"

"Were you just at the shop?"

"What?" I laughed. "No! I would have come in, if I'd . . . um."

There was silence. I closed my eyes, cheeks flaming.

"Nat thought she saw you peeking through the window," she said, her voice flat. "Must have been somebody else."

"I *am* downtown, just not on your block." That made absolutely no sense as an explanation, but I still dashed across the street and around a corner to make the lie true. "I'm working on this . . . speech. Thing."

"For the rally?"

I stopped walking. "You know about that?"

"Yeah! We're coming."

"Oh wow." I backed into a doorway to avoid a sudden onslaught of lost tourists. "*Hannah*. That means a lot to—"

"Ah, I've got a customer, but we'll see you later."

"Yeah! See—"

She hung up.

They're coming to the rally, I thought. *She* and *Natalie*. That had to mean something. If not forgiveness, at least a nod to it, right?

My heart started to race. *Rally. Focus. Everything is whatever.*

With the time I had left, I settled onto a bench outside a gated cemetery, swatting bugs, watching horse-drawn carriages clip-clop by, rereading my speech so frantically that basic words no longer made sense.

Am I pronouncing it right? Stoo-dent? That's really how you say it?

A text came in from Adam: *"Ready to rally? Need a pre-rally rally?"*

"No and YES," I texted back. *"HELP ME!!!!!!"*

Mom must have sensed that I was on the precipice of a breakdown, because she refrained from making any knowing comments about the young reporter she'd caught me with when she'd come to pick me up, our heads bowed over Adam's notepad as he reworked Cal's speech into something I could say without putting on a fake British accent.

Such was her self-control, in fact, that she did no more than wave from the driver's seat as I stood shakily from the bench.

"What do you think?" I asked Adam.

"It reads well," he offered.

"But the last part." I scratched it with my thumbnail, uneasy.

"Yeah." He kicked a twig. Looked up. "I can't answer that for you. On the one hand, it's what you agreed to do. On the other . . ."

He shrugged. I groaned, nodded. He was right. It was my impossible decision to make.

"Okay," I said. "See you there."

Four hours later, on the way to the rally, I was still trying to memorize my speech. The beginning was easy. The middle got murky. And the end . . . I still hadn't decided about the end.

"Will *Adam* be there tonight?" Mom asked.

"Yes. He's a reporter. He's reporting on it."

"Okay!"

I pretended not to see her wink.

The car radio started playing Kudzu Giants, and I turned it up. Adam didn't like this band. What kind of music did he listen to, if not Kudzu Giants? Classical? Polka? Oh God . . . jazz?

We rounded the corner to the town square and thoughts of

music fled my head. There was a roadblock ahead, police officers waving cars away. I knew we were expecting big crowds, but this seemed like overkill.

Mom turned the car around, muttering to herself about where she was going to park. I set my speech aside and tried to relax.

The radio went to a commercial break, so I changed the channel to an oldies station, Diana Ross singing:

"I'm coming out! I want the world to know. Got to let it show."

Mom parked the car. And looked at me. And we both burst out laughing.

"Come on," she said, grabbing a homemade placard from the backseat. "Time to rally."

26

The square was a crush of color, rainbow flags everywhere, on banners, shirts, crazy hats, beaded necklaces, a large piñata that I was guessing was supposed to be a pirate. The huge, cheering crowd was as brightly dressed as the signs they carried. But it wasn't their clothes that caught my attention. It was their hair.

All through the crowd, I caught glimpses of ponytails, bobs, braids, wigs—with the bottom few inches painted pink, green, purple, neon yellow, and more than any of those, my exact shade of cornflower blue. There were probably three hundred people here, and a third of them had dyed their hair to look like mine.

Entranced by the sight, and me being me, I almost walked smack into the drabbest person in the square—a large man in a black suit, with one giant hand pressed to his ear. For some reason, he was trying to block my way to the roped-off area beside the stage.

"Only authorized speakers past this point," he told me, his voice so authoritative that I nearly squeaked "okay" and scampered home. But then I felt Mom's hand on my back.

"This is Daisy Beaumont-Smith," she said, her chin craned imperiously. "And I'm her mother."

After a tense moment, the big man gave a nod. "You're cleared. You too, ma'am. Enjoy the rally."

It wasn't until we were a few feet out of earshot that I dared whisper to Mom, *What* in the what?"

"Secret. Service," she whispered back, and before I could figure out why in the world the White House would send us a security team as a gift, Kyle hopped into our path, tugging an older girl after him.

"Daisy! Before you go up, I wanted you to meet Lily?"

Kyle's sister shook my hand, then pulled me in for a stealth hug.

"Oh!" I said. "Hi!"

"Kyle's told me so much about you. Thank you . . . for everything." I could tell from Lily's eyes that she'd heard about the attack. And somehow, she didn't seem to blame me. She leaned in to murmur, "I was a little worried about him starting high school without me there. It's nice to know he's got a friend like you looking out for him."

The word "friend" hit me like sunshine. I was still basking in it when a blond boy walked up behind Lily with such a familiar face that I suddenly suspected none of this was happening.

"I think I'm on," the boy said, glancing behind him. "Daisy Beaumont-Smith, right? Can't wait to hear your speech. See you up there!"

He waved and jogged away, stopping on the stage's steps to kiss a tiny brunette I assumed was his girlfriend. But who cared about her?

"Is that *Andy Lawrence*?" I asked. "The president's kid?"

"I think he prefers 'First Son,'" Kyle said.

"Oh." I frowned. "Wow."

"He prefers 'Andy,' actually." Lily laughed and grabbed her brother's hand, pulling him away to watch from the square. "Break a leg, Daisy!"

"I will!" I shouted back. "I mean, I won't, hopefully, but thanks!"

"*Smooth*," someone said in my ear.

Grinning, I whirled around to punch Adam in the arm.

"Ow!" He cradled his elbow.

"Sorry. Sometimes I underestimate my own strength."

"This is what I keep trying to tell you."

I could make out a corner of the crowd over his shoulder. No familiar faces yet. Where were the Palmetto students?

Where was Hannah?

"So what did you decide?" Adam was peering at me with a strange expression.

"Um . . ." *Is that her?* I could have sworn I saw a black cropped hairdo next to a flash of bright red hair moving deeper into the crowd, but then in the next blink, I saw that they were both six feet tall and male.

Adam's hand grazed my back, startling me into blinking up at him.

"Either way, you've got this. Nobody's gonna judge you. Well—I won't." He winced. "This is not the pep talk I'd planned in my head."

I nodded, my eyes returning to the crowd. In my prep, I'd learned that the best way to give a speech was to imagine that you were speaking to one person in the audience. That would be easy, if I could just find Hannah. She had to be here. And if I saw her, I'd know what to do.

The crowd was igniting as the president's son—sorry, *Andy*—took the stage.

"I'm so happy to be here to fight for . . ." Andy had started to yell into the microphone, only to be drowned out by a surprising amount of screaming hetero girls. He chuckled and started again, but his voice warped and faded as I stared down at my speech, the shouts, laughter, applause of the rally hitting me in relentless waves, the ocean crashing against a boat's hull.

As a matter of fact, I felt like I was bobbing. Up and down, up and down.

"Interview after the rally?" Adam grinned. I couldn't focus on his face.

These people—they were thrilled to see celebrities up there, but they were really here to see me, weren't they? They thought I was just like them.

But I wasn't. I wasn't like anybody.

Andy Lawrence was blasting from the loudspeakers again.

". . . And so it's my pleasure to introduce the girl who stood on a chair to make sure that her voice was heard and that her rights—*your* rights—were not ignored. Daisy Beaumont-Smith!"

The noise rushed in with a crack. My imaginary boat hull had just smashed into splinters, and here I was, climbing to the stage, dimly noting Adam shooting me a thumbs-up and the First Son patting my shoulder to lead me to the microphone. And now I was standing staring at a mob of upturned faces that all seemed to expect something from me.

The banners in the crowd started to sink. The cheers became mutters.

And then, there she was—my best friend, rustling her hair, peering up at me, twirling one of the little rainbow flags that the Alliance was distributing throughout the crowd. Natalie was next to her, wearing a Braves cap so low I could hardly see her face.

Don't do it, I thought. *That's the answer.* Then, *Shut up, I have to. It's way too late for edits!*

"I have a confession to make." My voice erupted from the speakers and I almost didn't recognize it. It was so loud. So confident. The banners bobbed happily back into rally position.

I could say it. The truth. Right now.

And everyone would hate me.

I grinned. "It's a lot harder to give a speech when you're not standing on a chair!"

The crowd laughed so loud that it sent me staggering back from the microphone. I grabbed it closer.

"But since you all made the effort to turn up here and rally for America's Homecoming, I'll give it my best shot."

I stared down at my speech, drew a breath, and prepared to lie.

"As a gay teenager, it's not always easy to live in a conservative community."

"Hell no," somebody shouted.

"You grow up going along. Playing nice. Upholding 'traditional' values. You hold hands for grace at dinner. Say 'ma'am' and 'sir' when talking to adults. And you hold on to your secret with every ounce of energy you have. Until one day, there's no denying it. You can't lie anymore. You can't live a life that's been designed for someone who is not you. And in that moment, you're free."

I spoke right to Hannah, whose brow was furrowed, her expression otherwise opaque. Was she moved? Angry?

"Except you're *not* free," I went on. "Because in a place like this, everyone will fight to keep you traditional. To keep you quiet. Or alienate you to the point that you just give up and leave. Even after the Supreme Court guarantees your right to marry whomever you choose. *Especially* after that. They've doubled down, wherever they can. At the local level. The small-business level. The *school board* level."

The crowd grumbled in agreement.

"But look around. We're not leaving. We exist. This is our home, this is *our* school. And we deserve to be heard!"

The wall of faces seemed to pulse with one heartbeat as they cheered.

"And you know what? We're not alone. I've been blown away by the support this community has shown to our cause in the past few weeks. They've stood up alongside us and said, 'No. Hate does not represent us. Intolerance does not represent us. We are Charleston in the twenty-first century, and we are proud that you are proud.'"

The crowd roared their approval once again. So this was why Cal had written "applause break" under every paragraph.

Here went nothing.

"And so I stand up here today, just as I stood in front of the

Palmetto School Board, to say that I am proud to be a gay American and I am ready to live in a world of acceptance and love. I'm ready to dance with my girlfriend at homecoming. And next weekend, I will!"

Huge applause line. It was a good thing I hadn't changed it. I glanced at Hannah, desperate to see her reaction to that last, biggest, baldest lie—but it wasn't her face that froze my next breath.

Natalie Beck had started to cry.

"The . . ." My voice faltered. She was staring right up at me, one hand splayed against her mouth as if shoving a shout back in. I cleared my throat, dragged my eyes away. "The actions we take next weekend will pave the way for future generations of gay students, who won't have to fight, won't have to rally. All they'll have to worry about is whether their tux should be the same color as their date's or if that's too matchy."

Cal had written "pause for laughter." He was right.

"They will have the traditional high school experience—minus the hate. That's what we're here to fight for, and that's what we're going to get. So thank you for joining us and we'll see you at homecoming!"

I managed to get off the stage, knees wobbling, barely registering Adam's hand guiding me down the steps.

"Steady there," he said. "Got sea legs, Dread Pirate Daisy?"

I stared past him into the crowd.

Adam coughed. "Dumb joke. You were great, really."

"Thank . . . you." I nudged him to the side. "Sorry, I just need a sec."

288

I saw hurt flash across his face as I pushed out of the barricade and into the audience, but I couldn't double back, not without checking on Hannah first.

Sean walked backward into my path, whispering, "I *told* you you could do it!"

Jack ran up, iPhone outstretched. "I shot it for Cal. He already texted back."

The phone said, *"Nice tweaks! Impressive speech—talk more Monday."*

"It was Adam," I muttered. "Adam wrote the speech."

"What?" he shouted.

"I didn't do anything."

The crowd was pressing in, people patting me on the back, congratulating me, saying they'd be at homecoming. I couldn't focus, I couldn't see . . . there she was.

Hannah. Standing on the edge of the square under a flagpole that someone had draped with their own beaded banner.

"Hang on," I said to Sean and Jack, continuing deeper into the rally.

"You sure you wanna . . . ?" Jack's voice was drowned out behind me.

"Daisy? Daisy!"

Somebody else was calling. For a confused second, I thought it was Adam, but the accent was wrong. Another reporter, then. This was a bad time for an interview. Hannah was slumped, blinking into her rainbow flag, her face crumpling, her whole body shrinking. Something had happened. Something worse than my speech.

I needed to get to her.

"Daisy!" came that voice again, and this time, I recognized it.

QB ran out ahead of me. "I'm here! I came to support!"

"That's awesome, Chris, thank you!"

I tried to see past him, but the football friends he'd brought along were forming a wall of shoulders. When they shifted their weight, the spot where I'd seen Hannah was now filled with two girls in their twenties with long braids dipped green. It took me a few seconds to find her again, in front of a line of boys hoisting a long banner that said "LOVE IS LOVE" in Pirates colors.

Hannah grabbed for someone's hand but missed. A red ponytail whipped around. Natalie. They were arguing.

QB rocked onto his heels. "I thought maybe . . ." His voice died out, his eyes trailing mine over his shoulder. "She's here. *Natalie's* here."

"Daisy!" This time it was definitely reporters. "Can we get a shot?"

"Just a sec, if you don't mind!" I tried to smile apologetically, and they took that opportunity to snap a picture. Encouraged, more photographers gathered.

"Do you think she's seen me?" QB was muttering, swiping sweat from his top lip. "Oh man."

And then Natalie was backing away from Hannah, shaking her head, shuddering upright, heading straight for us. The crowd parted for her like it always did, total strangers sensing instinctively that this redhead was not someone you got in the way of.

Now Hannah was crying too.

I stepped forward, prepared to stop Natalie. She could mock me, betray me, but if she thought she could publicly humiliate my best friend and walk away, she was dead wrong.

"Nat," QB muttered, and just as I was reeling from the longing in his voice, the loss, I felt him grab my wrist so quickly that my ankle turned and sent me tumbling into his open arms.

I blinked. He was leaning over me. Why was he leaning over me?

He winced. Glanced at Natalie. Mouthed "Sorry." And pressed his lips to mine.

QB Saunders was kissing me.

And approximately one million cameras started to flash.

27

Either the crowd fell into woozy silence or I went deaf from shock.

My arms were still pinned under QB's chest, my face stuck to his like chewing gum. His eyes were open, locked on mine in mute panic. He was enjoying this about as much as I was.

Natalie, my brain gasped. *Trying . . . make . . . jealous . . .*

And then, like a taut rubber band, he broke away—nearly dropping me in the process of trying to discern whether his grand gesture had had the desired effect on his ex.

He didn't even seem to notice when I slapped him across the face. And neither did the reporters. They'd become a fallen beehive, frenzied, crowding, shouting orders to their cameramen, attacking me with questions I couldn't hear, some staggering back as if repulsed, most buzzing with barely disguised glee.

I'd just handed them a new angle.

Famous lesbian caught kissing a boy.

Raina was at my elbow in an instant.

"Let's recamp," she said, and not knowing what that meant,

I let her lead me away, her arms blocking one side of me while reporters swarmed the other. I ducked, my own hand raised, as we reached the edge of the square. The Secret Service were guarding Andy Lawrence's car. At the sight of them, most of the press dropped away, but the cameras kept rolling from a distance, getting footage of me leaving in disgrace.

I should stay, I thought numbly. *I should explain.*

Lie, *you mean. Again.*

It felt better to run.

I risked a glance back at the flagpole as we took to the sidewalk. Hannah was sitting on the flag's pedestal. Still crying. Natalie was gone. Had they broken up?

Raina's phone beeped with a text. She glanced down and quickly up, then tugged me faster down the block.

"Cal says good job, now go home and get some rest," Raina announced. "The photo's popped up online. He says we'll figure it out in the morning."

I stared at her phone as she pocketed it. The actual text read: "*SEND HER HOME.*"

"So, are you dating QB?" Raina asked the question past me.

"No." We turned into an alley. "Definitely not. At all."

"Then let's see about pressing charges."

"No!" I stopped walking to face her. "He's an idiot, but no. We can't do that to him."

"Why? *Why* can't we do that to him?" She dug her fingers into my shoulders. "That was *assault,* Daisy. Why won't you admit this to yourself? This seems to be a pattern with—"

"Trust me, this is totally different from . . . yeah."

"Why? What are you not telling me?"

"Nothing!"

She let go and spun away, then turned back. "Maybe we say you're bisexual." Raina ran her hand over her face. Paused. Peered past my shoulder. Voices rose up around the corner. "Come on, walk, this is about to get ugly."

Sure enough, the reporters had doubled around the security barricade to corner us.

"Daisy, are you dating that boy?" "Daisy, does this mean you've broken up with your girlfriend?" "Daisy, were you *ever* gay?"—and that one was so asinine that I actually looked to see who'd asked it.

Instead, I turned to find Adam Cohen staring at me from the center of the press horde. There was a closed look in his eyes that I hadn't seen since that first day at the Moonlight Coffee Shop when I'd sent his computer hurtling to the ground. Just as I was about to bum-rush the crowd, grab his hand, and make a break for it, both of us, together, he took one step back, tucking his iPhone into his pocket, and disappeared into the sea of faces.

A warm arm wrapped around my shoulder.

"No more. We're going home," Mom said into my ear, then turned to the reporters. "No comment, folks!"

Her hand shook as she walked us quickly away from Raina and the reporters, down the alley to the waiting Veggiemobile. My feet skipped every few steps to keep up with her. I could tell what she really wanted to do was sprint, but she was trying to preserve our dignity.

We had a second to breathe once the car doors slammed

shut, and then reporters surrounded us, shouting melo-dramatic questions, like *What does this mean for America's Homecoming?"*

Mom rolled her window down an inch, then thought better of it, yelled "Shoo!" and revved the engine. It worked. They scampered like rats, and away we drove. We'd made it two blocks, both of us still panting, when she turned to me with a painfully hopeful smile and said, "Your speech was excellent, sweetheart. I'm *sure* that's what they'll report on."

I didn't dare look at my phone until the next morning. And then I wished I hadn't.

The first message was from Jack. "We're in trouble. The only thing they're talking about is that kiss. Call me back. We need to fix this."

I peeked at the morning news. First headline:

**GAY ACTIVIST DAISY BEAUMONT-SMITH CAUGHT
WITH HUNKY BOYFRIEND**

I couldn't tell you what was more excruciating, their use of "hunky" or the photo that accompanied the headline. They must have found the one millisecond in which my eyes had closed from the shock of having QB's giant head squished against my own, so it looked romantic, like that World War II photo of the sailor kissing the nurse, probably as unwilling a recipient of affection as I'd been.

The second voicemail was from Adam. "You could have told me."

That was it. What the hell.

Third one from Mr. Murphy. Dear, reliable Mr. Murphy,

who was just "Calling to check in and see whether you might be able to finish that mural!"

I replayed that message three times as a distraction.

Fourth message. Hannah. Except she sounded more like the ghost of Hannah, her voice dry and raspy, wind through leaves.

"We broke up. Thought you'd like to know."

I was right. I felt a shameful rush of glee.

And then, on the message, a sigh.

"*QB*, Daisy? Just a rumor? Really?"

She should have known better than that. And yet . . . was she that far off? I'd gone on three pseudo-dates with the fool. I knew about his childhood, his hopes and fears, his everlasting devotion to his one true love, Natalie Beck. We were—perversely—kind of going out.

The last message was from the man himself. Romeo. Casanova. Pepé le Pew.

"I'm really sorry, Daisy. I feel like an asshole. Yeah, okay, I am an asshole. Call me if you want to talk?"

QB meant well, but he also meant "*listen to me* talk." I'd had just about enough of that.

I called Adam back first, partly because his beat poem of a message was by far the most intriguing, and partly because of reasons I wasn't willing to examine at this particular juncture. He picked up on the first ring.

"*What.*"

"Whoa," I said. "I'm calling to find out what exactly I *could have told you*. You already knew I was straight, yes? Thus the speech dilemma?"

"So you're dating this kid?"

"Kid?" I snorted. "He's like a year younger than you, college boy. And no. I'm not dating him."

"Just a casual thing, then. Were you with him last night? Is that why you're only calling me back now?"

"*What?*" I snapped, unwilling to dignify his crazy question with a rational answer. "Why do you even care? You've got your articles. Aren't you supposed to be maintaining a journalistic distance?"

I don't matter to you, I thought. *I'm only a story. Tell me I'm wrong,* please *tell me I'm wrong.*

I gripped the desk so hard it jolted, making that awful photo pop up again, this time in a new article questioning whether the whole event was a hoax.

"I will from now on, that's for damn sure." While I was processing that, he started to sputter. "*College boy*? I'm *college boy* now?"

"Why is that insulting?" I stood from my desk chair. "It's what you are, remember? Or have you spent so much time on James Island that you've forgotten where your own campus is?"

"I'm there right now."

He sounded confused. I made it clearer.

"Good. Maybe you can make some friends your own age."

I leaned against the desk and waited.

"You're right," he said.

Not what I expected.

"This whole thing . . . making friends, or whatever, with . . ." He sighed, cleared his throat, and when he talked again, it was with Reporter Voice. "It was inappropriate.

It won't happen again. So good luck with your event."

"Thank you," I said, my voice as polite as his. "Good luck reporting on my event."

"Bye, Daisy."

There was something wistful about the way he said my name, like he'd never say it again. I clutched the phone.

"Adam?"

But he'd already hung up.

Back to the news, I thought, drawing a cleansing breath that felt like tear gas. *Let's face this head-on.*

I made popcorn. Then I googled myself.

"Daisy's straight. She's been dating QB Saunders since . . ."

"The beginning of the year?"

"Yeah, at least. She's just doing this for attention."

"Definitely for attention. I mean, the whole country's talking about her, right?"

Jenna Jeffers and Kim Shoemaker, freshmen at Palmetto High School, interviewed by the *New York Post*

"She was gay. She was a lesbian with that Chinese girl—"

{Off-camera: "Hannah von Linden?"}

"I guess, yeah. They were dating for like forever and everybody knew it but nobody wanted to say anything. But then QB turned Daisy straight. She comes to all his games and they're always together. Like, making out everywhere. They're obsessed with each other. I don't know why she's pretending she's still gay. It's weird."

Whitney Jenkins, Palmetto sophomore, TMZ video interview

"Her soul is still in jeopardy, even if she's not an active homosexual. I'm praying for all of them."
Reverend Tom Rawlings, in *The Post and Courier*

"She's been straight all along. Since eighth grade, anyway. That's when we were together. I don't really want to kiss and tell, but let's just say she is very, very, very straight. It was intense. I'm gonna be honest . . . she broke my heart."
Seth-Freaking-Ross, basking in the News Channel 7 camera's glow

"Your heart? I broke your nose!"
Daisy Beaumont-Smith, Palmetto junior, screaming at the computer screen

"The barest, quickest web search reveals a worrying pattern of grandiose promises and outrageous assertions by Ms. Beaumont-Smith. Only two years prior, she made local headlines by claiming to have written an original opera on the life of famed pirate Stede Bonnet. Though she was hailed as a young prodigy, the opera never materialized. It begs the question—were we complicit? Too rabidly eager to laud and crown a sixteen-year-old whom the harsh glare of hindsight reveals quite clearly as the narcissist and pathological liar she was all along?"
Editorial in *The Guardian*

"We've been talking."

Sophie's eyes were kind, her voice soothing. It felt like I was being dumped by my fairy godmother.

"And we think it would be better for us to keep going . . . without you as our spokesperson."

I nodded. "I totally agree."

Sophie let out her breath in one big *shuh,* relieved that I didn't put up a fight. Sean patted my hand, but the old thrill at having him in close proximity was no longer strong enough to boost my mood.

"It's not that we don't appreciate what you've done, Daisy," he said. "It's just gotten so complicated, right?"

He leaned in, grimacing, like we were gossiping about somebody else.

"Yeah, I can see that." Everyone looked wary, half expecting me to go Hulk-mad and overturn the conference table. "So how else can I help?"

"You've done enough," Raina said, and it came out so harsh that she herself winced. "I mean . . . you've *helped* enough. You can sit it out from here."

I nodded as if I understood. "Sit it out, um, completely? Or—"

"It's nothing personal," Raina said, to a chorus of wild-eyed agreement from the group. "We should never have put you in this position in the first place. You're not a bad person, you're just . . . unqualified."

My mouth made an "oh," but the sound didn't come out.

"Sit with me at lunch," Sophie said, stretching her hand

out, not quite far enough to reach me. "You're still our friend, even if you're not . . . technically . . . an Alliance member anymore."

So I was out of the Alliance too. It took my lungs a second to recover from having the air smacked out of them.

I looked to Kyle, but he glanced away. It wouldn't be fair to ask him to go to bat for me. All I'd done was ruin everything he was fighting for. The narrative we'd been promoting all along was gone. The Alliance had gone from Gallant to Goofus in one stupid lip-lock.

"Got it," I said, and tried to leave with as much grace as possible—only to remember in the hallway that I'd left my backpack, forcing me to double back and round the table again to get it, before ducking out a second time with yet another sheepish wave *just* as the bell rang, at which point everybody got up and walked out with me. Awesome.

Sophie and Jack both gave a tiny wave good-bye, which made me feel a smidge less awkward, but then Raina, the last to leave the room, hit me with her backpack as she waltzed past. Didn't even look back, like I'd ceased to exist the instant she ousted me from the group.

Because it *was* her, wasn't it? She'd always wanted me gone. And now I was.

"Congratulations!" I shouted at her retreating back. She stopped walking. "I'm the villain after all. Right, Raina? This whole situation . . ." As she slowly turned, I drew a big circle in the air. "It's on me. I mean, it's not like you held a meeting and *voted* for me to pretend to be a lesbian. Oh! Wait!"

"What exactly are you fighting for, here, Daisy?" Raina asked, smoothing a stray curl into her headband as she strolled over. "The right to hang out with us?"

I flinched. She smiled.

"To help us put up tents? Hang streamers for the dance?" She pretended to consider. "Tell you what. You really want to do that? You can do it. There you go, you're hired."

"You can't rehire me," I snapped. "I quit."

She let out a laugh like a gunshot and pointed at me. "*There.* There it is."

I glanced down at my outfit. "Where what—?"

"Your *blind spot.*" She dropped her bag on the ground, spread her stance. "Here's what you don't get. You *can* quit. Because you, Daisy Beaumont-Smith, are *privileged.*"

"*Excuse me?*" I scoffed. Raina was looking at me like I was a princess. A mean girl. Natalie Beck. "Privileged? How am *I*—?"

She cut me off, eyes alight. "You really want to argue this with me? Let's see, Daisy." She counted off on her fingers. "You're white. You're cisgender, you're straight, you're rich—"

"I'm not rich!" I gawked at her. "We're *comfortable,* but—"

She sighed like it hurt. "Are you gonna go to college?"

This was ridiculous. "Yeah. But I don't see—"

"So you're looking into financial aid programs, then. Scholarships."

My mouth clamped shut. I looked away. "No."

"No," she parroted. "You're rich. And the fact that you think 'comfortable' isn't rich? That's your privilege showing."

I sank into myself, feeling like I was being cross-examined into a lengthy prison sentence. Raina was going to make one hell of an attorney. Not that I'd know her by the time that happened.

"You don't get it." Her voice grew gentle, almost sad. "You're never going to get it. Because this is the problem with privilege, Daisy. It's a blindfold with a pretty picture of the world painted on the inside. You think it's the truth. But it's just *your* truth. You think homecoming is something you can play with, be reckless about, never mind the consequences—because there have never *been* consequences for you. And you're lucky, I'm happy for you." As if to demonstrate, she shot me a grim smile that fell away instantly. "But that is not our reality. Our reality is that this fucking matters. Our cause is not a toy."

If she'd been holding a mic, she'd have dropped it. Instead, she picked up her backpack and continued down the hall, while I stayed shuffling in place like a lame horse, knowing that if I argued any further, I would only prove her point.

Besides, I agreed with her on one thing. I should never, *ever* have gotten involved.

28

Hannah once taught me the German word for vicarious embarrassment: *fremdschämen*. It sounded like an infectious disease, and for good reason—my entire school appeared to have come down with it.

No one acknowledged me—not to mock, yell, offer words of sympathy, hold the door before it smacked me in the face, call on me in class. QB was keeping his distance, as well he freaking should. No matter how many times I checked my phone, Adam wasn't texting. The Alliance was formalizing our divorce by pretending I'd never existed, and Hannah . . .

Hannah was really good at running.

"Hey!" I shouted, rounding the corner of the school toward the parking lot. She walked faster. "Han!"

I caught her by the shoulder and she turned with a bewildered headshake.

"Sorry," she muttered. "I didn't hear you."

"Then how did you know there was something to hear?" I grinned, nudged her, realized too late that joking around was the wrong tack to take.

She sighed. "What do you need, Daisy?"

One friend in the entire world?

I clung to my backpack straps, fighting to stay sunny. "I just wanted you to know that I got your voicemail, and if you need somebody to talk to, or a distraction, or anything else . . . I am here for you. And I suddenly have a lot more free time for hanging out. So yeah."

"Duly noted." She shifted her weight and looked away. "Listen, I need a week. Just to go to school and do my homework and go to bed and not think about anything. We'll talk after that." She crossed her arms, looked at me. "Is that okay?"

"Yeah, totally!" I backed away, hands where she could see them.

"Okay." She slumped, exhausted—but also visibly relieved.

As she walked off, I dropped the smile, the act, all of it. There was no point in pretending. She wasn't going to look back.

She left me the stoop. I'd noticed it sitting empty on Monday and Tuesday, but I'd snuck lunch up to the math wing to eat alone, knees tucked to make myself as small as possible. On Wednesday, the stoop looked so sunny and inviting that I took a chance, poked my head out, and reclaimed my old seat.

I'd sort of hoped it would be empowering. That I'd feel independent, self-sufficient, like this was still my own little corner of the universe. But the stoop just felt like a stoop—not mine, not Hannah's—a random architectural feature of an ugly municipal building.

I ate. I left. And on Thursday, I got over myself.

"Hey," I said, approaching the granola table. "Mind if I—?"

"Of course!" Sophie beamed, clearing the spot next to her.

I'd bought a salad for lunch, worried about offending their sensibilities, but now I looked around to find them chowing down on cafeteria burgers and chicken soup. Not what I'd expected.

Sophie tried to include me in the conversation, but it was all about some music festival they were going to and some guy named Gus who was lending them his van and was apparently *hilarious,* so there was really no entry point. I focused on my non-meal, grateful at least for the pretense of friends.

"Nope," said a dreadlocked girl at the end of the table. "Nope, nope, nope."

Everyone's heads turned right, a herd of gazelles sensing danger.

"Ignore them," said the boy to Sophie's left as she folded into herself. I glanced up from picking at my lettuce to see the Sexual Harassment Squad veering in our direction.

But they weren't here for Sophie.

"Daisy," cooed Seth Ross, his pompadour shellacked with gel, Roman nose begging to be re-pummeled. "I've missed you. We were hot together, don't you think? Did you see my *interview*?"

I bit into a cherry tomato. "Yup."

As far as harassment went, this was not impressive.

His friends were more skillful. "I heard you like dick now, is that right?"

"Or just football dick?" said the shortest guy in the crew, pulling on his ear as he tittered.

Leering, Seth picked up the thread. "Something about those sweaty jockstraps . . . do they remind you of—?"

"Oh my God," was all I could say.

Then, to my left came a sudden blur of movement as Sophie picked up the piping hot bowl of soup from a tray opposite her, stood, and tossed it at Seth Ross's crotch.

Her hands flew sweetly to her cheeks. "Oh, goodness. I'm so sorry, clumsy me!"

We all stood in amazement.

"What the *fuck*?" He was doubled over, spurting short-form expletives as his friends kneeled in a cluster, dabbing him with napkins. Realizing how it must look, he started hitting them to get them to stop. It was *incredible*.

Sophie fled. I followed. After a few rounded corners, I found her in the girls' room, perched on the windowsill, wiping her face with balled fists. I thought for a second she was laughing, but then she looked up, cheeks splotchy red and eyes streaming.

"That was so mean," she said, shuddering. "I can't believe how mean I just was!"

"You were defending me." I eased open one of her hands and held it. "*Thank* you. Now you need to start doing that for yourself."

She squeezed, shaking her head. "I can't."

"Why not?" I leaned in, catching and holding her eye. "Think about your anger issues. Wouldn't your mom be proud if she could see—?"

"She would be *horrified*. We're Quakers! We're supposed to be pacifists." She buried her face in her tucked-up knees, her symbol necklace swinging loose.

"Wait, you're a Quaker?" I squinted at her. "I thought you were, like, Wiccan. Or Hindu."

She peeked out, perplexed. "Why?"

"Your necklace," I admitted. "I couldn't figure out what the symbol meant."

Sophie blinked down at it. "*S*? For Sophie?"

"Oh." Now that she mentioned it, the curve did form a recognizable . . . yeah, I was an idiot.

When we left the bathroom, Principal Zimmer was shuffling uncomfortably on the other side of the hallway, hands clasped behind his back.

"Just heard there was an altercation in the cafeteria?"

Sophie's head sank.

Oh no, I realized. *They're gonna call her mom.*

I stepped in front of her. "*I did it.* Lost my temper. He deserved it, but . . . sorry?"

Principal Zimmer sighed. "Come with me."

Behind me, Sophie's eyes widened in shock, then relief. She mouthed "Thank you," and added out loud, "See you later, Daisy, I'm gonna get back to my friends." She spun back. "I mean—"

I forced a wan smile. "It's cool." *I know what you mean.* "See you later."

After shame-marching through the halls to the administrative wing, passing students grinning maliciously to see me getting into trouble—their *fremdschämen* morphing into *schadenfreude*—Principal Zimmer passed me to the starchy vice principal, who at least looked sympathetic as she handed down a one-week suspension, part of the school's "zero tolerance" policy against on-campus violence. I didn't bother to argue.

"Whom should I call?" the vice principal asked, lifting her phone from its cradle. "I need to notify one of your—"

"Dad!" I blurted. "My dad."

I forced my mind into a happy place while she spoke to him, then she motioned to a set of chairs in the hallway where I could wait.

The bell rang for seventh period. Raina walked past, typing on her phone. Then Jack, with Sean, who was demonstrating something with a series of elaborate hand gestures. Then Kyle. He dropped his bag, spilling books onto the carpet, and Sophie ran up to help. I lifted a hand. They didn't see me.

"*Daisy.*" My dad was standing over me, more ashen than I'd ever seen him. He looked like he needed to be quarantined, which he sort of already was. "Let's go. Explain in the car."

"It was Seth Ross," I said as soon as our seat belts were clicked.

Dad's mouth fell open. "The same—?"

"Yep."

He glanced around wildly, his face blotching with anger under his two-day stubble. "Do I need to have words with him myself? Or with his parents?"

I swallowed my grin. "No, Dad, I don't think we need another assault charge tacked on, but I appreciate the gesture."

He settled down and started the car.

"Could we . . . possibly . . . not tell Mom, though?"

His grimace deepened. "This seems like her area more than mine, Daisy. I don't see—"

"I don't want her to get involved," I said. "She would, like, start a petition on school harassment and . . . can we just tell her I'm home sick? Let her off the hook this once?"

"I see what you're saying." Dad glanced sidelong at me. "But she and I are partners, Daisy. I don't like cutting her out."

Really? I thought. *Because I can't remember the last time the three of us were even in the same room together.*

Was that what marriage was? Meet-cute in high school, share your dreams, launch a business, start a family, drift apart until you aren't much more than roommates? If that was the case, maybe it wasn't so sad that I hadn't seen Adam in five days. It wasn't heartbreaking at all. It was *fantastic.*

Watching my expression darken, Dad patted my shoulder and sighed. "All right, Daisy. Just make sure you're convincing."

After I heard Mom's car pull out of the driveway the next morning, I uncurled myself from "stomach virus pose," got out of bed, and stood for a few minutes in front of the bathroom mirror, debating whether to put on clothes, run a brush through my nest of hair, make some effort to feel human. But after a few bleary stares at my reflection, I opted for Plan B: wallow.

Here it was again, that old familiar feeling. Maybe it had always been with me, lurking in the background while I pretended to be happy. Empty house. Silent. Indifferent. I had the nostalgic urge to curl up with my old Giselle Chronicles books, but that would involve climbing into the attic. So instead, safely back in bed, I stared at Zelda as she flounced onto the end of my mattress and silently delivered a smug lecture: Hope: Avoiding It at All Costs.

"You knew this was going to happen," the cat said, blinking slowly. "It was only a matter of time before Hannah realized you weren't worth caring about. You're a psycho and everyone knows it now. Everyone in the entire country—including Adam. You're not gay. You're not asexual. You're not worth a designation. You're just nothing."

A tear rolled down my cheek, as close to a shower as I was going to get today.

"Stop crying," Zelda said, burrowing into the covers with a low purr. "Nobody feels sorry for you. You don't get to feel sorry for yourself. It's boring."

My cat, cruel tormentor though she may have been, had a point. Wallowing was really freaking boring.

So I got out of bed, pulled out my bio textbook, and started to read it, right from Lesson One: Darwin.

Once I'd worked my way through to one chapter past where we were in class, I took a break to check my email. Nobody had written. Then, stupidly, I clicked on the tab next to email—the one that took me to my brand-new Facebook account. Lots of people had written me there! All my new "friends." Saying what a liar I was, that they hoped I would crawl back in the troll hole I'd come from, that they wanted their donations back, that I'd set the gay rights movement back ten years, which seemed like a bit of an overstatement. But I wasn't gay, so I didn't get to decide that. Maybe they were right. Maybe I had just screwed up the lives of millions of people.

I deleted the account and shut down my computer for at least the day, maybe ever, and went back to having a staring contest with the cat. The cat won.

My mom's voice chirped, the stairwell echoing with a name that jolted me awake like a fire alarm.

"Hannah!"

Hannah. Here.

"So nice to see you again—it's been too long. How's the school year going?"

I tried to scramble from bed, but Mom must have come in and tucked me in extra tight while I was unconscious, so I got tangled in the covers and nearly sent the bowl of miso soup she'd put on my nightstand sloshing to the ground. By the time I made it to the stairs, I heard Mom saying, "I'll tell her you stopped by. I know she'd want to see you, but she's resting."

"Oh." Hannah sounded confused.

"Besides, she's probably contagious."

"Nope!" I yelled, taking the stairs two at a time. "I feel one hundred percent better! Thanks Mom, I'll take it from here."

Hannah and Mom both looked fairly stunned to see me careening to the front door in banana-print pajama pants and an oversized Minnie Mouse T-shirt, but at my chipper expression, Mom retreated and Hannah's face did something encouraging. It lifted, not quite a smile, but close.

"I came to give you these," she said, handing me a dauntingly thick packet of printouts from my teachers.

"Thanks?"

"And to see if you might be up for a sleepover this weekend?" Hannah stared at her shoes, as if frightened to see my reaction. Then her eyes darted slyly to mine. "Unless you're too sick?"

"No." I backed up a step and raised my voice. "I think all that *food poisoning* is finally out of my system!"

In the kitchen, I heard Mom mutter, "I knew it! That goddamn school cafeteria . . ."

"She doesn't know?" Hannah mouthed.

I raised my eyebrows. Like she even needed to ask.

Hannah laughed, but the effort seemed to drain her, her happy expression slumping into nothing.

"It hasn't been a week."

"I know." Her eyes were back on her shoes. She shrugged. "Close enough."

This doesn't feel right, I thought—then: *What is the matter with you? She's invited you over! Say yes, say yes!*

"Okay," I said.

"My place tomorrow night, then." She turned away. "It'll be fun."

Her voice was hushed. She was saying it to herself.

Mama Tan greeted me with a Euro-style double-cheek kiss when she answered the door. Then she leaned in to whisper.

"So glad things are getting back to normal."

"Me too," I said, dodging her dangling headscarf and wondering why she felt the need to keep her voice low.

Hannah stuck her head around the corner of the stairwell to wave me upstairs. As I shouldered my overnight bag, Tan winked and pointed, like we were Navy SEALs and this was our go signal.

Then I stepped into Hannah's room, and everything got even weirder. It was all laid out. Popcorn in a large bowl. TV paused on the first seconds of what looked like the season premiere of *Triplecross*. UNO cards stacked beside a Scrabble box. Hannah already dressed in neatly pressed polka dot pajamas.

She jumped cross-legged onto the end of her bed. "I've got the whole season—I don't know if you've kept up, but I am *way* behind—or we could rent a movie. Or both, like interspersed. Three episodes, movie, something like that? And I thought we'd order pizza, but I can probably coerce Mom into hitting up a kitchen for us, if you'd rather have something gourmet."

"Pizza's awesome." I pulled a container of peanut M&M'S from my overnight bag. "I brought some candy to mix—"

"With the popcorn?" Hannah grabbed the popcorn bowl and shoved it under my face. "Already did it! Totally prepared."

"Um. Great!" I turned to put away the candy, trying to pinpoint the source of my uneasiness. These things—the movies, the candy, the meal, even the pajamas, were supposed to unfold naturally. You talk about food when you get hungry. Talk about a TV marathon when you get bored of talking about other things. You don't line it up in advance.

But that wasn't the only thing bothering me. So far tonight, I could detect only the faintest impression of Hannah-weirdness amidst all the weird-weird vibes she was throwing my way. She wasn't even making eye contact.

Maybe because we'd fought. We hadn't actually made up

yet, either. We'd just stopped communicating and abruptly started again, skirting the far edges of things. I wasn't lolling on her rug like I should have been, burying my face in a pillow, saying, *Oh lordy Han, there's this boy who wants nothing to do with me now and I really miss him and I feel like a total idiot about it.* And she hadn't mentioned her ex at all. Not one word.

"Hey," I said, kicking my shoes off and crawling onto the bed. "I think we should probably talk about things."

Hannah's face went pale, but I pressed on, starting with the easiest apology.

"Look, I'm sorry about QB kissing me. I know that probably came as a shock, but I swear, we weren't dating and we still aren't. Never will be. I mean, he's a surprisingly nice guy, and ridiculously hot in a textbook-standard kind of way, but— pretty much a different species. It would be ludicrous for us to mate."

Hannah pivoted on one knee, her forehead scrunched. "It wasn't about QB. I mean, that was a capper, but it's not what I'm upset about."

I tucked my knees up and held them. "The speech."

She stared past me. "I never thought you would take it that far."

"It did get out of hand," I admitted, and hoped she could read the further apology in my eyes. That I'd lied. That I'd implied she was my girlfriend. That her real girlfriend broke up with her right afterward. But she was still looking away, so I added, tentatively, "Natalie seemed pretty upset too. Was it because of—"

Hannah's eyes flash-flooded. "Let's not talk about Natalie."

"Oh."

"Let's not talk about any of this, okay?" She forced a smile. "Let's just watch TV."

"Okay." I smiled. "Distraction it is."

A half hour into the season premiere of *Triplecross*, I started to twitch, ready to crawl out of my skin, or at least this room. Bad enough that I was watching this asinine show, stewing at the missed opportunity to meet the cast at homecoming, but Hannah was way too into this episode, narrating the whole thing like a ten-year-old on a sugar rush.

"What do you think of the new guy?" Hannah asked, leaning over my knee to pick an M&M out of the popcorn bowl. "I think he's a solid runner-up for hottest."

I stared at her. She ignored me.

"He's got kind of a dirty Prince Eric thing going on," she said. "Like, yeah, definitely a prince, but maybe the kind of prince who's legit and lived on a boat and knows all the sailor jargon and smells kind of briny but not too briny. I'd go for that."

"You'd *go* for that?"

Her smile drew in. She shrugged.

"Are you bi, Hannah?" I shook my head. "I didn't—"

"No." She turned to fluff a pillow. "I'm not . . ." She sighed. "I'm not bi. I'm just playing Hottest Guy on *Triplecross*."

"We can change it to hottest girl. Hottest person."

"Not as fun." Her face kept falling, a melting mask, until she grabbed the remote to pause the show. "I'm gonna check on the pizza order. Shouldn't it be here?"

She tried to scoot past me on her way to the door. I grabbed her hand.

"Hey. Stop."

She stared at me, eyes pleading.

"Take a breath," I ordered. "Pizza can wait. Hannah. We *have* to talk about what's going on with you."

"With me?" She let out a breathy laugh.

"You are not being yourself right now."

"Which 'myself,' Daisy?" She kept smiling. "Real me? Lesbian me?"

"Whoa, I . . ." I kept my grip on her hand. "Either one. What's the matter?"

Her arm went limp. She squinted at me, incredulous.

"The *matter*. Okay, let's see. Well . . . huh. Everything is fucked! Basically. My life is a freak show. Nationally televised. My mom asked me last night if Columbia was a '*lesbian* school.' Everybody at Palmetto looks at me like I'm a dog show contestant when I walk down the hall, and the one person who ever really knew me just completely crushed—"

She bit back the end of her sentence. A hard lump in my throat told me that she wasn't talking about me.

Hannah swatted at her streaming eyes. "I don't want to think about her, I don't want to talk about her, I just want everything to go back to normal. It wasn't supposed to get so messy. I just wanted it to stay the same. *Why* is that so . . ."

She huffed, shook her head, slumping against the edge of the wall. My breath caught. Hannah looked like Sean, like everything at once—swept away, jittery, poetic, and so, so very sad. She was in love. It was killing her.

"She's not that person," I said.

Hannah shook her head. "What?"

"The one who really knows you. I mean . . ." I leaned in. "Okay, yeah, maybe she is lately. But *we* used to be that close. Didn't we?"

Sudden sympathy shone in Hannah's eyes. "Daisy, you don't understand. It's different."

She brightened faintly, put her hand on my shoulder, and started saying, "You will understand one day, it just hasn't happened for you," but an idea had sprung into my mind. More a hope than an urge, but enough to make me bridge the distance, take her face in my palms . . .

And kiss her. Not an air-peck, like friends—something real. Our lips pressed together, noses grazing, as close as we could be.

I didn't feel *anything.* No spark. No answer. Just Hannah stiffening, then shoving my shoulders hard with her fists.

She staggered to the doorway, her face bloodred. I held on to my cheeks, waiting. When she finally spoke, it was with a whisper.

"Why would you do that?"

"I thought . . ." My own voice was hardly coming out. "It might be worth a try."

"And then what? We'd skip off into the sunset, because if *you* were gay, my life would be perfect."

Her voice was sharp enough to cut.

"Maybe." I attempted a smile, assembled from the scraps of all the other smiles I'd faked. "Would that be so bad?"

Watching me, her fury seemed to evaporate—leaving

something much more unsettling. Blankness. Politeness. A wall with no doors.

"Everything will always be all about you. You can't see past yourself. I do think you try, but . . . you just can't."

"Because of my privilege?" I asked quietly.

Hannah huffed, turning away. "I don't know what that means. We don't even speak the same language anymore."

Just as I was opening my mouth to tell her that I wasn't fully clear on the concept of privilege either, she picked up my overnight bag and handed it to me.

"You should go." She shouted over my shoulder, "Mom? Hannah's not feeling well, do you mind driving her home?"

"I'm sorry," I said. "Okay, I'm sorry!"

But I was already talking to the other side of Hannah's literal door. As Tan jingled her car keys, I touched my hand to the doorknob, then, hearing the sound of soft sobs beyond the wood, cradled my bag and plodded downstairs.

I took one last look at Hannah's house as we drove away, her lit bedroom window, the lanterns lining the front walk—committing it to memory, just in case.

29

Mama Tan was in a chatty mood.

"I'm sorry you weren't feeling well. I think Hannah really needed this, now that *Natalie* is out of the picture." Tan smirked, shaking her head, her long earrings jangling with the movement. "Glad she got that out of her system."

I turned to her slowly, chilled by her phrasing. "Got Natalie out of her system? Or being gay?"

Tan raised her eyebrows, indicating the latter.

"Because I don't think that last part is going anywhere."

She smiled sagely. "We'll see."

Was this why Hannah was playing straight? Why our evening plans looked like a wax museum version of the fun we used to have?

"You want her to be straight," I said.

Tan let out a song of a sigh and switched lanes. "I just want her to be happy."

"Then let me ask you something." I shifted to face her. "Do you really think she's happy right now? Without Natalie?"

Hannah's mother's face fell. For a split second, she looked her age.

"Because she seems *shattered* to me," I went on. "And you

know what? I've never seen her happier than when she was with Natalie. Being gay. Being okay with it."

As the words shot out of my mouth, the truth of them ricocheted against the windshield and struck me in the gut. She *was* happy with Natalie. Sleepless, nervous, neurotic, conflicted, and more herself than I'd ever seen her.

Tan pulled into my driveway, parked the car, and stared ahead.

"I'm trying to understand my daughter," she finally said, her voice plain, scrubbed of charm. "And I'm having a hard time lately."

She leaned against the steering wheel, a perfect zigzag of black hair falling over her face. Underneath, her smile was flickering, fluttering, dead. This might have been the first real conversation I'd ever had with Tan. Which meant that, at this moment, she was the closest thing I had to a friend.

"You're not the only one having a hard time," I admitted as I opened the car door and stepped out. "Maybe you don't have to understand her, you know? You just have to love her."

I shrugged. She nodded faintly, pulled the passenger door closed, and drove away.

Mom let out a startled shout when I ran into her in the kitchen. "What are you doing here? Where's—?"

"I'm still sick." I shut the fridge, realizing I didn't have much of an appetite. "It must be stomach flu after all."

Mom's eyes narrowed. Softened. "Did you two have a fight?"

"No," I groaned.

"Was it about Adam?" Her eyebrows lifted.

"*No,* Mom. What is the matter with you?"

She laughed, waving her hand in the air as she opened the pantry.

"Seriously, though," I huffed. "*Why* is my personal life so important to you?"

"Because I'm your mother!"

Her tone froze me. She clutched a can of soup with both hands and slumped against the pantry shelf.

"Because I am a member of this family, and I do *not* deserve to be teased. I do *not* deserve to be shut out. I am . . . *sick* of it!"

She shoved the can back. It slid and stopped.

From the ceiling came the sound of swords clashing, an ogre dying, a fake life lived behind a door that was always closed.

Her shoulders shook. I took three quiet steps and touched her ponytail, but she flinched away.

"Okay," I said, dropping my hand. "Okay. I'm straight, all right? I agreed to lie and say I was gay to help the homecoming cause, but it backfired. I'm not dating QB. I had a big crush on Don't Know Him From Adam, but he was just a friend, and he's not even that anymore."

She wiped her face and slowly turned.

"Hannah was dating Natalie Beck, but that's done too, and I feel like it's probably my fault. We *are* fighting. No, worse, we're done fighting. We're done in general, I think."

Mom took my hand.

"And I'm sorry I'm so self-absorbed. Everyone's been telling me I am, not just you, so it must be true."

"Oh, honey, that is not what I meant at all—"

"And I got kicked out of the Alliance and I've been suspended for a week for assaulting Seth Ross."

Mom's face went blank. She let go and wiped her hands on her jeans.

"Upstairs," she ordered. "I'll bring you some soup."

Before the organic gluten-free noodles were simmering on the stove, I was past needing them. I'd already sunk into a dense, dark sleep, dreaming of me, me, everywhere me, a homecoming where I was the queen and the king and the football team. A nightmarish world full of Daisy and no one else.

"You're so close, Daisy. Left, left, left! Get him with the lightning!"

The gamer chair ricocheted with the full-body effort it took me to push a couple of buttons in the right sequence, until at long last, the acid-drooling sub-dragon was dead at my sandaled feet.

Dad beamed. "You're getting good at this."

I nearly managed a smile at the compliment. I was now a level-seventeen *Everwander* elfin rogue with storm-calling mastery, well on my way to helping Player One restore order to the Kingdom of Xanthe. In my father's world, this was something to be very proud of.

"I want to hear what you think when we're done," Dad muttered, typing a note on his tablet. "Something's not working with the game arc."

"Seems fine so far," I said, buying healing potion from a

gnome in a pumpkin cart. *More than fine.* This game was cathartic. When I'd given it a half-hearted try on Sunday afternoon, I didn't expect how good it would feel to upgrade weapons and accessorize armor, to climb and slice and demolish
all in my path. I'd played games before, of course, here and
there, when Dad wasn't hogging every console in the house.
I'd never gotten addicted. But now, for the first time, I began
to understand why Dad was so loath to leave this room, this
portal into a world in which anything was possible if you just
obsessed over runes enough.

"You can level up," Dad pointed out, slurping from the coffee Mom had brought him on her way to yet another farm
group meeting.

"Should I boost my strength or my defenses?" I asked.

"Go for strength. If you're strong, you don't need as many
defenses."

"Got it."

"Choose carefully, though. This might be your last level up."

"Oh." I frowned. "Are we close to the end?"

"Yep, the *big battle* is right around the corner." He did a
butt-dance in his gamer chair, morphing into a little brother
in his excitement.

Meanwhile, I felt myself hollowing.

What would I do when this game was done? Return to my
minute-by-minute cataloguing of everything happening at
Palmetto in my absence? Continue this weekend's medita-
tion on how life marches on, indifferent and fickle, and how I
should become a Buddhist and practice detachment, and how
making my house into a weeklong hermitage was really a very

good starting point on my path to enlightenment? Except I wasn't detached. Not remotely enlightened. I was tormented.

At school right now they were celebrating Spirit Week. Today, they were probably announcing the official danceless-homecoming court. I wondered if QB would be king this year, or whether his odds were lessened without the school's princess by his side. Madison would probably be queen, just as a big old screw-you to everything we were doing across the street.

Speaking of which, the volunteers must have started to gather. The vacant field was probably a lot less vacant already—early arrivals from the East and West football teams starting to practice, helpers hoisting bleachers, tents, stands. That was the plan we had, anyway. Hopefully it was still going forward. The press might even be there already to document it. Maybe Adam too, his curling black hair waving in the breeze, his glasses slipping so maddeningly often that I just wanted to shimmy them off his face and . . . *Stop that thought right there. He hates you, remember? Along with most of the country.*

Had the protests died down or picked up? Were the counter-protesters still out in force, even after what happened at the rally? I could google it, but that would mean turning on my computer, and I'd already established that only bad things could come of that. I hadn't even turned my phone on since Saturday night. I was doing the hermit thing. It was going to be awesome.

At some point the awesome was bound to click in. Any minute now.

Besides, I had a war to win for the citizens of Xanthe.

But five more minutes into game play, just as we were grimly mounting the curving steps to the Dark Castle, moments from challenging the Primordial Beast-King, my controller rattled—and the action changed to a cut scene. I blinked in confusion.

On the screen, Dad's character, a level-eighteen warrior goblin, turned to me, laid a knobby arm on my lithe green shoulder, and started to speechify.

"We've come so far together, friend. Without you, I surely would have perished long ago. Not to mention . . ." The view widened to include the other characters he was naming, including a buxom priestess healer and a talking toadstool who made fart noises for comic effect. Then Dad's character filled the entire screen, blocking the rest of us out. "But from here to the castle, I travel alone. It is . . . my destiny."

"*Excuse* me?" I gawked at the screen, my controller dangling dead in my lap.

Dad couldn't decide whether to look at me or the game, where my character had suddenly been reduced to one member of a crowd waving from the dusty distance at Player One as he scaled the battlement and began to fight alone.

"*This is bullshit!*"

Dad paused the game and whirled around. "How so?" He cleared his throat. "Also, *language,* young lady."

"'Bullshit' is the right word for what this is," I protested. "This game sucks and I cannot believe I wasted all this time playing it."

Dad pointed to the TV with his controller. "This is what

I mean about the arc collapsing, but I can't pinpoint why."

"I can," I said, standing from the chair to better glare at the screen. "Why is this a multiplayer game? What is the point of spending all that time playing as part of a team, leveling up, throwing in with the other characters if you're just gonna get ditched? Tell me. Seriously. I want to know."

"Well . . ." Dad's brow crinkled like a paper bag puppet. "I mean, the opening scene establishes the story. Player One is destined to topple—"

"Who cares what he's destined to do? Maybe he's destined to do it with a bunch of other people. Maybe, now that he's reached the castle, he should think twice about ditching everyone who's come with him. They care just as much about the kingdom as he does! If it's gonna be him against the world, and that's the game, that's fine, but then why bring along all these other characters? It's stupid! I hate this game."

Dad's voice grew hushed. "Are you crying?"

I swiped at my face. "No."

But I was. And I wasn't sure why. I probably just needed to leave this room and see sunshine.

"You're right, you know." Dad shook his head as if dumbfounded, a smile beginning to bloom. "You're right! I've been coming back to this game for weeks and couldn't pick out the problem, but that's it. Someone else needs to be the hero."

My hand hesitated by the doorknob, his words reverberating up my spine.

"What if he's not the chosen one after all? He thinks he's important, but in the end it's another character. *Wait.*" Dad stood up from his chair on shaky legs and began to pace, pointing at me repeatedly. "This might be a big idea. Too big for this game. This might be . . ."

He crouched, holding my shoulders. I held my breath, waiting for the life-changing epiphany to come.

"A *new* game. Multiplayer. You're not just a team, you're *competitors*. Depending on the game-play, anyone could become Player One. You could integrate it into an online RPG format."

"Yeah!" I shouted, giving him a high five, no idea what he was talking about. His face was glowing like a billboard. He seemed ten years younger, like someone who exercised, who traveled, who got things done.

"Daisy . . . thank you," he said. "I owe you. Big-time. Name your price."

He waggled his eyebrows, joking, but I had an idea.

"Come down for dinner tonight. And tell Mom your game idea. I'm sure she'd love to hear it."

"Sure," he said, running a hand through his overgrown hair, then staring at it as if surprised he had appendages.

"Tomorrow night too," I tacked on.

Dad rocked back on his heels, eyeing me curiously. "I eat dinner with you guys already."

I raised my eyebrows.

"Unless I'm in the middle of . . ." He gestured to the paused screen, then sank. "It's not a big deal, though, is it? We're a *different* kind of family. Your mom's got her projects, you've got school . . . that's how we've always been. We all do our own thing."

"We do," I agreed. "But could we maybe take a break from our own thing? Just to see how we like it?"

As Dad stared at me, I felt like I could see the sun coming up behind his eyes. Then he blinked and extended his hand. "Deal."

I shook it and turned to go. "Plus ten percent of the revenues of any new company you form. See ya!"

"A new company?" Mom put Dad's dinner in front of him, then leaned on the table like she was dizzy. "But your non-compete—"

"Expired last year," Dad said, shoveling yams into his mouth with gusto. "I mean, I could sell this idea back to Bot-Co, or . . ."

"You could start fresh." Mom sat slowly. "I . . . *like* it."

Dad leaned back. "You do?"

"It's a no-brainer. You've stayed current, you're still a name in the industry, and with this idea . . ."

They started talking details, reminiscing about their high school startup days, their voices flying out of them, crackling with excitement—then lapsing into intermittent pauses, like they were conversationally rusty. Because they *were*.

"You wanna run out to the Chamber of Commerce?" Dad blurted. "Grab me a 'So You Want to Start a Business' pamphlet?" He winked at Mom across the table.

She snorted. "Oh Lord, I was so nervous."

"You bought a suit."

"A business suit! At Target, but still."

Dad grinned.

"I swore they were going to . . ." She buried her head, cringing at the memory. "Throw me out onto the sidewalk! And

329

then they just handed me the pamphlet. Didn't even ask how old I was. What a let down."

Dad reached for Mom's hand.

"Well," Mom said, and then just held on as she stared at him and he stared at her and I stared *anywhere* else.

I'd always worried that they'd known each other too long, that over the years their relationship shorthand had gotten more and more abbreviated until it became nothing at all. But at the moment, their silence was a lot more than nothing. It was full. Words, emotions, memories were flying across the table. I just couldn't hear them.

Even after they broke the silence, brainstorming next steps, chatting about a farming game app Mom wanted to make, I might as well have been sitting in a room by myself. It was disappointing in a petty way, but worth it for the way Mom's feet were tapping under the table.

Then I noticed her legs going still and my name coming out of her mouth.

"You need to check in with your friends, sweetheart," she said. "Councilman Franklin told me there's rumblings in the City Council about pulling the homecoming permit. They say the number of people planning to show up presents a fire hazard."

"But we're—*they're*—not doing a bonfire." I picked a speck of yam off my pajama pants, willing my heartbeat to return to a normal pace.

Mom shrugged. "These people just won't stop. They're clutching at straws."

I shrugged back. "I'm sure the Alliance will figure it out."

But at one a.m., I was still awake, mulling the scenarios that could be playing out in my absence. We could have lost the *Triplecross* cast. Or gained the entire NFL roster for our football game. Mole people could have risen from the ground and decimated our tents.

Maddened by not knowing and emboldened by my dad's return from the walking dead, I decided to take a risk. I clicked my phone back to life.

"*Two. New. Messages,*" robot voice said. My mind spun with contrasting hopes—Hannah, Adam, Raina, asking for help . . .

Raina. Right. I rolled my eyes at myself. *She despises—*

"Yeah. Daisy. It's Ray."

I dropped the phone. Scrambled to pick it up.

". . . did for Sophie. I was impressed. I have to admit, you really came through for her and it made me think . . ." She sighed. Practically growled. "Maybe I've been a little harsh on you. Possibly." She cleared her throat. "Sophie wound up telling her mom, by the way, like as soon as she got home. The girl thinks she's got anger avoidance issues, but what she really can't handle is guilt. She's *allergic* to it. She's been dabbing her damn eyes all week about your suspension too, so you might want to give her a call and tell her you're fine. I mean, I'm *assuming* you're fine, but if you're not, definitely call her. Or me." She cleared her throat again, so loud I had to move the phone away from my ear. "Anyway. Hope you're doing all right. Yeah, okay, bye."

Was that . . . an apology? From *Raina Moore*? My mouth was slowly forming the word "wow" when I realized she hadn't mentioned anything about homecoming. But why would she?

Homecoming was Alliance business—and despite the oddly conciliatory tone of her message, that door was clearly still shut to me. I was sinking straight back into glumdom when the robot voice said, *"Next. Message,"* and my heart skipped.

Adam? Hannah? I couldn't decide which of their voices I was most hoping to hear.

It was Mr. Murphy at the rec center.

"Just thought I'd try you one more time," he said, his voice more wooden than usual. "But I get the picture. You're busy. I liked your idea for that mural, though, kiddo, so maybe we'll have somebody else come finish it for you. Thanks anyway."

I gripped the phone, the world dropping away from me, pixel by pixel.

He'd given up too.

"No," I said. *"No."*

The night was dark, the house creaking quietly, the streets outside thick with silence as, for the first time in four days, I took off my pajamas and put on real clothes.

It was time to finish that mural.

30

In the far corner of the garage, behind Dad's rusting collection of bicycles, among my old ghost-hunting gear, my metal detector and coin sorting kit, the telescope I'd never figured out how to focus, and my loom, a whole shelf was filled with materials I'd bought to create the rec center's grand mural. Six buckets in different shades of blue, a gold paint that really sparkled, black for edges, red just in case. Brushes in a variety of sizes, for detail work after the broad strokes were finished.

But the broad strokes never got finished. Because after two days of painting, I'd panicked and stopped showing up.

The mural, I thought, tiptoeing past the Veggiemobile. Then I stopped, stuck to the spot for a second. *Hannah was right.*

Fumbling along the magnetized tool wall, I found a flashlight—the wraparound one Mom used when she was trying to get possums out from the bottom of our house. Once it was fastened on my own clammy forehead, I trained it at the mural shelf and picked out a single can of cerulean teal.

When Mr. Murphy woke up this morning, at long last, he'd have an answer to his voicemails. He might not see a completed mural, but at least he'd see an ocean covering that wall, and he'd feel pride for today's teenagers, hope for the next generation, and a renewed passion for his work that would in turn inspire each and every child who came to the rec center, many of whom would grow up to become Fortune 500 CEOs, international peacekeepers, and Academy Award–winning directors.

It was a five-minute drive from my house to the rec center, but hiking there took longer than I'd expected, and with fewer sidewalks than I would have liked. Since it was two a.m., only a couple of cars passed me along the highway, but, realizing I'd dressed in dark, incognito colors, I had to duck into the tree line to avoid them when they raced past. I put mental blinders on, like one of those poor carriage horses on Broad Street, until, at last, I saw the turn-in to the rec center parking lot.

The property was locked. I wasn't dissuaded. Cradling the can in the crook of my arm, the paintbrush sticking out of my back pocket, I scaled the low wire fence and hopped onto the asphalt, flush with the thrill of having overcome an actual, physical obstacle. It was just like the game—collect tools, hike, cut-scene, *action*!

When I got to the wall, I turned on my headlight. And there he was, swimming along the bottom right corner. My Moby Dick. The whale that had defeated me.

I'd painted him from a picture in a book. He wasn't half-bad, blue pleats, blowholes a-blowin', the whole deal. Unfortunately, after the seven hours it took me to create him, I'd stared at the wall, glowing with satisfaction—and in one chilling second, realized what I'd done wrong. One: I filled up a quarter of the wall with *a whale*. It was meant to be a fun detail, not a centerpiece. I'd made the thing monstrous! This was not what I'd promised. Two: I should have painted the background first, everything else after. Painting 101, right?

I mean, I assumed it was. I'd only taken Studio Art 1 at Palmetto, where my pieces had never once earned a spot on the "Honor Wall."

I began to slump with the renewed realization of my own inadequacy, but when my paint can hit the ground, I balled my fist around the brush, pried open the lid, and faced down the wall. Then came the painting—broad, joyous strokes, my ocean obscuring the whale, drowning him so the mural could be born anew.

This would be a masterpiece if it killed me.

Just as I was dipping into the paint can for the fifth time, wishing I'd brought a bigger light than this little dinky headband bulb, a huge white beam appeared on the far side of the wall and glided in my direction.

I reeled for a second, amazed at having gotten exactly what I'd wished for. A light! From nowhere!

Then I realized what it was.

"Hands where I can see them!"

I turned slowly around and raised my paintbrush above my head. Blue trickled down my arm.

"Drop your—!" The two night shift cops looked confused as they approached, hands on the hilts of their guns. I dropped my paintbrush like a hot poker. It landed on my head. Before I could wipe my forehead clean, my arm was yanked behind my back, cold metal circling my wrists.

"You're under arrest," the older and fatter of the two cops said, his Southern drawl dragging out each syllable of my Miranda Rights. The other cop was chuckling into his radio.

This couldn't be happening. "I'm not trespassing, I'm volunteering!"

In the back of the police car, I closed my eyes and listened to the chatter of the police radio. Apparently there was a 577 in progress and backup was on its way. For some reason, that struck me as hilarious, and once I started laughing, the fact that I had just gotten arrested while wearing a headband light got me snorting so hard, tears escaping from the corners of my eyes as if they were fleeing my body in terror, that the cops started to look scared too.

It was surprisingly awesome. I mean, if you're gonna get arrested, you want at least to have made an impression.

"We'd better run a drug test," one muttered to the other, which sent me into another giggle-fit that had me clutching my stomach to keep it from seizing up.

When we got to the police station, the cops kept me in the car for a few minutes while they did paperwork, or drank coffee, or whatever cops do right after an arrest. When they came back, I expected them to haul me into a cell where I would meet a hooker with a heart of gold and a brawler sleeping off his aggression. Instead, they took me straight to one of the glass-walled offices and seated me at an empty desk.

Was my crime really so bad that they wanted to interrogate me before locking me up? Or was this the way they handled convicts under eighteen? I wondered idly if I should have asked for a phone call, but then I remembered seven-year-old

Natalie telling me that the "one phone call" thing was a myth.

Natalie. I wonder what she'd say if she could see me now. She'd probably pat herself on the back for her good judgment in dropping me while she had the chance.

It took me the span of all of those thoughts to register the faces on the framed family photos strewn about this office. Groomed hair, smug smiles everywhere the eye could see. Natalie Beck. Cindy Beck.

My eyes landed on the nameplate on the desk: Chief Walter Beck.

The door opened, and the man himself lumbered in. His six-foot frame seemed to fill the whole doorway, but he deflated as soon as he walked through it. This must have been the end of his shift. Did police chiefs even have shifts? Oh God, did he show up just to deal with me?

He sat wearily on his side of the desk, laced his fingers, and leaned forward like he was warming them over a fire.

A sudden memory arose, so vague I wondered if it was just my imagination: Mr. Beck lighting a fire on the beach and me and Natalie handing him hot dogs to roast.

"Daisy," he said, his voice dry and weary. "What were you thinking?"

I've been hearing that a lot lately, I thought, but blurted, "I had an idea for the mural at the rec center, so I wanted to get a jump on it. You can ask Mr. Murphy. He'll tell you—"

"I did ask and he did tell me," Chief Beck said. "He's not pressing charges, but he wants to set up a firm schedule so that you'll get this durn mural done for him. Can you do that, Daisy?"

"*Yes*," I said, exhaling. "A schedule would be great. I think that's just what we need."

A small smile escaped Chief Beck, the kind that started in his eyes and spread slowly across his face. I liked him back then, didn't I? I remembered that now.

"You were always impulsive, weren't you, Daisy?" Chief Beck said, as if remembering the same thing. "Even when you were little, you'd get an idea in your head and you and Natalie would be off like a shot."

"Sometimes they were her ideas."

"That's what made you such good friends," he said. He looked as sad as I felt, and I couldn't understand why—until he told me I was free to go, then stopped me at the door.

"Nat's not doin' real well, Daisy."

I turned to peer up at him.

"I don't know what to do for her. But . . ." He shook his head. "If you'd look in on her, I think it would help. She could really use somebody to talk to."

I barely saw the rest of the police station as I walked out.

Had Natalie Beck's father seriously just asked *me*, a girl his daughter had hated for the past seven years, to reach out to her? He hadn't mentioned the homecoming campaign or his wife's role in opposing it. He'd just asked for help.

Things had to be even worse than I'd thought.

I pried my blue-shellacked hair away from my face. *Of course* things were bad for Natalie. She'd discovered she was gay, but been unable to talk to her parents about it. Her mother fought her at every turn, speaking out against gay rights in front of the whole country. Even after I'd outed her. On national television.

I'd always seen Natalie as perfectly in control. The one who held all the power—to hurt, to destroy friendships, to steel herself against everyone who stood in her way. But this was more than she could handle.

It was something I couldn't understand.

When I got outside, the cool air hit me like a shock. The parking lot was nearly empty. It was the middle of the night, and I had no idea where I was. I scrolled through my cell-phone, searching for rescuers, as a police car pulled up and two cops escorted a wriggling, cursing, spitting man out of the back and into the station. My eyes darted back to my phone.

Mom was out of the question. If I got home in the next few hours, neither she nor Dad would have any idea I was even gone, and really, it would be selfish to worry them unnec-essarily. I wasn't even arrested, exactly. Just questioned and released and asked to look in on the police chief's daughter if I had any free time in the next few days.

I couldn't bring myself to call Hannah. She probably wouldn't pick up when she saw the call, anyway. So, that left . . . who exactly? One of my old Alliance compatriots? They already thought I was a powder keg. Better to leave them with the memory of me as the friend who bravely took the fall for Sophie than the ex-ally who dragged them out of bed on a school night to rescue her from lockup.

Just as I was trying to figure out how to convince a taxi

to take me home without having any method of payment on hand, I noticed a missed call from Adam, from about an hour ago. My maniacal laughter in the police car must have drowned out the ringing.

"Hey Daisy," said his voicemail. I imagined I could hear the clink of ceramic coffee mug against a diner table as Adam drew a breath. "I just wanted to say—I overreacted. And . . . I think I'm partly to blame for how everything turned out with homecoming. Mostly to blame, maybe. And I'm sorry. And I'm sorry it took me so long to apologize. *And* I'm sorry I'm calling you in the middle of the night, so hopefully your ringer is off. Call me back if you want to talk. Off the record." He laughed nervously. "Okay bye."

Adam was awake. And he wasn't mad. I moved to the far edge of the station, plopped myself down on a bench, and called him back.

He sounded out of breath when he answered. "Hello?"

"Apology accepted."

There was a pause. I held my breath.

"Did my call wake you up?" he asked. "I should have waited until the morning—"

"I've been up. I'm sorry too, by the way."

"For what?" he asked quietly. "Honestly, Daisy, you haven't done anything wrong. If I made you feel—"

"No." I slumped against the bench, processing that. He was right. I mean, I'd done *plenty* wrong—lied to the country, appropriated someone else's cause to further my own, driven a wedge between my best friend and her first love . . . but as far as Adam was concerned, my conscience was pretty damn clear. "I guess I'm just sorry in a general sense."

"You wanna talk about it?"

"I was actually going to ask if you felt like hanging out for a bit?"

"Right now?"

"Yeah."

Probably wishful thinking, but I swore I could hear him smiling. "It's the middle of the night."

"And we're both awake."

"Interesting point. Are your parents okay with this?"

I made a "Pshhh" sound, and he seemed to accept it.

"You need me to pick you up?"

"Perfect. I'm at the Fourteenth District Police Station."

There was a very long pause, and then he said, "Daisy?"

"See you soon!"

31

After hearing the series of events that had led me to police headquarters at four a.m. on a Wednesday Adam wanted to see the mural.

"Right now," he ordered from the driver's seat. "Which way? Direct me."

Daylight was starting to creep up, a sickly early-morning glow from the fog off the rivers and marshes. I was curious to see it for myself, now that the mania had cleared and I could get a good glimpse at what I'd actually managed to do.

It wasn't until we pulled into the lot that I realized I'd been wearing my headlamp this whole time. Both Chief Beck and Adam had been too gentlemanly to point it out. I whipped it off, mussing my blue-crusted hair so that it hung over the indentation in my forehead.

"There." I nodded at the wall. "My masterpiece."

We sat staring at a largely blank cement block wall, where on one side, what used to sort of be a whale was now half-covered in messy strokes of blue paint. The can was still there, but had gotten overturned. I'd have to clean up the sidewalk now too.

"I can see it," Adam said, and I shot him a dubious look. He laughed, squinted. "I mean, it takes some concentration, but yeah. The sky, with a blimp. And there at the bottom, that's the land, right? It'll take some work, but it'll be great."

My groan turned into a laugh. "It's Atlantis."

He frowned. "I'm sorry?"

"The whale is too distracting, I'm taking it out, but the outline you can see there around the edge—it's all going to be the Lost Continent of Atlantis."

"Wow." Adam rested an arm on the steering wheel. "The Lost Continent of Atlantis. Like . . . the whole thing? An entire mythical continent? In one mural?"

I shrugged. "A panorama. A sweeping view, angled so you can see the destruction, the coral growing where buildings once stood. The breaching whale was meant to create a sense of perspective from the top of the ocean to the bottom, so the continent feels just out of reach, glimmering under the surface. And . . . yeah."

"Jesus," Adam said, blinking dizzily. "Atlantis. Not an abstract mural, not a picture of kids holding hands . . . a mythical continent. You plan *big*, don't you?"

"Gargantuan," I said, feeling the opposite of gargantuan as I stared at the mess of paint marring the rec center wall.

"Why don't you . . . ?" He winced like he knew I wouldn't like what he was going to say. "Change it to something easier?"

I was too tired to feel offended. "Hannah suggested the same thing."

He raised his eyebrows and I shook my head.

"It isn't my vision. I didn't want to paint *any* mural. I wanted to paint *this* mural. There was a little kid here who loved Atlantis more than anything and . . . I wanted to make it happen. Make it real. I wanted to make the most incredible mural he'd ever seen." I rubbed my eyes. "The funny thing is, I don't even remember the kid's name."

Adam was watching me.

"You think I sound arrogant, don't you?" I glanced away. "It's okay, I can take it."

"No." He pushed his glasses up, considering. "Not arrogant. More . . . self-defeating. Why does it have to be perfect? Nothing's perfect, Daisy. Not even Atlantis." He grinned. "*Especially* not Atlantis. That place used to be cool, I guess, but it's a total dump these days."

I laughed, leaning against the window, sifting through his words. *Self-defeating. Huh.*

"Seriously, Daisy, name me one perfect thing."

Catching his eye, I thought of an answer right away—and blushed like a lunatic. Then I turned away with a smirk. "The mozzarella sticks at the Moonlight Coffee Shop. Crisp. Golden . . ."

"Aha," he said, pointing at me. "But the coffee is an abomination. This is my point. There's always going to be *something* crappy you have to navigate to find your way to something amazing."

"Crappy," I repeated, staring at the wall. "Well, I've got that step covered." Then, with my next blink, the wall transformed.

I felt for the door handle. "The thing is—I really *can* see it."

Adam followed as I got out of the car.

"There's the temple to the gods," I said, pointing through the fence to a brick on the bottom left of the wall. "And there's the grand corridor that all the tall ships used to pass through on their way to the center of the island. And there, that's the toppled statue of Poseidon, being pulled back up by mermaids."

I blinked and it was gone. Just a collection of smears.

"It sounds beautiful," Adam said.

"There's just one problem." I pointed to myself with my thumb.

He opened his mouth. I cut him off.

"Raina was right. I'm unqualified."

"For what?"

"Everything. I can't paint. I can't compose music . . ."

"I beg to differ."

". . . I can't speak to gay issues, because I'm not gay. I'm not anything."

"You spoke to them well, I thought," Adam said. "Considering."

"They're way better off without me."

Adam's eyes drifted to the wall. "I'm not so sure about that. Have you been watching the news?"

"I peeked at CNN yesterday. They had a ticker that said 'Daisy's Gay Hoax,' so I turned it off."

"I would have too. Honestly, watching how you've been treated over the past few days has really soured me on journalism. Nobody seems at all interested in getting your side of the story. All they want to report on is that Beck woman and her quest to shut it down."

I shook my head, reality seeping in. "How, though? The 'fire risk' thing? That seems so flimsy."

"They're saying if the event has more than twelve hundred guests, they're shutting it down."

"Twelve hundred?" There were more than thirteen hundred students at Palmetto alone. And this wasn't just for them anymore. It was for *America.*

"The worst part is, the news is reporting it like it's a good thing," Adam said, squinting into the sunrise. "They've turned against it and I have no idea why. I'm trying to counter as best I can with my blog posts, but oh my *God,* the comments underneath." He pressed the heel of his hand to his forehead, then shot me a tight smile. "Let's just say I've learned a lot about avoiding comment sections in the past few weeks."

"Is this because of me?" I said quietly. "Because I screwed it up?"

Hannah's words echoed in my head, *"Everything will always be all about you."* I closed my eyes, wincing.

Adam sighed. "I think this whole event needed a face—one person to rally around. And now it's just got that actor guy popping up to say how awesome America's Homecoming is going to be. He's not a teenager. He plays one on *TV,* but . . . it's not enough."

A face, a teenager to rally around. Someone telegenic. Someone actually gay.

Player One is not the hero.

Adam squirmed and I realized I'd been staring. "Just my early-morning ramblings. I'm sure it's all going fine, Daisy, it's the coffee talking and the fact that the sun just came up, and—"

His glasses had slipped and I couldn't resist—I pushed them back into place. My fingers grazed his cheek and his hand darted up to catch mine and kept it there. Inside those black frames, his eyes ignited.

He was going to kiss me. This was unambiguous. It was going to happen.

"Daisy," he mumbled, and inched closer.

I could have stayed there and let it happen, enjoyed it happening, closed my eyes or whatever you do and forgotten everything but him. But the sun was bright now and I had been awake for a very long time and what I wanted in this moment, more than anything, was to let Adam see me.

So I leaned away. "Can I tell you something? Off the record?"

He froze, listening. Here went nothing.

"Hannah's . . . my person."

Adam nodded, having heard this before, but there was a new cloud of confusion in his eyes. I kept going quickly so he didn't get the wrong impression.

"I'm starting to realize that this is not a good thing. The truth is, for two years, I didn't have any friends. I went to the nurse's office every day of fourth grade in case there was some medical condition I didn't know about that would let me go home early. I did have *imaginary* friends. Stede Bonnet was one. We went on adventures. There was Table the Table, my dining room table. He'd ask me about my day when I got in. Grog the Dinosaur was another close confidant. I kept him in the closet so Mom wouldn't hear us talking. I tried to be best friends with my cat, which is more normal, but she hated me too. Still does, actually."

My legs had started to shake, so I sank into a crouch, but kept going. I needed to get this out.

"And then I met Hannah and everything was okay for a while. Better than okay. She saved me. Our friendship canceled out everything that happened before. But now it seems to be over, so I'm back to being the real me and . . . I just thought you should know who that was. I'm not the girl from the article. I'm not someone who can lead a charge and Do Great Things. I'm somebody who gets scared . . ." I smeared a tear away with my wrist. ". . . and flies under the radar. Doesn't make new friends. Clings to what's safe. But then I'm also someone who gets these *ideas*. Continent-sized ideas. And once they're there, I can't stop myself from chasing them—I'm like a . . . a *dog*, running after a car, realizing five blocks down that it was horrible idea and I need to go back home."

Adam laughed. I kept going.

"I fall on my face a lot. Like, *literally*. I say inappropriate things. I hurt feelings. I'm not brave, I'm not talented, I'm not together, I'm just . . ." I breathed in. "Me."

And with that last word, all my confidence vanished, leaving me flapping like a loose sail on a dead-calm sea.

I should have just let him kiss me.

I started to turn, drifting off to wreck on some sandbank— but he reached out and drew me in.

"No, Daisy." Adam's hands slid from my elbows to my wrists. "You don't get it. I'm sorry all that happened to you, but I knew who you were from the moment I met you. And okay, I might have fudged a few details in that article." He let go. "That was about me, not you. My ambition, I guess. Being a little too in love with my ability to bend the narrative, and . . . a whole host of other things I'm not going to go into now. I shouldn't have done it. It was lying by omission and it set you on a course for disaster. But in my defense . . . you make a *terrible* headline."

I peered up at him through stinging eyes. He grinned.

"You're . . . an experimental novel. An epic poem in Aramaic. The compiled lyrics of Sonic Youth."

"I have no idea whether you're complimenting me."

"I'm saying you're amazing, Daisy." Adam moved away, sticking his hands in his pockets as if embarrassed by the admission.

Heat swept my skin. "Oh."

"You were probably amazing as a kid too," he said, rolling a pebble with the toe of his black sneakers. "Going on adventures with pirates? What were the other kids doing? Playing foursquare? Trading stickers? I'd pick pirates too."

"You're just saying that to be nice," I said, mostly to hide my growing flush at the thought of Adam on a pirate ship, his glasses framing an eye-patch.

"I'm not really the 'saying it to be nice' type." He glanced over his shoulder at a passing car. "What I'm actually saying is that I understand. When Eli got heavy into music, he completely ditched me. Took our entire social group with him too. I was so thrown that I wasn't even sure what the mechanics were of making friends anymore. By the time I got to high school, I'd decided I was some kind of iconoclast, that nobody would ever understand me. A Byronic hero." He winced at the memory. "So I skipped the high school stuff. I had friends. Not close ones. I've hardly kept in touch with them since I got down here."

"But you've made college friends, right?" I nudged his knee with mine.

He laughed, eyes dancing over our knees, nudging back. "Actually, you were kind of spot on with the whole 'friends your own age' dig."

I shuffled back a step.

"I've sort of fallen into the same trap as before," he said. "Flying under the radar, as you said. Focusing on my work—among other distractions."

His grin rose slowly, one side of his mouth, then the other.

"Thank you," I said. "For relating. For not making fun of me."

"Never," he said. "Well, I shouldn't promise that. I promise not to make fun of you when it matters, how about that?"

"Deal."

We shook, and hesitated, our fingers comfortable against each other's. But it wasn't *that* moment. We were alert again. Cautious. The time for kissing had passed.

We didn't talk much on the way home. Even when we got to my driveway and parked, Adam gazed over his glasses out the windshield, lost in thought. It didn't feel right to blurt "Thanks for the ride" and dash into the house after everything that had happened, so I held my breath and touched his shoulder.

"You okay?"

He startled. "Yeah. I just . . ." A hint of a smile lit his face. "I need to call my brother."

Not what I'd expected. "Yeah. You should."

"And you should go to homecoming, Daisy." His voice had an intense edge.

I shook my head at my lap. "They don't want me there."

"I think you're wrong. I think a lot of people appreciate what you've done, straight or not. You've helped make this happen and you need to be there to see it take shape."

"I'll take your advice under consideration."

"Plus I'll be there, and I'll want one more interview."

"I'll give you an exclusive," I promised, and saw him beaming from the driver's seat as I made my reluctant way to my front door. Before I went inside, I watched him roll away, mentally mapping the distance—twenty yards, fifty yards, rounding the corner—like the numbers could rationalize away this twinge in my chest.

When I crept into the house, by some sort of miracle, my parents were still asleep. I made it up to my bedroom, tried without success to scrub the paint off my wrist and face and crawled into bed, exhausted to the point of thought-annihilation.

It seemed like I'd only closed my eyes for a second when a sound from downstairs jolted me awake.

Glass breaking. My father, screaming.

I fell out of bed and raced to the stairs just in time to see my mom sprint from her bedroom, equally terrified.

Did someone throw a brick through our window?

I was just about to yell "Call 911!" my feet thundering on the hardwood as I skipped the last three steps, when I caught sight of my parents standing in the living room. The windows were fine. The news was on. And a mug of coffee was shattered on the floor in front of Dad's feet.

"This is *our* Daisy?" He was pointing at the screen and yelling. "They're talking about *our* Daisy on *Morning Joe*?"

"Still? *Ugh*." Mom crouched to clean up the mess with a dustpan and brush.

"'Still'?" Dad's face went crimson. "How long have they been . . . ?"

He caught sight of me and his face returned to sickly white.

I waved. "How does he not know?"

Mom winced a smile and kept cleaning. "It's been a busy few weeks."

"I knew there was a *club* you were in and . . . buh . . . guh . . . you were throwing a *party*," Dad sputtered.

"All accurate so far," I said.

"I knew you were on the local news for it . . ." He waved wildly to the corner of the living room where we'd taped the Shawna Wells interview.

"Oh dear," Mom said quietly.

"I didn't know they were talking about it all over the goddamn country!" He turned and pointed three times at the TV. "And is that Cindy Beck?"

"Ugh," Mom repeated. "Yes."

I crept closer for confirmation. Yep, there she was in her cute pastel sweater set, sitting on a round sofa with the morning show hosts like they were old pals.

"More than anything, it's *sad*," she was saying. "I'm *sad* to see what's happening to this country."

The female anchor leaned over and touched her hand. I had to turn away to keep from vomiting.

"Do I need to go and have words with Walter?" Dad's chest was doing its best to puff.

"No," Mom and I said together, but she had this look in her eye like she and Dad were going to start making out the second I left the room.

"You know . . ." Cindy Beck's tittering laughter rang out over the chatter of the hosts. "I really believe they are going to wind up being hoisted by their own petards."

We all stared at the screen.

Mom was the first to laugh. "Did she just—?"

"That can't be how you pronounce that." I let out a giggle.

"Pee-tards," Dad said. "Pee. Tards."

"Can you fill him in?" I whispered to Mom, ducking back into the hallway. "I'm going back to bed."

She nodded, but Dad jogged up the stairs to intercept me just as I pulled up the covers.

"Daisy." He leaned against the doorway, huffing from the climb. "I've been thinking and—I'm gonna take some time off from consulting. A month. Mom and I are going to draw up a business plan, get the ball rolling on some new ideas, but . . . mostly I'm going to be around. And, ah . . ." He scratched his stubble. "Paying better attention. Whenever you want to talk about anything—I'm here. Sound good?"

"Sounds great," I said, smiling, then tugged the covers all the way over my head as the door shut quietly behind him.

Sure, he was here. Today, anyway. Maybe even for the next full month—until he poured himself into creating the next great imaginary universe and forgot all about the real one again, along with all the people populating . . .

Startled, I blinked alert, staring at the tiny pinpricks of sunlight sifting through my comforter.

Privilege? I thought.

Maybe. Or maybe just a blessing I'd been too whiny to count. I had two parents who loved me. Who tried. Hannah didn't even *have* a father in her life, just a single parent in stubborn denial about what her daughter was going through. And then there was Natalie—with a harpy of a right-wing nut job mother currently holding court on Fox News, and a father who seemed to want to help but was painfully out of his depth.

I'd told him I would talk to her. Another grandiose promise.

Something dimly connected in my brain, off in the neural distance, some truth I couldn't bring into focus before sleep overtook me.

But when I woke up, I knew. It was mapped in my brain, a beacon to guide me into the murky future. The way to fix what had been broken in me for as long as I could remember. And it *wasn't* that mural.

32

Natalie lived four blocks away, which was probably one of the reasons we'd become friends in the first place—neighborhood proximity. But I hadn't so much as driven past her house in years.

I waited until an hour after school had ended, guessing she'd be home by then and praying her mother wouldn't be. When Natalie herself answered the door, my first reaction was relief, followed closely by confusion. She was wearing sweats. Her auburn hair was matted in a scraggly bun at the base of her neck. Flyaways galore. I almost didn't recognize her.

"Home sick?" I asked.

She shrugged one shoulder. "Pretending."

"Ah."

"You still suspended?"

I shifted uncomfortably. "You heard about that, then."

Her mouth curled with something like appreciation. "Hot soup attack? Pretty badass."

I felt a treacherous thrill from the compliment. "Sophie Goodwin did it. I just took the heat."

"Oh."

"I'm supposed to go back to school tomorrow, but I'm thinking I'll round out the week."

"That's pretty much my plan," Natalie said numbly.

We both stopped talking, mute witnesses as our fledging conversation twitched and died. Maybe this was enough, though? Maybe she'd just needed to see someone outside her immediate family and chitchat for twenty seconds and that would fulfill my obligation to her dad. I could just turn around now and—

"Wanna come in?" She leaned away from the door.

"Thanks, yeah, awesome." My voice was so eager it made me want to slap myself. This might tie getting arrested as the stupidest thing I'd done this week.

It felt strange walking into her house. Some things were the same but seemed smaller, like the antique furniture in her formal living room, while others were factory-new. Her kitchen was brightly remodeled and there was a giant flat-screen on the wall of the family room where we'd once built a tent fortress that spread all the way into the hallway. I expected her to pause here, sit down on the sectional, but she trudged ahead of me up the steps, all the way to her bedroom.

When we were little, Natalie's room looked like the inside of a bag of Skittles. Now it was sleek monochrome, everything pale blue or off-white, like she'd paid someone to design it. It made me sad for her somehow.

She sat on the love seat under her window and motioned me to her plush desk chair.

"So . . ." I swiveled, unsure what the correct script was for check-in conversations you'd been pressured into having. *"How are things?" "Tell me about your feelings." "What does this ink blot remind you of?"*

"I know why you're here," Natalie said.

"You do?" I asked, hoping she would fill me in.

"I've screwed all this up. I know. I just can't seem to stop."

She covered her face roughly, like she was scrubbing herself off. When her hands relaxed into her lap, she looked different. She'd defrosted, somehow.

"What did you screw up?" I asked, then so as not to tip my hand, added, "I'd like to hear your side of it."

"Coming out? Your . . . event?" She sighed. "Hannah. My mother's career. You name it, I've ruined it. I mean . . . *heh*. You helped." She smiled sourly. "Pretending Hannah was your girlfriend, outing me on national television, making out with my ex-boyfriend in front of a million—"

"I did *not* make out with QB," I cut in. "Not on purpose. I did do the first two things. Not really on purpose either."

She grabbed an empty glass from her nightstand and raised it in a toast. "All hail the screw-ups. At least we make life interesting."

She turned the glass over, scowled at it, put it down.

"Hey, so," I started, examining my nails. "Speaking *of*, I did want to apolo—" Downstairs, the front door opened. I jumped from the chair, my eyes darting to the window in the hopes of finding a handhold for a second-story escape.

Natalie shook her head. "That's our housekeeper. Mom's in New York trying to convince everybody in the world to hate gay people."

"Oh, right," I said bleakly. "I saw her on MSNBC. Her outfit was really on point."

"My mother can rock a twin set. I will give her that."

I shook my head as I sank back into the chair. "Why is she doing this? Is she that mad at you?"

"Me?" Natalie cackled, tore the elastic from her hair, and shook her red mane loose. "Lord, no! I'm her perfect daughter. She's pretty pissed at you, though, for spreading all those lies about me on the evening news."

"Why does she think they're lies?"

"Because I told her they were." She pressed her lips together and looked at the floor, her hair wild around her face. "I told my parents I wasn't gay, that you had a vendetta against me and that's where the rumors came from." She glanced up when I didn't answer. I was too stunned. "So, yeah. Sorry about that. Didn't really expect Mom to go even more ape-shit than before, but I guess I should have."

I rolled closer. "But . . . you did come out. Right? I'm not imagining that."

"To my *friends*." The word was thick with irony. "And when that went—well, you saw how that went—I decided to hold off on telling my parents. My family is different from yours, Daisy. Your mom would throw a parade for you if she thought you were gay."

"Probably," I admitted.

"Meanwhile, my mom's gearing up to run for state senate as an ultra-super-duper conservative next year and I knew this would be, um, a *problem*. I tested her. Just in case. I said, 'Hey Mom, you remember Daisy Beaumont-Smith? I heard she's gonna lobby the school board to allow same-sex dates at dances.' And she said . . ." Natalie held on to her knees, fighting tears. "She said, 'That's disgusting. *Thank you* for bringing this to me.'" She looked at the ceiling until her eyes cleared. "Sorry about that too, by the way."

I shrugged in answer. What was done was done.

"Anyway, I thought maybe I could just get through high school and see Hannah in secret and get the hell out of here and *then* I could be myself? It was stupid."

"Is that why you broke up with her?" I asked. "So you could stay in the closet?"

"Hannah dumped me. At the rally."

I stared at her. "That was why you were crying? I saw you from the stage."

"I was crying because of your speech. There you were, lying your ass off, but your lies were a million times braver than mine. I've never felt more like a coward than hearing you tell *my* story in front of hundreds of people. I mean, it wasn't brave for you. You had nothing to lose, except maybe Hannah—who everybody thought was *your* girlfriend. I was so mad. I thought . . . kiss her, hold her hand, do something, make it obvious that *you're* the one she's in love with, not Daisy. But I couldn't. I couldn't handle it. When you were done talking, I turned to Hannah and I told her we needed to stay a secret until college. And yeah. She broke it off." At my sympathetic slump, Natalie shook her head. "I don't blame her. I was a total basket case the whole time we were together. I don't know why she even put up with me for as long as she did. I'm having a hard time putting up with myself at the moment. But I'm stuck with me."

"Why not be stuck with the real you, then?" I stood, feeling smothered by the blanket of self-pity settling over both of us.

"Natalie, do you remember how we used to dare each other to do things around the neighborhood?" It hurt to bring this up. "I'd dare you to leave a Twinkie on the hood of the car next door. You'd dare me to ring the doorbell of that crazy ex-Marine dude."

"I still can't believe you did that," she muttered to her lap.

"Well, it's my turn again. I dare you to tell your parents the truth. Preferably before the weekend so your mom can call off the attack."

Instead of immediately answering, Natalie watched me, searching for something in my face.

"Do you know why we stopped being friends?"

My breath went cold, frozen, shattering into shards. Why would she ask me this? And how did this girl still have the power to break my heart with a simple question?

She seemed to want an answer.

"Because I wasn't *cool enough*." My voice was like gravel. "Because you hated me. Or I embarrassed you. All of the above."

"No." Her eyes grew sharp, intense, like she was about to challenge me to a duel. "No, Daisy. It was because I loved you."

My mouth fell slack. Natalie had stopped making sense.

"I *loved* you," she said, her voice wavering. "Told my parents I wanted to marry you. They thought it was cute until my mom started getting worried. Called in some Christian re-programmers posing as child psychologists. I thought I was taking art lessons back then, but while I was painting pictures of the two of us together in ballet costumes, they were diagnosing me as deviant. That's why Mom and Dad took me away that summer, so they could get me away from you, tell me how girls loved boys, not other girls, how wrong those feelings were. And how *you* were the one who'd put all those wrong thoughts in my head. How something was wrong with you, not me. When we got back, I believed them. I just wanted so *desperately* to be normal. I didn't want anything to be wrong with me. So I stopped being friends with you."

I'd had so many theories about why she'd dropped me. That she'd suffered brain damage after slipping on the deck of the cruise ship. That I'd said something horrible to her and then *I'd* slipped and gotten amnesia and forgotten it. That I was a freak all along, who nobody in their right mind would want to be friends with.

"Natalie loves me" had never been one of my theories.

"And the worst thing was . . ." Natalie laughed, her pinkie darting up to swipe the corner of her eye. She'd been biting her nails. "You didn't care. You didn't fight for me. You found a new best friend, like, the same day, and forgot all about me."

"The same day?"

I gripped the back of the chair.

"Bad choice of words," she muttered, but it was too late.

"Natalie, I made a friend—*one* friend—*two years later.* For two years, nobody would be friends with me. Nobody even talked to me at school except to tease me."

"I never teased you," Natalie blurted, then bit her lip, as if to take it back. "Well, okay, the stuttering thing."

"Just that," I said. "And then you outsourced the mockery to your new besties."

"I didn't stop them," Natalie murmured.

"Didn't stop them? You *told* people not to be friends with me. You think I don't know that? That it didn't get back to me? You told them to pick sides, and everybody picked you."

Natalie didn't bother to deny it, so I went on, my throat stinging.

"Do you know that I didn't get invited to anyone's house in two years? Of course you know. You made sure of it. I *threw* a birthday party that nobody came to. After an hour of sitting there, waiting, my mom paid the DJ and the flamenco instructor—"

"Flamenco instructor?"

"And sent them home and took me to the movies to try to get me to forget. But I never did. How could I? That was my life, Natalie, because you declared war on me."

"I know," she said. "I was . . . what's the right word? An asshole, I guess." She coughed a laugh. "I mean, I *am* an asshole. There's no denying it. I blamed you! For everything. But you know the sick thing?" She scratched her hair, making it even wilder. "I missed you. Like, all the time. I hated you, because you hated me, which I realize is not the most logical thing. But—I don't know. All along, I wished things had been different. That *I* could be different. That I hadn't gone off the deep end." She turned away, like she couldn't admit it to my face. "I had my friends, or whatever, but . . . it was almost like I'd struck this bargain with myself that I would give them eighty percent. That was it. I'd be the same perfect fucking robot I was with my parents, my coaches, just . . . everybody." Her eyes dimmed. "Until Hannah."

I let silence settle over us as she turned to blink out the

window. Then, to my surprise, she looked right at me—and grinned.

"It's not like *either* of you is perfect. Hannah's crazy."

My temper flared in Hannah's defense, a well-worn instinct, but Natalie had begun to glow.

"She's beyond neurotic," she said tenderly. "She hates being stared at but she dresses like a J.Crew model, so of course everybody looks. She's terrified of conflict. *Cannot* handle it."

Wow, I thought. *That's spot on.* Why had I never registered it?

"She's so weird about that little notebook."

I cracked a smile. "The Moleskine."

"Yes." Natalie leaned forward, pointing at me.

"And the country music thing," I put in.

"Yes! What is *with* that?" She laughed. "I can take it in small doses, but *every* time we're near a radio? And she quotes it like it's Shakespeare . . ."

Natalie's eyes met mine and darkened. I wondered for a second whether she was downloading our entire history in one sad blink. But by now I knew the truth.

This wasn't about me.

"You miss her."

She swallowed like her throat was sore. Bit her thumb. Dropped it. "She's my best friend."

And with those words, something I couldn't name broke from me, lifted, an exorcised demon.

Let her go, I thought. *Let everybody go.*

"You need to tell her that."

She turned to look at me.

"Tell her that. Exactly that. And while you're at it, tell her what happened to you as a kid. What your parents did. I'm guessing she doesn't know?"

"Nope," she muttered, staring at her lap.

"So tell her. You can be full of shit out there in the world all you want—but not with her. Not with your best friend. Tell her the truth and I promise you, she'll understand. She'll cut you a break." I attempted a smile. "She's good at that."

"Maybe," she said, glancing up. "Thanks for—"

"I take it back," I blurted, my courage flaring. "Don't be full of shit. Don't let her cut you any more breaks. My dare stands. And come to homecoming! There will be so many people there who understand. You need to get out of this house and face up to the fact that you're not the special little snowflake you think you are."

She laughed—loud, unrestrained. It was Lida's laugh, all grown up. Fireworks went off in my chest at the sound of it.

"*Okay.* Jesus," she said. "I'll think about it."

Before she led me out the front door, Natalie grabbed my wrist.

"Listen, Daisy? Chris is a really solid guy. Be good to him, okay?"

I had to blink, breathe, reboot before I could answer. Out of everybody in the school, I'd have thought Natalie would have been the very last to believe that rumor. But apparently QB's plan was more effective than I'd given it credit for.

"He *is* a solid guy, isn't he?" I leaned against the doorframe. "It's bizarre. We're not dating, though. I'm sort of his free, unlicensed therapist . . . slash surrogate sister. Although that may be one-sided."

Natalie raised her eyebrows. "Sounds complicated."

I smiled. "I'm getting used to complicated."

When my feet hit the sidewalk, I heard her call after me.

"I'm still mad at you, by the way."

I spun around. "Same here."

She nodded. "See you at school tomorrow?"

There was an "I dare you" glint in her eyes, her hands clenching and unclenching at her sides. Apparently it was her turn now.

"See you at school," I said.

Speaking of dares, I thought, walking home. *Okay. Yeah. Here goes.*

I called Hannah. Got voicemail. Launched right in.

"You were right about what happened when you came out. I got fixated on the difference between us. Which I guess makes me the same as all the people I've been fighting. So I wanted to say that I'm sorry. And that you're *boring* and *ordinary* and I love you. And I hope you're doing okay."

She didn't call me right back, but that was fine. I'd said what I needed to say.

When I got back to my room, an incongruous sight awaited me—a purring ball of gray fur happily ensconced at the foot of my bed. This was the third time this week. As I peered down at Zelda, she stirred and blinked up at me.

Could this be happening? Could I have conquered all of my enemies in one fell swoop?

With a shaking hand, I reached down to pet her. Before I got within two inches, Zelda bristled like a Halloween decoration, attacked my bedpost, and bolted, her tiny paws tearing a thunderous path down the stairs.

But staring down at the dent she'd left in my comforter, I smiled. I knew progress when I saw it.

33

It happened.

There I was, outside school, staring at the smeared brass handle, steeling myself to reenter the fray, when the door eased open under my fingertips—and everything changed.

The transformation was subtler than I'd imagined but undeniable. The students I passed in the lobby caught my eye. Some of them smiled.

"Hey, Daisy," chirped Jenna, a senior I knew from Parapsychology. "You're back!"

"I *am* back," I answered brilliantly as three freshmen from French class waved and Darius Williams fist-bumped me on his way to homeroom.

I'd known these people for years. Passed them in the hallway, worked with them on school projects. But we'd never been on the hey level. The *fist-bump level*. Had we?

In the crowded intersection of the English and language hallways, I spotted a pristinely gathered red ponytail swinging its way through the crush of students.

"Morning, Daisy!" Natalie called out. "Lunch today?"

Everyone in the hallway started walking in slow motion.

This was unprecedented. Not just between me and Natalie. Between Natalie and anyone.

Her expression didn't waver.

"Sure," I said, pulling myself taller to match her false confidence. Then an idea bloomed. "Meet you on the stoop?"

I had to fight to keep from skipping as I turned the corner. It was like I'd woken up and stumbled into a parallel universe. I liked this one so much better. Had it been here all along, waiting for me to discover it?

But my step unstrutted when I reached French and found Raina waiting outside the door. I drew a breath and tried my best to fake nonchalance, raising my hand for a casual greeting. But before I could blurt it, she said, "Got a second?"

"Um, yeah." I shook my head, confused. "I mean, I have to get to class—"

"We're cool," she said, nodding into the room at my teacher, who smiled and waved me on.

I slid the door shut and turned to Raina, but she was staring into the distance at a group of black students clustered around their lockers, laughing at a joke one of them had made.

"When I moved here, I tried to make friends with those kids." Raina's voice was low, distracted. I didn't dare interrupt. "I just went up and introduced myself. You know, 'Hey, I'm Raina, I'm from Winston-Salem, I'm black, you're black, let's hang out.'"

Raina's face had relaxed with the memory. She looked younger, somehow. More like the actual teenager she was.

"I got stonewalled. They wanted nothing to do with me."

She leaned against the wall. "It was so easy for me to make friends back home. But *they* looked at me and saw northern, not Gullah, not us. Maybe they could tell I was queer, who knows. But I think the biggest thing they saw was privilege."

I stepped back, confused. Her eyes darted to mine and sharpened.

"I don't exactly qualify for scholarships myself," she admitted. "My dad's an attorney and my mom's got family money. She 'paints.'" She made air quotes, rolling her eyes. Then she sighed. "Listen, that's not what I came here to talk about. When you were out this week, people were talking about you."

I shrugged, not surprised.

"I didn't like what I heard," she said, crossing her arms. "In fact, it really pissed me off. And it made me realize that there is, in fact, some overlap in our Venn diagrams."

"You're saying we're alike." I pressed my lips together, ironing down my smile.

"In some ways." She sniffed. "You're you, no matter what people say, and yeah—I can respect that. Even when it becomes a major pain in my ass."

"About that," I cut in. "I'm sorry for jeopardizing everything. You were right, I was careless with something that didn't belong to me and—"

"Stop." She leaned against the lockers, her eyes boring into mine. "What happened at the rally is *not* just on you. The whole point of being an Alliance is that we become an 'us.' The kind of 'us' that stands up for 'us' when we . . . say . . . throw hot soup on some douchebag's crotch."

"Vivid example."

"I cut you out so I could scapegoat you. I shouldn't have. It was *facile.*" Her brow contorted at the word, like it was the ultimate insult. "Any mistakes we made—asking you to lie being the big one—they're on *us.* All of us. Okay?"

"Okay," I said. "Thank you." My head swam as she stepped away. "That was some intense bonding right there."

A grin flitted across her face as her posture returned to all-business mode.

"We're meeting after school. Same room, A2. If you're not too busy."

She smirked over her shoulder as she walked away, leaving that carrot dangling for me to chase.

Hannah was already on the stoop when I walked out, a steaming Cluck-Cluck bag on the cement beside her. I hesitated a split-second in the doorway, wondering what her reaction would be, but she rose before I could come up with a good opening line.

"You're back," she said. "At school."

I motioned to myself. "Voilà."

"Can we talk?"

"Of course."

"I mean, like, *have a talk.* Not, like, chitchat talk. Fair warning."

I walked closer. "I got that. And yes."

"Although hopefully we can chitchat *after.* I mean, I have nothing against . . ." She itched her chin, trying hard to smile. "Okay. Sorry. Starting over."

I could see now that she'd carefully left enough room on

the stoop for me—and that the bag of food was way too full to just be for her. Her Moleskine was dangling open in her hand. On top of one page, I could make out the words:

"*To say to Daisy:*"

"First of all, you were right—I haven't been myself lately, and I'm really sorry," she started reciting. "You're not the only one who's been self-centered."

Even in her written draft, she was calling me self-centered. For some reason, I found this so funny I had to bite my knuckles to keep from giggling as she went on.

". . . I've been so focused on what's been going on with me that I forgot how to be a good friend to you."

"That is so not true!" I covered my mouth. "Sorry. Ignore me, go on."

"It *is* true." Her brow furrowed, the notebook flapping. "I feel like, the last few months, I've been watching myself from a distance, with absolutely no idea what I'm going to do next. I *hate* it."

That sounded like me all the time.

She sat on the top step, tossing the notebook aside. "I've always seen myself as so rational and together and above it all. But lately I'm just one contradiction after another. I have no idea what I want from one moment to the next. I'm happy and then I'm, like, devastated. I'm . . ." I sat next to her. She mussed her hair. "A mess."

She'd stopped talking, so I offered, "Do you think this is because you came out?"

She tucked her legs up and hugged them. "Probably."

"Or do you think maybe you're just . . ." I thought of Sean

and Diego and loaded sighs and best friends and tapping pens and steering wheels and glasses. "In love."

It looked like it hurt her to breathe.

"Probably that too," she whispered. Her hand crept over to the Cluck-Cluck bag, picking at the edge of the paper. Then she crumpled it shut. "Listen, I miss you. Lots and lots. And I want to do whatever—"

Behind me, the door squeaked open.

"Hey Han?" I got up. "We'll pick this up later, I promise. But there's someone else who wants to talk to you just as much as I do, and if I don't give her a turn, she might burn my house down."

Natalie's fingers were pressed under her chin as if in prayer. Hannah's face had shifted from open to lockdown. After what felt like an epoch, she stuck her notebook in her backpack and scooted over—making room.

Natalie's eyes darted to mine. I motioned for her to take my place.

"See you guys later," I said, but they were already talking, quietly, carefully. I watched them from the doorway, then went to find my own lunch table.

Nobody bothered me while I ate. And nobody gawked out the windows at my friends. They were too busy staring out the giant glass walls on the other side of the room— at the massive party being erected in a once-vacant field across the street.

After lunch, we were excused from class to attend a home-coming rally in the gym. The cheerleaders cheered. The football team pounded the air. The homecoming court marched out wearing their silly crowns. I'd called it—Madison was queen. She didn't seem that happy about it. Darius was king. QB was doing his best to look excited to be in the court again this year. And everybody in the stands clapped and cheered, but mostly muttered, distracted, as if this were a dress rehearsal for homecoming, not the real thing.

The real thing was across the street.

The school's excitement only seemed to grow once the assembly was over.

"Are you gonna go?" a freshman boy asked the girl who was walking out with him. I knew in my bones he wasn't talking about Dana Costas's birthday party.

"I'm not sure my parents will let me," she whispered back.

"Don't tell them!" he said, and I very nearly hugged him.

But that was the dilemma, wasn't it? All these kids who wanted to participate—who sensed that this was important, a key moment, an exciting one, or just a good party—but didn't feel safe enough to be a part of it. That's why we were doing this. To change that.

In some small way, we already had.

Seventh period. Club period. *Technically they can't stop me* period.

I turned the doorknob to the administration's conference room, my heart racing with apprehension and hope.

My eyes were glued to the carpet as I walked in, so it took me a second to realize that something was different today. Talk about an alternate universe.

The room was packed. People were sitting on the window-sills, cross-legged on the floor, in extra chairs that they'd pulled from other offices. I recognized some of Sophie's friends, a bevy of drama girls, Dan Sawtuck and Mara Thomas *not* making out, three kids from my homeroom, a dozen other vaguely familiar faces. Unless the past week had seen a huge uptick in Palmetto students coming out of the closet, the Alliance had enacted some policy changes.

"Hey Daisy." Kyle swiveled a chair in my direction. "We saved you a seat."

A couple of guys in lacrosse hoodies scooted to make room.

Raina turned to the group with a tremulous smile—more nervous than I'd ever seen her. "Hi everybody, and welcome to our first meeting."

"*First* meeting?" I whispered.

"You've all known us as the school's LGBTQ Alliance for the past few years. But now that we're part of the Gay Straight Alliance Network, we're looking at today's meeting as a fresh start."

She stood, hands pressed against the desk.

"As you know, we've got kind of a big party scheduled for tomorrow."

Everybody laughed, settled.

"We never would have gotten as far as we have if it weren't for the help of supporters like you." She meant everyone, I knew, but she was looking at me. "And if we're going to see this through, make it happen, make it what we know it can be, we'll need your help tomorrow too. We've been so overwhelmed by your support, but as you know, some people in the community are not as—"

The door whined as it inched open.

"Sorry we're late!" said the most beautiful voice in the world. Hannah's eyes danced through the crowd until they found mine.

Natalie trailed behind, fingertips lightly touching Hannah's. Lunch must have gone well. I waved them over. They whispered to each other and slid down to sit against the wall behind me.

Raina motioned to Sophie, who took the stage.

"We do have a few requests," she said.

"Rules," Raina corrected.

"Anything anyone shares in this room is private. This hasn't worked out in the past, but we're trusting you now. Please don't violate that trust."

She had her grandma smile on. No one made a peep.

"Second, this is a supportive environment. If you have negative feelings about the things we talk about, please find a way to express them diplomatically. If we feel like anything is veering into harassment, we'll ask you not to participate anymore. And lastly, we ask that if you're an ally in here, you become an ally out there. If you see anyone being bullied, please speak up, speak out, do what you can to fight back . . ." Sophie flushed bright red. "In a *non-violent* way. Does everyone agree?"

As everyone nodded, Sophie sat and glanced at Sean, who was waiting by the door to dim the lights.

"And with that," he said, his voice dropping into a sultry hush. "Let's start this meeting by *testing* your *discretion.*"

Girls all over the room giggled with appreciation.

As he rejoined the table, Sophie pulled out her tiny fake candle and clicked it to life.

"I'll start," she said. "I'm Sophie. I identify as bisexual. So . . . things have been easier for the past few days. The guys who used to bother me have pretty much stopped, which is . . . really good. I'm grateful to my friends for standing up for me. I'm going to do more of it for myself now too."

She glanced at me so fleetingly that I almost missed it. Before I could shoot her a thumbs-up, the candle had passed to Jack.

"Update time: I told my parents I won't be going to church anymore," he started, and my next breath sputtered audibly out of me in my excitement. "Not their church, anyway. I said it was important to me to find a congregation I connected with, so I'd be going to the Unity Church's services down the street from now on. I . . ." He sighed. "I didn't tell them why. But they let me try it out and they asked what scripture we talked about and that was it, so I'm hoping it's a good first step. Or only step. I don't know, we'll see. But I like the new church. Reverend Jim and the youth group are all coming to homecoming, so I'll look forward to introducing them."

It was a small thing—and it was everything. He hadn't been totally honest with his parents. He might never. But he was wearing his cross proudly outside his collar today, as if those two parts of himself could finally coexist. I beamed over the table at him and he nodded, mouthing a silent "Thank you," that made me glow from my toes to the tips of my ears. Then his eyes sparked.

"Oh, right, and I'm Jack and hell *yes*, I'm bi!" He lifted the candle in the air like a torch and everybody whooped. *Nice*.

As he passed the candle to Kyle, I looked down, trying to keep my eyes from spilling over.

"Um. I'm Kyle? And I'm gay. Or . . ." He glanced at Sophie. "Queer maybe? Is that different from . . . ? I'm still trying to figure out, um, what all the words mean. So. My only real news is that they arrested the guys who jumped me."

The room erupted in cheers.

"But um . . . I decided not to press charges. I thought really hard about it, and I told my parents the truth." Kyle glanced at me as if to gauge my reaction. "But in the end, I just wanted to be able to enjoy homecoming. You know, focus on the positive."

I opened my mouth, full of arguments in the other direction. If it were me, I'd have found out their names and publically shamed them and *then* pressed charges and prepared a fiery speech for the courtroom—

But it *wasn't* me. I wasn't the one who'd been attacked. I wasn't the one who was fourteen years old and coming out of the closet with the whole country watching. I couldn't possibly understand what he was dealing with.

Privilege, I thought. This was Kyle's decision.

"First of all, I'm *so pumped for homecoming!*" Sean grinned, working the room as he grabbed the candle. "I'm calling it now—*party of the decade*. My only . . ." He slumped into a sigh. "My only issue at the moment is that I really wish my boyfriend were here."

The drama girls went "Awwwww," but Sophie hopped in her chair like it was giving her a series of static shocks. What was her deal?

"He'd love to see what we've managed to accomplish in such a short amount of time. Be a part of it."

"You must really miss him," Sophie said in a slightly louder murmur than usual.

"I do," Sean said. "A lot."

Sophie's eyes darted to the doorway. Just past the glass, I could see a skinny, floppy-haired silhouette.

"You must *really* miss him," she said again, marginally louder.

Sean stared at her. "*I do.* Anyway . . ."

The door didn't open, and by now I'd figured out her dastardly, wonderful plan. I stood.

"I think what Sophie's trying to say is that you must *really* miss him!!!" The windows practically rattled.

The door flew open, and in the hallway appeared a charmingly gawky Spanish kid, his eyes widening as they met Sean's.

"Holy shit, you did *not*!" Sean screamed to Sophie.

"Go," she said, shooing him. "We'll fill you in on the rest—"

But he was already gone, in the hallway, kissing his boyfriend in a stumbling twirl while the rest of us cheered. The drama girl closest to the door swung it quietly shut, sharing a sad smile with the brunette next to her.

When I looked up, Raina had the candle. I expected her

to click it off and start talking business, but her eyes were clouded. She glanced up. At me.

"I'm Raina Moore. I'm not a huge fan of labels, but for today's purposes, let's just say I fill out the *Q* and *L* in QUILT-BAG." Her voice cracked. She coughed to clear it. "When I moved to James Island, I wasn't sure what my place was. And then, after the first GSA went up in flames, I kinda stopped trusting people. I stopped . . ." She drew a breath, turning one of her legal pads end over end. "I stopped trusting that good things could happen. But what's happening in here, and across the street, and everywhere people are cheering us on, is good. I'm grateful for it. And you guys. And that's all I'm gonna say about that."

"Raina talked!" Jack said. "Woohoo!"

In the haze of camaraderie that swept the room, I hardly noticed that Raina had risen from her seat and handed me the candle. It took a few awkward seconds of everyone in the room staring expectantly for me to blurt, "Oh! No. I'm not—I don't feel qualified to share anything."

"Come on, Daisy," Jack said. "We're your friends. Give us *something.*"

His words hit me like a net.

"You're my friends," I said, glancing back to include Hannah, who was beaming, and her girlfriend, trying desperately not to. "I think that's my big news. You're my best friends. So thank you."

A warm silence fell. Sophie reached out for the candle. I pulled it back.

"Oh, and I totally have the hots for that reporter, so cross me off the asexual list!"

Raina smacked the table. "I knew it!"

"I hereby apologize to all asexuals I have offended by appropriating that title."

"The college reporter?" Hannah pulled on my chair to ask. "I have *got* to meet this guy."

"Is that the—?" Kyle glanced at Sophie. She shushed him.

I'd opened my mouth to ask what he was about to say, when Jack leaned forward.

"Wait, did you introduce yourself?" He glanced around. "We're supposed to introduce ourselves."

"Oh right." I waved to all the semi-strangers I'd known most of my life. "I'm Daisy. And . . . I'm not anything."

Jack snorted. "Straight, Daisy. It's called straight."

Straight. Duh. It was a sexual orientation. Why had I forgotten it?

My chair seemed to sink. The room seemed to grow.

Because straight was the default. Because it was the perceived "norm," no need to question it. Because everywhere I turned, I was blinded by privilege.

The room snapped back into proportion.

But it looked ever so slightly different now.

"I'm Daisy and I'm straight," I said, and everybody clapped, laughing, like I was the one coming out of the closet—except with none of the pressure and fears and irrevocable life-changes that came with it. I winced. I wanted to give each and every one of them a bear hug right now—starting with Raina, who was sitting closest to me.

As if sensing my intentions, her shoulders tightened and she stood just out of reach. "Okay. Now that touchy-feely time is out of the way, let's talk homecoming."

She gave us the rundown. Vendors were in place, except for a cowardly few that had dropped out in the last week. The mayor of Charleston was coming, along with a couple of senators and other Democrats I didn't care about. The cast of *Triplecross* was confirmed to be holed up at a hotel downtown, dodging paparazzi on their way to local clubs.

That news sent the drama girls into a flurry of whispers. I said a silent prayer that Chase Hernandez wasn't their new collective crush. It was time to move on to straight boys.

The parade was prepped, voting boxes set up for our gender-neutral queen, king, and attendants. The floats were "very colorful," Sophie said. And the dance was, in Jack's words, "Going to be in*cred*iballs."

"Except for the band," I couldn't resist putting in. "Sorry I couldn't deliver on that. What *is* the entertainment?"

"A DJ," Kyle blurted, just as Jack answered, "A local band."

"Both, actually," Raina said. "We got lucky."

"Cool!" This was awkward. "What's the local band called?"

Everyone stared at Jack. He must have booked them. "The Rhythm Squad."

Sophie started giggling and I couldn't resist a snicker myself. Not the most auspicious name, but at least we had *somebody* to entertain the masses.

"How many RSVPs so far?" Raina asked Jack, changing the subject. He consulted his handy phone.

"Thirteen hundred and seven." He glanced up, frowning. "Some of them will be no-shows."

"I hate to say it, but we'd better hope so. Okay, guys, thanks again for coming. We'll see you all tomorrow—eight a.m. sharp—to set up for homecoming."

I was following Hannah and Natalie out into the hallway along with the rest of the mostly straight crowd when Raina stopped me. "Daisy, we need to talk. I wasn't sure how to bring this up before, but . . . Cal wants you to become our spokesperson again."

I had to lean against the doorframe to keep from keeling over. "You have *got* to be kidding me."

She shrugged.

"Homecoming is tomorrow. Why do we even need a spokesperson?"

Sophie stepped up behind Raina. "If we don't have one tomorrow, the loudest voice the media will hear is Cindy Beck's. So no matter how well it goes, it will seem to the rest of the world like she's won."

"Okay. Yes. Fine. *But.*" I motioned wildly to myself.

Raina understood. "You're not ideal. But you're what we've got. I mean, *I'll* do it."

I hopped in celebration.

"I can't guarantee I'll *smile*. Or that I won't assault someone on camera for asking some *asinine* question—" Raina cracked her knuckles, incensed by the very thought of being interviewed.

I turned to Sophie. She did her best to hide behind her braid.

"*Okay . . .*" I clapped. "What about Sean? He's so photogenic. And all that theater training—"

"He's afraid of cameras. They don't even allow them at school performances." At my aghast expression, Sophie laughed. "I was surprised too!"

It was too tragic to contemplate at the moment. "Umm . . . the guy from *Triplecross.*"

"Not a teenager," Raina answered, glancing at her cell phone. "Cal says we need a Palmetto student. Listen, he suggested you say you're bisexual." I gawked at her. Her expression stayed guarded. "And that the way the media handled that kiss was just another example of how they misrepresent sexual identity in the press."

"I'm done lying, Raina."

She nodded. "I thought you'd say that."

"And anyway, you were right. I'm not the right spokesperson. I never was." I glanced behind me to see Natalie and Hannah laughing along with Jack. As the three of them disappeared down the hall, Natalie's ponytail swung back and forth like a flickering torch. "But I think I know who is."

34

"No."

A forkful of zucchini-wrapped grouper hovered a half inch from my mouth, forcing me to set it down in shock. "That's it? Just 'no'?"

Natalie had no problem taking a bite of her meal. "How about 'hell no'? That clear enough for you?"

Hannah eyed us nervously, her takeout still untouched on her lap.

I leaned over a pile of throw pillows to grab the remote and pause the TV. "*Miss* Beck. Have I not adequately described to you how important it is that we have a spokesperson right now?"

"And have I not adequately described just how very in the closet I am right now?" She took another giant bite of food as if to throw another obstacle in the way of this conversation. "I'm taking baby steps," she added through a full mouth. "Showing up to homecoming is a baby step. Going on national news to talk about how gay I am constitutes *throwing myself off a cliff.*"

"I get that," I said, using my kindest voice. "And I would never want you to throw yourself off a cliff."

Natalie lobbed a pillow at me, knocking the fork out of my hand. She giggled so maniacally that Hannah let out a giant snort through a mouth full of food.

"Okay," I groaned. "I tried. I'll tell them I tried."

"We'll be there early to volunteer," Hannah said.

"Yeah, about that," I started.

"Yes, you can have a ride."

Natalie shouted "Shotgun!" a millisecond before me.

"Gah!" I fell backward.

Hannah grabbed the remote. But before she pressed PLAY, she grinned. "This is fun."

"This is weird, is what this is," Natalie said, echoing what I was thinking. "*Weirdly* fun."

"This is what I pictured," Hannah added. "Except in like a castle where we're staying because we got lost backpacking in France in the *middle of the night* but the owner was really nice and gave us our own wing for the week. And there's a vineyard. With horses."

"A horse vineyard," Natalie said drily. "Yes. We should definitely do that."

"Spring break, maybe?" I suggested.

Natalie and I exchanged a veiled smile before our eyes darted away again. Fun might take a little longer for us. But seeing her happy made it worth the effort.

"So, hey." Since we were already in Hannah-weird territory, I turned to the two of them and asked, as casually as possible, "Which of you is better with scissors?"

Saturday morning, October the twenty-second, as Hannah

followed signs to the "America's Homecoming Staff Only" parking lot, a beautiful sight greeted us.

Protesters. Mobs of them. Hundreds, carrying hateful signs, chanting sick, offensive, cheerful rhymes.

Sigh. But hey—at least we were still relevant!

The press siege had begun in earnest too. Their vans formed a satellite-dish-festooned wall just outside the blue police barricades penning in the tent-covered field. Reporters hovered outside their vans, holding microphones in one hand and paper coffee cups in the other, chatting while scanning the parking lot for somebody to accost.

If they saw me, they'd stampede. Luckily . . .

"You're in disguise!"

At the sound of Adam's voice, I couldn't stop myself from doing a wobbling pirouette to greet him. He grinned and loped across the field, hoisting a Starbucks bag.

"This is the guy?" Natalie muttered. Hannah shushed her. "Surprisingly hot."

"Your hair," he said, motioning to his own head. "It's—"

"Blond," I offered. "Light brown, depending on how picky you are. Hannah cut it for me. It was time for the blue to go."

"Nice job," Adam said to Hannah. She smiled at her loafers in reply. "Smart too. They won't recognize you without the stripe."

"*You* recognized me."

He shrugged. "Of course."

"Awwww," Natalie said.

My hand flattened, slap-ready, and she danced away, grinning.

Adam glanced between us. "I was just at Starbucks, so I grabbed you your usual—fruity soda, cookie?"

"That's so sweet," I said, taking the bag from him. "Literally!"

He chuckled, pointing at me.

Natalie made a gagging noise.

"I think they're waiting for us," Hannah said over her, nodding to the volunteers gathering outside the main gate.

"I'll catch up in a sec," I said, waving them on.

Adam rocked back onto his sneakered heels.

"So . . ." My heart started to thud so hard I wondered if he could hear it through my Bertie and the Bots hoodie. Here went nothing. "I don't know if you were thinking of coming to the dance tonight, but I have an extra ticket. For a date. So it's yours if you want it."

His hands started tapping against his pockets. "Oh."

"I mean, I know you're over the whole high school thing, but it's technically an *all-ages* event."

"Yeah, of course." He glanced over his shoulder as if looking for the best path to run screaming, but I kept. On. Talking.

"We've got a DJ and a local band, I think. Not exactly the biggest band in the world, but oh well. Can't have it all, right?"

Whatever horrible thing I'd just said had sent his glasses careening off his face. He caught them as they were falling and shoved them crookedly back.

"Yeah, I don't know," he said, wincing. "I'll have to file my homecoming story tonight. My last one. Crazy."

"Crazy," I echoed, sinking steadily into the mud. "Yeah. You should do that. Just . . . let me know if you want an interview with anybody. I'm not the spokesperson anymore, so it won't be me!" I laughed for no reason. "But I'll see who I can get for you."

Adam looked regretful as I waved and raced away across the field. He must have meant to let me down more easily than that, but hey, at least I knew now, right? At least I wouldn't spend the whole day pining after somebody who I'd so completely, ridiculously, disastrously misread the entire time I'd known him.

It was a good thing. I appreciated his timing. I could focus on the day ahead, instead of daydreaming about the dance. The dance wasn't for me, anyway. It was for my friends. This whole event was about their romances, not mine. Which was convenient, because I was clearly going to die alone in a forest cabin where I would live out my life with only deer and songbirds for company. That actually sounded kind of awesome, so whatever, I'd be *fine*.

Raina pulled me aside as soon as I got to the clutch of gathered volunteers waiting for Sean and Sophie to hand out assignments. Before she could ask, I shook my head. "She said no."

"Just like that? Just no?" Raina glared at Natalie's head.

"It was a stretch, Raina. She's not out to her family yet, and her mom is—"

"Captain of the Hate Squad, yes."

I raised my eyebrows. Had Raina just made a joke?

She sighed and brushed her hands off on her jeans—by far the most casual thing I'd ever seen her wear. "Okay. We'll deal. I'll tell Cal that we'll all do interviews and pull people from the crowd to do sound bites. The important thing is the event itself, right?"

At my nod, we broke and joined the group, where Sean was looking dazed and Sophie was asking each person who walked up, "What would you enjoy working on this morning?" to which every single person was answering, "Parade floats."

Hannah raised her hand and ducked through the crowd. "I'm not sure if it's my place, but if this is helpful . . ." She handed Sophie a printed-out list of tasks, along with several sign-in slots under each category, from Ticket Collection to Vendor Management to Football Game Coordination. "Daisy told me a little bit about what needs to be done and I . . . well, I like to organize things."

"You're a *genius,*" Sean breathed, snatching it out of her hand and brandishing it like a flag. "Come! Sign up! Who's got a pen?"

"I already signed myself up to take photos." Hannah pointed to the bottom of the list. "Hopefully that's okay? Obviously *anybody* can take photos, on their phones or if they brought cameras or . . . yeah, I'm gonna stop talking now."

Natalie kissed her neck. "You're an excellent *visual* communicator, my dear."

Hannah glowed. "Thank you."

I watched her dig through her bag and pull out a camera. An unfamiliar one.

Her eyes flew up to meet mine. "It's . . . um . . ."

"A thirty-five millimeter," I said. "Nice."

"I got it for her. As a homecoming present. A *real* camera." Natalie popped gum into her mouth, grinning as she chomped, like a hyena gnawing on a zebra leg.

She offered me some. I snatched it out of her hand.

"Don't be mad," Hannah said.

"I'm not mad!" I chewed my gum. Chewed and chewed. "There is *no* getting mad today."

Natalie pouted.

I whapped her arm. "I'll get mad at you tomorrow."

"You'd better."

I was faux-growling over my shoulder at Natalie, scribbling my name onto the list under "Misc," when my mom's farm group ladies turned up wearing matching T-shirts saying: "We're proud of our gay children!"

A few feet away, Sophie's face went sickly green when she spotted them. It struck me that she was probably the only gay child they had between them, so the shirts should really have read: "We're proud of Sophie!" I was glad for her sake that they didn't.

A familiar face, pale and bewildered, was bobbing between all the women as they approached us. My mouth fell open.

"Dad?"

I reached out to steady his elbow, but he perked up at the sight of me.

"I'm here to support!" He shot me a shaky thumbs-up. "Plus your mom needed a date to the dance."

I snickered at the thought of the two of them dancing romantically to the dulcet tones of the Rhythm Squad. But then my fake smile became a real one. When was the last time my parents had gone out together, or danced together, or even spent a Saturday together, uninterrupted by video games?

Mom rested her head on his shoulder, poking him in the side. Even though it was heartwarming and everything, I thanked them both and darted away before they could ask to tag along with me for the rest of the day.

My first "misc" job was to set up trash cans throughout the venue, which turned out to be the perfect job. I got to wander the lot, marveling at its transformation.

There were multicolored tents everywhere—the biggest strung with fairy lights for the dance—aisles upon aisles of sponsor-branded food stands, booths selling America's Homecoming T-shirts and distributing free rainbow flags and buttons, and off to one side, a fully lined gridiron where, sure enough, teams were already lining up wearing competing fuchsia and silver uniforms. Our fifty-plus volunteers seemed like a skeleton crew as they milled through the sprawling grounds, checking off Hannah's "To Do" boxes. As I shook an industrial-strength plastic bag into the last trash can on my map, I spotted a laughing group led by Diego and Sean putting the final touches on astonishingly ornate floats—pirate ships and fortresses, a submarine float, a giant peacock—like Mardi Gras, with even more sparkles.

Just as I was wondering whether Diego ever got roped into building a pseudo bonfire, I wandered into the center of the lot—and stopped in abject wonder. Lovelorn as he was, Sean hadn't exaggerated one bit about his boyfriend's talents. Our bonfire was incredible, a colossal, swirling pyramid of gauzy orange and yellow cloth that caught the light and shone so brightly, you could swear it was emitting heat. It wasn't just gorgeous. It was *homecoming*.

Around noon—one hour from opening our gates and seven hours until the dance—I was hanging streamers above the unnecessarily large bandstand of the dance tent with Hannah and Natalie, when we all heard the same sound and paused to listen. Across the street at Palmetto, above the chatter of press and police and gathering crowds, the thrumming of a marching band.

"JV football game," Natalie said. She turned her head toward the school, eyes closed as if breathing in the soundtrack of her old life. If things had been different, she would have been Palmetto's homecoming queen. "I wonder if the Pirates won against Lewiston yesterday."

She was thinking about QB. Hannah quieted, probably with the same realization, but went back to pinning up streamers. She knew it wasn't a fair comparison, right? Natalie could never love QB the way she loved Hannah. Even so, she missed him. You could see it in her eyes.

The tent was positively mildewed with nostalgia. I felt myself backing away to the fresher air of the exit and the homemade gridiron beyond.

"I'll go find out who won," I said.

Hannah, Natalie, and I might have been the only Palmetto students who didn't attend the big homecoming game last night—Alliance included. Raina would know the final score. But when I found her by the newly erected bleachers, she was crouched beside a middle-aged man gripping his ankle in agony.

"We've got a first aid booth," Raina was saying to Jack. "Go grab them—he's gonna need help." Spotting me, she groaned. "Daisy, this is not a good time. We've got an injury, and unless you can throw a football . . . "

Before she could finish snarking at me, I'd darted away, cell phone in hand.

QB answered after one ring. "Daisy. I'm sorry."

I blinked. "For what?"

"For kissing you!"

"You don't have to apologize anymore, Chris." I sighed. "You were just trying to get Natalie's attention. I get it."

"Yeah, well, it didn't work. She didn't come last night either."

"She didn't come because she was hanging out with me."

"Very funny." His laugh died out in a moan.

"I'm serious. I'm with her right now. She's helping with our homecoming."

"Really?" He fell abruptly silent.

"She's worried about you, you know. She told me not to break your heart or she'd beat me up."

I could sense him grinning. "She said that?"

"Yep!" *Sort of.* "She does care about you, you know."

He didn't reply—but I could tell he was listening.

"If you want her in your life at all, you need to meet her halfway," I said. "Come to our homecoming. Help our cause. It'll mean a lot to her."

As he cleared his throat, I could picture him straightening his spine, cracking his knuckles. He'd been given a mission. This was the language QB spoke—the language of the pep talk, of the football field.

"What do you need me to do?"

"We've got an injury on one of the teams."

"You need a wide receiver?"

"Actually . . ." I grinned. "We need a QB."

I wasn't sure how this would go. QB had certainly grown a lot in the last few months, but he was still—you know—himself. Would he make it through the game without stroking out from culture shock?

The first test came as soon as his gleaming Mustang careened into the muddy parking lot. QB sauntered from the car, hauling his Pirates helmet and gear just as Jack started tiptoeing across the field, avoiding puddles on his way back from delivering the former quarterback to a waiting gurney. Their paths converged in front of me. I stifled a wince.

"Jack Jackson!"

I closed my eyes, only to realize a second later that QB hadn't said it in a high-pitched voice. He hadn't said it any particular way at all. When I opened my eyes, a peculiar sight greeted me—QB and Jack were midway through an elaborate hand-slapping routine, as if they'd spent weeks practicing it. The "buddy handshake" was one of those innate guy skills that someone with my particular chromosomes could not hope to understand. Or maybe that was just my cisgendered bias talking? Either way, this was going well.

Once QB was situated with his new team, throwing the ball in the world's quickest practice session, I went to find Raina and see how attendance was shaping up.

I could tell as soon as I got to the front gate that it was

going to be an issue. Cops were lining the property, waiting to pounce on gatecrashers—or on us if we allowed it to happen. A steady stream of attendees was spilling in, some wearing costumes, others in evening wear for tonight's dance, still others sporting homemade jerseys to support one of the football teams. They were all ages, all colors, arriving in rowdy groups that piled out of buses, others seemingly alone or with a significant other. At the front of the line, I saw two elderly gentlemen in tuxedos, pinning boutonnières lovingly on each other's lapels before offering their wedding-ringed hands for an entry stamp.

What I didn't see was a single Palmetto student.

I brushed the thought away. It was early. There was time.

And yet, the line to come in was growing like a beanstalk—and the clicker in Raina's hand was already dangerously close to our limit. She watched it in concentration, wincing every time she clicked. A roar rose from the football field, and Raina glanced longingly over her shoulder. The game was probably almost done.

"I'll take over," I offered.

Her brow furrowed. "You sure that's a—?"

"Go!" I grabbed the clicker from her hand without letting her finish the question. But just as she was jogging past a cotton candy stand and out of sight, I realized what she was going to ask. And what the answer was.

No. It wasn't such a good idea for me to be out here, greeting every single homecoming attendee.

What if they hated me? Felt betrayed? Wanted to hone their heckling skills?

They won't know it's me, I reminded myself. *Not with my new hairc—*

"Daisy," shouted a buxom local news reporter, brandishing her microphone like a tournament lance to break through the crowd.

Crap.

"Do you care to comment on reports that you were—quote—'playing gay' in order to get attention?"

"I do *not* care to comment, but thank you so much for asking!"

"Oh my God, are you Daisy?" A group of teenagers I didn't recognize poked their heads around the middle of the line, a few of them leaving their spots to get a closer look, edging the reporter out of the way.

I braced myself.

"What happened to your hair?" one of them asked. His had a lovely strip of purple along the bottom two inches.

"I switched it up," I said, dazedly. "But yours looks awesome."

"*You're* awesome," said the next girl in line, and I was so surprised and flattered that I almost forgot to click her group of six through after Kyle stamped their hands.

"This is crazy," Kyle said, shaking his head at all the people waiting to come in. "And the band hasn't even started yet."

"The Rhythm Squad? Do they have that many fans?"

Kyle stared at me.

Distracted, I forgot another click. The cops shuffled closer. *Whoops.* I needed to concentrate.

Raina ran back from the game, unruly curls spilling from her headscarf.

"Eastern Conference won," she announced through attempts to gather air. "They're carrying QB on their shoulders. You might want to rescue him."

Trading posts, I clumsily handed her the clicker and ran to see for myself.

From the edge of the field, it sure didn't look like QB needed rescuing. He was tomato red and, yes, a little panicked—but he was grinning too as the co-ed, all-ages, mostly queer football team carried him off the field to catcalls and whistles from dozens of guys in the bleachers.

"Come on honey, tell me you play for my team," shouted one young man in his twenties, wearing a faded Palmetto Pirates T-shirt.

But just as I thought QB was going to scramble down from his teammates' shoulders and run straight to the nearest exit, he craned his neck and affably shouted, "Sorry, man, I'm all about the ladies."

"For now!" one of his teammates yelled, to general applause. QB grinned, basking in the glow of adoration. He looked so much more like the QB I knew, glowing with self-assurance—a golden boy, through and through. Whatever piece of him Natalie had chipped away had just been restored at last—by a stadium of cheering gay men.

My services not needed here, I skipped deliriously back through the crowd, passing a crowd of boys in ball gowns, a trio of women wearing lettermen jackets, and a central stage, where the cast of *Triplecross* was posing for photos. I saw that

elderly couple sharing a funnel cake, careful not to get pow-
dered sugar on their tuxedos. I couldn't tell if the middle-aged
person in line to buy a T-shirt was male or female, and I loved
that it didn't matter.

People were laughing. People were spontaneously dancing.
People were eating and primping and meeting new people
and—relaxing. People were being themselves.

But when I got back to the front gates, Raina was sweating.
That wasn't exactly herself.

"We're close," she said. "I think we'll get everybody in,
but . . ."

"Any Palmetto students?" I asked.

"Not that many. Other than us, ten or twelve?"

We stared across the road at the school, its façade glowing
red with the sunset. As we watched, the light caught the sign,
making the Palmetto Pirate logo glow, a beacon we couldn't
quite reach.

The police officers looked almost disappointed not to have
any fights to break up or fire codes to enforce. The only one
not shuffling around, kicking the sod, was Chief Beck. He
stood watching the goings-on past the barriers with keen interest, a near-smile playing on his face. I wondered if he knew
his daughter was here.

It seemed odd that I hadn't seen Mrs. Beck. Was she off
holding her own press conference? Or outfitting the school
board with torches and pitchforks as a final offensive?

A second later, I got my answer. Cindy Beck appeared as if
out of nowhere—probably having arrived behind one of the
Dumpsters in a burst of flame—and stomped daintily to her

husband. His eyes didn't budge from the tents as she whispered angrily into his ear, gesturing to the field. He shrugged, pointed at me and Raina, and we both flinched backward.

Here she came.

As Mrs. Beck strode over, she stretched out her hand, contorting her face into an ill-fitting smile. Was she planning to shake our hands or punch us? Raina planted her feet and I forced myself to stand beside her, arms crossed, like I was her bodyguard. It made me feel tough for about half a second.

"Let me see it," Cindy said.

Raina smiled politely back. "I'm sorry?"

"The clicker. How many people do you have in there?"

Raina turned the counter around to face her, keeping it out of arm's reach. "One thousand, one hundred and seventy-two."

Cindy Beck's eyes narrowed. "You're lying."

Raina cocked her head, as if curious about the accusation rather than offended. "Prove it. Your husband and his officers have been monitoring our recordkeeping since the gates opened this afternoon. If you have a problem with our tally, take it up with him."

Cindy grinned, all slyness, as if we'd just handed her an ace card. "Oh, I will."

There was something very off about her, something that made me shiver as she stalked away. The cameras were on her, but she didn't even seem to notice. She'd lost her poise, that politician's veneer she'd shielded herself with since the school board meeting. Her eyes, her stride, even her hairdo seemed like they would rattle loose at the slightest provocation.

Was it because we were winning? Was destroying our cause so important to her that she was willing to look like a lunatic in front of all of the registered voters who were watching her go bat-shit, live on television? Apparently so.

And then, adding to the ramshackle charm of her march across the field, Cindy waved her arm. I thought for a second she'd tipped over into talking to herself, which made me giggle.

But then, something about the gesture struck me. It wasn't ramshackle. It was specific.

A cue. Not to the cops, not to us—to all the people across the street in the free speech zone, watching her like drone ants milling around their queen. At her movement, they erupted.

The Christian Values Coalition was coming, and Cindy Beck was their Moses. They streamed across the street to the barrier, singing cheery songs about hell, louder and more off-key the closer they got, until their faces were inches from ours.

"Let us in," said one woman with a long braid coiled around the top of her head like a snake. "We're paying customers, we have a right to be here too."

"Hey!" A gawky teen boy I didn't recognize, one of five people waiting to get in, fought to stay in line as protesters crowded him out. An elderly man smashed him on the head with his placard.

"Stop!" I screamed, Kyle's battered, frightened face flashing before me. I tried to jump over the barrier to shove them, but Raina's hand dragged me back by the collar of my shirt.

"You can't, Daisy," Raina hissed into my ear. "That's why they're here. To start a fight, get everything shut down."

She was right. I backed off. But it didn't matter.

Because as soon as we retreated an inch from our post, the two hundred members of the CVC jumped the gates and ran headlong into homecoming.

"You are over the limit!" Cindy Beck shrieked, clapping her hands. "And we are shutting! You! Down!"

35

For a second, everything was so loud it became silent, like a death scene in a war movie. If somebody told me later that I'd screamed *"Nooooooo!"* I wouldn't have been at all surprised.

Through a fog, I saw reporters crowding the gates, Cindy Beck granting interviews as if she were an actual elected official, Chief Beck waving his bullhorn to direct the dozens of cops to dispel the crowd, and whirling behind me, a mob of anti-gay protesters and attendees staring at one another in frozen fury—a look I knew instinctively was the precursor to punches thrown.

This had to be peaceful. It had to be perfect. Or after all of this, there would still be no dance.

"Daisy," someone was saying. Cal Montgomery. He was here? He must have been here, because he was shaking me. "We need you!"

I glanced around, frantic, picking out the faces that mattered most. Raina with her eyes closed. Sean beside her, holding Diego's hand with both of his. Poor Jack hiding behind Sophie, desperate to avoid the news cameras in case his family was watching. Kyle begging his parents to let him stay—and, approaching fast from the dance tent, Natalie and Hannah, their eyes widening with mounting horror.

"This is it," Cal said, taking my shoulders and pointing them toward the stage. "This is the moment. You need to move."

I peered over my shoulder one more time, hoping to catch Hannah's eye—but it was Natalie I couldn't stop looking at. Her face was steely. Cold. For the first time ever, I could step outside myself long enough to truly recognize the expression.

It was Natalie's game face. Her "nobody can touch me" face. I had never been so happy to see it in my life.

"Okay," I said to Cal. "I'll do it."

I watched as the crowd parted around me, people staggering from my path like there was a force field shoving them back. I nodded to the *Triplecross* actors who were climbing down from the stage, waving for me to take their spot. I walked quickly—purposefully—my eyes on that mic. I reached the steps.

Then I stepped aside so Natalie Beck could climb them.

As I folded back into the crowd, Hannah grabbed my arm. "What is this?"

I beamed up at Natalie as she crouched to take the microphone. "This is the girl I used to know."

"My name is Natalie Beck," she started, knees dipping at the sound of her own voice repeating from the speakers.

A crowd had gathered—our supporters, but some protesters too, banners drooping. Reporters had flooded around them, sensing that the barriers had been compromised. Their cameras were trained on Natalie.

"My parents are here today," she said, almost shyly. "By

now, you all know my mother, Cindy Beck, who's fought so hard against this cause."

I searched for Mrs. Beck, but couldn't see her past the crowd.

"And my father, Walter—here today as the chief of our James Island Police Force."

A wave rippled through the crowd and Chief Beck appeared, holding his radio, staring at the stage. A cop came up to him, probably to ask him when they could start arresting people, but he waved him away, shouting "Hold" into his walkie-talkie.

Natalie pressed her lips together, the closest she could get to a smile right now.

"I'm sixteen. I'm a junior at Palmetto High School. And . . . I'm a lesbian."

Jack and Raina started the cheer—it rippled outward, bright and almost frightening in its speed, a wildfire spreading from a spark.

"I realized I was gay when I was very young. My parents did too. They saw it as a problem to be fixed. And I *was* fixed, for a long time. I was a straight-A student, with a group of strictly platonic girl friends and an amazing boyfriend on the football team."

I glanced behind me, and sure enough, Chris was watching her speech with his jaw set, pained one blink and proud the next.

"But I wasn't me. I was an imitation. A knock-off, the kind that falls apart the first time you wash it. When I met my girlfriend—really met her—I started to unravel, slowly. *Too* slowly. I kept lying to my parents. Until right now, I guess? So, um, now that they're listening, I just want to tell them the truth. I am in love with a girl. *Scary* in love. And if you knew her, I promise, you would love her too."

Hannah gazed up, one hand clenched in her mess of hair as if to keep her head from floating off her body.

"Today is important—not just for me, but for millions of people like me who want to live their lives, enjoy a football game, and a dance without feeling hated. It's a basic right—not to be irrationally despised, vilified, bullied. I *deserve* it. And so does everyone here. We're not asking *you* to change. We're just asking you to let us be who we are. And . . . this is who I am."

Natalie crouched, offering Hannah a hand.

"Do you need a boost?" I asked, knitting my fingers together in preparation.

Hannah smiled, electrified. Grabbed Nat's hand. "We've got this."

She landed on the stage. They stared at each other for a second—two skydivers before the leap—and then, with a giddy giggle, they kissed.

Not a forced one, like QB's. Not a no-tongue peck. Not even a movie kiss where everything swirls around them. A real one—knees knocking, eyes half-open, hands clutching each other's backs like life rafts. Their lips smiling, glistening as they broke apart.

A hundred cameras flashed, and the crowd cheered, nearly drowning out the protesters, who booed like the children they were.

"Please," Natalie said, her arm around Hannah's waist. "Just let us have our homecoming."

Chief Beck's jaw was tight. Natalie watched him, eyes welling.

He nodded. Just a nod.

And then a wink.

And Natalie let out all her breath, stretching like a flower in the sun. Apparently, a wink from her dad meant a lot. I was just starting to beam along when I watched Natalie's smile waver and drop.

Cindy Beck strode through the crowd with her hand covering her eyes, a blinder against the sight of her daughter. She grasped her husband's arm over and over like it was slippery, hissing into his ear, gesturing everywhere but at Natalie. Her face was so taut it had become haggard, like whatever spell she used to keep herself camera-perfect had been broken by today's events.

Chief Beck stood still, not looking at her. Then he turned, hunching to say something to her that I wished like hell I could hear. She tensed, her mouth forming the word "no," but he shook his head and took her gently by the shoulders—and unbelievably, she relaxed against him, closing her eyes. He kissed her on the forehead. She nodded, blinking back tears, turned . . . and left.

And I exhaled.

The cops stood waiting throughout the field, ready to disperse, make arrests, whatever Chief Beck ordered. He raised his radio.

"Escort the protesters back to the Free Speech Zone. And

keep a better watch on those gates. Anybody who seems like trouble, get 'em out of here. Let's let these kids enjoy their homecoming."

The news spread slowly in wondering murmurs, nobody able to immediately process what had happened. The police had taken our side. Chief Beck had used the mysterious bonds of marriage to deactivate our arch-nemesis. We had won.

Chief Beck strode to the stage, offering Natalie a hand down.

"Thank you, Dad," she said, letting him lift her like she was a toddler.

"You got it, kiddo." Chief Beck extended his hand up to the stage once more. "Hannah, is it? It's nice to finally meet you."

She put her slender hand in his big one and smiled—a polite smile. A real one. "It's lovely to meet you too."

In the dance tent, Mom and her army of community farmers had just finished counting the ballots for homecoming king and queen. They were tittering, delighted by the chance to take part in something they probably would have turned their noses up at when they were actually in high school.

Like Adam. The thought of him sent my mood into the mud.

When Mom spotted me, she waved the slip of paper she was holding. "Congratulations!"

"Thanks," I said. "Yeah, everything seems to be going great."

"No." She took my hands. "You're queen, Daisy—you've been named homecoming queen!"

"*What?*"

I stared down at the scribbled tally. There it was, my name at the top with over eight hundred votes. It took me a bewildered second to figure out why. Popular or unpopular, gay or straight, I was the one who'd been on TV. I was the only name most of these people knew.

I pictured the view from our flagship Pirate Galley float, the crown glittering on my head as I waved to all the people who finally—finally—appreciated me, as I threw flowers to Hannah, who blew me a grateful kiss in reply. Then I opened my eyes, taking in reality—the tent, the lights, the ground beneath my feet.

"You counted wrong, Mom," I said. "Natalie Beck's homecoming queen."

Mom stared at me for a full second before the mind-meld kicked in. Then she gathered my ballots and tossed them into the trash bag under the table.

"Not Hannah?" she asked, watching me from the corner of her eye.

"No," I said. "She'd be mortified. But she'll be happy for Nat."

"*Ohhhhh*," Mom said. "We're calling her '*Nat*' again, are we?"

"What? No." I crouched, tying up the trash bag. "It's just . . . quicker to say."

"Okay." She was wearing her mom-instincts smirk again. She hadn't been right about me being gay. Or dating QB. Wrong about Adam too, in the end.

You never know, I thought. *This time she might be onto something.*

And so, I got to watch as Nat-short-for-Natalie donned a glowing neon headdress and pink feather boa to stand at the prow of Stede Bonnet's ship with Raina, our tuxedoed homecoming king by her side, and one step back, their attendants, Sean, Kyle, Chase Hernandez from *Triplecross*, and—the school secretary, Mrs. O'Brien? She was waving to a middle-aged woman in a maxi dress who was snapping photos of her from the parade route. I never would have guessed.

As we watched the float pass, Hannah cheered with her hands over her head. Then she linked arms with me, resting her head against mine.

"I never told you how it started, did I?" she asked. "Me and Natalie. That day in the car . . ."

I nudged her. "Tell me."

She grinned, leaning her arm on my shoulder. "Okay. So. We had an away match. A summer tournament at a clinic. She and I were playing doubles in the final—winning—and one of the girls on the other side of the net got mad and made, like, slanty eyes at me." She motioned to her face, then wiped her hand on her pocket.

"Are you *kidding* me?"

"I know! I was thrown. My serves were off. They got ahead. But then it was Natalie's serve. And . . ." Hannah wavered on her feet, remembering. "She was so angry. She looked like I felt. She served the fastest ace I'd ever seen—straight into that girl's head. We got disqualified. Nat stormed off the court. I followed her into the locker room and . . . she hugged me. We'd always been friendly. But this hug felt different. And when we broke away, she kind of looked at me and I looked at her. And then some of our teammates came in to get ready for the next match and we broke away, but we knew. And that was the start of it."

Even as she smiled, tears flooded her eyes.

"Oh, Han. I wish I'd—" I started, but she waved me off.

"Listen, the message you left me." She shouted over the roar of the crowd as the football team rolled by. "I don't think you even realize how much it meant to me to hear you say what you did."

"That you're ordinary?" I laughed. To anyone else, it would be a slap in the face.

"Seriously. Do you know how *we* started, Daisy?" She poked my forehead. "Why you and I became friends? You were the only one that first day who didn't ogle me like I was there for show-and-tell. Everyone else was like 'What *are* you? Where are you *from*? What's that *accent*?' But you . . ." She snorted. "You asked where I got my backpack."

"I have to be honest, Han," I said. "That might have been coincidental. I mean, you're 'exotic' and all, but that backpack was awesome."

"'Exotic.'" She made a gagging noise. Then her face fell serious. "I was so freaked out. My parents had split. I'd left the place I'd spent my entire life. Left my father. Everything was so different and all I wanted was for something to feel normal. Anything. And then I met you." She laughed. "Not that *you* were normal. You still aren't. You're always going to be you, Daisy, and I wouldn't want it any other way—grand gestures, crazy plans, musical interludes, all of it. I love the *you* about you."

Hannah reached out with both hands and I held on.

"But you and me," she said. "Can we be boring? Can we talk about backpacks and endangered birds and shreddie fries and kind of just be . . ."

She searched for the word. I supplied it.

"Ourselves."

"Yes," she said. "That. Exactly that."

"Deal," I said. "And I think we should start being ourselves by jumping the line for corn dogs. We *are* the organizers, after all."

Hannah looked back at the parade route. "You were right. This was worth it."

And suddenly it *was* worth it. The sleepless nights, the fights, the days I'd thought I'd lost her. It led here, didn't it? And here was fabulous.

While we savored our delicious foot-long deep-fried sausages, we watched the crowd. Down the parade route, Sean's boyfriend snapped an iPhone pic. That elderly couple had their hands clasped over their heads so they could wave together. Even QB had found someone to hit on—Sophie Goodwin! And it was working! She was laughing at something he'd said, twirling her braid around her pinkie. It was some kind of homecoming miracle—QB had managed to find the one lesbian in the school who might actually be interested. I smiled at him across the float, feeling hope for Chris Saunders at last.

And then another face seemed to replace QB's. One that wasn't here. One that was observing journalistic distance and had gone home hours ago. I hoped Adam had at least stuck around long enough to hear Natalie's speech and know that he had some part in it.

"You okay?" Hannah asked, taking my picked-clean corn dog stick.

"Me? Of course." I grinned. "I'm perfect."

"I'm gonna find Nat," she said, tossing our trash out. "Meet you at the dance?"

"You got it."

At a wave from Sophie, I sprinted to the Porta-Pottys to change out of my volunteer getup. Raina was already waiting, her tuxedo jacket slung on one arm and a zipped-up dress bag hoisted on the other.

As I was trying to slip into my dress without letting it touch the toilet walls, I heard a girl squealing outside my potty, her voice tinny through the plastic wall. "I can't believe Kudzu Giants are playing!"

I scowled into the door. Where had she heard *that* rumor? She was going to be pretty pissed when the Rhythm Squad took the stage. Unless they were awesome. I chose to assume that they'd be awesome. And if they weren't, who cared? Our dance was happening. And that was the point.

I erupted from my dirty stall, checking my high heels for toilet paper as Sophie descended elegantly from the one next to me, holding aloft the hem of a dress that didn't look much different from her usual day-to-day attire. Raina gave a whistle to see us—but my jaw dropped at the sight of her.

She was wearing a sleek, wine-colored gown that hugged curves her usual legal garb had never given a hint of. She looked like a movie star from the forties, flower in her hair and everything. Raina raised one shoulder coquettishly at my incredulous expression.

"Had to do it up," she said. "There are queer girls here from all over the country. This might be the best pickup opportunity I'll ever get."

"B-but . . . you were just in a tuxedo," I sputtered.

"I'm a bit gender fluid," she said. "A lot, actually."

"And your hair!" I gestured reverently to the ringlets forming perfect architectural spirals around her face. "Did you bring a curling iron? How did you—?"

Raina snorted, slinging an arm around my shoulders. "One day, Daisy, I'll walk you through the ninety-seven products I use on my hair. But for now, let's just call it magic."

She stepped away, examining my dress, a 1950s confection in the same shade of blue and gold as my former hairdo. When her eyes met mine again, they were approving.

"You clean up well," she said, and I beamed. Any compliment from Raina was worth twenty from anybody else.

As we started off, Sophie's flats slipped in the mud and Raina caught her. They glanced at each other, grinning. My eyebrows rose.

"Any chance . . . you two . . . ?" I waved my hands at them, feeling like a combination of Hannah's mom and my own.

Their arms still around each other, they burst out laughing, then said, in unison, *"No."*

"Just friends," Sophie clarified, walking off—but the "just" rang false. A friendship wasn't a consolation prize, was it? It was its own kind of miracle.

On my way into the bustling dance tent, I passed Natalie

and Hannah, exchanging corsages they'd bought for each other. I tried to get past without spoiling the moment—but Natalie grabbed my wrist.

"We got you one too," she said, sliding a blue carnation onto my arm. "Shut up, just wear it."

Then we all hugged, almost by accident, everybody going for everybody else, bonking hairdos in the process.

"Ow!" I stumbled back.

"That did not go as planned," Natalie growled, fixing her bun.

Hannah tugged on her arm. "Let's go!"

They waved and disappeared onto the dance floor, just as a DJ perched in a tall booth in one neon-lit corner of the tent started spinning songs that were way better than anything on our local radio stations.

I started away, then hesitated, unsure where to walk. I'd never been to a dance before, solo or otherwise. Some people in the crowd seemed to be bunched up, dancing as a group. Others were doing the spotlight dancer thing, like they were out at a club. And yeah, others, like me, were standing awkwardly on the fringe watching everybody else.

And then it hit me. I recognized them. The people along the edge of the tent—that was the freshman girl who sat next to me in French. And beside her, trying to flirt, a kid from Kyle's lacrosse team. In a cluster in the middle of the dance floor— oh my God, was that Dana? With a bunch of junior girls? Had she canceled her party? And was that Darius high-fiving QB by the door, while he politely introduced Sophie?

They were here. Palmetto had shown up.

I danced into the crowd until I found Raina, who grabbed my hand and spun me around. This was a group song—one of those awesome dance numbers that felt iconic and important until you paid attention to how stupid the lyrics were.

Then the next one was a slow song, and everybody paired off, so I ducked back to one of the benches lining the tent and kept counting familiar faces. There was Mrs. O'Brien, leading her partner onto the dance floor. And Principal Zimmer, dancing with Prof Hélène? Those two were an item? Wow. So much for gaydar.

And despite all my fears, there were my classmates, people I'd known for years, passed in the hall, waited behind in the lunch line, said hello to and barely noticed until they'd become everything to me. This was their event—the homecoming of the century. And even more wonderfully, the boys and girls dancing together didn't look at all uncomfortable dancing next to girls with girls and old men with old men and every combination in between.

Cindy Beck was officially wrong. She was probably sitting at home realizing how very wrong she was even now. Or not. Something told me that people like her were only held together by the gravitational pull of their false convictions.

I hoped it wouldn't be too hard for Natalie to walk back into that house. But for the next few hours, she wouldn't have to worry. She was here, out and proud, and even better than that, lost in a crowd, dancing with her girlfriend.

An image wafted up from somewhere deep in my memory.

Me and Hannah in sixth grade, hands clasped together as we ran across the room attempting grand jetés. And then I thought of Natalie, our many, many dances together, twirling until the garden became a blur of green, our hair whipping together so fast, it was hard to tell whose was whose.

How could I not have seen it? They were perfect together.

And I'm perfect as I am, I thought, tucking my high heels under the bench. *All alone. I'll be fine. It's better this way. I'm going to make an incredible Yosemite homesteader, communing with the deer and the birds and the bears. Yes—even* bears *will love and fear me.*

The music swelled, swooning harmonies mixed with pulsing beats, and I had the sudden sense that the DJ was cheering me on, my choice to live and die alone.

Then the music faded, the crowd murmuring, and the DJ leaned into his microphone to say, "Now here's the act you've really been waiting for. Let's hear it for Kudzu Giaaaaaaaants!"

Um. No. I had lapsed into hallucinations. Maybe somebody had spiked our punch after all. Because I'd suddenly gone deaf from the sound of everyone screaming, and up there on the stage, a group of musicians was picking up instruments, and they looked an awful lot like my favorite band in all the world. There was the lead singer, Stu, a banjo strung on his back and a guitar on his front; back-up singer Lucinda with her fiddle and tambourine; tall Keyko on the drums; Becket, Ron, and Charlotte manning the keyboards, percussion and brass instruments; the new guy Eli Cohen on the bass guita—

"Hang on a second," I said, but couldn't hear myself say it over the roar around me. "Hang! On! A second!"

But I heard it when someone whispered low into my ear, "Surprise."

And there he was, my ace reporter—not fidgeting, not slumped, wearing a tuxedo with such aplomb that I wondered suddenly whether he'd been a spy all along, sent here to report on me and defend my life if necessary.

Adam's hand slipped into mine, keeping me from flying away.

"You came," I said.

Adam laughed. "Kudzu Giants are playing, and *that's* what you want to say?"

"Your brother. He's in Kudzu Giants. I cannot believe I never made that connection." I blinked up at the stage, where they were strumming the opening bars of the lead single from their last album. "Why didn't you tell me?"

He swallowed. "You seemed to find me interesting. And everybody always finds Eli interesting. I didn't want that to change."

"Yes, you're interesting, Adam." I laughed. "You're completely insane! You did *this*."

He grinned. "I did do this."

I started to tear up. He grabbed my shoulder, but I shook my head, smoothing my crinoline skirt. "I thought you were done with me. Now that the story was over."

Adam winced. Then he shrugged, and in the tuxedo, the movement looked quite rakish.

"On the one hand," he said. "A journalist must never get involved with his subject. And on the other hand . . ."

His still ink-stained fingers rose to tuck my newly bobbed

hair behind my ear. The gesture rendered me immobile.

"On the other hand," he finished. "There was no way in hell I was going to miss your song's world premiere."

I was so dazed by his sudden appearance, and the rather impressive *appearance* of his appearance, that I nearly missed that last part.

"World premiere? What are you—"

The lead singer spoke into the microphone. "This next song goes out to Daisy Beaumont-Smith!"

Everyone at the dance started looking around for me. I gave a feeble wave.

"Not only was she the force behind creating this awesome party—she's also turned out to be quite the songsmith."

My breath caught. I grabbed Adam's lapel.

"You didn't."

He flashed a wicked grin. "I did."

There came a strumming from the stage, a sort of flamenco sound, and then a plaintive whistle from the lead singer—a tune I recognized as well as my own heartbeat.

"Out on the sea, you see the flag, the flag of Bloody Stede, and you know your fate is sealed as tight as a basket of woven reeds."

The band erupted. It was "The Ballad of Bloody Stede," my ballad, but so much better, jolted to life, every instrument dancing around the tune, teasing it, illuminating it instead of just playing it. My stupid song was now an actual song, a viable one, and everyone was dancing to it. Something I'd made up in the shower!

Adam dragged me into the fray. "Come on, Daisy. This is my first high school dance. We're not gonna sit it out."

His hand found its way to the dip in my back and pulled me close and it suddenly became incredibly difficult to focus. The biggest band in the world was singing my song, and Hannah was jumping up and down next to me, shrieking, "I cannot believe they're playing 'The Ballad of Bloody Stede'!" and Adam was just looking at me, a smile flickering over his face like light on water.

And before I knew it, the strangest thing was happening. Everything else faded, sunk, disintegrated. I could hardly even hear the song anymore, because this was real. Not a daydream or a delusion. This was the moment. We were here, pulling closer and closer in a riptide.

And then, connecting. His lips were warm, firm against mine and then parting them, his hands were in my hair and mine in his, then lower, tracing my shoulder blades, my waist—and holy *wow*, did I know who I was.

I was me. Daisy Beaumont-Smith. And I liked boys. But no, not all boys—*this* one—specifically and exclusively. Kissing Adam was terrifying one second and so perfect the next that my body forgot what terror even meant.

When I came to several hours later, only a few seconds had passed, and we were grinning at each other, Hannah and Natalie gawking at us in happy shock.

"Happy homecoming," Adam said.

36

We got to the Moonlight Coffee Shop just after midnight, once we'd thanked all the vendors and volunteers and staggered out to find some sustenance, our bodies still too giddy to go home.

A few booths were closing out their checks, but the reporters who'd swarmed the place were gone—probably off filing their stories or heading home, ready to find the next scoop, the next big hashtag movement.

Not Adam. As we settled into a corner booth, he announced his unofficial retirement from journalism.

"I'll stick with the major, but I might add in something like poli sci."

I frowned, tucking my feet so Natalie and Hannah could fill in opposite. "But you're such a good writer."

"Thank you." Adam squeezed my hand, then let his fingers linger against mine, more steady than I'd ever seen them. "Here's the thing, though. I thought I was cut out for journalism because I was so objective. I could remove my personal feelings from any situation. But it turns out I'm not as neutral as I thought I was."

I batted my eyelashes.

He laughed. "About any of it. Anything important, anyway. I can stay neutral about cat boutiques."

"So what's the career plan now, Mr. Journalism-slash-Poli Sci Major?"

"Cal Montgomery gave me his boss's business card? Said to call her firm when I graduate." Adam shrugged, turning the card over in his hand. "Sounded interesting."

"You could try it out."

"For a little while. And then maybe archeology."

"See, you're kidding, but I think that sounds like a perfectly good plan."

Adam put his arm around me and my voice sputtered into a pleasant nothing as I nestled against him in the booth.

Hannah watched us, her mouth twitching with the effort not to grin like a goon. She lifted a plastic menu as a distraction. "The usual?"

"I *love* the usual," Jack said, craning his neck from the next booth over. "What is it?"

"Mozzarella sticks, chicken fingers, and a salad," Natalie recited. "And I'm gonna add onion rings if nobody objects."

She looked at me, eyebrows raised in challenge, but I smiled. How could anybody object to onion rings?

"How dare you," Hannah said, grabbing Natalie's face. Natalie matched her grave expression for a half second, then darted in for a kiss. They smiled, still lip-locked. Hannah whispered something to Natalie and I cast my eyes away, happy for the opportunity to *finally* mock them for a glaring example of PDA. Not tonight, though. First thing tomorrow.

My fingers slid back between Adam's.

"I think I'll go for pie," he said. "What was that one you got the first time I interviewed you?"

"Coconut cream," I said, resting my head on his shoulder. "It was excellent."

Hannah raised her eyebrows, taking in the fact that Adam and I already had a history to reference. It was Hannah's turn to let somebody else into our carefully calibrated routine. I had a hunch she'd handle it a lot better than I had.

"So." Adam pointed at me with a spoon, his face taking on a stern edge. "Tomorrow. Driving lesson."

I whimpered.

Hannah clapped. "Are you *finally* learning?"

"Stick shift." Adam leaned back like he was already behind the wheel. "We might even try some defensive driving maneuvers."

"I don't think you're appreciating the magnitude of the challenge before you," I said.

Adam smirked. "Give me a month. You'll be ready for Formula One."

Incredibly, I could picture it. *Daisy Beaumont-Smith, idling at the starting gate of the Monaco Grand Prix, giving a gloved thumbs-up to the bespectacled hottie in the pit, narrowing my eyes through my helmet, revving the engine as the first flag waved.* Tonight, I could picture just about anything.

The booths quickly filled with GSA members and friends, the now-frenzied Moonlight waitresses bustling in and out of the kitchen with our orders, everybody buzzing from the concert, the game, the magnitude of what we'd pulled off.

"Today went well," Raina said, perched on her knees in the

booth behind me. Her voice was back to business but hoarse from screaming at the dance. "I think we should all start brainstorming next steps."

Sean, Sophie, and Kyle groaned in harmony.

"What?" She glanced around. "This isn't the end. We can leverage this, make even more of a difference."

"Prom?" Sean suggested, wincing more than smiling at the prospect.

"We're off the hook," Jack said, arms stretched grandly across the booth like he owned the place. "Before we left, Principal Zimmer told me same-sex dates are a go. I don't know if the school board got tired of reporters chasing them around Publix or what, but he said they're planning to officially cave at the next meeting."

We all fell into relieved silence at that news.

"Also," Jack said. "He and Prof Hélène are probably boning as we speak."

"Nasty!" I shouted. "Yeah, they probably are."

"He's not gay?" Kyle rubbed his temple.

Jack offered him a fry as consolation. "Even the experts are wrong from time to time."

"Next steps? Can we focus?" Raina capped her question with a noisy slurp from her strawberry milkshake, then scowled as everybody laughed. "What?"

"I'm up for it," QB said, interrupting his conversation with Diego about the relative merits of European vs. American football. "Whatever it is."

Whatever it is.

I cleared my throat.

"If we're looking for a way to make an impact on local youth," I started. "I might have a suggestion."

The Alliance turned to look at me, alert, ready for the next great challenge.

I smiled. "How do you guys feel about public art?"

And I could see this too, so beautiful, illuminating a once bleak, barren space—a grand ocean-scape teeming with life, a majestic temple, a fallen statue, an entire continent waiting to be discovered.

I mean, okay—not an *entire* continent. A glimpse of one, Messy strokes, flawed perspective, amateurish execution and yes, probably a random whale—I still had a perverse attachment to that whale—but still, *ours*. Days of working side by side. Jack and Sean keeping a laughing catalog of our mistakes. Me and Raina squabbling over whether the columns should be Ionic or Corinthian (*obviously* Corinthian). Sophie in the corner doodling fairies, which don't even belong in Atlantis but are absolutely lovely too. Natalie getting chartreuse paint on her face, this being *my* fantasy and all, Adam distributing shreddie fries and Hannah snapping photos and QB talking sporty-sport-sports with Kyle, and the lacrosse boys flirting with the drama girls, everybody adding a stroke to that wall.

The end result would be bright and hopeful. At the very least, bright. Neon. *Blinding*.

I leaned back in the booth and started to drift, picturing it. But then I blinked and focused. Here was reality: the curling corner of Adam's lips, laughter rippling through the air, a jagged, peeling crack in the royal blue plastic tabletop, friends (plural!) in every direction—like Kyle, his cheek faint green where the bruise hadn't completely faded, Natalie, whose eyes clouded whenever she glanced out the diner window toward home, and Hannah, drawing her back with clasped fingers and smiling whispers.

Tonight couldn't last forever. They'd walk out to face a different kind of reality from the one in here—not just joys and hopes and first dates and triumphs, but parents waiting in darkened living rooms, hurtful, tossed-off jokes, a hundred microaggressions a day, wounds I couldn't understand or even hope to heal. After all, I'd turned out to be a pretty crappy champion, hadn't I? But as Becky approached, sliding a massive plate of mozzarella sticks in my direction, I realized there was at least one thing I could offer.

Crisp. Golden. Its own kind of miracle.

It was a start.

ACKNOWLEDGMENTS

. . . In which I fall far short of conveying the depth of my gratitude to the people who brought this book to life.

First, to Jessica Garrison, an editor so wise, kind, and funny that she magically draws out the same qualities in everything she works on. Thank you for seeing the book of my heart underneath those early drafts and for having faith in me as it made its way onto paper.

To Katelyn Detweiler and the rest of the Jill Grinberg Literary team, who support me like we're family.

To Donna, Charlotte, and Pam, who do the same (although we actually are family—lucky me!).

To Mary Frame and Kim Liggett for your notes and encouragement when this story was in its earliest iterations, and to Lexi Beach, the Fearless Fifteeners, and everyone else in the book community who made my debut year (AKA the year I wrote this book) so memorably warm and vibrant.

Many thanks to the team at Dial and Penguin Young Readers Group, especially Regina Castillo, who made this book make sense; Dana Chidiac and Kristen Tozzo, who kept the trains running on time; Dana Li and Danielle Calotta, who must have found a mystical portal into the world of the book, because those cover models are my characters; Mina Chung, for her lovely design; Lauri Hornik and Namrata Tripathi, inestimable champions; the wonderful Lindsay Boggs, who, aside from all her publicity magic, makes me feel cooler just from knowing her; and Doni Kay, along with the rest of the PYRG Sales, Marketing, and Publicity departments, for all their hard work and dedication.

Finally, thank you to Lexi and Connie, Mike and Jeff, Mary Ann and Lisa, Ashley and Jen, and countless other swoon-tastic couples I count myself blessed to know. Thank you for letting me appear as an occasional comedic guest star in your love stories.

And to Rob, Ollie, and Henry, of course, for making my own story a love story too.

ABOUT THE AUTHOR

Jenn Marie Thorne graduated from NYU-Tisch with a BFA in drama and realized she was having more fun *writing* plays than performing in them. What followed was her acclaimed YA debut, *The Wrong Side of Right*. Jenn lives in Gulfport, Florida. Find her on Twitter @juniperjenny.